PALM BEACH BLUES

C.D. Boswell

Palm Beach Blues is a work of fiction—although a couple of characters may not realize it. Nevertheless, any similarity between the characters and situations within its pages and places or persons, living or dead, is unintentional and co-incidental.

For my family.

For my family.

PROLOGUE

"There's still a hand sticking out."

The Russian pointed the flashlight toward the freshly-filled grave. Sure enough, a clenched fist rose through the dirt, proclaiming either triumph or defiance. Knowing the Dead Russian, probably a little of both.

"Okay. What do you want to do?" the Russian asked.

"I don't see how we got much here in the way of alternatives," the Italian said. "We dig him up. We fix the body. We put him back in. We make sure he's covered. Basically, we start over."

He didn't want to do this; he was exhausted. He was dripping with sweat. He hadn't done this kind of work in more than twenty years; he'd forgotten what a bitch rigor mortis could be.

He was open to suggestions.

The Russian asked, "You have chainsaw or something like that in vehicle? A machete perhaps?"

"It's a loaner. With run flats. There ain't even a tire iron. We should've thought of this when we were in Home Depot."

The Russian sighed.

"Let's get him out. I will break joints, but I may need your help."

The Italian nodded, picked up the newly-purchased shovel, and began taking out dirt as the Russian lit the grave with the flashlight.

This is what happens when you don't plan effectively, the Italian thought. *This is what happens when you act impulsively.* When they'd thrown the Dead Russian's newly-cashiered corpse into the back of the oversized SUV, his arms had apparently splayed out in a sort of cruciform. They hadn't noticed as they hurriedly covered the body with a tablecloth and slammed the tailgate shut.

Six hours later, in a moonlit sugarcane field deep in western Palm Beach county, the Dead Russian's now-cold body had completely fossilized: his arms sticking straight out, his fists clenched, his eyes open, and his countenance twisted into an eternal fuck-you grimace.

The Dead Russian was still managing to make life hard for those who crossed him.

After a few minutes, the Russian stepped in to spell the older man. After all, this was his problem. He worked efficiently; seemingly unaffected by the 90% humidity. He finished, tossed the shovel aside, and motioned for the Italian to bring the light in a little closer.

Like a discarded action figure, the Dead Russian lay awkwardly at the bottom of the grave—one clenched fist dug into the dirt, the other pointing straight up. He looked like he was performing a cartwheel. The Russian grabbed the aloft hand and pulled, more or less standing the Dead Russian up. The Italian positioned the flashlight in the dirt on the edge of the grave, squatted down and put both arms underneath the Dead Russian's. With help from the Russian, he pulled the

240-pound corpse out of the hole. He walked backwards a few steps, pulling the corpse away from the grave, his arms wrapped around the Dead Russian's waist. After a couple of yards, he let go—expecting the Dead Russian to fall on his back.

Inexplicably, the corpse remained standing, his feet submerged in the thick Glades muck.

The Russian clambered out of the grave and walked up to the Dead Russian and the Italian. The three stood there silently for a minute, the Italian still panting, until the Russian reached out and pushed the Dead Russian over.

"Stand on the juncture of arm and shoulder, please, while I torque the arm out of socket." The Russian grabbed the Dead Russian's left wrist and assumed a positon that looked like he was going to do a deadlift. The Italian placed a foot on the Dead Russian's shoulder.

"Whenever you're ready."

It took the Russian three tries and all his considerable strength to break the joint, but when he was done, the Dead Russian's left arm folded obediently over his chest.

"Advance of rigor mortis is accelerated in tropical climates. And degree of rigor is directly proportional to muscle mass," the Russian observed. "The guy was no slouch, that is for sure."

The Italian thought he detected a hint of admiration in the Russian's voice.

After a few minutes' rest and a water break, the two men repeated the procedure on the corpse's right arm.

The Dead Russian lay in the muck, his body casket-ready, his eyes spewing hatred at the waning moon above.

"No time like the present," the Italian said, grabbing the corpse's ankles. The Russian put his hands under the shoulders, and with a few steps and a well-aimed heave, the Dead Russian came to rest neatly at the bottom of the six-foot grave.

As before, the Italian took the first shift with the shovel and the Russian spelled him after a few minutes. A half hour later, they were done.

"A nice, fat summer rainstorm tomorrow, and it's like we were never even here," the Russian observed.

They trudged back to the SUV.

Inside the darkened cabin of the car, the Russian said, "Thank you for your help in this matter. You are, if I may say so, a consummate professional—something that is hard to find down here."

"Which brings me to our agreement," the Italian said as he started the engine. "I help you, you help me."

"I am glad to do so," the Russian replied.

"So, you know where he is, then?"

"I will in a minute or so," the Russian said, as he pulled a cellphone out of his pocket and dialed a number. He spoke briefly in his native language and disconnected the call.

"He's in Boca Raton. Right now. A private home. The address is being texted to me as we speak."

"What about the account? You have the account number?"

"Also being texted to me."

"And you're sure? You're sure you got the right guy? You'd know him if you saw him?"

The Russian laughed.

"Trust me. I told you. I know Elliot Becker better than Elliot Becker knows himself."

CHAPTER 1

SIX DAYS EARLIER.

The thing is, when Ponzi schemes fail, they tend to fail *fast.*

"Okay...yeah...I got it...just thought I'd double check. Thought maybe there was a mistake or something...Right...okay. Yeah...bye."

Elliot Becker hung up the phone, took one last look at the figures on his screen, and pressed the power button on his laptop. The image collapsed into a single glowing pixel and faded, like a dwarf star imploding a million light-years away.

"There is no way that this is fucking happening. Tell me this isn't fucking happening," he said under his breath.

The phone on his desk rang. His eyes scanned the screen on the console and his stomach contracted as he recognized the incoming number.

It was definitely happening.

He counted off three rings and picked up.

"Elliot Becker."

"Mr. Becker? It's Noreen," replied an anxious female voice.

Noreen? Not good. Where the fuck was Burrell?

"Noreen? Well, how are you? And how's Burrell?

Did everything clear up?" Elliot asked, in his smoothest I'm-a-financial-professional-whose-only-interest-is-making-your-life-better voice.

"Well, as Burrell goes, I can't rightly say. He up and took off with that new girl that was working in the deli making the sandwiches. Up in Port Saint Lucie, last I hear."

Jesus.

"I'm so sorry to hear that, Noreen." Elliot said, adding unctuously, "If you have a number, maybe I can reach out. Help patch things up, as it were."

"Nah, that's okay, Mister Becker," Noreen replied. "Burrell was a lazy asshole on his best day—and as soon as he breaks out in that rash again, that deli girl's gonna send him packing anyway. Until Burrell, I ain't never heard of a skin rash that smelled. But his did—it smelled. Just like a jar of pickles left open on the kitchen counter overnight. About made me sick to my stomach, if you wanna know the truth."

"Uh, huh...well imagine that. That certainly doesn't sound pleasant..." Elliot trailed off, an uneasiness growing in his abdomen. Since the closing, he hadn't spoken a word to Noreen and didn't expect to—ever. Which raised two questions: why was she calling, and where the hell was Burrell? He was pretty certain he knew the answer to the first question.

"I'll tell you why I called, Mister Becker," Noreen said, interrupting Elliot's train of thought.

"Please do. How can I help you today?" As he spoke, Elliot waved frantically at his open door, trying to catch the attention of Sasha, his office administrator (a charitable title, if ever there was one.)

"Well, it's this bank. They keep calling here and leaving messages saying that I need to call them to go over my loan. And that I'm behind on my payments."

"Hmm...okay. Well, sounds like some sort of mix up to me,

Noreen. Let me get on the phone with the right people and see if— "

"So, you know, I called 'em, Mr. Becker." Noreen continued.

"You.... called them? I'm sorry, Noreen...I—I want to make sure I heard you correctly." Elliot closed his eyes tightly, inhaled through his nose, and exhaled slowly.

Slowly.

"You're telling me that you got on the phone and you...you called the bank? You called the bank after we talked about how you should never call the bank, never call anyone about that house, and never talk to anyone about anything that has to do with money when it comes to that house. That's what you're telling me?"

"Well now, wait a minute, Mister Becker. That loan has my name on it. That's—"

"—Your name? *YOUR NAME*?"

So much for the slow breathing.

"Lemme tell you about your name, Noreen..." He began more or less calmly, but picked up steam as he went on. "*Your name* is worth a Section Eight rental in a fish camp on Lake Okeechobee. *Do you understand*?!!" Elliot screamed into the phone, flecking his desk with spittle as his face turned a mottled red.

"Your name is not—I repeat NOT—worth a six hundred and fifty-thousand-dollar home in the good part of Delray Beach! Do you get that? Have you ever looked around your neighborhood, Noreen? Have your ever seen your neighbors? Do any of them look like they're a fucking *checker* in a Winn Dixie, Noreen? Huh?"

Noreen was silent on the other end. Elliot scratched the back of his head and dropped the receiver onto the desk and stared at his blotter.

"It's Publix, Mr. Becker. I work at Publix, not Winn Dixie,"

Noreen's thin voice squeaked through the handset. There was an unmistakable hint of pride.

Elliot rocked back in the chair, took a deep breath, shot forward, and grabbed the handset.

"Alright. Forget it. No harm done," he said.

Breathe. Slowly.

"So," Becker continued, "Who'd you talk to? What was his or her name? You got a number?"

"Don't you wanna know what they said?" Noreen asked.

As if that mattered. Among his many talents was Elliot's ability to run "what-if?" scenarios out into the hundreds of iterations. Which is precisely what he was doing as Noreen asked, "Mister Becker? Are you still there?"

He closed his eyes and took a breath.

"Yes, Noreen. I'm still here. I'm thinking. Something you should try once in a while. Now, who was the person at the bank with whom you spoke?"

"Hang on." He could hear the rustling of paper as—presumably—Noreen tracked down the name and the number. She came back on the phone, but Elliot was no longer listening. He vaguely heard her read off a name and the first few digits of a phone number as he slowly hung up the handset. Among the many, many things that had to happen in the next few hours, catching up with Noreen's customer service rep was not one of them. This thing—as Elliot had feared—had *escalated*. That was bad enough. Worse still was the fact that this was the third such call he'd taken this week. There was no mistaking it: the new real estate bubble was about to burst, a little more than a decade after the first bubble. Elliot remembered the fallout from *that* bubble.

More importantly, Elliot could run the numbers. And the numbers didn't lie. It was going to get very bad, very quickly.

CHAPTER 2

Silvano Mazzio stood patiently, but uncomfortably, in Row 23 of a parked Airbus A-320 emblazoned with a Jet Blue logo. An immense man, he was hunched over seat 22E, staring into the balding crown of its aging and still seated occupant. The back of Silvano's head rubbed against one of the air conditioning ducts installed into the luggage bin above.

Economy section. Economy airline. 3 ½ miserable hours from White Plains to West Palm. And the only seat in the entire goddamn aircraft with a malfunctioning video screen. So, no CNBC. No ESPN. No Direct TV. Nothing for 3 ½ hours but the farts and the snorts of his sleeping geriatric seatmates and an oily copy of *People* that a previous occupent of seat 23E had left behind.

Jesus.

At 55, Silvano was old enough to remember when flying was something special. You dressed up a bit. Even in Economy, you were at least given the illusion of being a VIP. Not anymore. He glanced sideways at the crowd stalled in the exit aisle. The shorts and the tank tops and the flip flips and the iPods and the backpacks. Might was well have been a Greyhound. Didn't these people have any pride? Pathetic.

The nozzle that was digging into his skull was not actually blowing air of any kind. Apparently, in some effort to economize, the air conditioning had been shut off the instant the aircraft rolled to a stop at the jet way. The cramped space was getting warmer by minute, a situation not helped by his dark suit coat and perfectly knotted tie. In his awkward pose, Silvano had a clear shot out the window in Row 22. It looked miserable outside—the heat rising off the tarmac in little undulating waves.

Florida in August. Who travels to Florida in August?

Before the trip, Silvano had scanned a dozen or so online weather sites, looking for the possibility of hurricanes. It would be typical of his luck as of late to fly straight into the teeth of a Category 5. The good news—if there was any good news that could be associated with this trip—was that the nearest thing to a hurricane was a tropical wave somewhere off the coast of Africa, literally thousands of miles away. If he couldn't get done what he needed to get done in the time it took for that little low pressure to make its way across the Atlantic, a hurricane would be the least of his problems.

That word:

Problems.

Lately, the problems had been piling up. One after another. Which actually wasn't that surprising, given the amount of time that had passed since Silvano's boss—a well-known Long Island mobster named Frank Pizzuti—had been out of the day-to-day operation of the family business, due to certain extenuating circumstances that included, among other things, an ongoing stint in federal prison. On top of that was Frank's incredibly spoiled and dysfunctional family— whose management and well-being served as Silvano's basic job description.

It was only a matter of time before little problems piled up and became bigger problems, compounded by new problems. That was the nature of things, and despite the management books and self-improvement tapes and personal coaching sessions, Silvano had realized long ago that for a guy in his position, the reality was pretty simple: most of his job was solving problems. Or, put another way, cleaning up after people. And planning meant very little when it came to cleaning up.

The crowd was starting to move a bit. Silvano shuffled sideways; just far enough to be able to stand up, straighten his tie, and tug his suit jacket into place. He held his place in the aisle and waved politely to his neighbor in the window seat, an ancient and frighteningly rouged lady who looked as if she weighed no more than 50 pounds. She waved back and said, "Thank you, young man. But they're bringing a wheel chair for me after everyone gets off."

Silvano smiled and said, "Yes, ma'am. I hope you enjoy your visit."

"Thank you," she replied and added coquettishly, "and I must say that it's very rare these days to see a man acting in a such a courtly manner."

Tell me about it, Silvano thought. *Who the hell can be a gentleman with those stupid goddamn white things sticking in your ears?* He smiled and nodded a polite "goodbye" as the line lurched forward.

He pulled his roll-on luggage from the overhead bin without breaking his stride, his mind already on the tasks ahead, the first of which was to find out where he needed to meet Richie. He had called from New York before boarding the airplane, and he had been very specific: keep an eye on the arrival time, park at the curb 15 minutes after that, and stay put—Silvano would call him as he exited the plane.

He pulled his cell phone from his pocket and hit the power button.

Hey A. Cdnt make it. Grab a a cab and Ill c u @ condo tnt.

Perfect. Another problem to deal with and he wasn't even out of the plane. He glanced back at his cell phone. Dealing with Richie over the last couple of years had created a certain fluency in the stilted language of text messages, but that didn't make him any more fond of them. He punched in Richie's number, but thought the better of it, his thumb poised over the SEND button. *What's the point?* he thought. *He's not gonna answer. And it wouldn't make any difference if he did. He's gonna do what he wants to do, anyway. Just like he always does.*

And *that* was problem number one.

Silvano assumed that "*tnt*" meant "tonight". So, he had half a day to kill. Might as well get a little work done and mix in a little pleasure while he was at it. He walked quickly down the terminal to the escalators, following the signs for "Departures" and "Ground Transportation."

Outside the airport, he found the taxi line and queued in behind a couple with an enormous pile of expensive luggage. Rather than wait and watch them attempt to wrestle all of it into the trunk, Silvano walked back toward the next cab waiting. On the car's roof was a garish advertisement for something called the "Cougar Club & Steakhouse." The ad featured four impossibly beautiful women in lingerie, standing behind what looked to be a bone-in Porterhouse.

He leaned down and looked into the passenger side window.

"Where to?" the cabbie asked. Silvano tapped the roof of the car.

"Here."

CHAPTER 3

Powered up and running at an optimum speed of 35,000 RPM, a good-quality commercial Dremel rotary tool is almost completely silent. Until it touches something. Especially something metal. Then, you can't hear yourself think—much less the ringing of a cellphone.

Anyway, that was the excuse I offered my wife (actually semi-ex-wife, or soon-to-be-ex-wife, or something along those lines) after she told me in an exasperated voice that she had been trying to call me every 30 seconds for the last hour and a half. I pulled the phone away from my face and scrolled to the "missed calls" screen.

Yep. That looked about right.

"Well, I'm sorry, sweetie. I offered. "What's up?"

"Jeez, Logan. Can't you put your phone on vibrate or something? What if I really, really needed you?"

"If you really, really needed me, I assume you'd call me every thirty seconds for ninety minutes, until I answered the phone. Like you're doing right now. So—what's up?"

I heard a quick intake of breath. To paint Emma as dramatic would be unfair but not inaccurate. Unfair in the sense that she's not particularly flighty or strident. She's actually quite balanced and levelheaded. On the other hand, she makes her living in advertising, so drama and hyperbole are part of her life. Unlike me.

"How does homelessness sound?"

It sounds overly dramatic, I thought, but replied, "Not good. But it's a nice headline. What's the product? A line of tents?"

"Ha, ha, very funny. You're a laugh a minute." She paused for a second. "Logan—I'm completely serious. I got a FedEx package from some bank today and I'm...I'm—I don't know what I am. I'm stunned, I guess. It says that I owe them a hundred and eighty-two thousand dollars." She paused, "A hundred and eighty-two thousand dollars, Logan. Some loan I supposedly took out a year ago—"

"Huh?"

Now, I was stunned.

"—that I never took out. That I know nothing about. If I had taken a loan for that kind of money, I'm pretty sure I'd remember it." She was talking rapidly and sounded a little out of breath, as if she were walking somewhere.

Quickly.

"So, what did they say when you called them?" I asked, quite logically.

"Do you actually think I talked to them?" she said, as the door to my studio swung open and she strode in, putting her phone in her purse. Without stopping, she dropped her purse on the floor, walked across the studio and into my arms.

She buried her face in my chest, before I could warn her that my shirt was probably coated with a very fine dust of metal— rusted metal, to be precise. Courtesy of the Dremel and a long-ago decommissioned Iraqi T-72 tank.

She looked up at me; her nose, cheeks and forehead now smudged a reddish brown. I fought the urge to laugh, because there were tears welling up in her eyes.

"You think I called *you* a lot? I must have tried to call them fifty times. I could never get through to anyone who could tell me anything—other than I owed them a hundred and eighty-two thousand dollars, that I've ignored all of their letters and phone calls, and now they're going to foreclose on my house. A 'notice of acceleration', they called it." She paused. "*Our* house, Logan. Yours. Mine."

"And Zack's. And Isabella's," I added.

"Right," she replied. "And Zack's. And Isabella's."

She returned her face to my chest. Once again, I didn't bother to tell her about the dust. Instead, I ran my fingers through her thick curls and stroked her neck gently. I could feel her sobs.

We stood for a few minutes, holding one another closely. Gradually, the sobs subsided. Emma turned her face to the side, and I could sense that she was looking at the piece. She pulled away and walked toward it. I noticed that my rust-reddened hands had applied a nice series of streaks in her blond hair, but I kept quiet.

"Whoa." she whispered. "Logan, this is amazing."

She was looking at something that had probably consumed a thousand hours of my life. Maybe more. I hadn't kept track.

It was the final piece in a series that I had spent a year producing. The same year that I spent watching my marriage unravel; the same year that I attended eight different military funerals in five different states; the same year that I watched my daughter toddle off to kindergarten, and my son hit his first home run (he hit it off a tee, but it was still a home run.) And the same year I watched my soon-to-be-ex-wife become a minor celebrity in the highly insular world of advertising.

The series was actually my debut as a sculptor. I'd had some moderate success as a painter—two gallery shows in the last three years and another one right around the corner—but I was still searching for my identity in sculpture. I had started the project with the assumption that it would be just that — a series of small pieces that were related, but not necessarily interdependent. As the year wore on, however, it had become increasingly clear to me that what I was really working on was an installation.

Which, by almost any standard, is a wildly ambitious idea for an unknown sculptor. An installation is the type of thing you see outdoors—usually in front of a skyscraper in New York City, or a nice museum in any mid-sized market (as my soon-to-be-etc. would say.) Big things. Bolted-down, expensive things. And usually done on commission by a nationally-renowned, highly respected artist expressly for the purpose of adorning the exact space in which it is installed.

As opposed to, say, this particular piece of work, which was "installed" in my ramshackle Florida studio, completed on my own dime, and on exactly no one's hot list to purchase.

She turned to me. The rust had mixed with her tears, so she had a slightly bizarre, clown-like appearance, which was really working with her hair. I debated telling her and decided to let it go for now.

"I mean, really amazing," she continued, as she walked around the largest element. "I haven't been over here in what —"

"Two months," I interjected.

"—A month or so. Okay—maybe a couple of months. But Logan—I wasn't expecting this. This...." she trailed off, looking for the right words.

"This tells me more about where you were—and what it was doing to you—than anything *you* ever told me."

"Well, there you go. And you're always telling me that I don't communicate. So, can we get back together now?"

"Nice try," she replied with a little smile.

As quickly as it appeared, the smile vanished.

"Logan, I am really, really worried about this loan thing. I'm not sure what I'm going to do. I don't even know where to start."

Certainly not with me, I thought. But of course, Emma already knew that. This isn't to suggest that I am irresponsible – which I'm not. A better way to put it is that for most of my life, money was something that I didn't really have to think about in the way most people do. Partly because my family is ridiculously wealthy (their words) and partly because I spent a big chunk of my youth in places where the (paltry) money you earned was shoved in some savings account—tax free—waiting to be withdrawn if and when you came home.

Nevertheless, since I was obscenely wealthy (technically) and still madly in love my soon-to-be-ex-wife and mother of my children, I said, "How about I just give you the money? All it'll cost me is a phone call." And most of my principles. But, screw it— this was my family. Technically.

"I know, sweetheart," Emma replied. "And I appreciate it— mostly because I know how much it really *would* cost you." Before I could reply, she added, "And it's not like that would really solve anything. The fact remains, someone put my name on a loan that I've never heard of. Someone got my identity, Logan. I don't know whom, I don't know how, and I don't know why. But someone has my *name*." She paused. "And who knows what else?"

CHAPTER 4

Silvano Mazzio sat in his booth at the Cougar Club and Steakhouse sawing away at the toughest piece of buffet prime rib he'd ever tried to consume. Occasionally, he'd direct his gaze toward the bank of televisions mounted above and around the bar. Amidst the soft-core porn and sports highlights, someone had—apparently inadvertently—tuned one of the sets to CNBC. Silvano was addicted to financial journalism, although he rarely traded stocks or bonds. In his line of work, the less he left in the way of a financial trail, the better for all concerned.

On screen, Sue Herera was wrapping up the day's results as the camera pulled back to reveal the ultra-modern set, as well as Ms. Herera's shapely legs. For Silvano, this was akin to a money shot. For as long as he could remember, he had nursed a lust for the venerable Ms. Herera. It was something he couldn't really explain. She was a moderately telegenic, basically attractive woman on the short side of 50, with a body made for Lane Bryant. Maybe it was the business suits she wore—or the fact that she spent her workday literally wallowing in money. She was certainly smarter than the women he normally associated with, present company included. But it wasn't really that either. Like every other cable news organization, CNBC seemed to have an endless supply of stunning Ivy Leaguers on its talent roster. And to Silvano, they all seemed pretty much the same person—young, aggressive, and dressed to the nines. A slightly lisp-y delivery matched with a coy half-smile that the studio honchos must have written into the training manual. And every one of them, Silvano was sure, dating some fucking hedge fund manager or private equity dickhead. A guy with the kind of cash you'd need to ferry a "10" from CNBC Headquarters down to St Bart's on a private jet for dinner and a 3-day weekend.

Those guys. Those fucking snotty faced, middle-thirties and early forties WASPs and Jews, with their Vacheron Constantins and Aston Martin DB9s double-parked every Saturday at the Citarella in East Hampton, filling their baskets with $30 a pound filet-mignons for a weekend barbeque. Like a regular Joe.

Right.

Silvano spent a good deal of time thinking about those guys. Like most middle-aged American men, the optimism he'd stubbornly clung to as a kid was now exhausted. He had either made it—or hadn't. It really didn't matter which, because there were no do-overs. Time was no longer on his side.

A depressing realization, to be sure—made all the more painful by the constant spectacle of these fucking Lords of the New Capitalism prancing all over the Gold Coast of Long Island and the nicer addresses in Manhattan.

It was obscene, on some levels, the way these people lived, with the beach homes and the Pre-Wars, and the Net Jets and Range Rovers. A couple of these guys—these hedge fund managers—he'd read, had taken home paychecks in excess of a billion dollars last year. Who on God's green earth could justify a billion dollars for a year's work? It was beyond comprehension. Across the Sound over in Connecticut—in places like New Canaan and Darian, they were putting up 50,000 square foot mansions for some of these dildos. To hold what? A wife, a couple of little kids, and a staff big enough to run a small hotel.

He'd seen the pictures in Forbes—these places had art galleries in them, for chrissakes. Like little museums.

How does a guy pull that off? What kind of talent, luck and training had to come together to put some otherwise ordinary Joe on the receiving end of a billion dollars?

Not to mention a couple of million. Thirty-five, forty-year-olds, pulling down two or three mil a year? Had to be thousands—even tens of thousands—of those guys sprinkled around New York, Jersey, and Connecticut. And that wasn't even counting the West Coast, Texas or down here around Palm Beach and Boca and Key Biscayne. Tons of money down here, too. Come to think of it, there had to be hundreds of thousands of two- million-dollar-a year nimrods out there.

And he wasn't one of them.

Eddie Money was wrapping up *Two Tickets to Paradise* on the PA. A strange choice, Silvano thought, until he glanced over at the main stage and noticed that the dancer had to be at least 50 years old. *Not bad for a broad at that age,* he thought, but still. He'd assumed that The Cougar Club was just a name—not a theme.

He shifted his attention back to his steak, deciding that a little A1 might help tenderize the hunk of meat. He grabbed a bottle from a wire stand in the center of the table that doubled as a Lazy Susan for condiments and a spinning promotional card holder.

FREE TABLE DANCE WITH EVERY ENTRÉE! WEDNESDAYS ONLY.

Absentmindedly pondering the bad timing that had led him here on a Monday afternoon, Silvano shook the bottle of steak sauce vigorously. On the second backstroke, the small white cap flew off the bottle and over his shoulder, immediately followed by a viscous brown arc of liquid that settled on his ear, the lapel of his suit, and finally, on the very natty light blue square nestled in the coat's breast pocket.

"Goddammit!"

He leapt to his feet, dropping the bottle, which clattered noisily onto his plate. Snatching a napkin from the table, he dipped it quickly in his half-finished vodka tonic and began wiping at the side of his face. Shrugging out of the suit coat, he draped it as neatly as he could over the back of the banquette, and began dabbing at the long brown streak that ran down its length. He turned and looked toward the drink station for his waitress, waving his arm back and forth. Somehow, she noticed him through the strobe lights.

"Another vod-ton?" she asked as she approached the table.

Silvano, who was furiously—but fastidiously—using the soaked napkin to attack the stain, didn't bother to turn around.

"Just soda. A big glass. And make it fast."

The waitress squinted at the order.

"Soda and what?"

"Soda and nothing."

"Just soda?"

Silvano swung around, furious.

"How many times I gotta say it? Soda! A big fucking glass of soda!"

She looked at him for a few seconds.

"You want ice?"

"GO!" Silvano yelled, pointing toward the drink station. "NOW!"

As soon as he barked the order, he regretted it. He knew what was coming next, and sure enough, the waitress waggled her hand at the bouncer, followed by a come-over-here gesture. The guy, who had been standing by the drink station watching events unfold, dropped his magazine on the bar and started toward the table. *Palm Beach Illustrated*, Silvano noticed.

For a man of his size, the bouncer was surprisingly quick and moved with a trained grace. He was at the table in a matter of a few seconds.

"Is problem?"

A Russian. Great. After more than 30 years of frequenting strip clubs on the East Coast, Silvano had become familiar with Russian bouncers—not to mention Russian owners. He hated both. He was, however, realistic, and he knew enough to avoid unnecessary provocation.

"Problem? Yeah, I would say there's problem," Silvano replied, in a calm, measured tone. "Someone on the staff here forgot to screw the cap down on the steak sauce and it got all over my suit. I wanted some soda water to get the stain out before the fucking thing sets and ruins the suit for good."

"Steak sauce? Like ketchups?"

"Yeah. Exactly like ketchups," Silvano replied.

The bouncer looked confused. He directed his attention to the girl: "Who is responsible for screwing down caps on ketchups?"

"I don't know, Vadik," she replied, rolling her eyes. "It's a strip bar, not an Applebee's. It's not like we have a franchisee handbook or anything."

Silvano sensed that this was going nowhere. "Look, it ain't no matter to me what your internal procedures are. I don't give a shit who did or didn't screw in the cap. But when it ruins the jacket on my Ralph Lauren Purple Label suit, then I got a problem."

Vadik nodded and moved a step toward Silvano, who immediately began to square up his feet—just in case things went south. Vadik raised his hands impassively, shaking his head. "Not to worry." He reached across Silvano, reaching toward the suit coat draped over the banquette. He flipped the lapel, squinted and nodded appreciatively. "Very nice. Purple Labels are made where? America?"

"England and Italy, actually. This particular one is Italian," Silvano responded warily, his eyes never leaving Vadik's.

"What is retail price for this suit? I see Purple Labels on the EBay, but I figure are for fakes."

"Retail on this one is around $4,500, I think. I have some connections in the garment district, so for me, a little less."

About $4,400 less, to be precise.

Vadik turned to the dancer. "New rule: No steak sauce, no ketchups, no mustard, no nothing on table without caps screwed on securely. Make it first step in table dance. Tell other performers. Now, go and get this guest soda water and then go to locker room and see if you can find Tide stick."

"But Vadik," the waitress began, "I've got like, four other – "

"Stop arguing," Vadik interrupted. "Others can wait. Have them see me if this is problem."

The man turned and trotted lightly down the stairs, never looking back. He called over his shoulder to Silvano, "Your tab is on the house. Sorry for damage to Purple Label." And with that, he went back to his magazine article.

On the main stage, a middle-aged redhead—and apparently her daughter—began a highly complex series of pole maneuvers to Rush's *Tom Sawyer* as the waitress returned with Silvano's soda water. He stood, grabbed his suit jacket, and strode out of the club, taking the glass of soda water with him.

Vadik never looked up.

CHAPTER 5

Burrell Malin strolled purposefully out of the Subway restaurant, a large plastic to-go bag in one hand, and the keys to his 1984 Oldsmobile Cutlass Sierra in the other. His goal, as always, was to move as quickly as possible from one air-conditioned space to another, and minimize direct exposure of his skull to the sun.

He was lucky in one respect—with the exception of his Cutlass, almost every square inch of interior space in the state of Florida enjoyed industrial-grade meat locker quality frigid air. Had since the 1950's. *Jackie Gleason, Flipper, and Miami Vice* aside, air conditioning was probably the single most important contributor to the state's late-century population boom.

The sun was, of course, problematic. There was simply no avoiding it—especially in late summer, when it hung blindingly in the haze, baking everything in sight, and turning the mid-day sun showers into steam rising off the asphalt.

Unfortunately, since the rash had migrated to Burrell's skull, hats were out of the question.

He was leaning over the car door, hurriedly fishing the keys from his pocket when he heard Elliot Becker's voice.

"What? You didn't think I'd find you?"

Not good. Burrell turned slowly to face the voice. "What are you talking about, Mr. Becker? I didn't know that I had to report in to you on everything I did, and everywhere I went." Burrell tried to glare menacingly as he spoke, but the effect was lost as the glare became a squint, and the raw and reddened patches on his scalp began to ooze in direct sunlight.

Becker stepped back. "Jesus, Noreen wasn't kidding," he said, as he fanned the air in front of him. "You smell like brine vinegar. Like a fucking pickle barrel. Is that really the rash?"

Burrell nodded abjectly. "Yep. Been to three docs in the last month alone—two of them derms. Some kind of yeast imbalance, one of them thinks. Probably from being exposed to insulation and stuff on inspections."

Becker snorted derisively, as he continued to daintily fan his hands. "Right. I've got to hand it to you, Burrell. You're the only person I've ever met who could make the home inspection business sound like a series on the Discovery Channel."

Burrell stiffened. "Hey, do you even know how many industrial chemicals there are in the average attic? Over fif—"

"Bullshit, pal." Becker interrupted. "Give it a rest. This isn't some West Virginia hollow, and you ain't got black lung. So, whatever scam you think you're going to pull against whomever you think is going to pay you, spare me. Save your bullshit, trumped-up asbestos-or-whatever-the-fuck-it-is claim for them." Becker paused and added. "Besides, you and I have enough problems, as it is."

"What are you talking about?" Burrell asked.

"Noreen."

"Noreen?"

Becker nodded. He looked skyward, searching for the right words.

"Well, I guess that's not completely accurate. Noreen's a problem. Definitely a problem. Maybe even the biggest problem. But Noreen's not the *only* problem."

Burrell was only half listening. His scalp was beginning to

itch unbearably. That was the problem with the sun—and the reason he tried like hell to avoid it. Sun meant sweat. And sweating made the lesions on his scalp itch like nothing else he had ever experienced—to the point that he wanted to literally claw the skin off his head. He had come close, in fact. Furiously rubbing at the already raw patches with anything abrasive he could get his hands on: a towel, the worn velour headrest in the Olds—it didn't matter.

Becker poked him in the shoulder. "Hey, Burrell. Are you hearing me? You need to be hearing me, because your name is on six different appraisals right now for a half dozen different loans, and they're all going south. Right now."

"I thought the whole idea, Mr. Becker, was to unload the houses—that way, there'd be no reason for anyone to ever look at the loans. Isn't that the way this thing is supposed to work?" Burrell was rubbing the Subway receipt briskly back and forth across his scalp as he spoke.

"Please, for the love of God, stop with the scratching. You're going to make me heave." Becker said. "And yes, that's the way this thing is supposed to work—except for one thing—and since you're in the business, lemme ask you: how many legitimate calls have you gotten lately for appraisals?"

Burrell thought about it for a moment. There had been that one job from SunTrust a couple of weeks ago. Maybe three total in the last month or so.

"Not many," he replied.

"Exactly. Not many. Wanna know why?"

"Well, I guess—"

"— Because the rest of the world has finally figured out— once again— that a fifteen hundred square foot ranch home on a lot the size of a postage stamp in the middle of Palm Beach County is not worth a million dollars. *That's* why."

"So—"

"—So, the market's drying up. Plain and simple. Nobody's buying. And if nobody's buying, nobody's selling. So...?" Becker paused and added, "You kinda see where I'm going with this, don't you, Burrell?"

"Um, yeah." Burrell replied.

"Good. So, let's recap: We are—did you notice my use of the inclusive pronoun there, Burrell? The *'we'*? Well, it's being used deliberately, as they say, because—again—*we* are now stuck with six different houses, which *we* bought for an average price of six hundred and eighty-nine thousand dollars. Each. A number I'm assuming you're familiar with, since it was your ridiculously over-valued appraisals that legitimized that price."

"Well, I'm not sure what you expect me to do, Mr. Becker," Burrell said, as he fought the urge to gouge himself with his car key. He needed to find some shade and some air conditioning —fast—or he was going to go bat shit. "You keep saying 'we' but I didn't buy any if those homes. My name's not on any of the contracts or deeds or loans."

"That true, Burrell." Becker replied. "Absolutely true. But it *is* on the appraisals. On every one of them. And when the shit hits the fan—and trust me, it will—that particular anomaly will be noted. If not by the Feds, then by me."

"Whaddaya mean? You'd rat me out?" Burrell was stunned – for about a nanosecond. Then he remembered who—and what—Elliot Becker was.

"Absolutely, I'm gonna rat you out. First chance I get, as a matter of fact. What – you think I'm taking your name to the grave? Like some mid-level Mafia guy from the fifties or something? Not hardly. And even if I didn't give you up, it wouldn't make any difference. This kind of stuff is *Federal*, Burrell. RICO-type stuff. FBI, and all that. You think those guys aren't going to run down every detail of every loan? How long do you think it's going take for them to spot a pattern? Jesus, they do this for a living, Burrell. The simple fact is, we're both toast unless..." Becker trailed off.

"Unless what?" Burrell asked, afraid of the answer.

"Well, there's an answer to that, Burrell. I'd ask you to jump in my car, but I couldn't take the smell. So, why don't you jump in your own piece of shit and follow me instead?"

"To where?"

No answer. Becker was already walking toward his car.

Burrell slid into the Olds and immediately began rubbing his scalp against the headrest.

CHAPTER 6

I pulled the door to the studio closed and snapped the padlock shut. Not that I had any concerns about theft—I couldn't really see anyone trying to make off with a couple hundred pounds of rusted anti-ballistic sheeting, or an old Millermatic MIG welder, but you never know.

I was still thinking about the conversation with my favorite ex.

Emma and I had spent the better part of an hour trying to reconstruct a process that had taken place more than three years ago, when we had bought our first—and as it turns out — only home. Not surprisingly, I was of absolutely no help in the reconstruction process. My lack of financial acumen notwithstanding, I hadn't been present at the closing and had only lived in the house for all of three weeks once "we" bought it.

Buying it had been an act of pure optimism on our part—an homage to the adulthood, responsibility and normalcy that we desperately wanted. At least Emma desperately wanted it. I had been in Afghanistan at the time and concerned with other things.

I'd suggested to Emma that we contact the police, reasoning that this was, in all likelihood, a case of fraud or identity theft.

"Really, Logan? You think?" Emma had responded.

I detected a hint of sarcasm.

"I called the cops first thing after hanging up with the bank."

"What'd they say?"

"Beyond taking my name and promising to contact the bank? Pretty much nothing. Wait—they did ask if I had lost a credit card or a driver's license recently. Or had my purse stolen."

"That's it?" I snorted.

"That's it. I got the sense that, unless they have something that they can pin down—like a theft—this is pretty much out of their area of expertise."

"They give you any suggestions on where to go?"

"Well, the desk sergeant that I spoke to said that cases like this tend to fall under federal jurisdiction, since they involve all sorts of interstate financial transactions—money wired from one bank to another. Blah, blah, blah."

"So, federal means FBI," I offered. "That's a good thing, right? Get the G-men on it. I met some of those guys back in the day. Serious people. Seriously competent."

"Well, if you know some of them, why don't you call them?"

"I'll see what I can do. The guys that I know were involved in...different stuff. Not financial crimes, per se. More along the lines of— "

"— Anti-terrorism. Yeah, I know, Logan. I wasn't born yesterday. I read the newspaper."

I briefly considered some of the things that I'd seen in the Middle East that would never make the newspaper and smiled.

"Yeah. Well, maybe one of them has a buddy here stateside that can help us out. Let me make some calls when I get over to the restaurant."

I crossed the alley, walked a hundred yards south down A1A, and turned into Casa Playa's. Van Morrison was singing about crazy love as I navigated the front bar and headed back to my office. I sat down, unlocked a file drawer, and flipped through a series of folders until I found one neatly labeled "255 Blue Water Lane." While I may not have an accountant's math skills, the organizational part I've got down cold. By nature, and by training, I keep things shipshape. The folder contained the mortgage and insurance documents on our home.

Opening the folder, I skimmed the paperwork for the loan. While my name was on the title, only Emma's was on the loan. At the time, it didn't seem to matter. Emma had just been given a huge promotion to partner and a big raise to go with it. She had easily qualified for the mortgage. I remembered her telling me over our weekly sat-chat that the loan agent had told her he could get her into a million-dollar mortgage if she wanted. She had said "no thanks", but I could tell—even over the phone —that she felt flattered. And very adult. I remembered mentioning that I could probably qualify for a $20 million loan if she wanted something bigger.

She had not been amused.

The loan was immortalized into an unwieldy document. Most of it was on legal-sized paper, folded, and shoved into a letter-sized folder. There looked to be about five copies of everything. Signatures, initials, counter-signatures. Insurances affidavits, confirmations of wire transfer, and so on. Basically, pages and pages of crap—the kind of stuff that makes lawyers wealthy, and the rest of us beholden to them. Not being an attorney myself, I soon gave up any pretense of looking for possible legal loopholes, reasoning that if I couldn't actually understand the document in the first place, it was pretty unlikely that I would recognize a loophole.

Instead, I found a pad of memo paper and a pen, and began jotting down the names and titles of anyone who had signed anything in the folder.

It seemed like a logical starting point: this was either a case of identity theft, or fraud or both. Which meant *people* were involved. Phantom, two-hundred-thousand dollar loans don't pop up as a result of a computer glitch.

Besides Emma's, there were handful of names and titles:

Nancy Greenberg, whose stamp attested to her 'in good standing' status as a Notary Public for the State of Florida... some guy named Elliot Becker, who appeared to be the loan agent from an outfit called "Modern Properties, Inc."...an insurance agent named Helen Deakman...a property appraiser named Burrell Malin...a locally famous husband and wife realtor combo whose name I recognized from a little ad they'd placed in the Casa Playa's menu: Gene and Jeannie Olmsted ("Call the Olmsteds for *your* Homestead!"), and finally, a guy from something called AA Top Title named Ted Hodges, Esq.

And that looked to be about it.

I stood up, closed the door to the little room, and pulled the desk away from the wall. Using a penknife, I popped out a small square of paneling, revealing a Secure Logic fireproof safe—complete with a biometric and five-digit pass code lock—mounted at about knee level. I knelt in front of the safe and placed my right ring finger on the sensor. The gravity-fed door opened a few seconds later.

Installing the safe was one of the first things I'd done after buying the little bar and grill; there were things that were a part of my recent past that were either too dangerous or too sensitive to leave laying around in a drawer at home.

I reached in and pulled out my trusty old Sig Sauer P226 and set it on the floor. I reached back in and retrieved a small, leather-bound book. A little black book of sorts, I suppose, but with an entirely different set of prospects. Replacing the pistol and sitting back down at the desk, I thumbed through the pages until I found the name I wanted: Ben Gray. National Joint Terrorism Task, Federal Bureau of Investigation. The last I'd heard, he was working out of the offices of the National

Counterterrorism Center in McLean, Virginia.

I'd met Ben years before—when he was known as Instructor Death. I was 23 years old, fresh out of OCS and a week into BUD/S 1st Phase when I was ordered by Instructor Death to hitch arms with the guy on either side of me and march into the Pacific. My first round of "surf torture." Eleven minutes later, I was shivering uncontrollably in the wave wash, trying to reel off sit-ups in time with Death's count and cadence. Falling behind, we were ordered back into the surf as a "wake-up call."

"You will learn to listen. You will learn to think. You will learn to follow instructions," Death intoned calmly and somewhat drolly into his portable megaphone. "Or, you will quit. Or you will drown. Either one is okay with me." I can still hear his voice, tinny and amplified by the cheap speaker, ordering us to "drop and push 'em out". Flat, factual, emotionless—a sort of soundtrack to accompany the seven weeks of hell that was First Phase in Naval Special Warfare training.

Many years later, we crossed paths in Bagram, of all places; I was rotating out of Afghanistan, while he was going the other way. I heard him before I saw him, but as I mentioned, I'll never forget that voice. In the few minutes we spent catching up, he told me that he was headed east—I assumed as part of a DEVGRU platoon.

DEVGRU is military shorthand for "Development Group." Which—in the great tradition of the Navy—is a complete misnomer, since DEVGRU doesn't "develop" anything. DEVGRU is actually the Navy's Counter Terrorism unit—a kind of SEAL Delta Force.

Sometimes (mistakenly) referred to as SEAL Team 6, DEVGRU is very black and very elite. And while all of its operators come from SEAL Teams, technically speaking, DEVGRU isn't even in the Navy's chain of command. It's actually part of the Joint Special Operations Command, which also includes the Army's Delta Force, the 160th Special Operations Aviation Regiment from the Air Force, a smattering of highly special-ized Army Rangers and hundreds of support personnel. JSOC reports directly to the Joint Chiefs of Staff and ultimately, the President. The command has its own budget, its own admin-istrative staff, its own equipment, and its own way of doing things. In Afghanistan, guys used to refer to JSOC as "Murder, Incorporated."

I wasn't surprised that Ben had landed there—he was about as serious as they came: smart, fit, thoughtful, creative, re-sourceful, relentless and blessed with an innate ability to dial up—and dial down—violence quickly and precisely. A team player. Perfect for DEVGRU.

At the time, Ben was probably somewhere in his late thirties or early forties, toward the end of the operational life of a SEAL. For most enlisted guys, that meant retirement. For Gray, I assumed it would simply mean a change of venue. The guy was a born warrior and an operator with few peers. You don't put people like that behind desks; you put them behind guns.

I found out how right—and how wrong—I was earlier this year, when we met again at a Navy memorial service in Charleston, South Carolina. The ceremony was to honor a fallen teammate named Brian Mathews. Brian had been my best friend since we'd entered the Navy. We had gone through BUD/S together and had spent much of the following ten years watching each other's back.

Ben had come down from Washington. He had indeed, re-tired from the Teams shortly after I'd seen him in Afghanistan. Still wanting to be active and operational, he'd joined the FBI, looking to become part of the Hostage Rescue Team. He'd put in his two years, earned his Special Agent badge, and gotten his berth in HRT. Within a month, he had managed to shatter both kneecaps in a fast-rope training accident—and suddenly found himself riding a desk in DC.

"Can you fucking believe it? Twenty years on the Teams and I barely get a scratch. A month here, and I'm a cripple."

I'd kept my mouth shut.

After the service ended, Ben and I, along with about fifty other frogmen, had gone out and gotten good and drunk at a local tavern. As I mentioned earlier, I've spent a lot time this year putting good friends in the ground—and that requires a lot of lubrication. A little more with every one, I'm finding out.

Maybe it's the thing itself—the service, I mean. Maybe it's the fact that these are the best people I'll ever meet—and I already know that without having to live the rest of my life. Or maybe it's the fact that I have the time to attend all of these services.

The time weighs on me. Because the simple fact is, I'm here when I should be there. And I can't be there because they're not going to let me go back. No matter whom I petition, no matter how many tests I pass, no matter how much paperwork I file.

Anyway, we got incredibly shitfaced. There are still parts of that evening that I don't remember. But I remembered putting Ben Gray's cell phone number into mine and copying the contents of his FBI Special Agent card into my little black book.

I dialed the number and it rang twice.

"Agent Gray."

CHAPTER 7

Silvano sat in an idling taxi outside a high-rise condominium in downtown West Palm Beach. He was intently scrolling through the emails on his BlackBerry. When Richie wasn't texting him, he was emailing him: *I need you to go blah blah blah...I never got the yada yada yada...* all hours of the fucking day and night, this kid. Like he never slept. Just punched buttons on a cell phone like some kind of over-trained chimpanzee. And when it wasn't Richie hounding him to death, it was Richie's mother, Darlene. Another piece of work.

It hadn't come to Silvano all at once, this realization that he actually *worked* for Darlene Pizzuti—and by extension, Richie and his idiot siblings. It more or less dawned on him, slowly, over the first six months or so of Frank's incarceration. Looking back, he wasn't really all that surprised that it had taken that long. He'd read enough self-help crap to recognize when he was blocking an uncomfortable truth. And to ponder the reality of this one—shitty implication after shitty implication—was enough to make anyone want to crawl inside a bottle and never get out.

First off – and this was the big one—there was no such thing as quitting in his business. Even if he had the money to say "Fuck you, I'm outta here," or maybe "Thanks for everything, but I feel like this is a good time for me to explore other opportunities," it wasn't going to happen. In this line of work, you were done when you were dead, or when they told you that you were done. Period. End of story.

Next was Frank Pizzuti—or more accurately, Frank's current status as a guest of the Federal Government. Bad news there, too. Federal raps had mandatory minimums, not much in the way of time off for good behavior, and no parole. In Frank's case, that worked out to a little more than eight years. This was as much a sentence for Silvano as it was for Frank. And given what Silvano now knew about Frank's family, an argument could be made that Frank got the better end of the deal.

Finally, there was the crushing realization of how little Frank must have actually thought of Silvano. This was a guy to whom Silvano had sworn a blood oath of fealty. Twenty years of being 100% unblinkingly loyal—to the exclusion of everything else that constitutes a normal life, like a wife and kids. For Silvano, there had been just Frank. And for what? To be pawned off as some second-rate, mobster-issue Mr. French for a bottle-blonde shrew from Bergen County and her half-witted offspring? For eight years, plus the duration? Who would do that?

When Frank went away, it wasn't like the business went away with him. Actually, quite the opposite. With Frank gone, the government seemed to lose all interest in the Pizzuti enterprise. They'd gotten the convictions, the headlines, and the head on the wall they had needed to justify their continuing drain on the taxpayer. Meanwhile, the Pizzuti organization needed new—albeit temporary—leadership. Fresh sources of revenue and enhanced strategies for capital preservation. Just like a regular multinational corporation.

Silvano felt that he had the experience and the ideas to take business to the next level—not to mention extensive training in financial management and personal productivity. He had planned on having the conversation with Frank between the indictment and plea agreement, as Frank was putting his affairs in order. Silvano was confident that he'd be rewarded for his years of hard work and dedication. Just like a regular employee.

Instead, he'd been shit on. Insulted. Pushed aside.

Frank, surrounded by lawyers, prison consultants, and members of his immediate and business family, was unreachable. Word of Silvano's new responsibilities had come to him through an associate attorney on Frank's defense team—a little Jew named Andrew something-or-other.

"For now, Mr. Pizzuti would like you to focus on working with Mrs. Pizzuti to maintain an orderly and positive environment for the family. As you know, the children are all at particularly impressionable ages, and it's important, Mr. Pizzuti believes, to promote stability and harmony at home. He feels strongly, Mr. Mazzio, that you're the right person to help in this regard."

What was he supposed to say to that?

"You going in? This is the address you gave me, man." The cabbie was looking at Silvano through the partition. "You need me to take you somewhere else?"

Silvano looked up from his email screen. He shut down the Blackberry and dropped it into his front pocket. "Nah, this is it."

Silvano got out, paid the cabbie and entered the building.

Richie's condo had once been an apartment. The whole place, in fact, had been just another generic, high-rise downtown apartment building with a generic high-rise apartment building name: Tower One. At the height of the real estate boom, however, an out-of-state development company had bought the property, with a plan to turn every rental unit into a high-end luxury condo. Starting prices for one bedroom "luxury-loft" efficiencies were in the two hundred-thousand-dollar range—and went up from there. This wasn't unique—it had been happening for years, and as the housing market gained momentum, so did the number of so called "condo-conversion" projects around the state.

Part of the reason that it was so popular was because it was so simple; there was nothing to build—and beyond a little carpet and a maybe some windows—nothing to tear out.

To create the "luxury", all it took was a coat of paint, a little tile, some crown molding, and eight hundred dollars' worth of granite in the kitchen. Throw in a fake cherry desk and a nice light fixture in the lobby and bingo! Luxury.

Creating vacancies was simply a matter of massive rent increases, combined with quick buyouts of the existing leases—as well as an "early buyer" incentive program for renters that wanted to buy their own unit. (The early buyer incentive was a total sham—pitched as a free "designer appliance upgrade," it basically replaced low-quality white kitchen appliances with low-quality black kitchen appliances.) The strategy worked perfectly and within six months, every apartment in the building was empty.

The real fun was in the actual renovation phase. Generally, the developer could generate enough free cash flow to start the work from the "pre-sales" activity alone. The concept behind a pre-sale was simple: buy the condo before it's built and get the "guaranteed" lowest price. Pre-sale buyers were typically real estate speculators interested in getting in on the ground floor and flipping the unit as soon as possible—usually within a year.

In South Florida—where real estate prices had risen so quickly it was hard to keep track—the practice made perfect sense: borrow the down payment at "teaser rate" of one or two percent, lock in a price, make as few mortgage payments as possible, flip the condo, and you had a good chance of doubling your money.

For developers, the deal was even sweeter: pre-sell enough units to get the renovations started. Keep most of the units off the market to take advantage of the inevitable price increases down the road. Secure a huge loan for the renovations necessary to turn rental apartments into luxury condominium homes. And pocket the loan money.

Regardless of what happened after that, the developer was golden. The renovations were usually so insignificant that they could be paid for—or at least started—out of the cash generated by the pre-sales. Once those were underway (and you always started with the lobby, the pool, and the "Sales Center") the prices on the units would start to rise. People would snap them up as fast as they could secure financing—which the developer also controlled.

Sell enough additional units to keep the renovations going, and the cash flow was amazing. In ideal circumstances, the developer would be completely flush before the first loan installment came due.

If it ran the other way, no problem. If prices stalled or dropped, if buyers dried up, —if a hurricane hit—it didn't matter. The developer would simply halt the renovation, stash the cash offshore, file bankruptcy, and haul ass out of Florida. It was a no-lose proposition and the most revered and copied real-estate scam in the state.

Silvano knew all of this because the developer in this particular instance was his boss, Frank. And it was precisely for these reasons that Frank's family—or more accurately, a real estate development firm owned by his family—had followed this particular business strategy to the letter in the process of taking Tower One condo.

Silvano walked across the foyer and approached the security guard, who was either peering intently at the security monitor in front of him, or sleeping soundly. Silvano gave him the benefit of the doubt by clearing his throat slightly as he drew near. The guard rustled and sat up a bit in his swivel chair.

"Can I help you?" he asked. A second later, a look of recognition flashed across his face, and he smiled. "Mr. Mazzio, nice to see you! Richie told me you was coming in. How are ya?"

Not great, but I'm not yet in your shoes, pal, Silvano thought. "I'm surviving—" Silvano stole a look at the man's nametag. "— Myron. I'm surviving." Myron looked pleased at Silvano's semi-instant recall of his name.

"Good to hear. Good to hear...You're, uh, looking for Richie, I guess? Want I should call up to his unit and let him know that you're down here?"

"That'd be swell, Myron. *Lo apprezzo.*"

Silvano wasn't above dropping a little theater into the act when the moment called for it, and he'd learned that a lot of these old coots down in Florida were still smitten with gangsters—a holdover from their glory days up north as union fixers and whatnot.

Old Myron looked as pleased as punch. "Lemme get him on the horn."

Thirty seconds later, Silvano was on the express elevator headed to one of the development's two penthouse units. Richie was there to greet him as the elevator doors slid open. "Hey, Big Sal. What's shaking, son?"

Always with this "son" shit. "Son" this, and "son" that—like some South Bronx eggplant hip-hopper. Silvano sighed. "I ain't your son, Richie. I'm your keeper. Let's us get inside and see what we can do to sort this shit out."

Richie's penthouse condominium managed to be expensive and cut-rate at the same time. It brought to a mind a story Silvano had read somewhere: the business manager for Ike and Tina Turner, at the height of their popularity, was rumored to have uttered upon stepping into their Beverly Hills mansion for the first time, "I didn't know it was possible to spend a million dollars at Kmart."

"You wanna a drink or something?"

Richie had shambled ahead of Silvano and called out from the kitchen. "I got some Patrón in here, some Remy, beers, wine...whatever."

"Jack Daniels. Neat." Silvano replied as he scanned the apartment. There were people all over the place. Lounging on the huge, tasteless, L-shaped couch in the middle of the living room; sitting on the floor rolling joints, standing by the entertainment center, flipping through the racks of 12-inch vinyl records and CDs. A deep, throbbing bass line rippled from the speakers, punctuated by a slowed-down horn chart from an old Motown staple.

Richie Pizzuti. Long Island's Original Gangster.

Richie handed Silvano his drink. Silvano noted the pale gold color as he brought the glass to his lips. Dewar's and water. On the rocks.

"Big Sal, meet the crew." Richie grinned lopsidedly at Silvano, clearly shattered. "Everybody? This is my man Silvano."

No one looked up.

"I think, Rich, we need to find a quiet place...whaddaya say? You know if anybody's back there in the bedroom?"

As he spoke, Silvano politely—but firmly—steered Richie down the hallway.

"Like I said, we need to talk."

CHAPTER 8

I finished my call with Ben Gray and stepped out of the office, closing and locking the door behind me.

Casa Playa's was hopping.

Both bars were packed, and most of the tables were taken. Someone had commandeered the sound system and Townes Van Zandt's classic *Pancho and Lefty* filled the room. I loved everything about that song, and I paused in the kitchen long enough to hear Townes, in his elegant and unsentimental way, tell the story of two aging bandits on the run and headed for their final stand against the *Federales*.

I said a quick prayer for Pancho.

The music lent a distinctive TexMex air to the place—which is what Casa Playa's had been when I had first walked into the bar two years earlier. At the time, I had been home a month; my marriage was crumbling and my career ending. Casa Playa's sat between where I liked to surf and where I liked to park.

After passing the little joint a dozen times, I finally decided to stick my nose in. The front door was propped open and a sign read "Live Music Tonight. Cold Beer Now."

It looked cool, dark and empty—a good place to get out of the heat, have a beer, and maybe do a little thinking. I figured it was time.

For weeks, I had been putting off sitting down and really facing my future. Workouts and surfing had filled my days—and since the workouts made me feel great physically, it was easy to turn feeling great into feeling "productive." Which wasn't the case at all.

I found a stool at the far corner of the bar. The Sir Douglas Quintet was thrashing its way through *Mendocino* on the jukebox. I hadn't heard that song in years.

"I'll have a beer," I said to the bartender.

"Got a preference?"

"Nope."

"Coors it is. Might as well have one myself."

He reached behind into the cooler, pulled out two bottles, opened both and handed one to me.

"Cheers, *mijo*."

We touched bottles. We were the only two people in the place.

The bartender continued. "I seen you walk by here every day. Wondered when you'd stop in. Flat?"

"No, the beer's fine." I answered. I got the feeling that I wasn't going to get much thinking done that afternoon in Casa Playa's.

"I meant the surf. No waves?"

"Oh. Yeah, it's totally flat."

Anyway, "a beer" turned into a bunch of beers and a long heart-to-heart with the bartender—who also happened to be Casa Playa's owner—an aging surfer from Corpus Christi named Rip. It was the middle of the day, the music was good, and neither of us had anywhere we needed to be. Apparently, Rip had been doing some thinking, too.

By about beer number five, he was telling me that he wanted out of the restaurant business and out of Florida to boot. Twenty-five years of sun, surf and booze had done its damage—he had tired of the crowds and bustle of South Florida, lost his passion for the restaurant, and wanted to get back to the Texas Gulf Coast.

Benign neglect and bad food had put a dent in Casa Playa's clientele, but the location was undeniable – across the street from the beach, just down the road from a legendary surf shop —and smack in the middle of one of the last truly unspoiled beach towns in the state.

I meant it when I said that money holds very little sway over me—but I have to admit that sometimes, access to unlimited capital is a good thing. This was one of those times. Joe Ely was singing about a waitress named Sherry when I wrote Rip a personal check for Casa Playa's—and he took it. I figured I'd gotten it for a song.

A month later, Rip was happily riding two-foot slop on Padre Island, and I was still trying to unravel the incredible train wreck I had purchased.

Starting with the food.

When Rip had opened the place a decade before, Casa Playa's was a gourmet Mexican restaurant. (Whether or not he deliberately misspelled the name remains a mystery.) Over the years, the place had devolved into an indoor taco stand of sorts. That in and of itself wouldn't have been a bad thing, had the tacos been any good—which they weren't.

I'm not much a cook, I'm not a restaurant critic, and the time I'd spent time in the military made me an expert on bad food – not good food. On the other hand, I had spent almost a decade (on and off) in San Diego, which is the taco stand capitol of the world. I knew what a taco was supposed to taste like.

Which was not like this.

I spent a week trying every dish on Casa Playa's menu. I felt a little bit like one of those ambush chef guys on a reality TV program. I'd sit at the table, and the two dreadlocked cooks—Devan and Peter—would bring out three or four things at a time and then stare at me while I tried them. They weren't friendly stares, either.

The deeper I got into the menu, the weirder the food became.

"Isn't a tamale supposed to be wrapped in like, a corn husk? This looks like a banana leaf."

"What's the difference? You don't eat it anyway," one of them would snap.

"What's that meat in the tortilla soup?" I'd ask.

"Goat."

"Goat?"

"Yeah, goat."

"Why is there goat in the tortilla soup? You know what? Never mind."

"No worries."

"And, now that I'm looking at it, why aren't there tortillas in the tortilla soup?"

"Tortillas are by request. You didn't request."

This got old fast. To break things up, I asked Peter and Devan what *they* thought of the food. Devan told me he wouldn't know – he had never eaten it.

"What do you mean, you've never eaten it?" I asked.

"I'm from fucking Antigua, mon. What de fuck would I know about Mexican food?"

Peter—named after Peter Tosh, the old Wailer, was—not surprisingly— from Jamaica. He, too, had never eaten the food he cooked at Casa Playa's.

"Only tortilla I ever ate was Taco Bell, and one of dem was plenty."

"How did you guys ever get a job cooking here?" I asked.

It turned out that Devan and Peter were fishing buddies who would occasionally sell Rip their catch. Which was why they happened to be standing in Casa Playa's kitchen the day that the entire staff quit *en masse* over the matter of a couple of bounced payroll checks.

Devan said, "Rip asked me if we could cook, and I said 'who you kidding?' I was a chef back home. Cooked for de high rollers at de St. Gene Club. Ah course I can cook. Peter can help with choppin' and such—"

"—So, Rip said to get cooking," Peter broke in. "Said he'd pay in cash, end of the night. And dat's what he did, and dat's what he was still doin' last month when you come in and buy de place."

That explained the hostility.

"Look, I'm happy to pay you guys," I replied. "And if you want me cut you a check today for what you're owed, I will. But to be honest—right now, I'm trying to figure whether I'm even going to *keep* you."

Devan and Peter had looked at each other as I continued.

"C'mon, let's be straight." I looked at Devan. "You're a chef. You know food. And you've got to know that this isn't very good food. So—as a chef—why don't you tell me what you think the problem is, and we'll figure out a way to fix it?"

After a few seconds of silence, he sat down at the table next to me.

"The problem is that this ain't the kinda food I know. Ain't the kinda food I love. You gotta love what you cook, mon.

Don't work any other way. I told Rip de same thing. Over and over. He never listen. Just tell me to make it more Mexican. What de fuck does dat even mean, mon?"

He leaned in toward me. "Let me cook you sumptin *I know*—sumptin from my heart—and if you wanna send me and Peter packin' after dat, ain't no hard feelings. Deal?"

What did I have to lose?

"Sure. Deal."

Devan stood up. "Okay. Chill a bit. I'm gonna make you sumptin that's gonna have you in tears."

I couldn't wait to see this.

Ten minutes later, Peter came back, bearing yet another plate. He set it before me.

"Dis your appetizah," he said, as he pulled a bottle of Kalik out of the cooler and set it on the table. He produced a quarter wedge of lime from somewhere, placed it in the neck of the beer bottle, and said "Put a little lime in both."

I looked down.

Three huge shrimp, beautifully pink and still steaming, were arranged delicately in the center of a shallow white bowl, drizzled in a light dressing of olive oil, black pepper, spices and garlic and finished with thinly-sliced fresh scallions, jalapeños and finely chopped cilantro. I squeezed a little lime over top, took a bite, and understood for the first time what those TV chefs meant when they talked about the "perfect balance of flavors and textures".

The tartness of the lime, a subtle hint of cumin, the crunch and bite of the jalapeño, and the peppery freshness of the cilantro were melded into something so perfect and so sublime that I almost cried. It was the best single bite of food I had ever experienced, and in that moment, I wanted nothing more than to eat Devan's shrimp for the rest of my life.

"You got to wash it down with the beer, mon."

Devan had come out the kitchen.

"After every bite. Then it's perfect."

I took a big pull off the ice-cold Kalik. He was right. It was perfect.

Devan's main course sealed the deal. A filet of sweet potato-crusted grouper, perfectly cooked and placed atop a bed of field greens, mangos, green beans and avocado, finished with a slightly-sweet citrus vinaigrette dressing. The crispy sweet-potato crust contrasted with the rich creamy texture of the fish perfectly, which in turn contrasted perfectly with the cool greens and crunchy green beans.

"What do you call this?" I asked, as I forced myself to slow down. *This was so fucking good.*

"Fish salad." Devan answered.

"Grouper and potatoes." Peter suggested.

"Tell you what—you guys worry about the food. I'll have Emma come up with the names."

Casa Playa's Caribe was born.

It started slowly, but over the next year, word spread that something special was happening with the food in that funky little Mexican place down on A1A. Devan refused to actually develop a proper menu, preferring instead to make up a list of daily specials based on the catch that was available and the mood he was in. Peter—who was blessed with oddly beautiful handwriting—would turn Devan's specials into an artfully chaotic daily menu that he'd run off onto oversized paper every morning at a local Kinko's. And since Emma thought the stupid names were kind of cool, "What's today's fish salad?" became the most commonly-asked question in the place.

At the end of the first year I had the opportunity to expand the restaurant when the owner of the little gift shop next door retired and moved to Maine. I used the space to add a second small bar, some additional tables and to expand the kitchen. Devan had started thinking big, and he needed room to maneuver. The smaller bar ended up becoming a second home for a slowly growing group of regulars, and I was proud that Casa Playa's had become the kind of place where a local could stop by, pull up a stool, and pick up yesterday's conversation without missing a beat.

My family, my restaurant and my rundown little art studio gave me the anchors I needed as I transitioned out of a decade of military service overseas; I had places to be, a purpose to fulfill, and a group of people that cared for me. On that score, I considered myself a very lucky man.

Pancho and Lefty segued into Bob Marley's *Simmer Down* as I headed toward the backroom bar, figuring that Devan or Peter had grown tired of country and western and had wrested control of the playlist from one of the regulars.

"Hey Shorty."

"Evening, Logan."

"Foley. Where've you been? What's up?"

"You're looking at it."

"Hey, Kyle. How's the Mustang, dude?"

"Still broke, but close."

My bartender Aaron handed me a beer I didn't want and a purchase order he needed me to initial. He'd wandered in one day after I had run a "bartender wanted" ad in the local paper. "America's Worst Bartender" was at the top of his resume. In the interview, he told me that his goal was to make any bar he worked in feel like it was in an airport. I figured I couldn't miss. Aaron had grown up in a trailer park in southeastern Ohio, earned a Masters in International Relations from Ohio State, spoke four languages, and distributed printouts of Ann Coulter columns every day to the regulars. No one ever read them, as far as I could determine.

Casa Playa's regulars were a seemingly random collection of surfers, charter captains, local business guys, musicians, artists and retired military. They represented no particular demographic; their backgrounds, tastes, and politics were all over the map. They ranged in age from twenty-five to the Greatest Generation. A few —like Rhonda, a sixty-five-year-old grand old dame of the ERA movement, and her boyfriend —a twenty-six-year-old DJ and ambient musician whose legal name was 19X—spent time together outside of Casa Playa's. But most saw the backroom bar as the last stop on the way home.

I liked them for their broad range of interests, the quality of the conversation, and the fact that no matter what the question, there was *always* an answer in the backroom bar. From proper bait color in overcast conditions to plumbing repairs; from the correct order of the Beatles discography to the spread on the Dolphins game, somebody in the backroom bar had an answer—or at the very least—an opinion. It was sort of like drinking with Google.

I sat down at the end of the bar and ran down a mental checklist of things that I needed to attend to.

"Hey," I asked Aaron. "Can you cover for lunch tomorrow? I've got somewhere I have to be."

Aaron looked up from the martini he was mixing and said, "*Oui.*"

"That means you gotta be here by eight, dude."

"*Ja.*"

"Also, I have that gallery opening next Friday night. So I won't be here that night. You're on your own."

"*Pas de probleme.*"

"Meaning?"

"Not a problem." He paused for a second and asked, "Anything else?"

"*Non,*" I said.

Aaron went back to work on his martini, and I took a long pull on my beer, thinking about art, love, war and commerce.

CHAPTER 9

Elliot Becker woke painfully, his body wrapped awkwardly around a sweat soaked pillow, his tongue stuck to the roof of his mouth. He was dimly aware of the sound of the shower running—and then being turned off—in the bathroom.

Sasha was up.

Becker rolled onto his back and stared at the ceiling as he weighed the merits of getting out of bed long enough to find five Advil and a glass of really fucking cold water. Asking Sasha was out of the question. The mere thought of the ways in which she could complicate something as simple as fetching a painkiller actually ratcheted up his headache.

RAH DAH DAH DAH DAH DAH DAH DAH! The sound of about 25 feet of toilet paper being pulled off the roll. "Sasha!" He called hoarsely. "What the hell are you doing in there?"

"Can't find a towel," came a muffled but high-pitched voice through the wall.

Becker levered his legs and swung them off the bed. He stood up and swayed slightly, waiting for his equilibrium to return. After a minute or two, he made his way across the condo toward the kitchen. The 5th floor unit looked directly east, with an amazing view of the Atlantic Ocean. At 10:30 in the morning, it also looked directly into the sun. As he shuffled past the balcony and the wall of floor-to-ceiling windows, Becker shielded his eyes like a vampire.

He shook a handful of tablets from the 1,000-count bottle of generic ibuprofen and gulped them down with a mouthful of water directly from the faucet. Trudging slowly back to the sanctuary of his darkened bedroom, he was cut off in the hall-way as Sasha emerged from the bathroom, glistening wet, and more or less naked.

"You okay?" she asked, standing in the doorway, look-ing oddly resplendent in a worn pair of Becker's Fruit-of-the-Looms and a set of cherry-red, seven-inch heels. Bits of damp toilet paper clung to parts of her body. Becker found himself slightly disgusted and strangely aroused.

"Jesus. A little early for that getup, don't you think?"

"What's the matter with what I'm wearing? The shower leaked out and got my panties wet. And you weren't complain-ing about the shoes last night, in case you've forgotten."

"That's because it was last *night*, you idiot. Night being the operative term." Becker furrowed his brow. "And, now that you mention it, I don't remember a whole bunch about last night. What the hell happened? And how did we get back here? The last thing I remember was being in the club."

Sasha maneuvered around Becker and into the pitch-black bedroom. As Elliot followed her in, he heard her say, "Let's get a little light in here. Brighten the place up." The sound of something—probably something expensive—falling off the dresser and onto the marble floor was immediately followed by a blinding white light as Sasha threw open the bedroom cur-tains. Becker recoiled in shock and pain and groped his way into the walk-in closet. He shut the door, whimpering slightly.

"What's the matter, Mr. Sourpuss? Time to greet the day. It's absolutely beautiful out there." Pronounced "theah," an echo of her Boston Southie upbringing. "I'm gonna go to the pool and work on my tan, and you've got a big meeting in a couple of hours. Didya forget about that?"

Oh, yeah. The "breakfast" meeting.

It was all coming back to him now. Becker, still crouching in the closet, grimaced at the memory. After wrapping up his business with Burrell up north, Elliot had felt an acute need to unwind and spend a little cash.

Barreling south on I-95, he'd called ahead to Nero's in West Palm and booked a Champagne Suite for the evening. Sasha had taken a cab up from Delray to meet him. She had a kind of good-spirited kinkiness that he sometimes found convenient.

Two hours in the Champagne Suite had done its damage. He dimly remembered drinking way too much—which, in a place like Nero's is a breathtakingly expensive undertaking. One thing led to another, and before he knew it, Sasha and a dancer whose shift had just ended had talked him into swinging by the Cougar Club. "It'll be fun," they'd said in unison as they helped Becker tug on his pants.

This was, for a variety of reasons, a horrible idea—the kind of thing he would have never done sober. Even half sober. Nonetheless, he'd gone along—or rather, stumbled along. He hadn't been in the place more than ten minutes when Vassili Dmitrievich—the Cougar Club's owner and a key "investor" in Elliot's rapidly failing real estate development business—materialized, a bottle of Ultimat vodka and four glasses in hand. Elliot wasn't sure what they were celebrating. Perhaps Elliot's imminent demise, since he had failed to make a scheduled "profit disbursement" payment to Vassili earlier that day. *Why in the hell had he agreed to come here?*

"Friend Elliot!" Vassili had boomed. "You visit my club without letting me know you are coming? You should have called ahead. I would have made Cougar Den ready for you and your guests!" Vassili glanced past Elliot and smiled. "How's the tricks, Sasha? Been a long time."

And so, an evening that began with such promise went

rapidly downhill. Between the noise, the liquor, and the enter-tainment, Becker quickly lost his footing.

Dmitrievich, seemingly unaffected by the enormous amount of liquor he was consuming, fired question after ques-tion at Elliot, while his creepy ninja bouncer—another Russian named Vadik—looked on impassively.

Elliot, who prided himself on his ability to bullshit anyone —any time, and in any condition—was coherent enough to realize that he wasn't nearly coherent enough to deal with this. His inner lawyer kept telling him that he needed a change of venue.

Hence, the breakfast meeting.

From the relative safety of his walk-in closet, Becker con-sidered telling Sasha to get on the phone and postpone the meeting. Push it off a couple of hours; give him some time to think through things rationally. As briefly as he considered it, he rejected the idea. Not wise. Possibly injurious, and, in the long term, potentially fatal. No, he had to show up.

He was worried, to be sure. But he wasn't panicking. Not yet, anyway. This thing still had some time left before it played out. Elliot needed to make the most of that time to engineer some maneuvering room and create a viable series of strategic options.

Options were important. And not simply in the sense of having a Plan B. Elliot figured he'd need at least five different contingency plans lined up to get out of this thing intact. In fact, he'd already gotten the ball rolling with Burrell.

He would use this "breakfast meeting" (who would sched-ule a breakfast meeting at two in the afternoon, other than a Russian?) to get the lay of the land and do whatever he could to buy as much time as possible before—as Vassili had put it last night—the time came to "settle ups."

Buying the time wasn't what had Becker worried. That part

was easy, because Vassili wasn't really in a position to argue. To have any reasonable hope of getting his money back, Dmitrievich needed Elliot alive and operating. They both knew this.

This particular enterprise was way, *way* out of Vassili's wheelhouse. For openers, it was an actual real estate development. Sure, there were some cooked books here and there, but at the end of the day it was more or less legit. And Vassili Dmitrievich was—first and foremost—a thug. A violent, unsophisticated, thug. And a foreigner to boot.

Once he got outside of illegal, cash-based enterprises like drugs, sex, weapons, extortion and influence peddling, Vassili was kind of a babe in the woods. Which made him surprisingly manageable, given his generally terrifying and unpredictable personality.

Dmitrievich suffered from an affliction common to successful East-Bloc gangsters: the illogical desire to be legitimate. Elliot understood why guys like Vassili craved this kind of mainstream assimilation. Whether it was just the natural human instinct to cover one's trail or some late-life epiphany, sometimes he felt the same way.

Whatever. The motivation was probably less important than the impulse. And the impulse was far less important than the fact that Elliot was on the hook to Vassili for a little under a million dollars.

That was what had Elliot worried. Because getting Vassili his money back wasn't an option, per se. It was an absolute. It was, in fact, the price for his continued existence. Russian gangsters were in an entirely different category when it came to ruthlessness. They made the Italians and the Irish look like choirboys. Even Columbians seemed sane by comparison. Elliot had no illusions about his fate if he couldn't come up with Vassili's money, as well as the "guaranteed" return on investment.

Elliot opened his eyes and cracked the door to the closet, letting his eyes adjust to the light pouring into the bedroom. He needed to call the lawyer. He needed to get moving.

CHAPTER 10

I finished the last half-mile of my morning run on a dead sprint. Bent over and panting, I punched the STOP button on my Casio G-Shock. 37 minutes and change. Not bad.

I headed around to the back of my studio—which I'd rented a few months after buying Casa Playa's— to a pull up bar that I'd installed and started a pyramid cycle—10 pull ups, followed by 10 seconds of rest, then nine pull ups, followed by nine seconds of rest, and so on, all the way down to one rep. And then back up to 10.

On a normal day, I'd tack on an ocean swim to this routine. Somewhere between a mile or two, depending on the surf. I realized that this routine put me pretty squarely in the "obsessive" category, but I was okay with that.

I had been more or less addicted to endorphins—that rush that comes from doing something intensely physical or inherently risky—since 17, when I'd surfed for the first time. It was one of the things that put me at odds with most of the members of my immediate family. They had long regarded me as some sort of wild-eyed thrill-seeker. And looking at it from their perspective, I could see their point.

Treverrow Capital Management, the family investment firm founded by my great-great-grandfather in 1906, had a reputation for solid, stable and conservative wealth management. A 'white-shoe' firm, as my father was fond of calling it. For more than a century, the firm had thrived—through two world wars, a depression, and macroeconomic cycles too numerous to count. TCM, as it is known, has also served as the sole source of employment for every Treverrow male since 1910. Except for me.

A majority interest in the firm had been acquired by a large investment bank in the early 1970's. That firm, in turn, had been acquired by a global banking conglomerate in the late 80's. *That* bank had merged with another bank in 2002—and so on and so on. Big fish gets eaten by a bigger fish. With every merger and acquisition, my family's net worth increased exponentially.

By my own (admittedly rough) reckoning, the family's initial stock-for-assets stake had probably trebled in value five or six times. We were, as I understood it, the largest private client of the international bank that now owned the controlling interest in TCM and its largest non-institutional shareholder outside of the Middle East.

We were too big to fail.

With my father more or less retired, the firm was largely managed by my older sister and younger brother. I had no real idea what it was worth, or by extension, what *I* was worth. Depending on market behavior, interest rates, and currency fluctuations, my personal wealth could vary by as much as $10 million in a month. Maybe more – I didn't really track it.

I finished my pull-ups, unlocked the door to the shed, and headed to the back of the big room, past the stacks of rusted sheet metal and welding equipment.

I pulled a Slingshot Darko 135 board and 6-meter Naish kite from an equipment rack I had installed a year earlier to hold the prodigious amount of sports junk I owned. Bikes, surfboards, wetsuits, dive gear, fishing rods, camping equipment, and the odd skateboard or two spilled off the plywood shelves.

A musically inclined acquaintance of mine once observed that this rack was my leitmotif. Maybe. While I'd like to think that I'm a little more complexly defined than by my collection of sporting goods, it's probably a pretty good place to start.

Some of the stuff was close to 20 years old: a Zuma Jay single-fin big wave board I had gotten in Malibu...an early Gary Fisher mountain bike that I still rode once in a while...a tattered sail from an old windsurfer, the padding on the boom long worn away. Each item represented another chapter in my obsessive quest to find The Greatest Sport of All Time. Lately, it had been about kite boarding, a sort of hybrid between surfing, wake boarding, and windsurfing.

A steady offshore breeze had been blowing for two days, and I had agreed to meet my buddy Junior south of the Deerfield Beach pier for a morning session.

Twenty-five minutes later, I was in 15 feet of water, making a heel turn jibe into the wind window. A split second after that my kite bit, and I was skimming across the top of the water at about 20 knots—cruising speed for a decent-sized powerboat.

I whooped like the teenager unleashed inside of me. God, I loved this sport. Outside of tow-in big wave surfing, nothing compared to it for sheer speed and power.

I manipulated the kite in a sine-wave pattern up and down, filling the kite with each pull on the control bar. The lower it rode, the faster it pulled me. I leaned back into the board and let go, riding a straight downwind line, parallel to the beach.

I had to be going 25 knots or more—in total silence.

I kept my eyes ahead of me. One look down at my board and I'd wobble and be in the water. Focus on the kite too long and I'd run into something—or someone. The key to kite surfing—which I had learned in a couple of epic sessions on Ann's Beach down in the Keys—was to always be looking toward the next maneuver.

See the wind, feel the board.

I pulled a little further back into the harness, shifting my weight from the board and into my arms and the kite lines. I glanced ahead, looking for the right wave shape.

There it was.

As the board crested the rise in the water, I drove my heels down into the board rails and then lifted. My knees came up, and my feet pulled into the straps on the board. Simultaneously, I pulled into the control bar, letting the kite rise on the wind. And just like that, I was flying. A hundred feet turned into a hundred yards, the waves racing below the board still strapped to my feet. I let some wind spill from the kite and set gently back onto the surface—still moving. Unbelievable.

Once in a while, after a morning on the water, after a ride like this, I would wonder about my younger brother. How it must feel to not know how *this* felt.

I didn't consider this maliciously—or from some smug sense of self-satisfaction. I wasn't deluding myself that my siblings were timid or unfulfilled, or unhappy. Quite to the contrary. My brother and sister were, by all appearances, contented, engaged, busy people doing work they considered important and meaningful. They took on enormous risk as a matter of routine in their roles at TCM. They had careers, families, charities, and hobbies. Their days were full. I loved them in my own way, and I was sure that they loved me. Our differences weren't rooted in malice, but rather, in a kind of shared confusion. We just didn't understand one another.

The sad bit of it was that we weren't really all that interested in understanding one another.

By 10:00 am, I was out of the water and stuffing my gear into the back of the old Bronco that I had driven since high school. I had just enough time to jump in the shower and get on the road to Miami, where I had a lunch meeting.

Courtesy of my buddy Ben Gray .

CHAPTER 11

By 10:00 am, Burrell Malin was packing the trunk of his Oldsmobile with every personal possession he could stuff into it. If it fit, it went. If not, *sayonara*. He was short on time, and he needed to get as far away as possible. And he needed to do that yesterday.

Elliot Becker was not a well man. While Burrell had suspected that for a long time—from the first time they had met, in fact—yesterday's encounter had confirmed it. What Becker was asking—no, *ordering*—him to do was beyond the bounds that even Burrell considered to be legally or morally reasonable. And Burrell was pretty flexible in that regard.

"Alright, let's both agree that Noreen is now a liability. A major liability. Can we agree on that?"

That's how it had started.

After leaving the Subway lot, Becker had driven south on I95 towards Jupiter. It was everything Burrell could do to keep Becker's Range Rover in his sights. The guy had to be doing a hundred miles an hour. Becker finally exited and made a beeline for Roger Dean Stadium, a minor league baseball field in the shadows of the freeway, and home of the Jupiter Hammerheads. Apparently, there was a game he wanted to see.

Becker had already parked at the far end of the lot and was walking purposefully toward the ticket booth. Burrell pulled in to the nearest empty space, jumped out of the Olds, and trotted to catch up. Becker didn't break stride.

At the booth, Becker purchased two General Admission tickets, went through the turnstile, and headed down a long walkway toward the bleachers along the first baseline. On the field, the Dunedin Blue Jays were tossing the ball around, warming up. Becker never looked back; with the exception of handing him his ticket, he had done nothing to even acknowledge Burrell's presence. Becker climbed to the top of bleachers and sat down.

Burrell struggled up the stairs, the sweat beginning to form at his brow line. He dropped heavily into the metal bench next to Becker. Shifting his gaze alternately from right field to Becker, he stammered, "Okay, Mr. Becker, I followed you all the way down here, so what—"

"So Burrell, here's the thing: Noreen." As he spoke, Becker never glanced at over. He simply looked out over the field, his gaze focused on some middle distance. Maybe the pitcher's mound. Or the far dugout where the Hammerheads were filing in and playing grab ass. Burrell couldn't really tell.

Becker continued: "Noreen is a problem. A big problem. In the context of our setting, you might say a major league problem. More importantly, Noreen's *your* problem, because you recruited Noreen." A silence hung in the air, punctuated occasionally by the distant sound of a ball hitting a glove.

Go, Dunedin.

Burrell Malin had always known, somewhere in the back of his mind, that this day would come. Becker was right—he had recruited Noreen. On paper, she couldn't have been more perfect—a hard worker who maxed out overtime in a stable, if not necessarily lucrative job, paid her bills on time, accrued little debt, and generally stayed out of trouble. By the time Burrell had found her, this quiet commitment to an exemplary life had netted her a missing husband, two children, a chronically aching back, little in the way of future prospects, and a nagging sense that somehow, life had been unfair to her.

On the last count, she had been right.

Burrell had been around. He'd seen his share of what he liked to think of as the human condition. And over the years, he had developed a good sense for a person's tipping point. After an hour or so with Noreen (in the Publix break room over a lunch of freshly made chicken tenders and Diet Pepsi) he knew that Noreen had reached hers. All she needed was the proper motivation.

A couple of sham "dates" followed: Chili's for wings and beer; a trip to Butterfly World with her kids. And that was all it took. Before she knew it, Noreen was signing her name (and 790 Transunion credit score) to a 30-year, adjustable rate, "no doc" mortgage on a four bedroom McMansion in one of the most desirable neighborhoods in Palm Beach County. Asking price: $625,000. Selling price $790,000.

"You can call it recruiting, Mr. Becker, but all I know is that Noreen's got herself and her two little ones in a nice place that they can call home. You may not think much of her, but I know...I know what it's like to wonder where your next meal's gonna – "

"Jesus! You never give the martyr act a second's rest, do you, Burrell?"

There was a brief silence as Burrell considered a series of righteous comebacks.

"What's that supposed to mean?" Burrell said weakly. He could feel the beginnings of an epic itch at his hairline. He fought the urge to scratch.

Becker continued to scan the field below. "You make it sound like you're running some kind of non-profit housing authority. Who are you kidding? You could give a shit about Noreen Everhart. Just like you could give a shit about Lorraine

70

Smith and her four brats. Or Joanne whatshername, down in Boca. What's she got—an alcoholic sister and her old man living there with her? What the hell was her last name, anyway?"

Sanders, Burrell thought, but his heart wasn't really in it, so he sat silently. Becker was right, after all.

The scam had been fairly simple and wildly successful—for the first few years, anyway. Lately, it seemed like the luck was running the other way.

Burrell had first come across Becker while doing an inspection on a 3-bedroom Cape-Cod style up in Port St Lucie—and it was clear from the start that Becker, who introduced himself as a mortgage broker—knew the score. Cards were exchanged, a couple of phone calls followed, and before long, Burrell had a sense that Becker was putting something together that went way beyond the same old scam. Becker seemed to be inventing an entirely new game—and Burrell wanted in. Which is where the trouble started.

Burrell had been in the appraisal racket for a couple of years by then, and it wasn't a bad gig, considering. The actual pay—meaning the legitimate fees that he earned for carrying out an inspection and doing the basic paperwork—wasn't all that great, but the off-the-table cash could be very lucrative.

Getting to it was even easier. All you had to do was under-appraise a property.

Burrell had learned this within his first six months on the job. He had turned in an appraisal for a property in Clewiston—a little known rural community favored by drug dealers and professional bass fishermen—nestled on the shore of Lake Okeechobee. The property sat at the end of a long dirt road, backed up against a stretch of scrub, swamp, and eventually, sugar cane fields as far as the eye could see.

Having spent the first 30 years his life in a hellhole corner of Indian River County that looked and smelled a lot like this property, Burrell couldn't see any value in it. The only thing out of place, in his mind, was that there was a *house* on the lot, where he would normally have expected a doublewide. He took a cursory look around, poked through the house and the attic, went back to his office and did a little comparative work online, filed his appraisal, and headed over to Tootsie's for a beer and a burger.

Twenty-four hours later, Burrell was at the same joint, finishing up another burger. Just as his third Bud Light hit the bar, his cell phone rang. A guy named Dave something-or-other. Said he was the "mortgage broker" for the guy buying the house out in Jupiter Farms.

"Okay," said Burrell. "What's that got to do with me?"

"Well, the thing is, I think you may have come in a little low on the appraisal."

"How so?" asked Malin. "I did the inspection, ran the comps. The place is pretty run down, and there ain't even a paved road out to the lot. Just dirt and gravel. They don't even run mail out to the house. Got to drive out to the main road."

"Yeah, I know that, Mister...um..."

"Malin."

"Malin—yeah, Mister Malin. Sorry about that. Anyway, I realize the property is pretty isolated and all, but to my way of thinking, that's actually a good thing, *a premium*, if you will, when you consider how overcrowded we are down here. I mean, that property is in more of a *sanctuary* than say, a regular run-of-the-mill neighborhood. You know what I mean?"

"A sanctuary, you say." Malin drawled. "Approached by a dirt road and backed up by a swamp."

"Well, it's all in how you look at it, I guess. Anyway, here's the thing— "

There was a pause on the phone.

"I'd like to ask you to take one more look at the property. I think you may have overlooked a couple of things. Intangibles, if you will."

"And why would I do that?" Malin asked.

"I don't know. Professional courtesy, maybe. Like I said, I realize that this is an imposition, and I'd be happy to do what I can to cover your time and expense. Say, five hundred dollars? Cash?"

Malin thought about it for a moment. "Okay, so let's say I go back out there, and I amend my appraisal? To reflect some of those—what did you call them— intangibles?"

"Intangibles, yeah."

"Intangibles. So, what do you figure, off the top of your head, those intangibles are worth to the overall valuation of the property?"

Dave answered, "Off the top of my head, I'd say those intangibles are worth an additional $95,000, give or take. Call it 98K just to be safe."

Malin considered the offer. He said, "So, help me understand something, Dave."

"What's that?"

"How come your client don't just take my appraisal to the guy selling the house and use it to get him to drop the price? You'd think I'd be doing him a favor. I mean, why do you want your client to pay more for the house?"

There was another pause on the phone. "Because I'm not in the house business, Burrell. I'm in the loan business."

Boom. There it is.

From that day forward, Burrell brought a new sense of entrepreneurism to the job. The way he figured it, there was more than enough cash to spread around in this new- fangled, real estate-driven economy, and he had found a way to get his. More importantly, he really couldn't find a rationale that said this was a bad thing. Housing prices go up and everybody wins.

Housing prices go down, everybody loses. If you thought of that way, then all he was really doing was his part to make the machine hum. Capitalism on the move.

His conscience clean and his bank account growing, Burrell went along happily for a couple of years. Lived better than he'd ever lived: ate out most nights; drank Heinekens. Picked up a used Cutlass from some gangbanger for a couple of thousand dollars and spent a little each month to pimp it out. Enjoyed the company of a lady once a month or so, and when not other-wise occupied, spent long nights on his La-Z-Boy, surfing all 500 channels on his Premium level cable subscription.

And along came Elliot Becker.

"Burrell. BURRELL! Did you hear what I said? Are you lis-tening to me?

Malin looked at Becker. "Huh? What'd you say?"

An organ trilled, "Charge!" on the PA system, as the Ham-merheads took the field.

"I said you've got to burn down the house."

What?

"Start an electrical fire in the attic or something. Short out the two-twenty box or whatever the fuck it is. You gotta burn the thing down."

Burrell squinted at him, not quite sure if he had heard Becker correctly.

"Burn it down? Burn *what* down?"

"Noreen's house, dumbass. What did you think I was talk-ing about? And that's not all, because after that, we gotta do the same thing to all of the other houses. One right after an-other."

Burrell looked out toward the baseball field. The Hammer-heads were playing a little last minute pepper as the pitcher— a lefty, Burrell noticed—ambled to the mound. Must be nice.

Play a little ball. Pick up a paycheck. Do it again the next night.

"Why the hell would you want to burn down a house? That's arson, Mr. Becker. That's a felony. A really big felony. Like, short of murder and rape, I think that's about as big a felony as there is."

"Oh, it's definitely a major fucking felony. Huge. May be right up there with wire fraud, racketeering, and embezzlement. Probably worse than honest services fraud, which, as a state-licensed home inspector, you're also guilty of—but who's gonna split hairs, right?"

Burrell closed his eyes, briefly. He was screwed. It was just a question of how.

"But why arson? Why burn the house down?"

For the first time, Becker turned and looked at him. He smiled. "To throw them off."

"Throw *who* off?" Burrell asked, still confused.

"Everyone, shit-for-brains. Everyone. The banks, the Feds, the cops, the fire department, the insurance people—everyone. "

Becker eyed Burrell closely, as if looking for a light to come on. "You don't get it, do you?"

Burrell shook his head. "Nope."

"Alright, look—once that house goes up in flames, everything goes into a tailspin: *What happened? Was it an accident? Was it arson? Who gets the insurance money? What happens to the loan? Who pays the taxes?* A million questions that gotta be answered, and thousands of man-hours to get to the bottom of it. And whatever they were looking at before—like *how did a checker from Winn Dixie buy a house like this?* All that goes out the window, at least for a while, because they've got all these other new problems to deal with."

Becker paused, to let this sink in. "Now, do you get it? We burn down the house, we throw them off."

Burrell got it, but it wasn't sitting well. "They're gonna know it was arson. That's the first thing they're gonna think. And I don't know anything about how to set a fire that doesn't look like arson."

Becker replied, "A—of course they're going to suspect it was arson. Absolutely. I want them to think it was arson. Do you know how long it takes to run an arson investigation? A long time. And B—you're a home inspector. You know a damn sight more about how fires start in houses than I do. And C— Noreen is *your mark*. Not mine. You got her into this, and she's fucking up all over the place. Calling the banks. Calling me. Calling —well, who the hell knows? She's a loose cannon, Burrell. And she's an idiot. And she's your problem. Not mine. So, that's why you're the one who starts the fire. Check that—fires." Becker drew out the "*s*".

Burrell hadn't said anything. He'd just looked out onto the field, thought about the day he'd met Becker in that Cape Cod, and wished he played first base.

CHAPTER 12

Silvano pushed his breakfast plate away and nodded at the waitress to warm up his coffee. One of the very few perks about "working" with the Pizzuti family was a longstanding and very high standard for hospitality. They liked nice hotels and expected everyone in their orbit to travel in similar style. As a result, Silvano was—for the third or fourth time this year—enjoying another stay in the Palm Beach Four Seasons.

As usual, the breakfast was perfect and the coffee without equal. Silvano decided to allow himself another cup while he finished up the Wall Street Journal. Might as well take advantage of the downtime while he still could. The way it was looking, he was going to be busy.

As he was scanning the "Heard on the Street" section, his phone rang. Silvano glanced down at the incoming number, sighed and went back to his article.

Twenty minutes later, he put his paper down along the edge of the table, picked up his cellphone, scrolled to the "missed calls" screen and punched the green button.

"You have reached Double A Top Title," an automated female voice answered. "If you know your party's extension, please press it now." A pause. "If you are an existing client, please press one now. For new contracts, please press—"

Silvano disconnected and scrolled to his "messages" screen. There it was. He pressed a button and put the phone back to his ear.

"Hi, Mr. Mazzio. This is Ted Hodges, with Top Title. You left a message with the service, um...it looks like yesterday in the evening some time. Just following up to see how I can help you. Please give me a call at your convenience—I'm at extension two eighty-five. I look forwar—"

Silvano hung up, redialed and punched in the extension.

"Ted Hodges," a voice announced after a couple of rings.

"Ted...Silvano Mazzio." Silvano paused a half second and continued. "Busy?"

"Well...I'm sure I have time to help, Mr. Mazzio." Hodges replied smoothly. "Your message didn't specifically mention what it was that you needed, other than some help with a large financial transaction."

"Yeah, Ted. I would definitely say it's large." Silvano replied.

"So, if you can fill me in on the particulars— "

"Richard Pizzuti." Mazzio interrupted. He let the name sink in. "Or, as I think of him, *Richie.*" Mazzio paused.

"You know who I'm talking about, right?"

Hodges cleared his throat nervously. "Um, I'm not sure..." Hodges trailed off, followed by a pregnant silence. "Let me, um...let me look him up in our system..."

Given his line of work, Silvano was intimately familiar with panic and its infinite manifestations. He could visualize Hodges frantically waving his arms at his desk, looking for any kind of help he could flag down. Probably pantomiming wildly and pointing at the phone, his eyes wide and darting everywhere. He waited a moment to see how Hodges would play it.

After a few seconds, there came an audible *click* on the line and some muffled whispering. "Mr. Hodges, can I interrupt?

I've got a judge from the county court on the line, and he says he needs you on line one *right now*," a female voice could be heard, more or less yelling into the phone.

Not bad, Silvano thought. A nice ruse, albeit a little over rehearsed. Hodges had even punched on the speakerphone to make sure Silvano could hear it clearly.

"Um, sorry Mr. Mazzio. Can I get back to you?" Hodges had picked up the handset. "If I miss this call, there's no telling when I'll be able to get the judge back on the line, and it's for a closing I've got scheduled later this afternoon."

Mazzio smiled to himself and said, "Sure, Ted. So, what time's the closing?"

"Um, I'm sorry?"

"The closing—the one you got later this afternoon. What time you got that scheduled for?"

He waited for Rains to catch up. "Um...let's see.... two...no – two-thirty. Yes, it's at two-thirty this afternoon." Rains stammered.

Jesus.

"Great," Silvano replied. "I'll be there at four."

"But— "

"And, Ted..." Silvano said, quietly.

".... Yes?" came Hodges' strangled reply.

"You'd better fucking be there, too."

Silvano disconnected the call, set the Blackberry squarely on the Wall Street Journal, leaned back and finished his coffee.

CHAPTER 13

"**I**'m sorry sir, Mr. Hodges is, as I mentioned, currently indisposed. Would you care to leave a message? I'm sure he'll return the call as soon as he is able."

Irwin Becker leaned back against his kitchen counter and gazed at the $12,000 a month ocean view. Thankfully, the ibuprofen tablets (helped along by a Percocet he'd found in Sasha's purse) were starting to kick in, and his headache and light sensitivity were beginning to fade. His impatience, however, remained acute.

"Okay, if Ted is trapped in a toilet stall, that's fine. I'm running on a very short timeline here, so here's what you're going to do. You're going to grab his cell phone off the desk, take it into the men's room, slide it under the stall or whatever, and tell him to call me on it. Right now. Tell him he's got five minutes before he finds himself in an entirely different kind of shit storm."

He hung up and glanced at the clock on the oven. Let the countdown begin.

Inside of three minutes, the phone rang. He could hear the unmistakable I'm-in-a-bathroom-stall echo behind Hodges' whispered voice.

"Why are you calling me here, Elliot? Are you out of your fucking mind? That was my wife who answered the phone—"

"Your wife?" Becker interrupted. "Really? Your wife works there with you? No wonder you're so jumpy. Huh. You never told me that."

"So I never told you that. So what? Big deal. She's my paralegal. I met her here." Hodges continued on in a whisper, accompanied by the sound of his bowels evacuating rather violently.

Grimacing, Becker pulled the phone away from his face and punched the speaker button. "Jeez, that doesn't sound good, Ted."

Hodges groaned and Becker smiled, feeling a little better about his little predicament. Misery loves company.

To the rest of the world, Ted Hodges was just a real estate lawyer—a closing attorney, to be precise. To Elliot Becker, however, Hodges was a private bank. An ATM with no withdrawal limits. In Becker's line of work, that was a beautiful thing to have—and all it had cost him was a blowjob.

Becker had met him at a property closing, almost two years ago to the day. At the time, Becker was in the early stages of his real estate "career" and Hodges' firm, Top Title (or AA Top Title, if you were looking in the Yellow Pages), had acted as the escrow agent for one of his first purchases. Typical escrow agent stuff— getting the paperwork in line, holding the down payment and other funds, and telling everyone involved where to sign and what to initial. It was—as home closings tend to be —a fairly long and tedious process, the kind of thing where you don't really think too hard about what you're doing, beyond responding to orders from some vague authority figure—*"And, if you'll just put your initials here, and here, and sign right there by the little yellow tabby...and now turn to Addendum A—yes, that one—and initial right there next to Paragraph C...."*—and so on.

Becker had quickly grown bored with the process. Although he had a law degree, various bureaucratic complications (including disbarment) precluded the actual practice of the profession. Rather than ruminate in situations like this,

Becker preferred to simply detach and think about other stuff. And the other stuff in this instance was Ted Hodges. Always an astute judge of character, Becker couldn't help but notice how little of that particular quality Hodges possessed.

Slovenly and unorganized, Hodges had sweated profusely throughout the proceedings. He wore an obviously off-the-rack, bargain-basement suit, the trousers of which were too short—a fact that became painfully apparent when he crossed his legs. The knot of his polyester necktie was pilled from the stubble of his double chin. Best of all, he sported a fascinatingly complex hairstyle best described as a pompadour/comb over—a sort of hybrid Fat Elvis/Donald Trump/Militant Lesbian thing that must have taken hours to achieve.

His administrative, social and conversational skills were a disaster. In the process of retrieving a document from an overstuffed accordion file, he had knocked the whole thing off the credenza, covering the floor in paper. It took him a half hour to pick it all up and put back into some semblance of order. The documents—amazingly, in this computerized age —were awash in Liquid Paper corrections and strikethroughs. During the signing and initialing, he would hand Becker a pen; the pen wouldn't work. He'd hand him another one; that one wouldn't work either.

Overwhelming all of this was the general *shiftiness* of his presence; a kind of low-rent hustler vibe that clung like body odor. Becker was smitten from the get-go. This was the kind of raw material he knew he could work with. He made a point to get an extra business card from Hodges at the end of the closing.

Within a couple of days, he had Hodges right where he wanted him—sprawled out in a private booth in the Cougar Club, with Sasha's head bobbing rhythmically between his legs, while Vassili's high end "security" cameras caught all of the action—including sound.

"Anyway, she seems like a nice gal, Ted. And very protective of you, that's for sure."

The toilet flushed. Again. "What do you want, Becker?"

Hodges was longer whispering.

"What do you think I want, Ted? A legal ruling?" Becker paused. "I need more cash. I need to make some kind of good faith payment to Vassili. And I need to do it today."

A splashing sound. Another flush.

Jesus.

"How much?" Hodges squeaked.

"I figure fifty grand ought to do it. It's a lot less than what he's looking for, but it's probably enough to buy us a couple of days. At least that's what I'm hoping. I'm kind of improvising here a little, Ted. Trying to keep both our asses out of the ground."

There was a long pause on the line. Becker waited.

"Well, we've got a problem on this end as well," Hodges said. "I got a call from some guy this morning who says he represents Richard Pizzuti."

Becker snorted. "Who's Richard Pizzuti?"

He heard Hodges draw an exasperated breath. "The account, Elliot. The guy on the account."

Oh yeah.

That guy.

Richard Pizzuti had established an escrow account at Top Title valued at more than a million dollars a few months prior. The money had been deposited to cover the down payment and closing costs for a Palm Beach mini mansion.

Needless to say, funds were, at this moment, a tad short.

Becker asked: "What do you mean, 'represents'? Like an attorney? A realtor? What?"

"Um, no. I'm pretty sure that this guy isn't a lawyer," Hodges replied.

"Then what?

"Well, here's the thing," Hodges said. "Richard Pizzuti."

"What about him?" Becker asked.

"Well, you know, I never actually saw the guy, right? Just the guy selling the house. He put me in touch with Pizzuti and we only talked over the phone. He never came in. The escrow money was a wire transfer."

"Yeah, so?"

"Yeah, so I never thought too much about it until this morning until this guy called," Hodges replied over yet another flush. "His name was Silvano Mazzio, and he said that he represented '*Richie* Pizzuti'"

Becker thought about that for a moment. Why did that name mean something, all of a sudden?

"*Richie*. Not *Richard*. You with me?"

"I'm trying, Ted. Why don't you save us both some time and just catch me up?" Becker replied, as he rubbed his temples, trying to remember what was so special about Richie Pizzuti.

"MTV. That show – that fucking reality show...what'd they call it? *Mob House*? *Mob Kids*? Something like that? That show where kids from Mafia families share a house at the beach or whatever?"

Becker suddenly remembered.

Fuck.

"*Mobster Beach*," he replied, quietly. "The show's called *Mobster Beach*. Richie Pizzuti was—or is—that asshole little DJ-looking kid with all the tattoos and earrings and his hat on sideways. Calls himself Richie C."

Becker sighed. *Could this really be happening?*

"Right," Hodges said. "And his dad—you're not gonna believe this, I thought those shows were a sham, but his dad is— "

"Yeah, I know who his dad is." Becker interrupted, tiredly.

Becker could hear a faucet running. Hodges was apparently finished. The water stopped.

"What time is this guy—what was his name—Mazzio? What time's he due over there?" Becker asked.

"He said he'd be here at four. So, I've gotta, you know, be here when he gets here, I guess." Hodges trailed off, sounding like a wounded five-year-old.

Becker said, "Alright. I can be there in the next hour or so. We'll figure something out, but I've got to get moving, because I've gotta meet this Russian at some joint down in Lauderdale at two or two-thirty at the latest. That's an extra hour of driving, so I'm headed up to you now—and you've got to get me that cash, or we're looking at *another* problem. One I don't even want to think about right now."

He heard the whooshing of an electric hand dryer. "HODGES! DID YOU HEAR ME?" Becker practically shouted into the handset.

Nothing. He disconnected the call, took a long look at the ocean, and pondered his next move.

CHAPTER 14

I was sitting quietly in the lobby of the North Miami Beach offices of the Federal Bureau of Investigation, trying ever so subtly to get the sand out my ears, when the nice lady at reception called my name.

"Mr. Treverrow?"

I glanced up, my pinky finger still buried in my ear. I suspected that I looked more like a Confidential Informant than a Concerned Citizen, but there you go.

"Hi, that's me," I said, as I deftly brought my hand back to my lap.

"Agent Slavnick is ready for you, sir. He's on the way down right now."

I stood and smoothed my hair. One of the few facets of military service that I had never come to grips with was the whole hair length thing—although once I found myself in Afghanistan that had pretty much gone out the window. In Asia, SpecOps personnel from every branch were encouraged there to grow out their hair and beards—the longer and more unruly, the better. Within limits, of course.

Once out of the service, I had let my freak flag fly a bit, keeping my hair just to the left of what is usually considered appropriate for an adult. Whatever. A bit of harmless personal expression, and since I'd never been the tattoo type, one that was easily modified.

Agent Slavnick—at least I assumed that it was Agent Slavnick, since he was a dead-ringer for the guy Gray had described —strode into the lobby, his right hand leading the way, his smile broad and welcoming.

"Lieutenant Treverrow, it's a pleasure to meet you," he said as he walked past me and right up to the only other person in the lobby's waiting area, a respectable-looking fellow in a dark gray suit and an adult-appropriate hairstyle.

I cleared my throat politely. "Um, excuse me, but I'm Logan Treverrow, Agent Slavnick." Their hands clasped, both men turned to look at me, differing levels of confusion registering on their faces. I gave Slavnick a few seconds to catch up, which he did. He walked over, the hand still extended, leaving the guy in the suit doubly perplexed.

"Sorry about that, Lieutenant. My mistake."

"Not a problem," I replied. "And please call me Logan. Ben probably told you that I'm no longer on active duty with the Navy."

"Yes, he mentioned that to me."

As we shook hands (firm, steady, right out of the law enforcement guidelines) Slavnick continued, "And, please on behalf of the Bureau, let me tell you how grateful we are to you and your colleagues for your service to our country."

This was another reason why I had maintained a decidedly non-military appearance since coming home.

"Thanks, I appreciate it."

And I did. Unlike the returning veterans of previous wars that I could mention, most of the men and women who had served in Iraq and Afghanistan were accorded a modicum of respect and—well, *gratitude*, I guess. And that was appreciated by everyone I knew who had come home from overseas.

On the other hand, there were no good reasons for anyone

to know anything about what I had been doing in the military. OPSEC guidelines are pretty clear when it comes to war stories. Which was fine by me, since apart from my art, I have never been one to seek out praise and attention. In fact, both generally made me uncomfortable—present circumstances being the perfect example.

Slavnick seemed not to notice. Still grasping my hand, he looked directly into my eyes. The other guy—the one that Slavnick had mistaken for me—was also looking at me. Awkward.

"So, Ben gave you some background on what's going on with my wife? "I asked, immediately regretting the phrasing. The guy in suit perked up, clearly interested in what Lieutenant Treverrow's wife had been up to while Lieutenant Treverrow was out serving his country.

"Wife? Agent Gray indicated that it was your ex-wife," Slavnick replied.

"Sorry. We're kind of still in the process and all, so I'm not really sure what the right terminology is." This was just getting worse by the sentence. The guy in the suit was doing everything but cupping a hand to his ear. Finally, Slavnick noticed.

"I have a conference room booked for us. It's just down the hall."

The Suit was crestfallen.

CHAPTER 15

By 11:30 am, Elliot Becker was barreling up I95 toward Hodges' office, still reviewing his options—and still finding his options wanting. He hoped fifty thousand was going to be enough, but he had a sneaking suspicion that wasn't even going to be close. And while Dmitrievich wasn't the least of his problems (which was ironic, since pissed-off Russian mobsters usually rank right at the top when it comes to problems) Dimitrievich was, unfortunately, only *one* of his problems.

Becker allowed himself a few seconds to wallow in self-pity: All that upside. A few lousy decisions. An economy that didn't want to cooperate. And now it was all coming down on top of him.

The original scheme had been simple—and to his way of thinking—sort of elegant. It was based on the universal reality that real estate transactions are complicated, confusing and never quick. The paperwork is ridiculous; the due diligence equally so. Along the way, a million things can go wrong: a house can burn down, a seller can change his mind, a buyer can go bankrupt. And on and on.

Which is why most real estate transactions start with a deposit of some kind as a hedge. Typically, deposits are put in escrow for safekeeping and maintained by a title company. The title company acts a legal guardian for the money while all the details of the transaction are getting ironed out; and on closing day, the closing attorney from the title company makes sure that everybody gets paid what they're supposed to get paid.

Given the sheer volume of real estate transactions that go on every day, an average title company might be the custodian to millions of dollars—which was why Becker had been on the lookout for a closing attorney that he could leverage—and why Hodges was the perfect idiot for the scheme.

In the beginning, they ran it as a classic Ponzi scheme: skimming money from one escrow account, and paying it back later from another escrow account. The key was to pay each escrow account back before it was actually needed for the closing. As long as the money was there on closing day, who gave a shit what happened with it beforehand? And as long as new cash was always coming in—in the form of new escrow accounts—there was never a problem.

To make sure their tracks were covered, Becker recruited two out-of-work web designers—Devin and Dustin— to create fake statements for the escrow accounts they raided. Tucked away in a single cube in the back of AA Top Title's offices, drinking vast amounts of Red Bull, and listening to gangster rap, the two geeks would create dozens of letter-perfect counterfeits each month, seemingly untroubled by the moral or legal ramifications of what they were doing. Their only request—which Hodges was happy to oblige—was to have a PlayStation installed in the break room.

Becker would use most of the money he skimmed to fund different real estate scams—from straw buyer schemes, where he would recruit low-income buyers with impeccable credit scores, like Noreen, to apply for loans—to flipping pre-construction condos down on Biscayne Boulevard in Miami.

Becker had also figured out the he could apply for home equity loans on behalf of former AA clients. Completely forgetting what had happened with home equity loans a decade earlier, banks once again practically giving those things away —and Hodges already had everything he needed to pull it off: social security numbers, tax returns, paystubs and credit histories. Fake a signature or two, have a girl in the office notarize the whole mess, and boom! Instant cash.

For a year or so, things clicked right along. Nobody got caught and everybody got paid.

But that hadn't been good enough for Elliot Becker. It made sense, he believed, to continually diversify. Real estate was running hot in South Florida, and if you had access to cash, it was easy to take advantage of the opportunities.

Unfortunately, it was that kind of thinking that had Becker presently entangled with a homicidal Russian tittie bar magnate, building (from the ground up) a brand new development of mid-priced, Tudor-styled homes, twenty miles from the nearest Walgreens and on the edge of the Everglades. It was going to be called English Glades, and it was going to make Elliot Becker legit.

Big mistake.

It turns out that *developing* real estate is completely different from buying and selling real estate. Between the contractors, the county, the inspectors, the regulators, the school board, and the lawyers, Becker didn't have a prayer. The whole thing was a soul-sucking money pit: seventy-five acres of reclaimed swamp, thick with mosquitos, Australian Pines, palmetto scrub and a rapidly-growing population of Burmese pythons. Not a single home completed. Not even the models.

Given his questionable background, the only outside financing Becker had been able to secure had come from a shady little three-branch bank down in Broward County that made most of its money brokering subprime mortgages. The terms were shitty and the milestones unreasonable. Nonetheless, he had completely tapped out the initial draw and figured that it was only a matter of time before they started snooping around, cutting him off and foreclosing on the land. So he had dug into his own pocket to try and to staunch the hemorrhaging. It was every cent he had; money that he had been carefully stashing away in the Caymans. The Retirement Fund.

It was gone in a heartbeat.

It was only then that Becker had turned to Dmitrievich. Vassili had demanded a 50% stake to start, and his terms were even more egregious than the bank's. Worse still, Dmitrievich had Becker on the hook to start repaying the loan immediately. *Immediately.* Before a single home in English Glades was finished, let alone sold.

He called them "guaranteed profit disbursements."

What the fuck?

Still, Dmitrievich was the only game in town, and Becker figured he could find a way to make it work—which he did, initially, by skimming a little more money, a little more often, from the escrow accounts. Becker ignored Hodges' worried clucking that they were cutting it too close, and for a while, he managed to keep up with Dmitrievich's repayment schedule *and* keep things moving forward with the development.

Then the housing market took its first dainty steps toward a correction.

This should have spelled the end of the game. As home sales slowed, fewer new escrow accounts were being opened. Which meant fewer sources of fresh capital were coming into AA. Becker and Hodges had to scramble to get funds replaced in the existing accounts before those funds were needed for a closing.

The straw-buyer scheme, which depended on Becker being able to flip a home before the 1% teaser mortgages reset, also started to collapse, as demand slowed and home prices started to flatten and head south. Suddenly, Becker was on the hook for almost seventy thousand dollars a month in mortgages—which he had no ability to pay—and a half-dozen houses with sinking values. Including Noreen's.

Same thing with the fake home equity loans. As long as he and Hodges kept up with the payments, they were fine. The "borrowers" were clueless that they even had a loan with their name on it, because banks don't call you unless you miss a payment. And in the beginning, the payments were tiny: a 1% interest-only payment on a hundred-thousand-dollar loan was nothing. But when those loans started to reset—and the payments went up—Becker and Hodges didn't have the cash to cover them. Suddenly, phones started ringing all over Palm Beach County as banks went looking for their money.

As his carefully laid plans began to collapse, Becker would watch his future playing out on documentaries and biopics of the previous generation's Ponzi-schemers—whether it was a Bernie Madoff, or some Milwaukee huckster ripping off his fellow parishioners, these collapses were simply the fulfillment of a foregone conclusion: that once the cash inflow stopped, *it was over*. And when the housing economy slowed—even slightly—cash inflow stopped everywhere.

A lesser man would have given up; thrown in the towel and high-tailed it out of there. But not Becker. (First of all, giving up wasn't really an option. Once he stopped paying Dmitrievich, he was dead. Period. Even in a federal lockup. Probably even in solitary. There was no escaping the guy.)

The answer to his prayers came in the form of a $1 million escrow account established in the name of Richard Pizzuti. It was the deposit for a $2 million, all-cash purchase. Some Palm Beach mini-mansion being sold "by owner." Within a day of its funding, Hodges and Becker raided the account for a hundred grand, using the proceeds to get two older accounts back up to their original levels the day before they were needed for a closing. A little close, but Hodges and Becker were elated—they had dodged a yet another bullet.

Two days later, the owner of the mini-mansion called Hodges to request that the escrow account be closed and the money returned to Mr. Pizzuti. He had changed his mind and had decided to hang onto the house and leave it to his grown children. The contract and sale were cancelled.

Hodges was a mess when he finally reached Becker.

"What are we gonna do? We're out of cash. I have three accounts left here, that's all. And they're all scheduled to go to closing in the next couple of days. We're toast, Elliot. Elliot? Are you listening to me?"

Not really. Becker had been thinking.

"Alright, here's what we're gonna do." He paused for effect. "Nothing."

There was silence for a second or two.

"Nothing? What do you mean, nothing?"

"Just what I said. You're gonna do nothing. And in a couple of days, I'm gonna have Sasha call this Pizzuti guy and tell him that she's the seller's personal assistant and that he's changed his mind; that he'd still like to go through with the sale. And that unfortunately, he has been called out of the country for the next month or so, which is why he had his personal assistant call him. I may even have her do it in person. If the guy has a working penis, he'll buy everything she says, lock stock and barrel."

The phone was silent, but he could hear Hodges thinking.

"And then what?"

"And then you're gonna call Pizzuti and tell him that the seller also called *you* with the same news, and you just want to confirm that you're keeping the escrow account in place."

Hodges asked, "You think he'll agree?"

"Probably. Why wouldn't he? He wants the house. He put down the dough in the first place."

"And then what?"

"Then, we string him along for as long as we can: the seller's delayed overseas, there's a problem with the title, there's a lien against the property. Blah blah blah. All the shit *you're* supposed to be worrying about on his behalf about as a title attorney. Since there's no realtor involved, we can tell him anything we want. There's no one out there to tell him different. And it'll look to him like you're actually doing your job."

Becker could sense that Hodges was catching on and warming to the idea, so he continued.

"We use the money to get out of this hole. Once we start selling in English Glades—which will hopefully be in a couple of months—we'll be home free. The key is to keep our hands on that escrow account, because the cash in that account is gonna be our lifeboat for a while."

"A couple of months?" Hodges asked hopefully.

"At most," Becker reassured him. "Just make sure the web guys keep sending him legit looking statements, and we'll be fine."

Hodges had agreed to go along with him. At the time, it was his only choice.

As he hit the exit for Hodges's office, Becker found himself asking the question again. Was $50,000 going to be enough to keep Dmitrievich at bay for a while? He hoped so, because he needed time for Burrell to put the pieces in place for the burns, and he had plans for the rest of Richie Pizzuti's escrow money.

It was no longer a lifeboat. It was a ticket out of town.

CHAPTER 16

"**S**o." As he spoke, Agent Slavnick squared up a small stack of business cards with the edge of his cell phone.

"Agent Gray gave me a little bit of preliminary information on what looks like a case of identity theft and/or financial fraud regarding your, um, estranged wife."

It was rare to hear someone actually use the phrase 'and/or' in the course of normal conversation—even official conversation—but Agent Harley Slavnick was that kind of guy. According to Gray, Slavnick had achieved a sort of minor fame in the Bureau after it was determined (unofficially) that as a GS-10 level government employee, he was the lowest-paid Harvard MBA in the country.

It didn't seem to bother him.

Thin and intense, with a rapidly receding hairline that added about ten years to his appearance, Slavnick looked like he'd stepped out of an old black and white movie about Prohibition bootleggers and J. Edgar Hoover—right down to the pencil thin mustache. He radiated the kind of manic energy unique to supremely bright people.

"Around here, he's considered a freak of nature," Gray had told me. "Like a human mainframe. You know those cardboard boxes that bankers and lawyers use to store their files? I've seen Harley chew thorough twenty of those things in a couple of hours and find the *one thing* in there we needed to make a case, or start an investigation, or get an indictment. Not a needle in a haystack. A needle in *hundred* haystacks."

I'd wondered aloud why he wasn't working out of the Manhattan bureau.

Gray answered, "From what I understand, the brass is terrified at the prospect of losing him. And I guess they figure the fastest way for that to happen would be to put him on Wall Street. Can you imagine the kind of dough one of those investment banks would throw at him? A guy who's first in his class at Harvard, with an IQ that's off the charts, *and* happens to be an expert in financial fraud? What do you figure that's worth to say, Goldman Sachs?"

"Yeah, but with the government, you have all of that job security."

Gray laughed.

"To tell you the truth, I'm not all that sure Harley would even be tempted. The guy loves—*I mean loves*—being a G-man. Carries a little snub nose on a leather shoulder holster, right out of one of those old James Cagney movies. I'm not sure he could beat his way out of a wet paper bag, but he's got style—and he's got balls."

I had to ask. "And his name is really Harley Slavnick? Really?"

"Yep," Gray replied, chuckling. "I just call him Harley, mainly to keep from laughing."

Harley Slavnick: G-Man took a sip from his bottle of Aquafina and— again—tried to make Special-Agent-eye-contact with me.

"In a case like this—as I'm sure you understand—the first place law enforcement would likely look is to the estranged spouse. In other words, *you*."

Thank you, Elliot Ness.

"I actually do understand that; on the other hand, I'm the one reporting it to law enforcement." I replied. "I'm not sure if you did any preliminary research before meeting with me, but it should take you about five minutes of Internet time to conclude that I have absolutely no interest in, or need to steal one hundred and eighty thousand dollars from my wife."

"Ex-wife."

"Whatever."

"I'm sorry, Lieuten—er..Mister Treverrow. I didn't mean to imply anything. I'm actually quite familiar with your family's firm—and I'm well aware of your financial status."

"You are?"

"Yes," he answered. "I did a case study on TCM in graduate school. Although that's going back almost 10 years, now." Slavnick gazed off wistfully, apparently pondering the path not taken.

I slid a file folder with the mortgage documents across the conference table, along with a cover sheet listing the names I'd pulled, and the FedEx package Emma had gotten from the bank.

"I have originals of everything back in my office safe; I thought it would be better to give you copies to start," I said as Slavnick picked up the folder.

As he leafed through the documents, I recounted my conversation with Emma. Slavnick never looked up, grunting occasionally, interjecting a polite question here and there. Occasionally, something would catch his eye; he would frown, leaf back through the deck, and nod. Then he would flip the folder over and make a small notation on the cover.

Within fifteen minutes, I had finished my recap, and Slavnick had covered my once-pristine folder with his scribbled notes. He looked up at me.

"Alright. First things first: discrepancies. There are a number of them in this file. Some of them are related to property law, along with several questions that are financial in nature. I need to look into all of them, along with the names you noted."

"You found all of that in 15 minutes?" Ben Gray was right. The guy was like Rain Man.

"Uh, huh. A lot of very sloppy stuff in here. The kind of stuff that points to either very shady people, or very poor practitioners. Given the phone call Mrs. Treverrow received, I'd say the former."

I replied, "You said *legal* and financial. And you mentioned property law. Are you a lawyer, too?"

"I am," he replied. "Picked up a night degree a couple of years ago when I was posted in DC. And I'm licensed by the Florida Bar to practice here as well."

Agent Harley Slavnick, Esq. looked down at his notes as he continued. "One of the more interesting conundrums here is the fact that documents in the folder are for the home mortgage. The loan on the house. What bankers call the *first,* meaning the first loan against the property. Yes? You understand? "

I nodded, and he continued.

"And even though the mortgage is clearly a mess, it may not necessarily have anything to do with Ms. Treverrow's fraud case."

"How's that?" I asked.

"As I understand it, Ms. Trev— "

"Emma," I interrupted. "Just call her Emma." The title sensitivity thing was starting to grate on me a little.

"Right. Well, the way Emma put it to you was she got a FedEx package from 'some bank' regarding a loan on the house that had gone past-due."

He held up the envelope. "This package." He dropped the

letter back onto the pile. "The loan that's referenced in this document isn't for the mortgage in this folder. It's for a home equity line of credit. Bankers call them HELOCs. A HELOC is kind of cross between a credit line and a second mortgage. You take money out as you need it, it has a credit limit, and it's secured against your home. Whatever you draw out instantly becomes a loan—which you're liable for. You understand so far?"

I nodded again.

"Okay, good. The bad news is that whoever secured this particular line of credit has withdrawn everything. It's completely tapped out."

He moved a couple of other papers around as he spoke. "So, that's problem number one. Problem number two is that HELOCs are not typically protected with title insurance."

"I have no idea what that means," I said.

Slavnick looked a little surprised, but soldiered on.

"Title insurance indemnifies buyers from obligations that might arise with mortgage-related problems—like fraud."

"In plain English, please, Agent Slavnick."

Slavnick blushed. "Sorry." He paused a few seconds as he searched for the right words.

"What that means, Mr. Treverrow, is that there is no backstop here. Even if you prove fraud in this case—and I fully intend to get to the bottom of this and prosecute the perpetrator —but even if that happens, no one's going to magically swoop in and make this disappear. That's what title insurance does, basically. It covers you in case of fraud. It makes good on the loan—it pays the bank what the bank is owed."

He paused again. I knew it wasn't going to be good.

"But this loan doesn't have that insurance. For whatever reason, it wasn't required. Which means that at the end of the day, Emma is on the hook for this loan. And the loan is secured against the house. And if the loan is not paid, the house will go into foreclosure. Which is why you received this letter."

Terrific.

I couldn't wait to share that bit of good news with the little missus.

I said, "So, should I be looking for an attorney?"

"Probably, but let me do a little digging first."

"Okay." I said.

Slavnick continued. "Now, as far as the people who signed various documents in here, I think your first instincts were probably right–they're a good place to start—but probably for different reasons than you considered. The way I'm looking at it—some of the names in here—for example, this closing attorney, a Mister— "

He took another sip of water as he scanned the documents looking for the name.

"—Hodges. Ted Hodges. I'm interested in Mr. Hodges because he's the person who prepared these loan documents. Which means, among other things, he had access to all of the information necessary to fraudulently apply for the HELOC."

"So, he's the guy you'd start with?"

"Probably." Slavnick answered. "And if it makes you feel any better, Mr. Treverrow, this isn't all that uncommon. We're starting to see more and more of these cases crop up across the country, and we expect that to continue. The banks seem to have forgotten what happened the last time they did this, because—once again— they've made money far too easy to access, with far too little documentation on who was getting it. You combine that with the fact that most people have parts of their identity spread all over the Internet, and you've got a recipe for disaster. And it's going to get worse before it gets better."

He looked at me, clasped his hands together and said, "But, let's table that for now and start at the beginning. When you two first bought the house."

"What do you want to know?" I asked.

"Everything."

CHAPTER 17

"So—fifty-thousand dollars. That's the number?"

Vassili Dmitrievich thumbed the stack of bills, holding them up and gauging the thickness through squinted eyes.

What a thug move, Elliot thought.

"Fifty-thousand dollars is considerably off what we agreed to for profit disbursement schedule, Elliot. Considerably."

"I know, Vassili. I know." Elliot leaned back in his chair in an effort to look relaxed and unconcerned. Neither of which was the case. The two were sitting in a rundown café off a side street near the beach in Fort Lauderdale. With the exception of a single employee and Vassili's ever-present bodyguard, the place was empty. In retrospect, Elliot should have seen that as a sign that things were not good.

"I'm just as unhappy about this as you are, Vassili. Remember, if your disbursement is down, so is mine." Elliot shrugged, "Unfortunately, projects of this magnitude have a tendency to start slowly, and real estate is one of those things where you can't predict every expense. There are some unknowns going in."

Elliot's strategy was to dive quickly into technicalities and minutiae in an attempt to get Vassili out of his depth—dealing with unfamiliar jargon, exotic accounting techniques, and just plain bullshit. From the look on Vassili's face, he wasn't having much luck.

"Once we're past this series of one-time, upfront and fixed costs, then we should start seeing a more reliable and pre-dictable income stream. Remember, these costs are actually amortized over the life of the project from an accounting per-spective, but are realized up front from a cash flow perspec-tive," Elliot went on, fully aware that everything he was saying was absolute gibberish.

Vassili took his eyes off of his stack of cash and shifted his gaze to a point over Elliot right shoulder.

"Vadik. *Idi nozhnitsy*," he said, as he let the stack of cash drop to the table. Elliot sensed movement behind him and turned to look over his shoulder in time to see Dmitrievich's creepy ninja bodyguard walk out of the café's front door.

Vassili turned his gaze from the money on the table to Becker.

"Elliot? Here's thing: for some reason—reason I don't understand—you have decided that Vassili Dmitrievich is kind of guy you can outsmart. As if I know nothing about business. So, Elliot, as they say in business, let's recaps." Dmitrievich brought his hands together under his chin as if he were about to pray.

"At last count, I owned four different corporations which, in turn, owned six different night clubs, two car rental agencies, five parking lots, and three restaurants—one of which you are sitting in." Vassili paused. "And this is just the legal part of— what do you sophisticated business guys like to call it? Oh, yes. My portfolio."

Elliot started to interrupt, but Vassili silenced him with the slight wave of his hands.

"You are not only accountant or lawyer I sit with to review business deals, Elliot. I am disappointed that you take me for such a *durak* that you think you can confuse me with double speak and legalese."

Elliot heard the door open behind him.

"You like to talk accounting, Elliot. Good. Let's talk accounting. We agreed that payments would be for two hundred thousand dollars, *da*?"

Elliot nodded.

"This means that you now owe me one hundred fifty thousand dollars, *da*? On top of the original investment that you still owe me."

He leaned forward.

"*Da*?"

Elliot nodded again. He swallowed nervously.

"And, as I understand it, responsible accounting and lending practices would stipulate that I require some sort of collateral, just to be safe. To keep everything on the up and ups, as they say. *Da*?"

Elliot reached into his pocket and came out with his car keys. "I've got a Land Rover parked out front that you can keep. For collateral, I mean. Brand new. Beautiful. Every option. Custom paint. At least a hundred twenty retail." He loved that car—*fucking loved it*—but this wasn't the time for petty attachments.

"Elliot, first of all, if I took your Land Rover, you would have no way to get to emergency room. Why would I do that to a friend?" Vassili said, as Vadik sat down next to Elliot, effectively pinning him into the booth.

"Secondly, that's far too much to ask in collateral. What I'm going to hold of yours is much smaller."

CHAPTER 18

By the time I left the Bureau, I was exhausted. Not physically, but mentally. What had started as a routine fact-gathering session had quickly turned into an inquisition—despite Slavnick's best efforts to the contrary.

"I apologize, Lieutenant, if it feels like I'm grilling you. I'm simply trying to line up the facts, and I know my style can sometimes leave a little bit to be desired."

I replied that I understood, and that I was happy to answer any questions that he had.

Not that I meant it.

Driving south on 195, I scrolled through my phone's directory looking for Emma's work number. Her assistant answered after a couple of rings. "Emma Treverrow's office. This is Constance."

"Hey, it's Logan. She around?"

Constance had been Emma's right hand for the last five years. She knew more about her day-to-day life than I ever will. And not just her work life—when I was deployed overseas, Constance helped Emma manage everything from getting Isabella and Zack to daycare to waiting for the cable guy to show up at the house.

"She's in with the Under Armour guys. Store displays. She's got her cell with her, if you want to call her on that. Or I can pop in there. It's not like they're splitting the atom or anything."

"No, that's okay," I replied. "It's just that I'm right down the road and thought maybe I could swing by for a few minutes."

"Is this about the fake loan thing?" Constance asked. "She said you were meeting with someone from the FBI."

I wasn't particularly surprised that Constance knew about the loan; advertising people tend to advertise everything. Still, a little discretion once in a while would be refreshing.

"Partly, I guess," I replied. "I figured it would be a shame to waste a perfectly good drive down here without stopping in. Maybe take her to lunch or something."

"It's two o'clock in the afternoon, Logan. Why don't you take her to an early happy hour or something?" Constance replied.

Ten minutes later, Constance was ushering me into the inner sanctum of Day+Lancer & Treverrow. "Hey, I was thinking about it," Constance said over her shoulder. "Why don't you take both of us to an early happy hour? It's Friday, and a martini feels very much in order. That's what they would do on Mad Men."

We rounded a corner and stepped into an enormous open space buzzing with people and activity. The agency (which insiders called "D-LaT" for short) had moved its growing operation into an abandoned old cinema the year prior. While this seemed like a really cool idea at the time—and very in keeping with D-LaT's reputation for being quirky – it also created one of the weirdest workspaces I'd ever seen. I could never understand how anyone got anything accomplished at D-LaT.

The partners had decided, for example, to leave as much of the original theatre intact as possible. While it's possible, I suppose, that this was simply an artsy commitment to authenticity or kitsch, my guess is that it was more of a PR stunt – calculated to generate a maximum level of free and adoring press. And like most PR stunts, the problems persisted long after the buzz wore off.

Since the actual theatre served as the creative hub of the agency, virtually everyone at D-LaT spent much of the day trudging up and down an indoor hill. Junior talent worked down the bottom of the hill—where the original front row movie seats had been. Senior people worked further up the hill —toward the back of the theatre. Management was perched in the balconies.

Rather than removing all of the chairs and creating workstations or cubes, someone had the bright idea of using the original theatre seats as work chairs and grafting little pull down shelves onto the seatbacks—sort of like the tray tables one finds on an airplane. This, of course, had the immediate effect of making the agency about as productive as a packed flight to Atlanta.

It took a few huge missed deadlines, but within a week, crews were busy tearing out the theatre chairs, leaving people to sit on cushions and throw pillows, laptops balanced on crossed legs. Which, in turn, made the agency about as productive as Phish concert.

A couple of missed deadlines later, and the agency was the proud owner of almost a hundred, brand-new, custom-designed ergonomic workstations built to maximize workflow— and still arranged on an indoor hill. The press coverage was, of course, maximal, free, and adoring.

I followed Constance into the front of the theatre. Behind me, on the giant cinema screen, a seemingly random stream of advertising and pop culture paraphernalia—ads, videos, movie clips, photographs, Tweets, animations—looped silently. As I gazed up into the balconies looking for Emma, I could feel the logo for an energy drink being projected onto my check.

"Hang tight, Logan. I'll go find her," Constance said, as she trudged up the hill.

Rocket science or not, it took Emma a little more than a half hour to extricate herself from the Under Armour Guys. I killed time by pestering the junior art directors in the front row about color theory. They seemed relieved when Emma and Constance came and collected me.

By 2:30, we were sitting in an outdoor café in Coconut Grove, nursing a couple of beers. At least Emma and I were nursing a couple of beers. Constance was enjoying her martini.

"Well, I know it doesn't sound like good news, but it's all in the way you look at it," I said, trying my best to sound upbeat and positive.

"You—actually, *we've*—got the FBI on this thing. A case like this is so far below their usual threshold, I'm surprised they even agreed to meet with me, much less put time in trying to get to the bottom of it."

"Logan," Emma began in a measured tone. "I've had my identity stolen. I've had someone run up almost $200,000 in bogus loans in my name. Which, apparently, I'm on the hook for, even if they find the assholes who did this. If you think somehow the difference between this being really, really bad news—or you know, a little thing that'll *pass*—is just in the way I look at it, you're dreaming." Emma looked at me. "This is really, *really* bad news. And you know it."

She was right, of course—but my instinct to protect her was always going to be there—together or apart. (Which was, of course, one of the fundamental issues in our brief, but torrid marriage: how do you protect people who resent the implication that they need it in the first place?)

"Okay, you're right. It's not good." Both Emma and Constance nodded in exasperation. "Look, Slavnick's going to do his thing—and whatever that is, and however long that takes, it is what it is. In the meantime, I'm thinking that I want to talk to some of the names that were involved in that closing. The names I got off the closing documents. Maybe the realtors, but definitely the mortgage broker and that closing attorney."

"Why them?" Constance asked.

I was starting to feel, if not out gunned, at least a little outnumbered. Like I had two ex-wives who had somehow teamed up.

"Common sense," I said. "I started thinking about it—those two are the only ones that had access to all of the information on Emma you'd need if you were an identity thief—her Social Security number, all of her banking info, credit reports, income taxes – stuff like that."

"You figured that out? Pretty sharp, Logan," Constance said.

"Well, there's that—and it's also what Slavnick told me." I replied.

"Aha!" Constance laughed. "Now, that makes more sense. Emma said you'd never been to a house closing in your life."

"True, but I'm not an idiot. I went to some of the most exclusive boarding schools in the country and graduated cum laude from Princeton," I said, a little defensively.

"Really? I didn't know that. What did you major in?" she asked, as Emma pulled on her Kalik and rolled her eyes.

"Philosophy."

Constance raised her eyebrows.

"It's a real major - trust me. And there's more math that you'd think."

Constance snorted, finished off her martini and raised her hand to get the waiter's attention. She made a twirling motion with her hand, indicating one more, all around. I settled back into my chair, trying to clear my head a little. It was a little past three it had already been a long day.

"So, Emma," I said as I rubbed my eyes, "Do you remember

anything about either of those guys—Becker or Hodges?"

"Not really," she replied, as she took a swig off her fresh beer. "One of them—I can't remember which one—was really squirrely looking, I do remember that. Had like an Elvis haircut. Or a bad toupee, I couldn't tell. Also, he was really sweaty."

I had no idea what that meant. "Are you saying that he looked shady? Or suspicious?"

"I don't know, Logan. He was just…weird. That's all. Kind of creepy."

I thought about that for a moment. Singling people out in South Florida for being weird, or creepy—or even sweaty, for that matter—wasn't going to get us much in the way of narrowing the field. On the other hand, it was something.

"How about the other people there that day? Anything else stand out?' I asked.

Emma's brow furrowed. "Not really. Suits, cell phones, tons of paper. Everyone kind of blended together. Wait—I do remember the sweaty guy had one of those big square briefcases —the kind lawyers carry. The kind that *only* lawyers carry. I remember because he tripped over it."

"So that would make sweaty guy…" I opened the folder and flipped through a couple of documents.

"…Ted Hodges."

"So, there you go, Sherlock. Now go get him." Constance said.

"Let's not get ahead of ourselves," I said. "I'll swing over there and see what I can find out. He works a place called Double A Top Title."

CHAPTER 19

When Elliot Becker was seven years old, he walked into the wrong end of a baseball bat that Tommy Elmore was swinging as he warmed up on deck, waiting for his turn at the plate. That was the last time Becker played baseball, and the first time he'd been to the emergency room. In the 40-odd years since, Becker had seen more than his share of emergency rooms—due, in large part, to his career choices.

When Elliot had rolled out of bed that morning, he'd considered the distant possibility of ending up in the emergency room at some point in the day. And so it had turned out. On the other hand, (no pun intended) he never imagined what would transpire to put him there.

Vadik had moved so quickly and so forcefully, it was almost over before Elliot knew what had happened. After pinning Elliot between the wall and the café table, he had wrapped a viselike grip around Elliot's left wrist. Keeping him pinned with his hip, Vadik pulled Elliot's arm close into his body, and in a single motion, snipped off his pinky finger with a pair of pruning shears. The finger fell to the table with a little clatter, still wearing its signet ring.

For a second or two, all three men stared down at the finger; Elliot with horror, Vassili with interest, and Vadik with professional detachment. As Vassili plucked a French fry off his plate, dipped it in ketchup and ate it, a geyser of blood began to shoot from Becker's hand. Vadik pulled a dirty dishrag from somewhere and clamped it on the tiny nubbin of finger that remained. He grabbed Elliot's right hand, clamped it over the towel and said, "Steady pressure. Don't let up, or you'll bleed out. From pinky."

Vadik sounded disgusted that someone would be so cavalier as to bleed out from an amputated finger.

And then the pain came—followed by nausea and an enveloping darkness that was about to take over—until he was slapped hard across his face. "Hey! Stay awake! I wasn't kidding about keeping pressure."

Vadik snorted, got up from the table and walked out of Elliot's line of sight. Vassili ate another French fry.

"Elliot, by the way, I was just kidding about keeping finger for collateral," Vassili said, through a mouthful of food. "I mean, I'm going to keep it—and I may even give it back to you later—but, there's no putting it back on. You are nine-fingered guy for life now, Elliot. And for what, I ask you? A short payment?" As he spoke, Vassili wagged a ketchup-coated fry in an admonishing manner.

"I'm betting it wasn't worth it. Am I right?"

Vassili pulled a flask from his jacket pocket, dumped some of it into his coffee, and took a sip. "Ah, there we go. Hair of the dog, Elliot. You were some life of party last night, buddy—you and Sasha, I got to tell you." He took another sip and shrugged.

"Today, not so much."

The pain in his hand was so intense that Becker began lose control of his bowels. He was too shocked to scream, too terrified to stand, but more terrified of the beatific Russian sociopath sitting across from him. He had no idea what was going to happen next. For all he knew, Vadik had gone outside to fetch a chain saw.

Vassili solved his dilemma by pushing his chair back and standing up. Becker looked up at him, sweat running down his face, his good hand clamped on a greasy rag that was quickly going scarlet.

"Not to worry about the bill, Elliot. On the house. See you in the funny papers."

And with that, Vassili walked out.

CHAPTER 20

S ilvano Mazzio sat quietly in the lobby of AA Top Title, pondering what it would be like to have to come to this office every day in order to earn a living. The lobby was exactly as he imagined it would be—a dark, wood-veneered coffee table festooned with long-out-of-date lifestyle magazines, a couple of bad fox-chase prints on the walls, and an abandoned front desk. An LED camera mounted over the reception desk captured, Silvano assumed, the entire area. With the exception of the security guy napping behind the desk, the lobby could have been transplanted to Richie's condo building and it would have fit right in.

Silvano had a number in his head: 10.

Ten minutes was the exact amount of time that he was willing to sit quietly in the lobby, on the pretext that this visit was a perfectly normal part of a perfectly legal real-estate transaction. At minute eleven, all bets were off.

After two decades of shaking down local businesses in and around Long Island, Silvano knew that this idiot lawyer was also in the middle of his own countdown. He'd seen it a thousand times—particularly on collections. These little guys loved to make him wait. Not long enough to piss him off, but long enough to establish the fact that they were not intimidated by him. To remind him that they considered his presence – and his collections—as simply a cost of doing business.

115

Table stakes.

Fine. Silvano understood. Do what you gotta do. As long as it wasn't too overt, or too long. And generally, "too long" was about 11 minutes.

He was four minutes in and considering picking up an ancient copy of *Forbes* when the solenoid on the door to the inner office clicked, and a pleasant-faced, middle-aged woman appeared in the frame.

"Mr. Mazzio?" She smiled.

"That's me," Silvano said as he stood and smoothed the front of his other Ralph Lauren Purple Label suit—a nice two-button, dark grey ensemble with dotted-pinstripes.

"Mr. Hodges is wrapping up his conference call right now, and he asked me to escort you to the conference room, where he thought you might be more comfortable. Can I offer you anything—coffee? Water?"

As she ushered him into an inner hallway, Silvano took note of the fact that the conference room—another bad English Private Hunt Club affair—was actually separated from the office proper by a second, electromagnetic-locked door at the end of the hall. A key card reader was mounted on the wall to the right, and a small security camera hung over the doorframe.

Counting the front door, that's three electromagnetic locks and at least a couple of cameras between the sidewalk and this guy's desk, Silvano thought. That many cameras, that many locks —that's the kind of thing one usually sees in cash-intensive businesses, like pawnshops or check-cashing places. Not law offices.

What the hell?

Taking a chair at the head of the table, Silvano said, "I think I've had my quota of coffee for today, but bottled water— sparkling, if you have it—would be very nice."

The woman smiled. "I'll see what I can do. Mr. Hodges

should be along shortly."

The door closed and Silvano reached down into the brief-case at his feet and pulled out a legal-sized manila envelope. He set it squarely on the table, reached into his jacket pocket for his reading glasses, and began to organize the documents from the folder into three neat stacks. When he finished, he nudged the stacks lightly to square up the corners, removed his glasses, set them precisely on top of the middle stack, folded his hands, and waited.

For another four minutes.

At what Silvano figured was roughly the 10-minute mark, a poorly-dressed man wearing a terrible hairpiece blew into the room, his arms wrapped around an accordion folder of paper —some of which fell out as he dropped it onto the conference room table. Right behind him was the woman who had escorted Silvano in, carrying a tray with a bottle of San Pellegrino sparkling water and two crystal tumblers.

A nice touch, Silvano thought.

"Mr. Mazzio, I'm Ted Hodges. We spoke earlier this morning. It's nice to meet you," the man said, as he slid into a chair at the far end of the table.

Silvano could tell that Hodges was confused. In these sorts of meetings, clients invariably sat in one of the chairs along the side of the table, ceding the position at the head to the host. That's the way it always worked—and why Silvano always took the head of the table. Nothing like starting things out with the other guy confused and off his game. Thank you, Tony Robbins.

Silvano said nothing, preferring to let Hodges struggle to fill the silence with blather. Which, of course, he did.

"Sorry for the wait. I have had one doozy of a day, let me tell you. One call after another—sometimes it seems that things just stack right up—you don't even have time to take a breath or grab a bite for lunch— which I think I actually missed today —"

Silvano held his hand up, and Hodges stopped. Silvano raised a finger and waved it slowly in a "give me a moment" fashion as he glanced down at the stacks of paper in front of him. He pulled a single document out and studied it closely. He looked up at Hodges.

"So Counselor, can I assume you've done your due diligence this morning, and that we can dispense with the whole who-the-fuck-is-this-guy and what-the-fuck-is-he-doing-here bit?"

Hodges swallowed once and stammered, "Um...yes. Mister Pizzuti called me shortly after we hung up this morning and explained how you were, um...helping him with his transaction. And... that you had some, um..."

Silvano regarded Hodges with hooded eyes. "Questions?" He tilted his head slightly and smiled. All charm. "That I had some questions about the account? Is that what Richie told you?"

Hodges looked down into the depths of his accordion folder. Silvano could see the mesh of his toupee. "Yes. Questions. Mr. Pizzuti said you...had...questions."

"Spot on, Counselor. I *do* have some questions about the account. Lots of questions, in fact. But before we get to those questions, let's start with *this* question. It's kind of a techie question, and in this day in age, it's probably a rhetorical question, but let's ask it anyway and see what happens. You ready?"

Hodges look up, confused and frightened. He nodded slowly. "Yes."

"Do you know what a jpeg is?

CHAPTER 21

I t turns out that pinky fingers are not simply decorative. Elliot Becker had never thought about the important functional role that pinky fingers play in day-to-day life, but he was now.

Take driving, for example. Pinky fingers are crucial in making the subtle adjustments to the steering wheel that spell the difference between driving smoothly up Interstate 95 and weaving all over the place. This holds true even when the steering wheel in question is attached to a fully customized, $120,000 British sports utility vehicle with power-assisted everything. Which, to his surprise and chagrin, Elliot still owned. Looking back on it, he would have gladly traded the Range Rover to have his pinky still attached to his hand. *But that deal hadn't been on the table, had it?*

Elliot was pushing the car north on I95, determined to put as much distance as possible between him and the hospital. The physician on duty had been understandably curious as to how Elliot had managed to both amputate—and lose—his own finger. Elliot had claimed a landscaping accident—namely, that some electric hedge clippers had gotten away from him and in the process pulverized his finger into an unrecoverable mess. Blah blah blah.

It wasn't a great story—and the fact that Elliot was wearing a tie detracted from the idea that he had been landscaping—

but it was the best he could come up with, considering the limited amount of time he'd had to think about it, the overwhelming pain he was in, and the general dizziness and lack of mental acuity that came with significant blood loss. The doctor had told him that he was in shock.

Really?

If there had been a silver lining to the whole thing, it was that the hospital staff still had no idea who he was. He had managed to get in, get treated and get out without ever having to fill out a form, or give anyone his name. Getting treated immediately had been simple, actually. He'd walked straight up to the front desk, removed the rag from around his hand, and sprayed a fountain of blood four feet high across the counter and onto the row of filing cabinets behind it.

No triage. No registration. Just a gurney and an express ride to Examination Room D.

"I would strongly recommend that we admit you for at least the evening," the doctor had said. "Losing a finger is very traumatic. It's not something that you just bounce back from, like a sprain."

The idea of crawling into a hospital bed and turning up the morphine drip was seductive. What he wouldn't give for ten hours of sleep, safely stashed away from homicidal Russians, brainless straw-buyers, yammering girlfriends, and rash-covered bagmen. Ten hours of painless, dreamless *silence.*

But that wasn't going to happen. What was going to happen was that this ER doctor was going to put the finishing touches on Elliot's tiny little stump, wrap it up, and head off somewhere to make some notes about the guy with the missing finger in Exam Room D.

At which point Elliot would haul ass.

That part of the plan hadn't run so smoothly. For one thing,

Elliot had actually been hooked to an IV. Not for painkillers, but rather, for two units of whole blood, Type O negative. Prudently, the doctor had run the IV into the arm opposite his mangled hand, which made it easier for him to clean, prep, suture and wrap what little remained of the finger. Unfortunately for Elliot, that had meant trying to tug the IV needle out of his arm with a four-fingered hand wrapped to resemble a boxing glove.

It hadn't been pretty.

Next came the challenge of leaving the ER unnoticed. Elliot had considered—and overruled—a rush to the exit doors, for the simple fact that there were, in fact, three different sets of doors between where he was sitting in Exam Room D and his Range Rover out in the parking lot—some of which were probably locked. Emergency rooms also had orderlies. Big orderlies.

Instead, he had opted to go the other way—toward the back of the ER, pushing through random doors until he found himself alone in an entry corridor which, he assumed, would take him deeper into the hospital. He had walked for about 10 minutes, making random turns, looking for exits along the way, until – surprisingly—he found himself in the hospital cafeteria. From there, a single set of double doors opened to an outdoor picnic area and freedom.

As he raced toward Palm Beach County, Elliot regretted not taking an extra few minutes in the ER to lift some painkillers. The local anesthetic the doctor had administered was starting to wear off, and his hand was throbbing. Elliot had read about phantom pain associated with amputated limbs, and he was now learning that this applied to fingers as well. *Who knew?*

Elliot punched a button on his steering wheel. A BBC-accented female responded over the Range Rover's sound system.

"Number, please?"

Elliot dictated the number to his office, while thanking the gods for hands-free technology. The phone rang twice and

Sasha came online.

"Modern Properties. Can I help you?"

"Hey. Don't say anything. Just get a pen and a piece of paper, and write down exactly what I tell you. Okay?"

There was silence.

"Sasha—okay?"

More silence.

"Are you there? Did the fucking call drop? Sasha?"

"I'm here," came the reply over the Range Rover's stereo system.

"Well then, why didn't you say anything?" Elliot asked.

"Because you told me not to say anything." Sasha said.

Elliot sighed.

"You got the pen and paper?" he asked, as he swerved the Rover back into the middle lane.

"Nope. Gimme a minute." Elliot could hear Sasha shuffling through drawers. "Okay, got it."

"First, send Hodges the routing number to the checking account for Modern Properties, Inc. And make sure that it's absolutely *that* account. None of the other ones. It has to be the one for Modern Properties. Tell him he needs to do a wire transfer to us, today. And that it's gotta be for..."

Elliot did a little quick math in his head and rounded up. "Tell him it's gotta be for four hundred thousand. Not a dime less. If he can do it, four-fifty would be even better."

He paused a second and added, "You have to do that in the next fifteen minutes, and you gotta tell him he has to do the wire before five pm today. Period. Tomorrow's too late. So, call him, tell him you're sending him the info, and then call him back and make sure he got it and that he understands it's gotta get done today. And tell him I'm headed up to him right now and that I'll be there in the next thirty minutes or so. Once you get that done, I want you to send a text to that appraiser Burrell—the number's on a Post-it note in the top drawer of my desk. Burrell Malin. He's the bald guy with the rash. The text needs to say that the timetable's been moved up, and everything needs to be ready to go by this weekend. Exactly like that. Timetable's been moved up, be ready to go this weekend."

"I don't get it."

"— I told you to shut up and write. He knows what it means. You don't have to."

 Silence.

"Sasha? You got all that?"

"So, it's okay for me to talk, now? You're all done with your little rant?" the Range Rover asked.

"Just tell me you got all that, please." Elliot said, as he scanned ahead for the exit he needed.

"I got it. Call. Email. Bank routing number for Modern Properties. Wire transfer for four hundred thousand. Text Burrell." There was a pause. "Four hundred thousand is a lot of money, Elliot. A lot."

"No kidding."

What had Elliot worried wasn't that it was a lot of money. What had him worried was that it wasn't enough money.

"Alright, you're wasting time. Get moving."

Elliot disconnected the call and stomped on the accelerator.

CHAPTER 22

"**A** jpeg? Like a picture? That kind of jpeg?"

"Exactly that kind of jpeg."

Ted Hodges had a very bad feeling about this man —and this meeting. He had purposefully made him wait in the conference room for about ten minutes, hoping that it would appear that Hodges was a busy man, a man with important responsibilities, and that he had agreed to the meeting simply as a courtesy.

It hadn't worked. It was clear from the moment that he had set foot in his own conference room that this big Italian was in charge. Hodges wasn't sure he had ever actually met a Mafioso (was that even a word?) but he was pretty sure he was meeting one now.

Mazzio, who was sitting at the other end of the conference table like he owned the place, picked up his reading glasses and settled them delicately on the end of his nose. He glanced down and pulled a document from one of the folders in front of him.

"Here's a good example of a jpeg, as a matter of fact." He slid the document down the table toward Hodges.

Rather than reaching out and pulling toward him, Hodges hesitated, knowing somewhere deep in his heart that once he touched it, everything was going change. And for the worse.

"Go ahead. Take a look."

Hodges reluctantly leaned over and pulled the document toward him. It was a printout of an email. The email was addressed to "Richard Pizzuti." The sender was "AA Top Title." The subject line read "Account Statement."

"Look familiar, Counselor?"

Hodges coughed. "Well, I'm not sure that I'm familiar with this particular statement, but yes, this looks like the account statements we routinely send out to our clients, particularly if their escrow accounts are held over a longer period of time, which sometimes happens, say in a case where— "

"— So, take a look at the attachment that's listed there at the top," Mazzio interrupted. "The one that says "RPEscrow.jpg."

Hodges looked down.

"You see that?"

Hodges nodded.

"Well, I saw that, too. It was one of the first things I saw when I started rooting through all of this shit. Which I was rooting through in the first place because Ritchie gave me call asking me to figure out why it was taking six months to close on a house he was putting a 100% cash offer on."

Hodges waited for what he knew was coming next.

"More importantly, Richie's a young guy, hasn't really been around the block and all, so he was wondering if it's normal to have to put 50% down on a cash offer and for some fucking attorney to be able to hold his money for six months."

Mazzio smiled charmingly and sat back in his seat.

"So, I'm coming to this a little late, you know? And I've known Ritchie and his family for years—both personally and professionally. And I know Ritchie's been prone to some errors in judgment over the years, the kinda things you expect in a young guy full of piss and vinegar—and that's okay. And personally, I'm not sure why a single guy who's barely out of high school needs a two-million-dollar house in Palm Beach County, right? — "

Mazzio raised eyebrows and held his hands up. Hodges nodded along in nervous agreement.

"—but who am I to judge? It's his life, his money, and I'm just here to help in any way I can. Know what I mean?"

Mazzio began leafing through the folders in front of him, his gaze directed downward as he picked up and scrutinized one document after another.

"So, I said, 'Sure Ritchie, I'll see what I can do.' And incidentally, me being an older guy—one who's been around the block a couple a times, unlike young master Ritchie — I'd never heard of it taking six months to buy a house you're paying cash for, either. Seemed kinda odd, you know what I mean?"

He closed the folders and met Hodges' gaze. He was no longer smiling.

"And then there's the whole thing about you keeping a million dollars of Ritchie's money for six months. There's something definitely odd there. Wouldn't you agree, Counselor?"

Hodges began to stammer a reply, but Mazzio cut him off.

"Let's pretend you just gave me a hundred legal instances in which it would be perfectly reasonable to keep a million bucks of some kid's dough, okay? I'm sure you can reel them off. And since I'm gonna tell you they're all bullshit anyway, we can just skip over that whole thing. Save us both a buncha time. Yeah?"

Hodges nodded, and Mazzio resumed.

"Okay, where was I? Oh yeah—jpegs. So, I'm looking through all of this paperwork, all these emails with all these excuses from you on this delay...that delay...this thing... that thing—on and on, you know? Did you know there are fifty four emails from this office to Richie in here?"

Mazzio held up one of the manila folders.

126

"I know because I counted them when I printed them out. Ritchie, he don't print things out—maybe he's trying to reduce his carbon footprint or something, I don't know. Maybe it's a youth thing."

He flipped through the folder and quickly pulled out a document.

"But the way I see it, you print things out and you catch things you might skip over if you're just looking at it on tiny some computer screen, or, if you're like me, on a Blackberry. I don't know about you, but I can't see a damn thing on a Blackberry. Screen's too small. But with a printout—"

Mazzio held up the document.

"—you see stuff. Like this account statement here. Kind of like the one you've got there, Counselor, just a different month —but the same kind of attachment. Which is a jpeg. So I asked myself, what kind of program makes jpegs?"

He looked at Hodges.

"Do you know what kind of program makes jpegs, Ted?"

Hodges figured the worst thing he could do was to answer the question, so he simply shook his head.

"How about Photoshop?"

Those fucking idiots, Hodges thought. The web guys—Devin and Dustin. They had told him and Becker in no uncertain terms that no one would *ever* be able to tell that the account statements were doctored. Because, as Devin and Dustin liked to say, they were "Photoshop Masters."

"Counselor?" Mazzio interrupted his thoughts.

"Um...Photoshop? Yes, I think that's a program that makes jpeg files. I'm sure there are many different programs that make —— "

"You ever hear of a bank program that makes jpegs, Counselor? Because I haven't."

Mazzio looked at Hodges expectantly. He said nothing. He obviously was waiting for Hodges to say something. Anything.

"Well, I can't say that I'm familiar with the kinds of programs that the banking system runs, Mr. Mazzio, but you have my word that I'll look into why the statements in question here are using that kind of file immediately—although I'm not exactly sure why a particular file type is something that should be an issue. I'm sure that there's a simple explanation, but nevertheless, I appreciate you're bringing this to my attention this."

Hodges stood, hoping that his pledge to investigate "immediately" would give him an excuse to head into the back office, effectively putting a door with a lock between himself and this fucking Mafioso.

Mazzio held his hand up and made a gentle motion for Hodges to resume his seat. Which he did, rather reluctantly. Mazzio tilted his head slightly and smiled.

"You know Ockham's Razor? The theory that the simpler the hypothesis, the higher the likelihood of it being the correct hypothesis? They teach that in law school?"

Who the fuck is this guy? Hodges thought, as he nodded.

"Good. So you'd agree with me that the simplest hypothesis to explain our little jpeg mystery is that someone in your office is making up fake bank account statements in Photoshop and sending them out to clients like they're the real McCoy. Simple."

Mazzio leaned across the table, as if bestowing a confidence.

"That, in and of itself, doesn't bother me. In my line of work, you see this kind of thing all the time. Some guy trying to squeeze a little extra juice out of the orange. Taking a short cut here and there. Doing something that may or may not be on the right side of the law—whatever that law is. It happens more than you know. But *I* know. And like I said, I don't really care. How someone makes his dough is his business. To each his own, I always say."

Hodges felt a faint glimmer of hope, as Mazzio leaned back into his seat, his smile fading.

"Until I find myself on the wrong side of it. Then, I care."

So much for the glimmer.

"What actually surprises me is that you'd be stupid enough to pull this shit on Ritchie. *Ritchie Pizzuti*. Forget everyone else you're scamming, but I can't believe you didn't know who the fuck this kid is. Where his money comes from. Who's behind him. And most importantly, what would happen to you once we found out you were scamming him."

Mazzio paused for a moment and let that sink in.

"And while we're on the subject of things I can't believe, let me add one more: I can't believe you actually thought you'd get away with it. That no one in Ritchie's family would see through this half-assed scam. I mean, are you kidding? We practically invented this kind of stuff, Ted."

Hodges began to stammer an explanation, but Mazzio held his hand up. Hodges shut his mouth.

"Which brings me back to my original point. That there's no way you coulda known who Ritchie was. Am I right?"

Hodges, realizing that to protest would be simultaneously pathetic (not that he cared) and useless (which he did) simply nodded.

"Well, that's about the only good thing I can find in any of this, Ted. That at least you did this without actually knowing the people you were scamming. So—you get a little credit for being ignorant instead of insane. But it's only a little credit. Because the fact of the matter is that you fucked up, Counselor. You fucked up big time. And it's gonna cost you."

The room was silent as Mazzio his point sink in.

This is it? Hodges thought. *An Italian mobster whacks me so that Elliot doesn't have to get whacked by a Russian mobster? This so unbelievably unfair...*

Hodges began to cry. He screwed his eyes shut so that he didn't have to see what was coming next. Whatever was coming next.

"Counselor?"

Instinctively, Hodges brought his hands up to block what he assumed was a gun pointed at his face. What a last moment. Please God let it be over quickly. He thought briefly of his wife. She'd be fine, he knew. That realization actually created a little resentment.

"Counselor?

Hodges continued to whimper.

"Ted...TED! I'm talking to you. Stop crying. Put your hands down."

Hodges slowly opened his eyes and lowered his hands. Mazzio was looking at him with an expression that was somewhere between amusement and disgust.

"Man up, for Christ's sake. I'm not gonna kill you. What? You think that's the way I work? That I'm some kinda animal? Give me some credit."

Hodges felt his heart rate began to moderate a bit.

"I've been strictly on the up and up here, Ted. Unlike some people I could mention," Mazzio said, arching an eyebrow. "Called in ahead of time, set up an appointment, showed up on time with all of my paperwork in order. That's far from an animal, Ted. That's a model client, if you ask me."

Mazzio leaned back, crossed his arms and waited for a response.

"Um, yes. You've been a model client, Mr. Mazzio," Hodges said shakily.

Mazzio continued to look at Hodges. He raised his palms in a *go-on* gesture.

Hodges continued, "So, I guess we need to discuss your thoughts on how best to, um...*straighten out*...this irregularity."

"Well, first things first, Ted," Mazzio responded. "I'm assuming the reason you've been sending fake account statements is because you've been skimming money from that account. Yes?"

Mazzio leaned forward.

"It's okay. I know. *You know*. We both know. Let's not waste a bunch of time jerking each other off."

Hodges nodded reluctantly, and Mazzio continued.

"So—first things first—I need to know what's actually in that account. You know, the real number, before Photoshop. Once we know that, we'll know what you gotta put back in to bring it up to where it was. Next, we gotta figure what you owe Ritchie for the use of the money you borrowed. That part's easy, since Ritchie's family is already in the loan business. We got interest calculations and collections down to a science."

Mazzio smiled.

"Now, from one loan professional to another, I'm sure you know that our interest rates are a little different from what you're used to seeing here." Mazzio smiled as he held up a hand with his thumb and finger spread apart.

"They're a little bit higher."

Hodges wondered if he might actually be better off dead.

"Speaking of documentation," Mazzio continued, "that's another area where our operations differ. And I think you're gonna like the way we do it – which is with very little documentation. All this stuff you gotta put together? Gotta be a nightmare. All these forms? These government forms? We got none of that. We got almost no paperwork, as a matter of fact. A little note in a little book, and you're good to go. And in this case, since you've already taken the money, there's no approval process. You're already pre-approved, as they say."

Hodges knew there would be more, so he simply nodded and waited for what was inevitably coming next.

"Alright, so after we got all that squared away – and that shouldn't take long—all we gotta do is get your corporate papers here at the title company amended to reflect our new partnership."

Hodges coughed. "Partnership? What do you mean partnership?"

Mazzio was no longer smiling. "You know exactly what I mean, Counselor. As of right now, we fucking own you. Get used to it. You deserve it."

Hodges let his head drop. His toupee began to slide slightly starboard, covering his ear.

"Hey, Ted. I bet I know what you're thinking. Wanna know what I think you're thinking?"

Hodges, his eyes closed, just nodded.

"I'm betting you wish that I'd just gone ahead and popped you. I'm betting you figure that you're better off dead. Wanna know something else?"

Mazzio didn't bother to wait for Hodges to respond.

"You're right."

CHAPTER 23

An hour after leaving Coconut Grove, I pulled the Bronco into the parking lot of a dilapidated strip center in Boynton Beach. I made a mental note to check the oil level on my aging truck, which I was certain was low, considering that I had driven it through three counties—twice—in the last eight hours.

Having no plan other than showing up and asking to speak to Ted Hodges, I swung out of the Bronco, crossed the lot to AA Top Title's front door and pulled the handle.

The door was locked.

I checked my watched: 5:15 pm. I looked around the door and windows for the company's office hours. Nothing. I noticed a button set in the frame of the door, which I promptly pushed and stepped back. I noticed a security camera installed above the door, so I moved a few steps further back and looked directly into it, hoping that there was someone on the other side looking at me.

It must have worked, because the door buzzed few seconds later.

I grabbed the handle before the buzzing stopped, opened the door and went inside. The lobby was empty, but there was a sign beside a telephone that read *Please Call Extension 115*, which I did. A pleasant sounding woman answered.

"Hello. Can I help you?"

"Hi. My name is Logan Treverrow, and I'm wondering if I could speak to Ted Hodges," I said.

There was a brief pause on phone and I could hear the rapid clickity-clack of a keyboard in action.

I said, "I don't have an appointment, but I was in the area and I have a couple of questions on a contract that Mr. Hodges worked on in connection with a home that my wife purchased."

"Oh," said the woman, with a little chuckle. "That would explain why I couldn't find your name in our system."

"Her name is Emma Treverrow."

More typing and then silence.

"You found her?" I asked.

"Uh, yes. I found her, thank you." She sounded a little surprised that I was still on the line. "Mr. Treverrow, can I ask what your visit is in reference to?"

"Actually, I'd rather talk to Mr. Hodges on what my visit is in reference to. Is he available?"

The pleasant voiced woman answered, "Actually, he's currently in conference with a client and I'm not sure how long that he'll be in there. If you'd like to wait, I'll pop in and see if I can get better idea."

"Sure," I said. "I'm happy to wait."

"Please understand, Mr. Treverrow, Mr. Hodges has a very tight schedule, and it's usually a good idea to schedule an appointment with him in advance. This is purely for your convenience, you understand, as we try very hard to be cognizant of our client's time."

"Thank you, but as we've already established, I'm not a client. My wife is—or was," I pointed out.

Another pause. "I'll see what I can do. Please make yourself comfortable." With that, the line clicked off.

Aside from my morning workout and kite surfing session, I had spent the majority of the day on my ass. Sitting in cars, sitting in lobbies, sitting in conference rooms, sitting in cafes. I was tired of sitting and my body was starting to kink up from inactivity. I leaned onto the reception desk, grabbed my left ankle, and started a quick stretching routine to loosen up my legs. As I contorted, I noticed another security camera, this one mounted above the desk. I stopped stretching.

Camera outside. Camera inside.

I looked behind me at the door that opened into the office. Solenoid lock and the same kind of buzzer button that was out front.

Lock outside. Lock inside.

I understood operational security. And from an operational security perspective, this seemed a little excessive for what was, for all intents and purposes, a law office. I stood on my tip-toes and peered over the counter of the reception desk, searching for a door release button. There wasn't one as far as I could tell—at least one in plain view. I debated heading behind the desk to see if there was one hidden in a drawer or underneath the desk itself, but decided against it, reasoning that whatever I did in the reception was being logged to a hard drive somewhere. Besides, even if I got into the office, what was I going to do? Wander around? Ask every male who looked like Elvis if he had a few minutes?

Actually, that didn't seem like such a bad idea—but I decided to shelve it for the time being. Better to start this thing out on the right note, I figured.

With nothing left to keep me occupied, I sat down in one of the faux cherry chairs, glanced over the reading materials on the faux cherry coffee table, saw nothing of interest and decided instead do a little smart-phone research AA Top Title.

CHAPTER 24

Elliot Becker waited about fifteen minutes before calling Sasha back.

"Gimme an update," he barked.

"I couldn't get Ted on the phone. His wife—you knew that was his wife, right? —anyway, she said that he was in some meeting and wasn't answering the phone in the conference room or on his cell. I didn't know whether you wanted me to give her the message instead, but I figured I'd better ask you before I did anything."

Despite his misery, Becker actually smiled. Sasha was beginning to show good judgment and might prove to be a valuable asset over the long run. On the other hand, if he couldn't get things moving quickly, there wasn't going to be a long run.

"Alright well, I'm about a minute away from his office, so I'll see what the hell is up and handle it in person. Did you get the text off to Burrell?"

"I did. He's already sent back like, twenty responses."

"Read 'em to me," Becker ordered. "Actually, fuck that. Forward them to my phone. I'll deal with him after I deal with Hodges. In the meantime, stay close to the phone."

"Okay," Sasha replied. "Also, that woman from the other

day keeps calling—Noreen. She says that she's gotten a bunch of letters from the bank about the house and doesn't know what to do with them."

"Like I've got time for that," Elliot snorted. "Call her back and tell her to cool her jets. I'll get back to her in a couple of days."

Yeah, right.

"Alright, I'm here."

Elliot disconnected the call and swerved into the parking lot facing AA Top Title like he was taking an exit on the turnpike. The oversized brakes on the Range Rover managed to drag the beast to a halt in surprisingly short order, but not before he nearly sideswiped an old Bronco parked near the firm's front door.

Out of breath and sweating as if he'd just completed a marathon, Elliot pawed futilely at the car's driver's side door handle with his boxing glove. Reaching over awkwardly with his right hand, he managed to get it open and more or less fall out of the big SUV. That doctor hadn't been kidding when he said that losing a finger was traumatic. Becker felt horrible—the pain from his hand was now radiating up his arm and into his shoulder. The adrenaline rush that he had been riding since breaking out of the hospital had dissipated, and now he was nauseous and vaguely disoriented, as if he had just stepped off a carnival ride. His eyes darted all over the shopping complex, looking for threats, as he lurched towards AA's door.

Which was locked.

With his good hand, he yanked at the door violently, to no avail. Nearly weeping in frustration, he punched at the buzzer, again and again.

Nothing.

Becker cupped his one good hand around his eyes, binocular style, and peered through the window to the right of the door. Some surfer-looking type was sitting quietly in the lobby, staring back at him. Elliot rapped on the window sharply and yelled, "Open the door!" with as much authority as he could muster.

The surfer didn't move—he just continued to look at Becker for a moment, and then dropped his eyes to the mobile phone he was holding. Elliot rapped on the window again, but the surfer simply ignored him.

Un-fucking-believable. The sheer rudeness of people.

Becker started looking for a brick or a big stone—something that he could throw through the window—when the buzzer finally sounded. He grabbed the handle and yanked. The door opened easily—so easily, in fact, that the momentum sent him reeling backwards, off the sidewalk and off his feet. The back of his head took the brunt of the fall, and his world went black.

CHAPTER 25

There wasn't much to learn about AA Top Title on the Internet. The company's website looked to be about ten years old, with big buttons and flashing banners—the kind of thing that would have Emma shaking her head. I clicked on the "About Us" section and found a profile for Ted Hodges, Esq.

The headshot that accompanied his bio showed a handsome and well-groomed executive in his middle forties. The picture didn't match the description Emma had given me for Hodges, but that didn't mean anything. If everybody on Match.com looked like their profile picture, there would be no need for Match.com. His academic background was—to my standards, anyway – unimpressive. State land grant university undergrad and a law degree from a school I'd never heard of. Beyond that, I learned that Hodges' "expertise" was in real estate and commercial law, and that he was licensed to practice in both Florida and Tennessee. Maybe that explained the Elvis infatuation.

I was in the process of putting Hodges's name into the search field on LinkedIn when someone started yanking on the front door of the office, which apparently had relocked itself. Although my view was partially obscured by the big "AA Top Title" graphics, I could tell that he was not a happy camper. The buzzer sounded repeatedly.

I watched as the guy moved to the window and peered inside. Our eyes met.

"Open the door!" he yelled as he pounded on the window.

I looked at him for a few seconds.

Not counting my out-processing, the last order I had taken had come from a Lieutenant Commander on a chase boat in Puget Sound—and it was my intention to keep it that way. My focus at the moment was on getting answers to the questions I had about Emma's loan, and I sensed that this guy would get in the way of that.

I went back to LinkedIn.

A minute later, I heard the solenoid on the door trip and the door swung open.

Violently.

The next few seconds looked like something from an old Pink Panther movie. Through the open door, I saw the guy stumbling backwards across the sidewalk and then going ass-over-tea-kettle into the parking lot. Unlike Inspector Clouseau, however, he didn't pop back up. He simply lay there, apparently out cold.

What an idiot.

I sighed, got up and went out to check on him.

He was splayed out, his heels up on the sidewalk, the rest of him in the fire lane. It looked like the edge of the door caught him on the forehead, to judge by the angry red welt that was beginning to bloom. There were brown stains on his shirt and tie—clearly dried blood, which I assumed came from an injury to his left hand, which was over-wrapped in gauze. The field medic in me noted the professionalism of the job.

I squatted down and put my hand in front of his open mouth to check for respiration. He was breathing—shallowly

—but he was breathing. I checked his carotid artery for a pulse, which was a little rapid, but strong. As I was leaning over him, his eyes slowly opened.

"What happened?" he croaked, his eyes blinking rapidly.

"It looks like you pulled too hard on the door and got yourself tripped up." I replied. "You fell off the back of the sidewalk, and I'm guessing you cracked your head. You were out for a few seconds, maybe a minute. How do you feel?"

The guy blinked his eyes a few more times as his senses returned. He was clammy and in a cold sweat, which was to be expected. I continued to lean over him, knowing that he'd get his sea legs back in a few minutes. Over the course of fifteen years of pre-deployment training and patrols, I'd seen this kind of stuff on an almost daily basis—whether it happened to one of my teammates, or to me. It was a bump on the head, nothing more.

"Can you get up?" I asked. "You're going to feel better if you get up. Not to mention, you're going to get run over if you *don't* get up. You're laid out in traffic."

The guy groaned and rolled over onto his side, pulling his knees up into a fetal position.

"C'mon man, you need to get up on the sidewalk, at least." I stood and looked down at him. "Do you need some help, or do you want to do it on your own?" That probably sounded insensitive, but that's the way it was done in the Teams, and so that was the way it was done with me. You didn't help unless you were asked to help.

I had learned this the hard way, more than a decade earlier, in one of my very first work ups. We were doing small unit tactical training deep in the woods somewhere and I was the new guy. We were on a single-file foot patrol in the middle of the night and wearing night vision goggles, which swing down from the front of your helmet and project perpendicularly from your face—sort of like having a pair of binoculars grafted to your nose. Anyway, we were moving pretty quickly, when the guy in front of me tripped over a root and went straight down. His hands were occupied with an M4A1, so he had had nothing to break his fall–which meant that the NVGs hit first. As they collapsed, the goggles broke his nose, tore the skin off his check, and finally, took out two of his bottom teeth. Reflexively, I reached down to help him up as I whispered, "You okay, Chief?"

He was fine. So fine in fact, that he popped up and beat me within an inch of my life—very quietly and in total darkness. He was bleeding so profusely from a deep gash on the bridge of his nose that—at least through my NVGs—it looked like he was crying black tears. Spitting out blood and teeth, he pummeled me up and down the trail while everyone else watched. Even though—technically—I outranked him. When it was over, I was laid out on my back, exhausted and bleeding from more places than he was.

"If I need your help, sir, I'll ask for your help." That was all he said.

I picked myself up, wiped the blood off my face, adjusted my kit, and said "Copy that, Chief." And we moved out.

How you dealt with pain and injury said a lot about you as an operator and as a teammate—and nobody wanted to be That Guy who slowed a patrol down when he twisted an ankle or got his bell rung.

This guy laying in the parking lot was clearly That Guy.

I sighed and held out my hand. "Let's go," I said. "Grab my wrist and pull yourself up." He grabbed hold with his good hand and slowly pulled himself to his feet. He swayed a little, but stayed upright.

I looked over my shoulder. The door to the office had swung closed and I assumed it had locked again.

"I'm going to buzz us back in. You good?"

The guy was still trying to clear the cobwebs, but he nodded. I hit the buzzer couple of times and pulled him into the range of the security camera and motioned to whoever was watching to unlock the door. Again.

The solenoid clicked and I pulled the guy with me into the reception area.

As we entered, the door at the back of the lobby opened.

Two men stood in the doorframe. One of them was Hodges.

He was (pardon the pun, Emma) exactly as advertised. And judging from his expression, he was not in an upbeat frame of mind. His eyes were red-rimmed, as if he had been crying. He looked deflated and scared, and it was obvious that he wanted the man on his right to leave. The other man was very large, very well-dressed, and clearly not someone to be trifled with. I knew violent people when I saw them. He was holding a big folder of documents and had the kind of hooded eyes I associated with certain tribal elders I had run across in my previous life.

The big man nodded to Hodges, looked carefully at the two of us, nodded again and left the building. We stood there awkwardly for a second, until Hodges turned his attention toward us. I literally watched his day go from bad to worse. He obviously knew the man next to me, and he didn't seem happy to find him standing in his lobby.

Hodges looked at him and asked, "What are you doing here, Elliot?" The man began to say something, but I cut him off.

"You're Ted Hodges. I'm Logan Treverrow. My wife, Emma Treverrow, used your firm to buy a house a couple of years ago. A problem has come up with paperwork associated with that purchase, along with a couple of other issues I want to discuss. I don't have an appointment, but it's the end of the day, and I was here before—" I nodded at the other guy. "—Elliot. Besides, Elliot here could probably use a minute or two to get his head together, considering that he was laid out cold in your parking lot a few minutes ago."

By now Hodges was completely confused. He looked to my new friend Elliot for some help.

"I'm fine, Ted," he said. Which was definitely not the case.

"I've actually been here for a while, but this guy wouldn't let me in the door. I had to break the lock to get in."

I laughed.

"Just gimme a second," Elliot said. "And maybe a glass of water. We need to talk, Ted. Now. "

"Great," I said. "Let's get Elliot some water, let him chill out for a few, and you and I can go over the stuff that brought me here. I'll be out of your way before you know it, and you two can have the rest of the afternoon to catch up."

Before he could protest, I steered Hodges back through the door and into a hallway with a conference room running along its length. Before we had taken another step, something occurred to me. I stepped back toward the lobby and looked at Elliot, who had taken a seat and was leaning back as far as he could, his head against the wall. His eyes were closed.

"Elliot. Excuse me, but what's your last name?" I asked.

"Who wants to know?" he replied, his voice thin and his pallor alarming,

"Is it Becker? Elliot Becker?" I watched the corners of his closed eyes closely for a reaction.

There it was—a quick and unconscious flinch. It was gone in a flash, but it was there.

Gotcha.

"Like I said, who wants to know? Who are you, anyway? What's *your* name?"

"Logan Treverrow," I replied. "But you should already know that—you were standing right there when I introduced myself to Mr. Hodges."

"Yeah, whatever," Becker replied tiredly. "You're a rude guy, Logan Treverrow. I gotta tell you that. Didn't even open the door for me. And now you're cutting in line."

Cutting in line?

I had no interest in arguing with him. "Okay, well, it'll only be a few minutes and I'll be out of your way."

I rejoined Hodges, who was standing beside the conference room door. He gestured toward the room and asked if I'd like to wait while he fetched the water.

"Nah, that's okay, I'll just tag along and wait for you in your office."

The fact that two of the people who had signed my wife's faulty home closing documents were actually right here in front of me got me thinking—and an idea had popped in my head. I wasn't sure if it was a good idea, or even a completely legal idea, but in order for it to work, I needed to meet with Hodges in the same place that he would be meeting with Becker. And that, I figured, was much more likely to be his office than the conference room.

Hodges shrugged and swiped his key card across the reader next to the door at the end of the hall. I looked up and noticed another security camera over the door. He opened the door and gestured for me to enter ahead of him.

"It's the office there on the left," he said, pointing. "Would you like some water as well?"

"Sure," I said.

Why not?

"I'll be right back."

Hodges turned right into a little kitchenette area, and I headed down the hall and into his office, which was incredibly cluttered. Books, files, surveys, plans, folders, magazines, coffee cups, pencils, and various and assorted debris covered every surface, including the chairs.

I smiled.

Perfect.

CHAPTER 26

Hodges rooted through the mini-fridge for a couple of bottles of water. In his wildest dreams, he could not have imagined a day where so much had unraveled, so quickly. *Who was this Treverrow guy?* Had something gone wrong on his wife's closing (it wouldn't be the first time) or had Treverrow actually tracked that bogus loan back to him?

And what the hell was Becker doing here? And what had happened to his hand? He looked horrible—a kind of horrible that went beyond the hand. He looked like he was on the edge of some sort of meltdown. Hodges hustled the water out to lobby, handed it to Becker and asked, "What in God's name is happening here, Elliot?"

Becker took the water and gulped deeply. He held the bottle against his forehead and said with closed eyes, "You need to get that surfer guy out of here in the next five minutes, Ted. And while you're in there, you need to have someone wire four-hundred and fifty grand to my corporate checking account. Check your email. Sasha sent you all the info. You've got about fifteen minutes to make that happen, or we're both fucked."

Becker opened his eyes and help up his bandaged hand.

"I'm not kidding, Ted. That crazy fucking Russian took off one of my fingers at lunch today—with a pair of garden shears. That's what I got for fifty grand. I'm pretty sure that he won't be that nice next time. To either of us."

Hodges leaned in, his face close to Becker's. "Where do you expect me to come up with that kind of money, Elliot? Four-hundred and fifty thousand dollars? In fifteen minutes? You've lost your—"

Becker had closed his eyes again. He appeared to be nodding off. A tiny bit of drool fell from the corner of his mouth.

"Wait here," Hodges said to the sleeping con man. "Let me get this guy out of my office and I'll be back in five minutes. We'll figure something out."

A minute later, Hodges strode into his wife's cubicle. "Do me a favor, and pull that guy's file and bring it into the office. It's his wife—I think her name is Emma something— "

"— Emma Treverrow," she said, and handed him a folder. "It's all in there. I pulled it when he showed up."

Hodges opened the file and looked it over. At first glance, everything seemed to be in order. All the boxes were filled out, anyway. A little correction tape here and there, a strike-through or two, but nothing to get too worked up over.

"You know, Ted—and I understand I'm just a paralegal, and you're the big smart lawyer—but, one of these days, this kind of shoddy work is going to get you disbarred. I mean it."

"You're right Marcy. You're just a paralegal. So keep your opinions to yourself."

As quickly as he said it, Hodges regretted it. Although they both pretended otherwise, Marcy had her suspicions about what was actually going on at Double A. And if she ever really wanted to know, it wouldn't take much digging. Neither of them really wanted it to come to that, he assumed. Or at least hoped.

The good news was that, as his wife, she couldn't be legally compelled to testify against him—something he was counting on if things ever went completely south. Which was where things appeared to be going at the moment.

"Sorry—sorry. Sorry, Marcy."

He wilted under the fire in her eyes and had an uncomfortable mental image of a future ex-Mrs. Hodges on the witness stand.

"I didn't mean to snap at you. There's just a lot going on, that's all, and I'm a little frazzled." He hoped that would be the end of it.

It wasn't.

"I saw Elliot Becker on the video feed," Marcy said. "Is he still out in the lobby?"

Hodges nodded.

"What's he want?"

Hodges ignored the question. Instead, he asked, "Can you pull up the escrow account balances and print out a quick copy for me? I need to get this Treverrow fellow in and out of here, so just bring it in my office when you have it."

"Ted, you need to be very careful around that Becker guy. I don't trust—"

"—I know. I know. Thank you, honey. Even so, can you check on him ? He wasn't looking so hot a few minutes ago."

Hodges left Marcy's cube and walked the fifteen feet to his office. Treverrow was sitting in one of the visitor's chairs facing the desk, a pile of folders and paperwork on the floor beside him.

"I just moved that stuff off the chair, Mr. Hodges. It's all right there in that pile. Hope you don't mind."

Rained nodded absently as he took a seat in his office chair.

"Alright, Mr. Treverrow, you said that you had some ques-

tions regarding a home purchase that my office allegedly executed for you."

CHAPTER 27

I like simple plans. Simple plans are easier to execute, have very few moving parts, and tend not to go haywire. Simple is good—and this plan was simple. Even better, the only gear required was already sitting on the home page of my cell phone.

It was an app called *iRecordit*. I had downloaded it months earlier, figuring it might be a good way to send reminders to myself and keep a running log of items that I needed to order for the bar. It was a free, simple and created surprisingly high-quality recordings. I had used it religiously for a week and then forgotten all about it—until I was standing outside the conference room in Hodges' offices.

With Hodges in the break room fetching Becker's water, I punched RECORD on the app and slid my cellphone into the middle of a pile of folders sitting on his desk. The dust on top told me the folders hadn't been touched in months—which meant that they probably weren't going anywhere in the next hour, either. I positioned the phone face down in the stack so that the microphone, which ran along the bottom edge, would pick up Hodges—who would probably be sitting at his desk—and Becker, who would be sitting across the desk in the only chair not covered with various and assorted detritus. The chair I had just cleared.

A few minutes later, Hodges hustled into the office, clearly intent on getting me out there as quickly as possible. I was fine with that. In fact, I cooperated with him; nodding along as he told me he'd look into the "alleged issue."

"Alleged." I loved that.

I took his card, shook his hand, and told him I'd look forward to his call.

Hodges escorted me out, picking Becker up in the lobby and taking him back into the offices. I considered doubling back and peeking through the glass to see where they were headed, but thought the better of it. *Have faith. Let it play out.*

Five minutes later, I was sitting in the Bronco across the street from AA Top Title, with the engine running, the headlights out, and a Wilco cassette in the tape deck.

Twenty minutes after that, the lights along the right side of the AA building began to go dark. Closing time. Flipping on the headlights, I swung the Bronco in a broad arc through the parking lot. After heading down the street a couple hundred yards, I u-turned and brought the truck barreling up the road that fronted AA Top Title.

My timing was good.

Screeching to a halt in front of the AA door, I climbed out of the Bronco just as Hodges and Becker exited the offices.

"I'm glad I caught you!" I called out as I walked toward them. "I'm pretty sure that I left my phone in your office. Can you let me back in to go grab it? I didn't notice until I was half-way down ninety-five."

After a choked sigh and a little eye rolling, Hodges said, "Follow me, Mr. Treverrow," and the two of us re-entered the building. I pushed past him as we entered his office, so that my back would effectively block his view. A few seconds later, the phone was safely in my pocket.

"Found it, thanks."

Hodges eyed me a little suspiciously as we headed out to the lobby, but there was nothing he could really do, other than to tell me again that he'd be calling me.

"Great. Well, thanks again. And I hope you're feeling better, Mr. Becker." I gave the pair a little wave as I sped away.

It was dark when I pulled into the shell parking lot behind Casa Playa's. I was exhausted in that way that's peculiar to a full day of tedium. Too much driving. Too much sitting. Too many meetings. And probably one too many mid-day cocktails. I was tempted to bolt across the street and hit the beach for a quick run to clear my mind, but remembered that it was Friday, which was Casa Playa's busiest night.

And Emma was on the way over.

I reached over onto the passenger-side seat, retrieved my iPhone and pulled up the *iRecordit* app. I scrolled to the last file, and—for the third time in an hour – hit the big green PLAY button. I was rewarded with the mellow sounds of Ted Hodges and Elliot Becker having a collective meltdown.

CHAPTER 28

For the second time in less than 24 hours, Elliot Becker was standing in his robe in the kitchen, wrestling with a 1,000-count bottle of generic ibuprofen. Given that he had two good hands when the day had started, this time round proved to be a bit more challenging.

"Sasha!"

Fucking childproof caps. Short of sawing the bottle in half with a bread knife, there was no way he was going to get into this thing without her help. Sasha bounded into kitchen. He handed her the bottle.

"Here. Open this."

Sasha twisted the cap and asked, "How many do you want?"

Elliot grabbed the bottle and tried to read the miniscule type on the label, looking for the maximum recommended dose. He planned to double it. The problem was that his eyes had been twitching so rapidly since he'd escaped the ER, he couldn't focus on anything. He handed the bottle back to Sasha.

"What's it say there about the max dose? How many?

Sasha squinted at the label, her lips moving as she read.

Jesus.

"It says here you can take 3,200 milligrams a day."

Elliot did the math.

"That's what? 16 tablets? Alright, fuck it, give me thirty."

Sasha looked at him.

"Are you sure, Elliot? That seems like an awful lot."

"Yeah?" Elliot retorted. "You got anything better? A Percocet, maybe? Vicodin? Anything?"

Sasha frowned. "All I got are birth control pills."

Elliot snorted. "The way my fucking hand feels, I might take a couple of those as well. I'm serious, Sasha. I can feel this thing all the way up my arm. I feel like I'm gonna pass out from the pain, and the one thing I can't afford right now is to pass out. I got too much to think through, too much to do."

He held out his good hand. "So, give me thirty of those little fuckers."

Sasha reached into the bottle and began depositing the tablets into Becker's outstretched hand on at a time, counting as she went.

"There's one...two...three—Elliot! Wait!"

Becker had grabbed the bottle from Sasha and guzzled a bunch of tablets like he was slamming a beer.

"Are you crazy?" Sasha asked.

He sloshed the tablets around in his mouth. It felt like there were about 30 in there, give or take.

"Wa-her," he said to her, through the mouthful of pills.

She looked at him. "Huh?"

"Wa-her!" He pointed at the sink. "Wa-her!"

Sasha rushed to the sink, filled a dirty coffee cup full of water from the tap and handed it to him. By now, the red dye from the pills had melted in his mouth and had begun running down his chin. Combined with his boxing glove-like bandage and the robe, the overall effect was that of a badly beaten and balding welterweight prizefighter.

Becker washed the wad of painkillers down, set the cup on the counter and used his good hand to rub his eyes. The news from AA Top Title wasn't good, but it could have been worse. It could have been devastating. And while he wasn't generally a glass-is-half-full kind of a person, in this instance he was happy find that he still had a play or two left with AA. But that was about it.

On the glass-is-half-empty side, he was horrified to learn that he had inadvertently picked a Mafia Don's kid to fleece as a part of this thing. It was bad enough trying to stay ahead of the fucking Russians; now he had to worry about the Italians as well. And it wasn't as if being in South Florida was going to do him any good in that regard: half the organized crime guys in New York probably had homes down here and if not, their mothers had condos.

One thing was for certain: Becker needed to cut all ties with Hodges as soon as he could. He figured that once this Mazzio guy wormed his way into AA's books and records, his name would be all over the place. And it would only be a matter of time before Mazzio figured out that the Pizzuti kid had actually put a contract and a million dollar down payment on a house that *hadn't* actually been for sale, technically speaking. When that little fact came to light, Becker wanted to be very, very far away.

The way he figured it, if you got caught fucking over the Don's kid, you were dead. One way or another, they were going to kill you. It might not be today, it might not be tomorrow, but the outcome was inevitable. And it didn't matter if it was fifty bucks or fifty million. You fucked with the wrong people, and you paid the price. That's the way it worked. He was philosophical about this because at the end of the day, what was done was done and even if he could go back in time, he would have done the same thing, because at the time, he and Hodges had run out of options.

That said, there were still practicalities to consider.

Five minutes after Hodges recounted the details of his meeting with Mazzio, Becker had him transferring the remainder of the Pizzuti's escrow account balance into his Modern Properties account. Just short of $400,000.

"Don't worry, Ted. Half that's for you and your wife," he'd said. "And you need to be thinking about getting the fuck out of dodge with that money."

He couldn't believe that Hodges had actually bought that whole spiel from Mazzio about turning what they'd skimmed into a loan. How could he be that gullible? There was no way that Mazzio was going to keep his word. He'd keep Hodges around long enough to get some shell corporation he'd set up added to AA as an owner and partner, then use the Hodges' firm to launder Mafia money for a month or two while he ransacked whatever accounts were left, and then he'd kill Hodges for failing to come up with the first impossibly high payment on his marker. Then, Mazzio would just walk away, leaving some local police department to dick around with it for a month before figuring out that the whole thing was over their heads, and calling the feds.

Regardless of how it played out, Becker had no intention of being anywhere near AA Top Title when it did. It was time to get the hell out the state of Florida, and probably the United States altogether. And when you needed to get lost in a hurry, cash was king. The 400K was a good start; Burrell Malin's budding career as an arsonist was essential. Most importantly, he needed to find a way to get out from under Dmitrievich. Hiding from him was out of the question—he'd never pull it off. Vassili would find him eventually. What he really needed to do was get Dmitrievich to *stop looking for him*. The possibilities were limited, but there *were* options.

Option 1: Fake his own death. Maybe...Burrell was getting ready to burn down five houses and he could probably get his hands on a cadaver if he needed to. But with DNA testing as far along as it was, he couldn't be certain that a body plant would hold up.

Option 2: Witness Protection Program. Probably the most surefire way to disappear, but there were no guarantees that the Feds would greenlight it. Who would he rat out—Vassili? Besides, Elliot couldn't see himself running a carwash in Topeka for the next 30 years.

Option 3: South American plastic surgery clinic and identity reassignment. Great, if you're a German war criminal. In addition, long-term success required learning a second language, and Elliot wasn't sure he had that in him.

Option 4: Have someone kill Dmitrievich. This seemed like far and away the best solution. The problem was that Becker, despite being an utter criminal, was a purely white collar criminal. Violence made him nauseous. He had no idea how to find or hire a hit man. Still, there was something there.

He needed to think about it, and he needed to get Burrell rolling.

He picked up his phone and dialed a number.

CHAPTER 29

I figured I had a little bit of time before Emma showed up at the restaurant, and I wanted to put it to good use. I made a beeline for the back bar.

Brad Shephard, a middle-aged corporate tax attorney and a Casa Playa's regular, was leaning against the bar talking to Nick Munoz, a thirty-year old ex-Army Ranger and first mate with a passion for kite fishing, Radiohead and libertarian politics.

"You got a minute?" I asked.

"Sure, what's up?" he asked, as I motioned him down toward a couple of empty seats at the far end of the bar. He got up and followed me.

"A little informal legal advice." I said as he climbed on the stool.

Generally speaking, Casa Playa's regulars had a sense of what I had been doing before I bought the place, but as I mentioned, I'm not the war-story type, and I was more than happy to be considered the least interesting person at the bar.

I said, "I've got a—let's call it a hypothetical question— about recording something; a conversation, let's say. But the people being recorded *don't know* they're being recorded. And so, they're having this conversation and let's say that some of the stuff that comes up during the course of that conversation is, um…" I was struggling with the best way to characterize what I'd heard.

"Incriminating?" Brad asked.

"That's the word. I guess."

"Okay, so I'm guessing you want to know—hypothetically—if that recording can be used as a basis to implicate someone in the commission of a crime? Even though the recording of this conversation was made without his or her knowledge. Is that the hypothetical question?"

"Um…yeah. That's pretty much it," I replied.

"Well, it's complicated," Brad said. "Generally speaking, as a private citizen, the only people you can record or video tape without prior consent are cops and public officials. You have a constitutional right to do that—it's part of the First Amendment, weirdly enough. Freedom of the press. But recording a *private* conversation between private citizens without consent or a warrant is considered wiretapping, basically. Which is a crime."

"So, not only is that inadmissible as evidence, but it's also—
"

"A crime. And very often, a federal crime." Brad finished. "Not good."

"Okay, well, what about an instance where this hypothetical conversation is actually being recorded by a third party? As in— "

"As in you—hypothetically—recorded a conversation between two parties, neither of whom were you? And neither of whom consented to being recorded?"

I nodded.

"What, are you an idiot? That's completely fucking illegal,

160

dude."

He looked at me with wonder.

"I thought you went to Princeton."

That stung a little.

"Like I said, this is all completely hypothetical." I said.

"Yeah, well, it's a good thing I helped you with your taxes last year, so that I can claim client privilege. What the fuck, Logan?"

Brad looked like he had something else to add, but was apparently thinking the better of it.

"What? Out with it." I said.

"Alright, assuming that all of this is hypothetical, and knowing that this alleged recording is completely useless in a court of law, I would urge the person responsible for this recording to destroy it. If it's on tape, I'd tell that person to erase it and throw the tape in the ocean. If it's on a cell phone, I'd tell the person to delete it—and then delete the app as well. Do not, under any circumstances, transfer this recording to a computer. Most computers these days have some kind of back up service and this person does not want an illegally obtained recording floating around the Cloud somewhere. So, if said recording is important, my best advice would be to memorize it, maybe transcribe it—and then fucking get rid of it."

"That sounds like solid hypothetical advice, Brad. Thanks."

"Logan— "

"Yeah?"

"Everything alright?" Brad made a point of looking me in directly in the eye.

"It's like Kyle's Mustang," I said. "It's broke right now, but I'm pretty sure I can fix it."

CHAPTER 30

E mma began tugging off her work clothes the minute she hit her front door. She had gotten a call from Logan on the drive home, and he had asked her to meet him at the Casa Playa's that evening. Apparently, something had happened, or he had found something out at the lawyer's office. She didn't know what it was because he wouldn't say.

"I'll talk to you in person. At the bar. Just swing by."

Like he was a spy or something.

"Hello? I'm home! Where are you guys?" she called out from the foyer.

"In the kitchen, Miss Emma!"

"What are you guys up to?" Emma asked, as she walked into the kitchen. Elyssa, the babysitter, was standing at the stove stirring a pot of mac and cheese, while Zack and Isabella stared raptly at an old SpongeBob episode, which was way too loud.

In Boca, Elyssa would be referred to as 'the nanny', a term that set Emma's teeth on edge. This was real life, contemporary America—not *Upstairs, Downstairs*. Real life people didn't have nannies. Real life people had babysitters. And that's what Elyssa was—a normal, full-time babysitter who—admittedly—had had her own bedroom upstairs, her own Emma-supplied automobile, and her own Emma-supplied operating budget.

Still, perfectly normal.

"You guys okay for a while?" Emma asked, as she wriggled out her skirt, unbuttoned and removed her blouse, and left the clothing, along with her heels, in a pile on the kitchen floor. No one seemed to notice.

"I have to run over and see your dad for a little bit, but I won't be very long." she said, as she walked into the laundry room and fetched a Roxy Music T-shirt and a pair of shorts from a stack on the dryer.

She walked back into the kitchen. Onscreen, Plankton was threatening world domination at a volume that rivaled a Spinal Tap concert.

"Did anyone hear a word I said?"

Nothing.

ZACK! PLEASE TURN SPONGEBOB DOWN!" she yelled.

The children turned around and looked at her, as if noticing her for the first time. Zack grabbed the remote and turned down the TV.

"Hi, mom," they said in unison.

Emma shook her head. "Hi, my babies. I'm running out to see Dad. I'll be back in a bit."

"Okay." Their little heads spun back around and SpongeBob went back up to eleven.

Emma patted Elyssa on the shoulder as she passed. "See you in a bit."

Elyssa nodded as she continued to stir mac and cheese and sing along with the SpongeBob gang in heavily accented Spanish.

"Are choo ready, keeds? Aye Aye Cap-i-tan! Ohhhhh..."

Emma walked out the front door, slipped into old pair of flip-flops sitting on the front porch, jumped in her car and pointed it toward Casa Playa's.

Poor Logan. I shouldn't have done this, she thought as she navigated the bridge over the Intracoastal. When she had first met him, she had known that he was the one. She had loved him completely and without reservation. As time went on and she began to consider the idea of being married to him, she had assumed that the big challenges would come from the obvious: the danger of the job, the long separations, the constant worry and the never knowing what was going on in his life.

She was also very aware of the fact that, for Logan, the Teams came first. Duty trumped all. Because that's the way it was. More importantly, she understood that that was the *way it had to be*—it didn't work any other way. You were all in—or you were out. She accepted that. In a backhanded kind of way, it probably made her adore and admire him all the more. Part of what made Logan unique was his remarkable singularity of purpose; and in the process of becoming a Team guy that trait had crystalized. She had watched it happen; from the moment he graduated BUD/S to his first real deployment.

The funny thing was, as he became more deeply committed and focused on becoming what he was born to be—a protector —Emma, knowing that she would need to be completely self-reliant once Logan got deployed, became someone who needed less and less protecting. In a way, he freed her from being the kind of person that needed him.

The disconnect would become more apparent each time he came home between assignments; he'd rush headlong into whatever was happening in the household, barking orders and taking over. Thinking that he was helping; fulfilling his role. Early on, she had let him take charge. Over time, however— particularly after the kids came along—she came to resent it. And she'd resent herself for feeling that way, because she knew there was nothing he could do about it; his need to help and protect was as ingrained as the color of his eyes.

To try to keep conflict to a minimum, and to make sure that the precious few months Logan had at home between deployments were stress-free and focused on time with his family, Emma would push off big decisions until he was away, and then present them to him as a fait accompli in an email, or when they had their weekly satellite phone chat. Usually he was so distracted by whatever he was immersed in over there he'd simply say "That sounds like the right decision," and they'd move on. Whether it was buying a car or deciding which daycare they should put Zack in, she'd wait until Logan was gone, and then pull the trigger.

Which was part of why this identity theft had her so undone; buying the house was another one of those things that she had consciously waited to do until Logan was gone. She had found the house, applied for the mortgage, done all the paperwork and moved in while Logan was in Afghanistan. By the time he first set foot in the house, she and the kids had been living there almost three months.

Within a week, Logan had started at least three or four major home improvement projects, each of which was abandoned when he went off on some training evolution three weeks later. Emma had gone nuts. She had told him that if he had been a contractor, she would have sued him. And if he'd been a normal husband, she would have withheld sex until he finished what he started.

"But with you, Logan, it doesn't even matter if I tell you I'm not fucking you until you fix it, because you're not gonna be here to fix it—or fuck me—anyway! I fucking hate you and I fucking hate the Navy! Go play in the woods with your buddies, asshole! I'll go to Sears and get a new refrigerator!"

He had just stood there in the foyer, his bags at his feet.

"I'm sorry. I just wanted to help."

A year before the accident, she had come to two conclusions: she would never stop loving him and it was over.

She had planned to bring up the subject of separation between his overseas assignments. He would be stateside for months; initially at home on leave, then off with his team doing workups, then back at home for a bit before redeploying.

She waited until a few days before he was scheduled to be out for a two-week training evolution. It was one of those I-can't-really-tell-you-much-about-what-I'm-doing workups, but he'd said that it shouldn't be longer than a couple of weeks and that he'd be stateside the whole time.

Predictably, the conversations hadn't gone well. Logan couldn't understand what had changed; he felt unloved, unappreciated, and—worst of all—unneeded. Emma, who made a living by communicating, couldn't find the right words to convey her love, her appreciation—and her certainty that this was what needed to happen. Zack wasn't quite three at the time, and Logan was apoplectic at the idea that his little boy was going to grow up without his father; that Isabella might be walked down the aisle someday by a stranger. Emma ached for him, but she wouldn't—couldn't—give in.

The last two days were emotionally draining and physically exhausting. They never slept, instead talking into the early morning hours; Logan trying to find a way back into the marriage, while Emma was trying to find a way to close it—graciously, gently, but finally. Emma awoke that last morning to an empty bed; Logan had left for his workup before dawn, probably on about an hour's sleep. Emma spent most of the day in bed, crying and inconsolable, feeling like the worst kind of bitch, but knowing that what had to be done was done.

Five days later the phone rang, and everything changed.

Logan and his team had been doing routine training on a

special underwater device called a SEAL Delivery Vehicle, or SDV, in Puget Sound. Something had gone wrong with his breathing apparatus in 60 feet of water.

All they would tell her was that he was alive.

CHAPTER 31

Burrell Malin was crouched down in the paint and solvents aisle of a True Value hardware store, hunting for the biggest can of acetone he could get his hands on. Not that he was actually going to use it. At least, he hoped that he wasn't going to have to use it. At this point, he had no idea what he was going to do.

Burrell was unraveling; he wasn't mentally prepared to be an arsonist—much less an arsonist five times over. That was the number of homes Becker had given him as 'priorities'. Five houses with five families—each of whom Burrell had recruited to be a straw buyer in Becker's burgeoning real-estate empire.

Contrary to what Becker insisted, he was no expert when it came to arson. It wasn't like there was an "arson" section on the State of Florida Home Inspector Examination.

Since the ballpark meeting, Burrell had been in a sort of daze. After packing his car to head out of town, he'd come to the inescapable conclusion that running anywhere was useless. His Cutlass wasn't going to get him very far—that was for sure. The fucking thing broke down every hundred miles or so. He was as close to completely broke as it was possible to be—there was a little room here and there on a credit card or two, but that was about it. Becker—assuming he kept his promises—owed him something like ten grand, but Burrell didn't expect that to ever be paid. And last but not least, the rash that covered his hands and face made him nauseatingly recognizable.

He was reduced to doing whatever Becker asked him to do and hoping it worked out. The lack of control over his own destiny was maddening—glancing at his cell phone every thirty seconds or so, waiting for something—anything—from Becker. It was like being a condemned prisoner strapped to the electric chair, staring at the phone on the wall and waiting for the Governor to call.

Well, the phone had rung, and it wasn't with clemency.

Timetable has been moved up. Be ready to go by this weekend. Elliot will get back to you.

That was it. A single text, from a number he didn't recognize.

He had texted back, madly.

What does that mean?

I don't know how to do this.

What about the people inside?

What happens after?

Please call me ASAP.

Why are U not texting me or calling me?

How do I get supplies?

Do U have supplies?

All of them this weekend?

I have car trouble. I cannot get supplies.

Got car started. Credit card is maxed out. Will need cash 4 supplies.

And on and on, to no avail.

From the pocket of his Dickie's work pants, Burrell pulled a handwritten list of items he'd copied from the Internet—each item considered essential to a successful arson attack by some random online firebug he'd come across in his research. Some of the stuff probably *was* essential, but Burrell had no way of knowing which stuff was—and which stuff wasn't.

He had spent hours online researching a myriad of topics, ranging from electrical fires to accelerants. With every result that Google had returned, something else to consider would pop up, and Burrell would dutifully follow the new trail. He reasoned that in the (hopefully unlikely) event that he'd actually have to torch a home, his mastery of the details would be the thing that kept him off the radar of law enforcement.

It never occurred to Burrell that his frantic fact-finding and search activity on topics ranging from "getting away with arson" to "untraceable accelerants" was, in fact, setting off alerts all over the American law enforcement and intelligence communities—his IP address automatically being added to watch lists maintained by the FBI, NSA and the Bureau of Alcohol, Tobacco and Firearms.

Sitting on the True Value floor, Burrell studied the list as he absently scratched a hot spot on the nape of his neck. Terms like "fire triangle" and "oxygen concentration" cluttered his thoughts.

From what he'd read, there wasn't a lot of *"Was it arson or was it an accident?"* going on when a house went up in flames. They pretty much knew—or suspected—from the get-go when it was arson. As a matter of fact, most arson cases were identified by the firefighters actually responding to the scene, based on everything from the way the fire behaved, to the color of the smoke.

Great.

Burrell had gotten so discouraged that he'd abandoned his research for a couple of hours, turning his attention instead to the Internet's other primary purpose—surfing porn. For the first time in days, he was able to set his worries aside and relax, only to awaken a couple of hours later—a little chafed—and facing the same set of bad choices he'd been facing all week.

Everything on his initial list was now either in the trunk of his car, or in the True Value shopping basket sitting on the floor beside him. He pushed himself up, grabbed the basket and went to check out. As he waited, he took one final look at his list. He began to worry that he hadn't gotten enough shop rags to stage "multiple points of origin" in each house, which the Internet insisted was the key to a successful arson attack. He considered getting another dozen or so.

"Personal-sized acetylene torch and a gallon of acetone. You an arsonist?"

Burrell's stomach dropped. He looked up. It was the cashier, smiling at Burrell as he scanned the items in the basket.

"Say again?" Burrell asked, rather meekly.

"I asked if you were an arsonist. It was a joke." The cashier replied, still smiling. According to the tag on his jaunty red vest, the kid's name was Rich.

"No—no…ha ha ha," Burrell answered meekly. "Just a little work on the car and some painting projects in the garage."

Jesus. He'd already managed to get fingered and he hadn't set a single fire.

He thought briefly about going to Becker's condo and burning it down. That might solve everything. And even if it didn't, it would probably feel great. But the more he thought about it, the less viable—and more insane—it seemed. Becker lived on the fifth floor of a huge oceanfront condo building, which had security—which meant he'd never get in. On top of that, there had to be a thousand people living there, and if the fire got out of control, he'd go down as the greatest mass murderer in the long and checkered history of Palm Beach County.

He considered Becker's offices as a contingency plan and rejected the idea almost as quickly as it came into his head. Sure. A lot of records with Burrell's name on them might go up in flames, but he assumed those same records were maintained electronically somewhere else. And in the end, he didn't want to see Becker's little admin girl Sasha get hurt if something went wrong. He'd never met her personally, but he liked her voice on the phone.

Ultimately, he decided that the only thing he could do was to hope that Becker changed his mind—and if that didn't happen, do everything he could to make sure nothing could be traced back to him.

He also needed to make sure that the houses were unoccupied when he torched them. How he was going to make that happen was still a little fuzzy.

It took him three different charge cards to find enough credit to pay for his True Value purchases. There were other customers queued behind him, and the pressure of the transaction made his rash flare up. Burrell noticed that Rich was holding his breath.

Burrell scooped up his bag and left, walking through the fading evening light toward his Cutlass, which he'd parked under a street lamp. He popped the trunk and threw the bag in with the buckets, the rags, the burner phones, the batteries, the firing caps and the Dura Flame logs he'd purchased earlier. He looked at the pile of stuff in the dim light. Combined with the stuff he had at home, he had everything he needed. He just needed to figure out how it all worked together.

Then his phone rang.

CHAPTER 32

I was standing at the back bar, still thinking about what my lawyer friend Brad had said, when I saw Emma walk in through the front door. She scanned the room looking for me. I waved my hand and she headed toward me. Along the way, she was stopped several times by friends and acquaintances, a few of whom got up from their seat to hug her.

While I was a relatively recent transplant, Emma was a local through and through. She had grown up on these beaches, gone to the local high school, and had gained some measure of fame as that girl who had gone off to Princeton—where I had met her—and was now some high-powered advertising executive. The locals loved her and she loved them—which partially explained why she was willing to make the one-hour drive each way to and from Miami. This was her neighborhood; this was where she belonged.

A half dozen "Hey Emmas!" later, she was standing next to me at the small bar. Aaron slid her a Corona Light, from which she took a long pull.

"Weren't we doing this exact same thing in the Grove like, six hours ago?"

I smiled and said, "Let's go back to the office."

She picked up her beer and followed me through the restaurant and into the kitchen. Devan stopped stirring whatever it was he was stirring to come over and give her a hug.

"If dis one don't treat you like a queen, you tell ol' Devan, and I straighten him right out," he said, as he wrapped her up and lifted her off the ground. His huge white teeth shone against his ebony skin, and his dreads were piled atop his head and stuffed into a brightly colored Rasta cap. Counting the hair, he had to be 7 feet tall. "We don' see enough of you, young lady, and we gettin' tired of dis worn out ol' swabby."

Emma giggled and said, "I know, right? I'm tired of him too, and I can't seem to get rid of him either."

The both started laughing and pointing at me.

"At least Peter loves me." I said.

Peter, standing at the far end of the kitchen filleting a hog-fish, said with a perfectly straight face, "I barely tolerate you, Logan. And dat's on a good day."

Everyone had one more hearty laugh at my expense as I steered Emma into the office.

In the interest of privacy, I closed the door behind us. Given how tiny and cramped the office was, it had the effect of being locked in a walk-in closet. There was barely enough space for both of us to stand, so I sat behind the desk to create a little breathing room.

"So, what's up, Logan?" Emma asked. "Why all the cloak and dagger stuff?"

"Well..." I began. "It's a little complicated."

Emma looked up at the ceiling in exasperation and sighed. "Logan, I drove up from Miami at like, a hundred miles an hour, saw the kids for all of ninety seconds, and high-tailed it over here because you said you'd been to that title attorney's office and I wouldn't believe what you found out." She looked at me. "Not that it's 'complicated'. I've got enough complicated, baby. I need *uncomplicated*."

"I understand that, Emma. I'm just saying that there may be some ramifications to what I'm going to tell you, and you need to be aware of those ramifications."

"Like what kind of ramifications?" she asked.

"Legal ramifications, I guess. Or not, if that's what we decide."

"You're losing me, sweetheart. Why don't you just tell me what's going on, and we'll figure it out from there?

"Fine." I responded. I took a breath.

"What would you say if I told you that I went to the lawyer's office, and not only was Hodges there, but that the mortgage broker—the guy named Elliot Becker—was there as well?"

Emma said, "I'd say 'so what'? They probably work together all the time. That's the way that stuff works. They feed each other clients, and pay each other commissions. For someone whose family is in investment banking, you have absolutely no business sense, Logan. It's a wonder this place is solvent."

"Well that may very well be the case, Mrs. Trump, but what would you say if I told you that I actually heard them acknowledge that they were running a fake loan scam and using their clients' names and identities to make it work?"

"How on earth would you have heard that, Logan?"

I ignored her and continued: "And that *you* were one of the clients that they ripped off? Now what would you say?"

"I'd say the same thing, Logan. How did you hear this? You didn't beat them up, did you?"

She looked at me and her eyes widened. "Or torture them, or something? Do you know how to torture people, Logan? Is that what you were doing over in Iraq and Afghanistan? Torturing people? Is that what you did to those two guys?"

She was practically yelling; loud enough, I was sure, to be

overheard by half the restaurant—and all of the kitchen staff. I had a vision of Devan and Peter rethinking their career choice.

"No! Of course not!" I snapped. "You think I'm crazy or something? Jesus, why would you even ask that?"

"Okay...okay. I'm sorry." Emma said.

She leaned across the desk and took my hand.

"I'm stressed. I'm worried. I'm tired. And you made me drink beers in the middle of the day, so I have a headache to boot. I'm not firing on all cylinders, alright? And not for nothing, but I really *don't* know what you did over there. For all I know, you guys tortured people all the time."

I gave her a little smile.

"We're getting off the subject here, Emma, but for the record? No. We didn't torture people all the time over there. That wasn't what we were doing, okay? And I'm a private citizen now, in case you didn't notice. I'm a fine artist and the owner and operator of a nice, financially insolvent little bar and grill called Casa Playa's."

She smiled back.

"Okay, so you didn't go beat up the bullies who stole my lunch money. Still, I have to ask: How did you ever get them to admit that they were behind all of this? Seems kind of a stupid thing to do, if you ask me. Like number one on the list of stuff you never do if you're a criminal."

"Okay, so here's where it gets complicated." I said.

She looked at me expectantly.

"They didn't actually tell me any of this stuff. They were just talking about it between themselves."

Emma raised her eyebrows. "And what? You happened to overhear it?"

"Not exactly." I paused for a second, having a pretty good sense of how this was going to go down.

"I happened to record all of it on my cell phone."

She just kept looking at me.

"Which I hid in Hodges' office."

She closed her eyes and shook her head. "Are you out of your mind, Logan? Do you know how unbelievably illegal that is?"

I said, "I don't think there's such a thing as 'unbelievably illegal.' I think there's just legal and illegal. But yeah, I talked to Brad about it— "

"You told him about this? Are you— "

"— *hypothetically*. Only hypothetically. I didn't tell him anything specific. But yeah, it turns out that recording a private conversation between two parties without their knowledge is illegal. Maybe even unbelievably illegal."

We sat there in silence for a few moments.

Emma took a sip of her Corona and said, "Okay, Logan. Why don't you tell me the whole story?"

Which I did.

CHAPTER 33

A ll things considered, Silvano Mazzio felt that it had been a productive day. By Monday, he'd have Ritchie's money recovered and AA Top Title added to Pizzuti's portfolio of companies. In business terms, he'd transformed a singular challenge into multiple opportunities. He'd unlocked synergies. Just like Steve Jobs.

He couldn't believe how easily Hodges fell for that bullshit about turning the skim into a loan. Seriously? Didn't he watch the Sopranos? It never ceased to amaze Mazzio how powerful the tiniest sliver of hope could be to a desperate person. And he knew that the only thing Hodges had left was the tiniest sliver of hope that if he rolled over, opened up his books, and gave Mazzio every single cent he had access to, Silvano wouldn't kill him.

Well, there's hope, and then there's false hope.

Silvano sipped at his vodka tonic and took a leisurely and contented puff on his Olivia Serie V Melanio. *Fifteen bucks apiece. Cigar Aficionado's* 'Cigar of the Year', and worth every penny.

After finishing up with Hodges, Silvano had driven up to Ritchie's place, let him know that his little problem was solved, and that he needed to be ready to meet Silvano in the lobby at 8 am sharp Monday morning. He figured that the only way he'd ever get the kid over to the title company on time was to give him three day's advance notice and then send him regular reminders over the weekend. For that, he had deputized Myron, the security guy, whom he knew would take to his new assignment with relish.

For supper, Silvano had treated himself to a filet at the Palm Beach Grill. He'd read somewhere that the restaurant was James Patterson's favorite place on the island, and he made it made it a point drop in at least once each visit. Still no Patterson sightings, but the food and service were excellent, as usual.

After he finished his meal, Silvano had considered his options for the rest of the evening. It was still early, and he had no desire to return to his room at the Four Seasons and channel surf. He had few friends in Palm Beach County, and he wasn't really in the mood for a bunch of chitchat. He'd talked enough for one day.

He wanted to relax, unwind, smoke a cigar, and have a drink. And despite the incident with the A1 sauce earlier in the week, the Cougar Club fit the bill. Besides, the Russian had picked up the tab last time, and it was good form to repay the gesture.

Silvano signaled his girl for another vodka tonic and reviewed the talent on the stage. He was half hoping to catch a reprise of the mother/daughter act he'd seen earlier in the week, but they didn't appear to be working that evening. They probably keep it limited to the day shift, he thought. Easier to get childcare.

Although he was actually trying to clear his mind, he kept drifting back to his meeting with Hodges. There was something that thing felt a little *off*, but he couldn't put his finger on it. He reran the entire afternoon in his head; other than the overly paranoid security set up, everything else was pretty much what he'd figured it would be. Hodges had turned out to be exactly and pathetically in line with his expectations, but again, no big surprise there. Silvano had run across thousands of guys like Hodges over the years; guys looking to take short-cuts, get as much as they could with as little effort as possible.

It was the American way.

So, no—that wasn't it. Silvano kept going through the meeting in his head. Hodges owns up to skimming...Hodges starts to cry...Hodges gets the new lay of the land...meeting over. Everyone packs up their stuff and a sniveling Hodges walks Silvano out to the lobby.

The lobby.

The two guys in the lobby. A sweaty little menschy-type with a big bandage on his hand and some kind of beach bum. Two guys who definitely didn't belong together, but there they were, the beach bum sort of holding up the little guy who, the more Silvano thought about it, looked like he'd been hit by a fucking freight train.

So, that's one more question to bring to the table on Monday morning at the "orientation meeting" at AA Top Title, he thought. Silvano had actually called it that: an orientation meeting. For a second there, it had looked like Hodges was going to start bawling again. Then again, telling some guy who woke up that morning owning his own business that come next Monday, he needs to be on time for an orientation meeting at the same business—which he no longer owns, incidentally—has a way of doing that.

A subtle gesture, but an effective one to be sure.

Silvano took a sip of his fresh drink and a long puff from his cigar. The waitress was leaning over him, making change from the pile of twenties lying on the table. Despite the thick cloud of tobacco smoke, she worked quickly and deftly, confident in the fact that Silvano's eyes were not on her hands, but rather, on her tits. For all he knew, she was short-changing him. Which was fine with him, actually.

It was the American way.

Silvano put his cigar in the ashtray and picked up his Black-Berry, which had been vibrating intermittently as it lay face down on the table.

It was Richie, asking him if he could please send a limo to the condo to pick up him and his posse.

Silvano sighed and raised his hand to get the attention of his cocktail waitress.

"Whaddaya need, hon?" she asked, as she approached the table.

"I've gotta make a phone call or two, and I can't hear myself think in here. Think you could keep an eye on my drink and cigar while I step out front? I think we're all paid up, so I'm not jumping the tab on you. And I want to make sure the big guy up front—I think his name's Vadik—doesn't think I'm walking the check, either."

"Vadik? Don't worry about him. He's fine. But sure, sweetie. I'll make sure your stuff is here when you get back."

"Thanks. What's your name again, sweetheart?

"Jeannie."

"Alright, Jeannie. I'll be back in a few." Silvano said as he struggled out of the booth. As he walked toward the front door, he punched in a number into his Blackberry. He let it ring as he exited the nightclub.

"Star Studded Limousines."

CHAPTER 34

Aleyev Vadik Antonovich—so named by his father to honor the revered Soviet General Aleyev Vadik Pur-hayevion— sat lightly at his station near the far end of the bar, reading an article about Karl Lagerfeld in French Vogue. Unlike every other male in the Cougar Club, he was not there for pleasure.

This was his job.

"Vadik, there's some guy over at table twenty-seven complaining about the TV."

Vadik looked up from his article. It was Jeannie, one of the two cocktail waitresses working the floor that night.

"Problem with TV? What is problem with TV?"

"He says there's some game that he wants to see. The LA whoevers are playing the Houstons. Or something like that. I don't even know what sport. But he's a good tipper and he says that's what he wants to watch."

Vadik just looked at her. Jeannie raised her eyebrows.

"What? Why are you looking at me like that? He just wants you to change the channel on— "

She pointed across the bar to the flat screen television directly in front of them.

"That one. The one with—what is that? A cooking show? Is that the Cooking Channel?"

"Food Network," Vadik clarified. "And I'm watching it. That guy up there onscreen is trying to beat Bobby Flay. And I am guessing that he will not beat Bobby Flay. So no – there is no changing channel on that TV."

Jeannie gave him a blank look.

"I don't know what you're talking about, Vadik. I never know what you're talking about. No one does. But that guy—" she pointed in the general direction of table 27, "—wants to watch the Houstons and The LAs play— "

Vadik interrupted. "You see that guy up there?" He pointed at the television.

"To beat Bobby Flay, that guy must choose a single dish for them both to make. He makes his version. Bobby Flay makes Bobby Flay's version. Judges pick best version in blind taste test. This guy chose *Coq Au Vin*. Chicken with wine. It's French. This is good strategy to beat Bobby Flay, because Bobby Flay is not French. He is from New York, but he makes mostly southwestern cuisine. Very cagey this guy, with the *Coq Au Vin*."

"Vadik?"

"But, thing is, Bobby Flay always wins on this show. I think judges are tipped off. They'll be looking for a *Coq Au Vin* that has jalapeños or something. That, I think, is how Bobby Flay tips off judges. With jalapeños. Or chorizo. Bobby Flay will put chorizo in anything. They see that kind of stuff in dish, they know that's Bobby Flay's dish. And boom! Bobby Flay wins."

"Vadik? What do you want me to tell the guy?"

"Tell guy to fuck off. Is tittie bar. He wants sports bar, tell him to go to Hotters."

"Hooters."

183

"Whatever. Back to work. You're costing Cougar Club money with all your chitter chat."

Jeannie stalked off and Vadik returned his attention to Bobby Flay and Karl Lagerfeld. He knew that the guy at table 27 wasn't going to try and push his luck. They rarely did with him.

It was his gift.

In the five-odd years he had been "managing" the Cougar Club, Vadik rarely resorted to violence. He didn't need to; over time, the word had gotten out that it was a bad idea to fuck up in the Cougar Club.

"Vadik?"

Vadik looked up. Jeannie was back.

"You got to be kidding me. Tell guy to come here, and I'll show him what I think of his fucking sports game."

She said, "It's not him. He's fine. It's those three guys up in booth fifty-three. Fucking bikers. Look what one of them just did to my ass." Jeannie turned so Vadik could see. A bright red welt in the shape of a handprint was blooming on her hip. She turned back to face him, and Vadik could see tears welling up in her eyes.

"What makes guys think they can do shit like that? Fucking animals." She stared across the room. Vadik followed her eyes.

Growing up in the old USSR, Vadik's idea of American bikers had been Dennis Hopper and Peter Fonda in *Easy Rider*, which he'd seen on a grainy VHS tape when he was fifteen. These guys weren't those kinds of bikers; they were huge, hairy—and despite the many signs in the club imploring patrons to leave their guns at home—probably armed.

As Vadik watched, the biggest guy waved and got the attention of a dancer passing by the booth. He motioned her in close, as if to whisper in her ear. As she leaned over, he wrapped his arm around her waist and yanked her into his lap. One big paw grabbed roughly at her breast, while the other pulled her hair, forcing her head back onto his chest. The harder she struggled to free herself, the more tightly he held her. The whole while, he was looking across the room directly at Vadik.

He was smiling.

Vadik closed his magazine, took a sip of his ice water, hopped off his stool and began a leisurely walk toward the table; his hands in his pockets, his eyes never straying from the leader.

As he crossed the floor toward the booth, the three bikers stood and crossed their arms, forming a sort of fat, hairy wall. They were swaying slightly. The dancer—who'd been unceremoniously dumped on the floor in the process—scampered toward the back of the club.

Vadik took quick stock of the tactical situation. The table wasn't going anywhere. It was bolted to the floor. Good. The swaying and the glazed eyes indicated either alcohol or drugs. Also, good. And the crossed arms meant that they weren't expecting violence. Not yet, anyway. The way Vadik figured it, these guys were probably accustomed to taking over every establishment they entered. Which he could understand: get the average bodybuilder-bouncer type outnumbered, and the first thing that bouncer wants to do is de-escalate the situation. Try to talk it out; get everyone smiling and promising to be on his best behavior—all while doing his level best to get the fuck out of the line of fire.

He hoped he'd figured correctly, but in the end it didn't matter. Vadik was not the type to de-escalate.

Rather than stopping to face them across the table and chat, as they clearly expected, Vadik moved quickly to the left. As he did, he withdrew his right hand from his pocket. It held a cheap ballpoint pen—which he jammed as hard as he could into the soft spot underneath the leader's chin, just inside the Submental artery. The pen emerged through the floor of the biker's mouth and continued on through his tongue. Vadik let go of the pen, grabbed the man's hair, and drove his face onto the table. His nose split open, and he flopped back into the booth, covered in blood and clawing at his neck in a futile effort to remove the pen, which was buried in the tangle of his beard.

Before either of the remaining men could react, Vadik brought the heel of his hand up sharply, hitting the middle biker squarely on the point of his chin. Vadik could hear teeth breaking. He stepped back, walked around the front of the table toward the third biker, who had sat back down in fear. Vadik looked at him for a second and drove a roundhouse kick into the side of his head. The man fell over into the lap of the guy with the broken mouth, who proceeded to bleed all over him.

The entire confrontation had taken less than 20 seconds.

Now, Vadik was ready to chat.

He leaned over the table, directing his words toward the biggest man, who was still struggling to wrench the pen from underneath his chin.

"Not to worry. You'll live. I missed all major arteries on purpose. Actually, you're bleeding more from nose than from mouth."

He stepped back and looked at the three of them.

"So, here's deal. You are to leave Cougar Club in a few minutes when I say is ok. You are not to come back to Cougar Club. Ever. No one from your club is to come into Cougar Club. I have name of your club, because you are stupid enough to wear vests in here with name of club on them. You guys are not from here, I'm guessing. Is probably a good thing."

Vadik looked at each of them for a few seconds.

"Everyone understands this?"

The men, bleeding and petrified, nodded.

"Next, you owe Cougar Club all of your money for damages to both club and to dignity of employees. Cash. Now."

He waited for a second.

"Now!"

The bikers struggled to find wallets and wads of cash. They piled it on the table. Vadik took the cash and stuffed it in his pocket without counting it.

"Last and most important: worst thing you can be doing right now is thinking about getting friends together for paybacks. Bad idea. I see paybacks, all of you are dead. Yes? You understand?"

The men nodded. He looked at them closely, his head tilted slightly.

"I am not convinced of this."

Vadik leapt up on the table and delivered a quick series of snap kicks to the face of each man. He knew from experience that the best way to prevent future violence and retribution was to instill complete and utter fear from the outset. He needed to fuck them up so badly that they'd never think about coming back.

As he paused for a moment to survey his work, the cellphone in his pocket vibrated briefly. He pulled it out and looked at the screen.

It was Rheese.

He put the phone to his ear.

"Hi. Kind of busy. Let me call you back in a few minutes— "

"—Okay, but DEFINITELY call me back."

There was a pause.

"We got it, Vadik. *We got it.*"

Vadik hopped off the table and walked a few feet away. The bikers were sprawled out, moaning in pain. Vadik held up a finger to his lips, admonishing them to be quiet as he returned to the call.

"We got it? Not to be messing with me, Rheese. Seriously."

"I'm not messing with you Vadik. I can't believe it myself, but *we got it.* They took the offer."

Both were silent for a minute.

"We're going to own our own hotel, Vadik. You and me."

Rheese's voice cracked slightly.

Vadik took a deep breath.

America. What an amazing place.

"I'm not knowing what to say. I am having trouble um... what is word?"

"Processing it? Me too. But it's real. *It's happening*, Vadik. It's everything we've talked about, everything we've dreamed of. It's happening. Right now."

Vadik was silent for a moment.

"Vadik? Are you there?"

"I'm here. Trying to get handle on my feelings."

He glanced over at the bikers. They were struggling to untangle themselves and sit up. The one with pen in his neck had apparently given up trying to remove it.

"And I still have stuff to finish here. Let me call you back in a little bit."

Vadik paused.

"Rheese— thank you."

With that, Aleyev Vadik Antonovich—former Senior Warrant Officer, Spetsnaz GRU, recipient of the Medal of Valor for the Russian Federation, current mob enforcer and future part-owner of a high-end boutique hotel in the heart of Palm Beach —disconnected the call, slipped the phone back into his pocket and turned to the writhing mass of bikers in booth 53.

"You are now free to leave. Not to ever come back. Please drive safely."

CHAPTER 35

"Hey, Johnnie. It's Sal Mazzio."

Silvano pulled a handkerchief from his jacket pocket and mopped his brow. Ten o'clock at night and it still had to be ninty-five degrees.

Fucking Florida.

"Mr. Mazzio! I was wondering when I'd hear from you," Johnny answered.

"And here I am, calling you," Silvano responded, as he walked toward an area in front of the Cougar Club reserved for valet parking.

"Amazing how that works, isn't it? Anyway, I need you to get a town car out to Tower One. They wanna go somewhere. Where, I don't know. Probably some club down in South Beach."

Silvano paused, expecting Johnny to reply.

Nothing.

"Johnny. You still there?"

More silence.

"Um, Ritchie didn't tell you?" Johnny asked uncomfortably.

"Tell me what?   What's going on?"

He waited as Johnny carefully picked his words.

"Look, Mr. Mazzio, I didn't wanna do it, but sometimes you got no choice."

"Whaddaya mean? No choice about what?"

More silence.

Silvano was growing impatient as he imagined his expensive cigar burning down to a stub, the ice in his drink melting, and the mother/daughter team potentially taking center stage without him in the audience.

"Alright, so last week, when they rented the big stretch," Johnny finally began. "You know, the Hummer?"

Silvano grunted.

"Anyway, somebody – I'm not saying it was Ritchie, probably wasn't—"

"Somebody what?" Silvano interrupted.

"Somebody spilled one of those big tall bongs in the back. Fucking bong water everywhere, Mr. Mazzio. *Old* bong water. You ever try to get that shit out of automobile carpet? It's impossible."

Silvano sighed and said, "So, I'm assuming that means you ran the Amex card for damages. Is that it?"

"Well, yeah. I mean, that Hummer is a big revenue generator, and we can't afford to keep it out of—"

"How much?" Silvano interrupted.

There was a pause and then:

"Thirty-five hundred."

"Thirty-five hundred? For fucking carpet? Are you kidding me?" Silvano asked in disbelief.

"It's a triple stretch Hummer, Mr. Mazzio." Johnny replied, nervously. "Way more carpet than a normal car, or even a stretch. They hadda take out all the seats *and* the bar. I can show you the invoice from the rep—"

"Alright. Alright. I get it." Silvano said. "Don't worry about it."

A clearly relieved Johnny said, "Thanks for understanding, Mr. Mazzio."

Mazzio snorted. "It's not my money."

He turned away from the club entryway, facing the darkened parking lot. There were at least ten cars filing through, looking for a spot. Near the valet stand, three oversized Harley roadsters were leaning on their kickstands. The night was picking up.

"So, you got something that you can send over there? A stretch or something?"

Johnny said, "I got the Hummer. That's it."

"Jesus."

"It's the only thing I got here other than a couple of Crown Vics, Mr. Mazzio," Johnny said defensively. "I'll do it for the stretch rate. Save you like a hundred bucks."

Silvano rubbed his eyes and said, "Yeah, okay. But I want the driver to tell Ritchie I said NO FUCKING BONGS. None. They wanna get high, they can smoke a fucking blunt. Like real rappers."

"Yes sir. I'll make sure the driver passes on the message."

"Alright, Johnny. Thanks."

Silvano heard—rather than saw—the doors open, as *Hot for Teacher* began pouring out of the club's entrance. He stayed where he was, focused on getting a text off to Ritchie saying that a car was on its way. Behind him, he heard the heavy shuffle of boots on pavement, along with various and assorted muffled groans, grunts and curses. He hit SEND on the phone and turned to see three bleeding bikers making their way down the entryway, apparently headed for the Harleys parked up front.

They were a mess. There was blood everywhere; matted in their beards, their hair, down the front of their shirts and dripping onto their motorcycle boots. One of them had something sticking out of his neck; Silvano couldn't be sure, but it looked like a Bic pen.

The bikers were moving in a kind of six-legged wad toward their cycles; Silvano wasn't sure that they would be able to drive them. He watched, silently and impassively, as they struggled to untangle themselves and mount and start their Harleys. He didn't offer any assistance.

This wasn't his problem.

As the bikes roared to life, Silvano turned and headed back into the club. He wondered if the bouncer named Vadik had inflicted the damage. If so, the guy was in a league of his own. Silvano had been around; he could count on one hand the number of bouncers he'd met who were crazy enough to take on three bikers alone.

As he re-entered the club, Silvano saw a male employee busily mopping the floor beneath a booth, while another was wiping down the seat and table.

Like it never even happened.

At the back of the club on his usual perch at the bar sat Vadik, his face placid, his body relaxed. Their eyes met, and Vadik politely waved Silvano over.

What the fuck?

Silvano approached Vadik a little warily.

"Hey, how you doing?" Silvano began as he approached the

bar. "I didn't get a chance to thank you last time for comping the tab. I appreciate it."

Vadik waved his hand casually. "Was nothing."

Silvano gave Vadik a polite but slightly quizzical look. "So, how can I help you, um—it's Vadik, right?"

Vadik nodded. "Yes, Vadik. Pardon my boldness, but I had a question I wanted to ask you. Kind of question that I believe you are uniquely qualified to answer."

Silvano tilted his head. "Unique? What's unique about me?"

Vadik said, "You are not typical Cougar Club guest, if you take my meaning. Most guests in Cougar Club are more—how to say it? Low class? Yes? They are not great wearers of Ralph Lauren Purple Label suits, for example." Vadik paused as if searching his limited English for the perfect words.

"You, on other hand, appear to be someone who is accustomed to a more refined lifestyle. Yes?"

Silvano narrowed his eyes a bit as he nodded slightly. "If you say so, sure."

"And I believe you are also from out of town," Vadik continued. "Would this be correct?"

Where the fuck was the guy going with this?

Silvano said, "My full time residence is in the New York metropolitan area, but I'm down here pretty frequently. But yeah—technically speaking, I'm just another tourist."

"Thank you, yes." Vadik replied. "So, my question for you is about hotels. I am sorry, but I never got your name in last incident here in Club."

"Silvano. Call me Sal."

"Sal. Thank you. So Sal, when you are visiting us here in Palm Beaches, is there a hotel you are fond of? One you stay in regularly?"

Silvano thought about that. In his line of work, it wasn't very smart to telegraph where you're sleeping every night. It was the kind of thing that could get you killed.

On the other hand, Vadik could be some kind of snitch for the feds or local law enforcement, keeping tabs on all the wise guys that wandered into the club. Possible—but Silvano didn't think so. There was something *off* about the guy, though; Silvano couldn't put his finger on what it was, but there was *something*.

Fuck it.

"Well, for the past year or so, I've been pretty loyal to The Four Seasons over on Palm Beach."

"And you like Four Seasons for why, if I may ask?"

"The staff, the accommodations, the food, the service. I mean, everything about the place is top drawer," Silvano replied.

"Top drawer? I am not familiar with this phrase."

"It means first class. You know—the best." Silvano clarified.

"Ahhh. Thank you. Top drawer." Vadik said as he nodded. He paused. "So Sal, here is question I wanted to ask: In your travels to Florida, would you ever consider staying in a smaller, independently-owned boutique hotel in downtown Palm Beach? Assuming this smaller hotel is just as top drawer as Four Seasons, but has unique personality all its own?"

This guy just beat three bikers to within an inch of their lives. He's not amped. He's not angry. He's not sweating. He's not even breathing hard. Instead, he's doing market research on hotels.

There was definitely something off about Vadik the Bouncer.

Vadik was looking at him expectantly.

"Well, I guess it'd depend. Maybe. I'd want to check it out first, probably."

Vadik asked, "So, a high-end guest like you would maybe expect a free night's stay to try place out?"

"Not free," Silvano replied. "Maybe an intro rate or something. A bottle of champagne in the room at check-in. A fruit basket. That kind of thing."

Vadik was busily writing all of this down.

"Okay," Vadik said, as he continued to write. "This is good stuff. I appreciate your help in this, Sal."

Silvano asked, "Can I ask you what all this is about?"

"Well," Vadik replied with a smile, "It is possible—more than possible, actually—that I might be in hotel business very soon. And I want to make sure that I am crossing I's and dotting T's so that hotel is of kind of quality that attracts guests of your caliber. So, I am taking opportunity to collect some facts. And in gratitude of your cooperation, I am comping your bill again tonight."

Vadik smiled. "You must be first guy in history of Cougar Club that drinks for free two nights in row."

He held up his hand.

"All I ask is that you tip your server. That, I cannot cover."

Silvano thought about the fact that he'd paid for his drinks as they had been delivered—in cash—but let it go. *Why make it more complicated?*

Vadik continued, "Also, if you leave your server with email address, I will send you a note when we open."

This was possibly the most surreal conversation that Silvano had ever had in a strip club. Which was saying something.

"Thanks, Vadik."

Silvano started to walk to his table, hesitated a second, turned back and said, "Those three guys I saw leaving the club. The bikers. They didn't look too good."

Vadik looked up from his notebook.

"They were not supposed to look good, Sal. They were supposed to look like three guys that fucked up in wrong place at wrong time. With wrong manager."

Silvano replied, "Well, just so you know, that's the kind of thing you're probably not going to want to do with guests that piss you off in your hotel. Know what I mean?"

Vadik smiled. "That is precisely why I am so excited about hotel business, Sal. Those guys show up in my hotel lobby looking for a room? I say, 'Sorry, we are full up tonight, gentlemen.' And off they go. Only this time they go with all of their teeth still in their head, not wearing ball point pen sticking out of their neck."

It was Silvano's turn to smile.

CHAPTER 36

I can't say that I worked my way back into Emma's good graces after recounting my little adventure at AA Top Title, but I got the sense that I had piqued her interest.

"Logan, I can't believe you did something this harebrained. There's a lot about you that drives me nuts, baby, but you usually have very good judgment. What were you thinking?"

"So," I said. "Do you want to hear the recording?"

I knew her body language. She was dying to hear it. She just wasn't ready to roll over quite yet. We were sitting at a small table just off the main bar. As the evening wore on, the restaurant gradually emptied out, while the bar stayed busy. The effect was almost complete privacy; we were too far away from the bar for anyone sitting there to overhear us, but close enough that the bar chatter kept anyone sitting at a nearby table from being able to hear us, either.

I watched her squirm in her seat, wrestling with the moral and legal implications of listening to my half-assed wiretap.

"C'mon. You know you want to. Tell you what: we'll do what Brad suggested. We'll listen to it one time, take down notes, and you can watch me delete it and erase the app. No one will ever know we had it, but it'll help us figure out what we need to do next."

Emma leaned back in her chair and crossed her arms. "Okay, but before we do, let me ask you this: what are you going to do about your friend at the FBI? Are you going to tell him about this?"

I hadn't thought about that.

"I don't know, to tell you the truth.' I said. "Maybe there's a way to tell him what we heard without telling him how we came to hear it in the first place."

"Yeah, that makes sense, Logan. Because FBI agents *never* ask questions. They just take everything you tell them at face value."

There is a time and place for everything. Including irony.

I said, "Well, I guess we'll figure that out as we go along. In the meantime, do you want to hear this thing?"

Emma sighed. "Why not?"

Recalling my conversation with Brad, I said, "It might be a good idea to do this in the office. I don't think we need a bunch of witnesses."

As we entered the office, I pulled out my phone, scrolled to the *iRecordit* app and pulled up the recording.

"There's a bunch of dead air at the beginning. Give me a second."

I dragged the scrub bar about an inch to the right and hit PLAY. I had listened to the recording a couple of times already and knew what to expect.

I said to Emma, "They start talking—arguing, really—as they're walking down the hall into Hodges' office. It starts off kind of faint and indistinct, but clears up in a few seconds, after they get into his office."

"—never seen the guy in my life, Elliot. He just showed up out of the blue, told me he had some questions about a home equity loan that his wife never took out."

"That's Hodges," I said.

"No duh," Emma replied.

Like I said. A time and a place.

"—You know why, Ted?"

I said, "And that's Becker."

Emma nodded, clearly fighting the urge to roll her eyes.

"Because the banks are starting to call the marks, dumb-ass. We stopped making payments on those loans sixty days ago. And banks are like clockwork with that shit. I'm surprised it took them that long to call her."

Hodges and Becker had clearly entered the room at this point, as the audio quality improved considerably. I set the phone on the desk.

HODGES: I told him I'd look into it. Not that there's anything to look into, but we've got to get some kind of story together. I don't know when the guy's going to come stomping back in here looking for answers.

BECKER: Yeah? Well, fuck that guy. Fuck Logan whatever-his-name-is. By the time he comes back here, you and I need to be long gone, because his wife's piddling little loan is the tip of the iceberg, Ted. The tip of the fucking iceberg.

HODGES: You think I don't know that, Elliot? I'm not even sure I *own* this place any more. I think that big Italian stole it from me this afternoon. He just walked in and—

BECKER: —Yeah, yeah, we'll get to that. But you gotta find me a fucking aspirin or something, Ted. Like right now. Between my head and my hand, I can't take it anymore. And you got any booze hiding in a drawer somewhere? Vodka? Bourbon? Anything.

The sound of a drawer opening.

HODGES: Here. Don't drink it all. Save me some. I need it as badly as you.

Hodges' voice trailed off as he left the office, presumably to find a painkiller for Becker.

BECKER (YELLING): Gimme at least six of whatever you got! And bring me the paperwork the Guinea brought with him!

The unmistakable sound of booze being guzzled directly from the bottle.

BECKER (COUGHING): Fuck me. Jesus.

The sound of Hodges re-entering the office.

HODGES: Alright. This is all I could find. There's six.

BECKER (STILL COUGHING): What is it?

HODGES: Pamprin. I found them in my wife's desk.

BECKER: Pamprin? What the fuck is a Pamprin?

HODGES: It says it's for cramps. Women stuff. It's her time of the month, I think.

BECKER: What the fuck, Ted? Is this gonna hurt me?

Pause.

HODGES: Are you kidding me, Elliot? Have you looked at yourself lately? You can't get any worse, trust me. Take them. Don't take them. I don't care one way or the other.

The sound of another long pull on the bottle.

HODGES: You want a glass? No? Give me that.

Emma was looking at me. "Is this the part where we're supposed to be taking notes? Want me to write down that Becker ate six Pamprin?"

"Give it a few minutes," I said. "It gets better."

The sound of the bottle being set on a table.

BECKER: So, take me through what happened with the guy from the Pizzuti family. I'm assuming that was him in the lobby with you, right? The big guy in the dark suit?

HODGES: Yeah, that was him. So, he parks himself at the head of my conference room table with a stack of folders and a note pad from the Four Seasons. Then, he starts pulling out account statements—I didn't make copies of the stuff, but it doesn't matter, since all he had were printouts of stuff we've sent him. Anyway, he starts pulling out one statement after another and he asks me why the account statements are jpegs. Get that? Jpegs. He knows right off the bat they're fakes, but he wants me to *tell him* they're fakes.

BECKER: Hold up—how did he know the account statements were faked?

HODGES: Because when we email the statements to clients, the statement itself is an attachment. You know, the email says something like 'Your account statement is attached.' And right there on top—where you click on the little icon thing to open the attachment—it says right there that the attachment is a jpeg. Clear as day. And apparently—as I found out today—the only computer program that makes jpegs is Photoshop. Fucking Photoshop.

WECHLER: Well, that was fucking stupid, Ted.

HODGES: Yeah and hindsight's twenty-twenty, Elliot.

The sound of someone taking a pull from the bottle.

BECKER: Alright, so getting back to—

HODGES: So, long story short, he's coming back in on Monday morning with the kid. I've got to give him an accounting of how much we skimmed, and I'm on the hook to pay it back. He also told me to have my corporate documents ready to amend, because he was now my 'partner.'

BECKER: So, you're fucked.

HODGES: Yeah, I'm fucked. On the other hand, I could be dead, I guess.

BECKER: True. Doesn't mean that he still won't try to kill sometime down the road.

HODGES: Well, he told me that since I didn't actually know who I was skimming, he was cutting me a break. Giving me a chance to make good.

BECKER: And you believe him?

HODGES: I don't really have much of a choice, Elliot. I mean, consider the alternatives.

Sound of booze being poured.

BECKER: Alright. First things first: how much did we skim off that account? Three hundred? Three-fifty? Something like that?

HODGES: I wish. Closer to six. Five hundred and change just over the past four months.

BECKER: Oh yeah—I forgot. There were a couple of big payments to that asshole Dmitrievich in there.

HODGES: Yeah. At two hundred and twenty grand a shot. And then all the other stuff, too.

BECKER: So, what's left in the account?

HODGES: A little over four hundred thousand dollars.

BECKER: Well, if that's what we got, that's what we got. We're gonna have to make do. What do you have to do to liquidate it? Can you do a wire transfer to my checking account at Modern Properties tonight, so that it'll hit first thing Monday morning?

HODGES: What do you mean? I told you—he's coming back on Monday with the kid to go over all this. I show him an empty account, I'm pretty sure he'll just shoot me on the spot.

BECKER: Which is why you're not gonna be here, Ted.

HODGES: —but—

BECKER: —but nothing. I got news for you, Ted: he's gonna kill you anyway. Once he's gotten his hands on every cent you've got stashed away here, he's got no use for you. What did you think? He's gonna approve you for a mortgage? Give you thirty years to pay him back at five percent? You didn't learn anything from this deal with Dmitrievich?

I paused the playback and looked at Emma.

I said, "I don't know what all that's about, but it sounds like everything's falling apart with these guys and they're looking to disappear as soon as possible. Like, over the weekend."

Emma said, "So, maybe the best thing we can do it just let them disappear. Go to the bank, tell them we've been the victims of fraud or identity theft or something, and let them take over.

"That's great, Emma but it still doesn't absolve us from the fact that we're on the hook for two hundred thousand dollars. I told you what that FBI agent Slavnick said: we have no backstop."

I paused and said, "I don't know about you, but that pisses me off. As far as I'm concerned, they picked the wrong people to rip off and I intend to make sure that they find that out *and* pay us back."

I hit PLAY and said, "Not to mention this:"

HODGES: I don't know, Elliot. He and the kid show up Monday and I'm not here— what do you think he's going to do?

BECKER: He's gonna start looking for you, that's what he's gonna do. Which means your ass better be tucked away somewhere he can't find you. Starting tonight. You and the wife.

Shouldn't be hard. Just find a cheap-ass motel and park yourself for a couple of days. It's South Florida—there's a thousand little joints between here and Miami. Check in one, sit on the bed, bang the wife, watch free HBO. This guy's not the FBI—he can't put an APB out on you; he can't trace your credit cards. He's just a wise guy in a nice suit.

HODGES: And then what? What happens Monday when I'm a no-show at my orientation meeting—that's what he called it, by the way, an 'orientation' meeting—what happens then?

BECKER: You're on the move with a pile of cash. You and the wife. And if you're smart, you're headed the hell out of Florida.

HODGES: And what about you, Elliot? What are you doing come Monday?

BECKER: Pretty much the same thing. Although I've got a couple of other things I've got to put in motion. Stuff I hope will cover both our trails for a while. Give us a chance to get a head start.

HODGES: Like what?

BECKER: Like you don't wanna know.

HODGES: Don't pull that shit on me, Elliot. I'm already in enough trouble as it is, going along with your brilliant ideas. If you've got something else going on that implicates me, you can bet your ass I want to know about it. What are you planning?

Becker sighing.

BECKER: Alright. But remember—you asked.

I hit PAUSE and looked at Emma. She had stopped taking notes.

"This is the part that I was talking about," I said as I hit PLAY.

BECKER: On Monday or Tuesday—depending on a couple of things—I'm gonna have Burrell start torching the flip houses.

All of them, over the course of the week, one at a time. He's been in every hardware and hobby and Army Navy store in Palm Beach County pulling supplies together, and based on the last text I got from Sasha, he's got everything he needs to get the job done. Gasoline, torches, kerosene, rags. The works.

I looked at Emma and raised my eyebrows.

HODGES: Elliot, have you lost your fucking mind? What do you think you're going to solve? Why would you want to burn down a bunch of houses?

BECKER: Because they're all going into default, Ted. Because we got straw buyers for all of them. Because we overpaid for all of them—and pocketed the difference. Because we skimmed money—from your escrow accounts—to buy them in the first place. And it's gonna take the Feds all of about two weeks to put it together, unless we come up with a way to keep them distracted from looking at the obvious.

HODGES: And that way is…is *arson*?

BECKER: Yep.

HODGES: You're fucking nuts, man. You're certifiable. And I want nothing to do with this.

BECKER: Too late. You asked. I told you not to, but you did. Now you know. And that makes you an accessory. Fact is, you were *already* an accessory; pleading ignorance isn't gonna change that any more than telling—what was his name? Mazzio? Telling Mazzio that you didn't know you were skimming off a kid whose dad is a fucking Mafia boss. You're in, Ted. Up to your fucking ears. The question is, you got any better ideas on how to get out?

Long silence.

BECKER: Didn't think so.

HODGES: I can't believe this is—

BECKER: —Believe it, Ted.

More silence.

I hit PAUSE again.

I said, "So, the rest is about transferring the money into Becker's company checking account. They leave the office in a few minutes and it gets kind of hard to make out, but that's the gist of it."

Emma asked, "And that's when you showed back up, grabbed your phone and came back here?"

"Pretty much, yeah."

"So what is it you want to do with this, Logan? It's not like we're cops. Or the FBI. Like Elliot said, all they have to do is check into some cheap motel somewhere and as far as we're concerned, they might as well have dropped off the face of the earth."

"True," I said, then quickly amended: "Well, partially true, anyway. There are a couple things we learned that could help us."

"Like what?"

I held up my hand and counted off the particulars.

"One: we know the big Italian's name—Mazzio—and we know where we can find him: The Four Seasons. Two: even if Hodges disappears, we know where Becker's going to be on Monday—at Modern Properties, Inc., waiting for his wire transfer. And I'm pretty sure that we can get the address for Modern Properties from the loan documents I've got in here."

I opened a file drawer in my desk and pulled out the paperwork for the loan on 255 Bluewater Lane. I flipped a couple of pages.

"We also know the arsonist's name is Burrell," I said as I scanned the document. "Which, if memory serves, is also the name of the property appraiser on your original loan document."

I found the line I was looking for.

"Yep," I said, tapping the page. "Burrell Malin. That's got to be the same guy. And not only do I have Becker's address, I've got his business card. With fax and phone number."

I looked at Emma and smiled.

"What do you think?"

"What do you mean what do I think? I think we'd be sticking our nose into something we have no business sticking our nose into. And I think you're crazy to think you can do anything to change the outcome on this. I think you should call your FBI buddy on Monday and see what he's come up with, and hope he's come up with something—anything—because this is *way* out of your realm. That's what I think."

"Out of my realm?" I asked incredulously. "Are you serious? I spent almost a decade chasing down guys that were *way* worse than this—murderers, basically—based on intelligence documents in Persian, Dari and Pashto. We wouldn't approach a hut over there without at least four weapons up *and* an interpreter. In Iraq, we walked double columns, with one guy walking backwards, looking up at rooftops for snipers. We'd have to clear every stair well and every basement window because otherwise, they'd shoot out our legs. This is easy compared to that. It's The Four Seasons and a mortgage company. They speak English, and I can *drive* there. Alone."

"That's not my point, Logan. And you know it."

"Then what's your point?" I asked.

"Well, I know you, and I think the only reason you want to get involved in this is you're bored. That and you want to protect me. But mostly because you're bored."

I thought about that for a minute.

"It's not boredom, Emma. It's principle. I'm not bored. I'm pissed. And pissed for me doesn't mean call the cops and hope for the best. It means call the cops and we'll see who gets there first."

"But—" she began to protest.

"But nothing. They picked the wrong people. And it's gonna cost them."

She sighed.

"So, what do you want from me?"

CHAPTER 37

Special Agent Harley Slavnick picked up the pace on the treadmill, determined to finish his Saturday morning workout with a new personal record. During his time at Harvard, he had run the Boston Marathon twice. His finish times weren't anything to write home about, but he *had* finished. Because that's what Harley Slavnick did: he finished things.

The treadmill was located in the corner of the small workout room on the ground floor of his apartment complex. Harley wasn't the gym type, and normally, he'd run a route that took him from his building on Biscayne Boulevard to the American Airlines Arena. If his timing was right, he'd catch a glimpse of a random Heat player driving his Bentley in for Saturday morning practice. But since it was coming down in torrents on the streets of Miami—and Harley wasn't one to skip proscribed exercise routines—today, the treadmill would have to do.

As he ran, Harley thought about his conversation with Logan Treverrow. The request for the meeting had come directly from Ben Gray , with whom Harley had worked on a money laundering case the previous year. The fact that Treverrow knew Gray was all Harley had needed—he idolized Gray and would do anything for him. Nonetheless, the case itself was fairly small potatoes. A single case of mortgage fraud

—a crime that Harley knew little about.

Not that mortgage fraud was unimportant—in fact, the opposite was true. Mortgage fraud had become so widespread that the Bureau had actually chartered an official network of task forces and a working groups to take on the problem. Something like 300 Special Agents were working full time on this. Which made him wonder why Gray had called him.

Although he knew it was unfair to paint it this way, the simple fact was that $200,000 was more or a less a rounding error in Logan Treverrow's checking account. It wasn't like he was going to miss it; he was one of three direct heirs to one of America's great family fortunes. Not Microsoft or Facebook money, but if Logan Treverrow had felt like buying the Heat instead of his little bar, he probably could have gotten close.

He had called Gray after the meeting to give him an update, and he was surprised to learn that Gray had no idea that Treverrow came from that kind of money.

"He's worth *what*?" Gray had asked, incredulously. "I've known Logan for at least ten years, and he's never once mentioned that to me. Ever. I figured he was like everybody else I served with. I figured two hundred grand was probably every cent he had."

Harley thought about that, and felt all the worse for writing Treverrow off as some poor little rich guy. But that didn't take away from the fact that this was an awfully small case for the FBI.

And for him.

Harley Slavnick was fully aware of his limitations as a Special Agent for the Federal Bureau of Investigation: He did not cut the classic figure (at least from the current era.) He was not the least bit physically intimidating. His political and social skills were almost non-existent. And he had scored the absolute minimum required to pass the FBI Qualification Course of

Fire.

Nevertheless, Harley Slavnick was one of the busiest Special Agents in the entire Bureau. His assignment to the North Miami field office notwithstanding, Harley's work took him all over the world. His superiors spent more time managing his priorities than they did trying to manage him. In a way, he was viewed as a sort of super high-powered rifle that was only taken out of the case for really important, high impact shots.

He understood this because Harley Slavnick was also fully aware of what made him special—so special, in fact, that he had more or less lapped the other 48 agent-trainees that had gone through Quantico with him: He was preternaturally bright. He had the ability to assimilate vast amounts of data and sort it in a way that made rapid-fire analysis instinctive and unerring. His undergraduate degree had been in applied mathematics, and his focus in business school had been in hard-core quantitative finance—as opposed to the relatively lightweight tracks like management or operations or (worse yet) entrepreneurship. But most importantly, Harley Slavnick never stopped asking questions until there were no more questions to be asked.

He was a finisher.

It was that trait that led Harley Slavnick to stop dwelling on the fact that Logan Treverrow's case was too small for him, and to instead ask himself a question: what if Logan Treverrow's case *wasn't* that small? What if Logan Treverrow's case was just the tip of the iceberg? He thought about that a bit as he ran, and the more he thought about it, the less likely it seemed that someone would pull this stunt for a single case of mortgage fraud. Too much to set up, and too many risk factors for a fairly paltry payoff. What *did* make sense, actually, was the idea that this was some kind of programmatic fraud: bad guys identifying an opportunity, coming up with a process and procedure, and setting up an infrastructure to exploit it—over and over. As he had learned in business school, the best business plan was a scalable business plan.

Harley spent the rest of his run putting together a list of questions to follow up on Monday. There were a lot of questions, because Harley Slavnick questioned everything—starting with the assumption that key elements of the victim's identity were stolen. Instead, he asked himself: What if the victims had *supplied* that information willingly? Once he asked that question, lots of things started to fall into place.

Quickly.

CHAPTER 38

I woke up in the most unlikely of places.

Emma's bed.

I pulled my arm out from under the covers and checked my watch: 6:45 am. Through the bedroom window, I could hear the rain coming down in droves. I was tempted to roll back over, pull Emma in close to me, and sleep until one of the kids came rambling in. But I knew that my touch would wake her, and once awake, the recriminations would start, and I'd be up and out before the sun rose.

I didn't want that; I wanted to stay in her bed for as long as she'd have me.

We had followed Brad's advice, more or less to the letter. We had listened once more to the recording, with Emma taking notes in her precise, uncluttered handwriting. After we reviewed them and agreed that nothing important was missing, I deleted both the recording and the app. I felt a slight pang as I thumbed the "x" on the icon; I had grown fond of *iRecordit*, and I knew I'd miss it. *So long, little buddy.*

With the weekend upon us, our options for next steps were limited. Modern Properties, Inc. would, in all likelihood, be closed, but I figured there was nothing to lose by doing quick drive-by either Saturday or Sunday. The odds of finding Mazzio in The Four Seasons were probably pretty good; the question was what I would say if and when I found him:

"Hi Mr. Mazzio, I sort of met you in the lobby of Double A Top Title yesterday. I was holding up a little squirrely guy with blood all over him and a bandage on his hand. Remember? Anyway, it looks like people we both care about got ripped off by the same set of guys: you found one of them and I found the other one. Anyway, judging from the illegally obtained recording I listened to last night with my wife, it looks like you've got your end pretty well wrapped up. Good job. But, seeing as how I've still got a couple of issues to get resolved—not the least of which is to recover the two hundred thousand dollars they stole from my wife, and considering these guys are planning to burn down a half-dozen houses next week— I'm wondering if you could hold off on actually killing Ted Hodges until I get my end all squared away? Oh, and by the way, I wouldn't count on Ted being there for your Monday morning meeting."

This was a bad idea on a hundred different levels. On this, Emma and I were in complete agreement.

"Not to mention, if Hodges is right, Mazzio is some kind of organized crime guy, Logan. *A criminal.* You really want to go play Crime Busters with a *criminal*? Doesn't that offend your sense of rationality?"

Maybe. Maybe not.

We had made our way out to our little table by the back bar. The restaurant was empty save for a few diehards in the front room. Aaron had put a shaker of martinis and two glasses with olives on the table; a mixtape of old Columbia and Blue Note-era jazz standards played as he idly surfed conspiracy sites on his iPad.

"We could leave an anonymous message on a police tip line. Just tell them there are going to be some arson attacks next week, and the names of the people connected to them," Emma said, as I poured drinks.

"We could do that," I allowed. "But we have no idea where

the homes are, or when they're supposed to go up. We can give the police Becker's name, but even if they showed up at his office, I'm betting there's nothing there that would incriminate him for arson. So, we'd be back to where we started."

"You think your FBI guy has made any progress?"

"Doubtful," I replied. "I only spoke to him this morning."

We sat and sipped our martinis for a moment. Miles Davis was working his way through *Round About Midnight*. I thought back to what Harley Slavnick had said earlier about the explosion in identity theft crimes. There's a certain irony in the notion of a crime being deeply personal and completely depersonalized at the same time. Criminals knowing the most intimate details of your life without ever having met you; utterly secure in their anonymity, cloaked by a thousand redirected computer servers and black market websites.

*Well, guess what, Ted and Elliot...*I thought. *I've got you. I know who you are. And that's bad news for you.*

I could feel the part of me that I had struggled to repress for two years beginning to manifest. It felt good.

"What are you thinking about, baby? You're a million miles away."

"Huh? Oh, nothing." I said. "What to tell Agent Slavnick. Next logical steps. That kind of thing."

This is the part of me that Emma *does not* know—and will never know. The part of me that has seen and done things that normal people with normal lives will never see, and never do. And that's fine. More than fine, in fact. It's *necessary*. It's something that's drilled into every soldier that leaves the service: if it was CLASSIFIED over there, it's CLASSIFIED here. Be a good citizen, shut the fuck up, and blend in.

The "shut the fuck up" part is easy.

Blending in? Not so much.

Despite the 'transitional' counseling programs the military tries to put you through before you come home, it's impossible to just to turn off switches that have been hardwired over time and circumstance simply because you're back in civilian life— where life is predictable and violence is almost *never* necessary.

You end up having to find your own way to deal with it.

For some of the guys I served with, that meant staying away from people altogether; becoming hermits, essentially. They would tell me that it was the only way they knew to protect the people they cared about from the rage that would boil up within them. For others—including me—it was more about trying to repress the person they had become; searching for the long-lost version of themselves; the one who has never heard a shot fired in anger.

Isolation. Or repression. Not exactly what the average shrink would consider "healthy choices."

I had never even thought about my transition out of the military, because my career in the military came to a surprising and abrupt halt: I was on a training dive off the coast of Washington. A filter on the closed-circuit rebreather I was using got some water in the wrong place and I got a lungful of caustic liquid. It burned my trachea and lungs before I blacked out, ran a mini-sub into the ocean floor, drowned, and died. My teammates dragged me out of the water so quickly that all of us suffered the bends—even though I was technically dead. I was actually revived in a recompression chamber.

The first couple of weeks after the accident are still a little hazy. A month later, I sat before a review board, where I was cleared of any wrongdoing. An examination of the rebreather unit revealed that a micro-tear in the lining of a hose had expanded under pressure and fissured.

Shit happens.

I assumed that, after some rehab and a hundred different

physicals, I'd be cleared for active duty and returned to my platoon. I assumed wrong. There were concerns from the medical people that I might have some sort of long-term respiratory problem "as a result of acute corrosive tissue injury", which apparently, is not something you want cropping up at 13,000 feet on the side of some mountain in eastern Afghanistan.

If I had been an aviator, they would have grounded me. But since I was an operator, they simply fucked me.

I was attached to the staff of a Rear Admiral in the Pentagon, tasked with putting together PowerPoint presentations for the office of the Secretary of the Navy. It was mind-numbingly dull work, and I used every spare minute filing appeals and filling out paperwork for reinstatement to an active SEAL Team. Every request I sent was denied or ignored. I lasted three months in DC before I resigned my commission.

I was the only time in my life that I had quit anything.

"So, have you come to any conclusions?" Emma asked, snapping me out of my reverie.

"What do you mean?" I asked.

"About the next logical step in all this?" Emma asked.

I thought about that for a minute.

"What about this appraiser guy?" I asked. "I can't remember, but maybe there's something in that closing document that would help us track him down: the company he works for; a work address. We've got his full name; there can't be a lot of Burrell Malins in Palm Beach County. Maybe we can we Google his home address."

Emma took a sip of her martini as she nodded. "And from what Becker said, it's a good bet you'd find him at home this weekend. So maybe Burrell Malin's your next logical step."

Surprised by her response, I asked, "Just so I understand, Emma, you're not trying to convince me to find his address, call the cops and walk away? You understand that's not happening, right?"

Emma looked at me, smiled gently and said, "I know Logan. Even though I really do think that's what you *should* do, I know it's not what you're *going* to do."

She looked down into her drink and swirled the olive.

"I know you better than you give me credit for, sweetheart. I know how you're built. It's a big part of what made me fall in love with you in the first place."

"Really? I thought it's what made you fall out of love with me."

She smiled, a little sadly. "Logan, I still love you. I'm still *in* love with you. And I will always be in love you."

We sat silently for a few minutes, lost in our own thoughts.

"A couple of weekends ago, I had Zack and Izzie out on the beach, and these three boys—who were probably twelve or thirteen—were standing in the wave wash, throwing globs of wet sand at each other, just messing around." Emma said quietly, lost in the memory. "So, Zack and Izzie were down there playing on their skim boards, and the two of them kind of ended up in the line of fire of this sand fight, and Isabella got pelted."

She looked at me and laughed.

"So, Izzie starts acting all wounded, like you'd expect from a six-year-old little girl. Zack sees that and just *charges* these kids —who were all a head taller than him—yelling 'leave my sister alone!', his little arms flailing away."

I smiled.

"So, I had to wade in and pull him back out of the water. He was red-faced and tearing up, and those teen boys were just staring at him, kind of in shock. And I thought: that's the

Logan coming out in him—protecting what's his, completely fearless, oblivious of the odds, and damn the consequences."

"And?" I asked.

She laughed. "And I *loved* it. I loved knowing my little tiny boy has got his sister's back. Every time. No questions. No hesitation."

She looked at me. "Just like I know you have mine."

I poured what was left in the shaker into our glasses. "And those teen boys?"

Emma smiled and said, "They couldn't apologize enough. It was hilarious. I think they were so freaked out by this little tiny kid stomping out there they didn't know what to do."

"Little bastards." I said, and we both laughed.

By now, Casa Playa's was empty.

Aaron called out from the front door: "You two need anything else? If not, I'm going to get out of here, go home and watch Tucker Carlson."

"It's one in the morning, Aaron." I said.

"I Tivo'd it. Season pass."

"Of course you did. Good night, Aaron. I'll lock up. Thanks for the martinis."

"Good night, Aaron." Emma called.

I watched her as she smiled and gave a little wave to Aaron. She looked incredibly— impossibly—beautiful in the low, warm glow of streetlamps shining through the front window. Even dressed in a t-shirt and flip flops, there was an undeniable elegance to her; an old fashioned movie star-like quality that had befuddled and dazzled me since we'd been nineteen years old. I had known from the moment I met her that I would love her for the rest of my life—and although everything had changed, that had not.

I felt an overwhelming urge to lean over across the table and kiss her—not as her ex, not as the father of her children, and not as her best friend. Instead, I pushed my seat back and stood.

"Well, I guess we need to lock up and get you home, sweetie." I said.

Emma stood and looked at me.

"Take me home, Logan." There were tears in her eyes.

I hesitated a second and asked, "Are you sure?"

"Take me home."

Emma lives a block west of the Intracoastal Waterway, just over the bridge from Casa Playa's—about a mile as the crow flies. It's at best a five-minute drive. But neither of us could wait that long.

"Pull over into the beach parking lot, baby. *Please*." Emma had said, an edge in her voice.

We made love in the car—passionately, desperately; trying to make up for years of lost time—a tangle of clothes on the floorboards. We came violently and simultaneously, sweat pouring off our bodies.

We dressed, found a blanket in the trunk, and went down the long flight of steps to the beach, where we made love again, this time more slowly, nestled behind a stand of sea oats. After-wards, we lay on our backs, holding hands, listening to the waves, and watching the moon trace its way across the eastern sky.

"Let's go home," she said, after a while. And so we did, slipping silently upstairs and into her bed, my arms pulling her close, my face buried in the tangle of her hair.

CHAPTER 39

Ted Hodges held his breath, clinched his teeth, and turned the key.

This was the crucial moment; if he was going to get caught, it was going to be right now, as the engine in his Camry sputtered to life. He coaxed the car gently into gear, his eyes fixed on the master bedroom window that looked directly onto the driveway. His wife was a notoriously light sleeper—which had been the reason that he had been banished to the guest room years before.

Well, one of the reasons, anyway.

He was hoping that the rain would create enough white noise to cover the car engine, and that by time Marcy woke up, he'd be well out of Palm Beach county, tucked safely away in an anonymous roach motel with a bottle of Johnny Walker Red and some pay-per-view porn on the room TV.

It wasn't easy, leaving Marcy in the lurch like this, but Hodges had come to the conclusion that it was for the best. Taking her along would inevitably make her an accomplice in the eyes of the law, and if everything went south, he didn't feel it was fair for her to have to face prosecution for something that she had nothing really to do with. More importantly, were she to ever be charged, she'd roll over on him in a heartbeat. No, better to leave it in such a way that Marcy could plead ignorance and cling to spousal privilege.

Although Hodges had never actually been on the lam, instinct told him that his chances were better if he were alone; he could move quicker, his cash would last longer, and he wouldn't be subjected to the constant criticism and second-guessing that Marcy was expert in dealing out. They had no kids to worry about—just a yammering little Pekinese that was Marcy's dog, anyway.

 In a way, he kind of looked forward to the whole thing; it might actually be peaceful.

He had packed light, figuring he had enough cash to pick up the odds and ends he might need as time went on. He'd also left his toupee in the dresser, in the hope that he'd be virtually unrecognizable without it. It was the first time he'd left the house without a hairpiece in probably thirty years, and he felt both naked *and* liberated. His first order of business after checking into a motel would be to take a long, hot shower and scrub away the last vestiges of adhesive still clinging to his scalp.

After his conversation with Becker the previous evening— and after the first waves of panic had subsided, something in Hodges clicked: he had gone from denial to anger to acceptance —and straight into survival mode. It had surprised him how natural it felt, but he assumed it was simply a manifestation of how human beings were programmed.

Fight or flight. Or in this case, both.

Even as he was transferring what was left of the Pizzuti kid's escrow deposit to Becker's corporate account, Hodges knew he'd never see a penny of it. Regardless of his promises, Hodges knew that Becker was going to screw him—one way or another. Not that this was some sort of epiphany; over the course of their two-year "partnership," Becker had made a habit out of screwing him.

With the specter of the Cougar Club blow job—and nasty

and expensive divorce that would result if Marcy found out about it—Hodges had always been hesitant to confront Becker directly and demand what was rightfully his. Instead, he'd found another way to get it: through Devin and Dustin, the self-anointed "Photoshop Masters."

AA Top Title's customers weren't the only people getting doctored account statements. So was Becker. By routinely understating the actual value of the accounts they were raiding— and skimming off the difference—Hodges had managed to sock away an additional $300,000 without Becker—or Marcy— ever catching on.

The money had been sitting quietly in a no-frills money market account, slowing accruing, and earning a paltry half percent interest. Hodges didn't give a shit about the interest rate. It was liquid, and that's all that mattered.

So, who's screwing who now, Elliot?

Hodges turned the Camry south, figuring it would be just as easy to disappear in Fort Lauderdale or Miami as it would be to disappear in Atlanta, with the added benefit of being a whole lot warmer come November. And if didn't work out on the mainland, he'd keep heading south, toward Key West.

The rain was coming down in sheets, forcing Hodges to slow the car to a crawl. He had been putting off replacing his windshield wiper blades for months, and it was coming back to haunt him now. He turned up the radio to cover the squeak of metal on glass, and squinted through the thin strip at the bottom of the wiper's arc where some rubber was still making contact. He couldn't see a fucking thing.

As he negotiated his way around a Cadillac that had stalled out in the middle lane, Hodges thought about his odds. Once Mazzio showed up on Monday and discovered that Richie's account had been emptied, the implosion would come fast and furious, leaving poor Marcy holding the bag. With nothing of value to shake out of the firm, Hodges figured Mazzio would immediately turn his attention toward finding him. Within a day or two, law enforcement would descend on the place, and in very short order, they'd start looking for him, too.

The more he thought about it, the better the Keys looked. Put some miles between the himself and Ground Zero, as it were. People disappeared in the Keys all the time, because it was easy to disappear in the Keys. A totally transient population, a cash-based economy, and no one gave a shit who you were, where you came from, or what you did to end up there.

He grabbed his iPhone off the passenger seat and pulled up the Google Maps application. Marcy had given him the device for his birthday the previous month, and he was still trying to figure out how the thing worked. He thumbed awkwardly at the screen, trying to figure out how to calculate travel time. After a few missed attempts, he somehow landed on the right screen: Weather and traffic permitting, he could be in downtown Key West by early afternoon, give or take an hour or two.

Perfect.

Hodges imagined himself a year from now: a roguishly handsome, tanned and mysterious stranger holding court in a tropical waterhole, charming locals and tourists alike with his wit and erudition.

Screw the hairpiece.

Jimmy Buffet was bald, and look how it had worked out for him.

CHAPTER 40

Elliot Becker lay naked on the Italian marble floor in the living room of his condo, alternately sweating and shivering. The good news was that his hand no longer hurt.

The bad news was that he wished it did.

Anything was preferable to the way he felt. Hindsight being 20/20, Becker still wondered what prompted him to take thirty ibuprofen tablets without even a cursory Google search of the possible adverse effects. First up would probably have been "ringing in the ears," followed closely by blurred vision, unbearable gastric distress, and an inability to regulate body temperature. And that was just for starters.

The night had been an adventure ride of misery; starting in the bedroom and migrating to the living room just before dawn, when Becker had deliriously concluded that cool tile was just the thing to get his core body temperature down. He had fallen out of bed and crawled into the living room, a blanket clamped in his teeth as he pushed a single pillow before him. He curled up in a fetal position on the cold tile, his battered hand splayed out, his body wracked with cramps, his eyes jittering wildly. A sort of foam had started to form at the corners of his lips; he let it slide out onto the floor.

"Sasha!"

Becker waited a few moan-filled minutes before calling out again.

"Sasha! Wake the fuck up!"

Fat chance of that happening. Sasha was the most circadian person Becker had ever known. She could sleep through anything, provided it was dark. She never snored, she never tossed and turned, and she never mumbled. She simply closed her eyes and went catatonic. The only thing that ever woke her was light, and the blackout curtains on the floor-to-ceiling windows in the bedroom guaranteed that wasn't going to happen any time soon.

Becker felt something warm and liquid between his cheek and the pillow. He touched his cheek with his good hand, and held it up to his twitching eyes.

Great. Add nosebleed to the list.

Like a wounded infantryman, Becker shimmied his body toward a wall panel of light switches mounted between the living room and a hallway that led to the bedroom. He didn't know what he needed—other than a towel for the nosebleed—but he knew he needed something, and he knew he wasn't going to be able to get it was on his own. He needed Sasha.

He flopped over on his back and pushed the top of his head against the wall, directly below the wall panel. Looking up, he tried to swing the pillow toward the light switches, hoping to hit one in such a way that it would flip on. Since he was limited to one working hand, the attempts were awkward and ineffectual. He couldn't get the pillow moving with enough speed to reach the wall, much less the light switch. The only thing he did manage to hit was his own face, which opened up the other nostril. Rather than facing the ignominy of drowning from a double nosebleed, Becker rolled over to his side, and considered a Plan B.

From his vantage point on the floor, he saw what he needed,

dead ahead.

A floor lamp.

Turning back on his stomach, he resumed his infantryman crawl toward the lamp, his nosebleed leaving a scarlet trail on the Italian marble. Reaching the lamp, he grabbed the base and pulled the lamp over and down to the floor. He shimmied the four feet to the switch, turned the lamp on, and then began to drag it toward the hallway outside his bedroom. His hope was that the lamp would pour enough light into the bedroom to rouse Sasha.

"Sasha!"

He jiggled the lamp outside the doorway, which created a disco-like effect on the bedroom ceiling. The effort left him exhausted.

"Sasha! Get up! I need help!" His head dropped back to the floor.

He heard a stirring in the direction of the bed, but he was too tired to lift his head and look.

"Elliot?" Sasha asked, sleepily. "What's the matter?"

A few seconds passed and Becker heard the rustling of bed sheets as Sasha pulled herself awake.

"Where's the bedspread? And why's the lamp from the living room on the floor?"

Elliot moaned and asked, "Can you please get your ass out here? I'm in the hall."

Although he had braced himself for the scream that was inevitably coming, it still unnerved him.

"For the love of God, Sasha, pipe down, will you? It's a nosebleed, that's all. Looks worse that it is." Becker had reassumed his fetal position, his good hand pawing for the blanket.

"My God, Elliot! What happened? What's wrong with you?" she asked as she stood over him.

Becker looked up blearily.

"Is this from all that Advil?" she asked.

"I hope so," Becker said. "If it's something else, then I'm really fucked."

"What can I do?" Sasha asked.

"I don't really know, to tell you the truth. Everything on me is fucked up. I need a wet towel for sure. And if you can help me get to the bathroom, I can get in a hot shower. Maybe that'll help. And some ice water or something. I gotta get something to drink."

"Okay," she said, holding her arms out. "Stay right here."

Seriously? Where else was he going to go?

A minute or so later, Sasha was sitting on the floor cross-legged beside him, gently moving his head from the pillow and cradling it between her knees. She laid a cool wet towel gently over Becker's forehead, and put an ice-cold bottle of Evian water to his lips.

He drank greedily, coughed, and drank again. A few deep breaths later, and his equilibrium began to return. While he didn't dare stand, at least he didn't feel like he was going to die any second, which was a step in the right direction.

He looked up at Sasha, who was staring intently into his face.

"Alright, gimme a second or two, and we'll see about getting to the shower."

He shuddered a little and said, "You may wanna look on that ibuprofen bottle and see if there's an eight hundred number or something. They may be able to tell you what to do in case of an overdose, like drink milk or something."

"*Drink milk*? Sasha asked incredulously. "Are you crazy, Elliot? They're gonna tell me to get you to an emergency room."

Becker shook him head. "That ain't happening. I've been to enough emergency rooms for one week. No way. Besides, I skipped out on the one yesterday after they fixed my hand. For all I know, they've got some kinda hospital APB out on me."

Sasha moved the towel from his forehead to his nose in an effort to staunch the nosebleed.

"You're a mess, baby," she said. "Do you think you can move yet? A shower might do you good. You got nose blood all over you."

Elliot slowly rolled off Sasha and assumed a crawling position.

"Go ahead and get it started and I'll see if I can make it there."

Sasha nodded, stood up and trotted off toward the master bathroom, as Becker began his crawl.

Ten minutes later, Becker lay at the epicenter of three intersecting, high pressure/high volume hot water streams—a rainfall sheet coming down from the ceiling, and one each from the opposing walls of the custom-built steam shower he had installed—at great expense—in the master bathroom the year before. At the time, the only practical application he could see for such an extravagance was as a sort of oversized sex toy. After a couple of test runs with Sasha, the novelty had worn off; the granite floor was uncomfortable, and his water bill was through the roof. He had written the entire thing off as a waste of money—an expense he hoped he could someday recoup on resale.

The events of tonight, however, had given him a new appreciation for his steam shower. With every torrent of steaming hot rainwater falling on him, he felt a tiny bit renewed. The powerful jets from the side walls scrubbed the dried blood from his body as if he were being pressure cleaned. The steam cleared his clogged nostrils. And the granite felt warm, soft and inviting after three hours on Italian marble.

He gradually found the energy to pull himself into a sitting position, his knees up, his head bowed, the water cascading over his back. He sat that way for at least an hour, and as he felt the drugs leach from his body, his mental acuity slowly returned. His ears were still ringing, but the sound of the water drowned out the worst of it. For the first time in twelve hours, he was actually able to think.

The glass door to the shower opened. It was Sasha, holding a glass of ice water and a washcloth.

"I thought you might be thirsty." She looked at him and tilted her head slightly.

"You're sitting up. Does that mean you're feeling better?"

"A little," Becker answered. "What did the ibuprofen people say?"

"They asked me for a lot number." Sasha answered.

Figures, Elliot thought.

Everybody is just trying to cover their ass.

CHAPTER 41

Emma woke to the sound of rain, but kept her eyes closed. A muscular arm was wrapped protectively around her, pulling her in close to a body so familiar that it felt like it had never left her bed. She wondered if she'd ever let him leave again.

She didn't want to move. Didn't want to stir him. She wanted to lay in bed forever, on the limen of sleep, listening to the rain fall, and Logan breathe. For perhaps the first time in years, she felt what it was to be completely in the moment. Nowhere else. With no one else but him. It didn't frighten her —or reassure her. It simply was.

In the two years following their separation, Emma had made it a point to never stand still long enough to wonder whether she was doing the right thing. She knew that to sec-ond-guess her decision was to invite doubt, and she refused to put Zack and Isabella—not to mention Logan— on the seesaw of uncertainty that doubt would create.

"I know Daddy spent the night sweetheart. I can't tell you if that means Mommy and Daddy are going to live together again. We'll see, sweetheart."

Followed by:

"I know Daddy was here last night, and he's not here now. That's because Mommy and Daddy are still trying to figure things

out, sweetie. I know you like it when Daddy's here. I do, too."

Followed by:

"I don't know what's going on sweetheart. We're just trying to figure it out."

She had vowed to never let that happen, yet here she was. She wondered why she wasn't anxious; why she hadn't rolled over, jabbed at Logan until he opened his eyes and told him that he needed to get out of there before the kids woke up.

Logan stirred and rolled over onto his back. Emma stayed still, hoping that he would continue to sleep. She didn't want him to leave.

She hadn't known that this would happen when she set out for Casa Playa's the previous evening. It was just another place she had to be in a day full of obligations, appointments, decisions and destinations. The kind of day she created every day: too much to do, too little time to get it done and (blessedly) too little time to think about anything other than what came next.

And then, the evening had slowed down.

Aaron had left a shaker of martinis on the table, the crowd had filed out, the lights were turned low, and there was a jazz record playing.

Who plays jazz records?

By the second martini, something had begun to stir in her; not simply a longing for what she had lost—she would have understood that. It was more. It was her first and smallest inkling that maybe she had made a mistake; that "compatibility" might be an overly-simplistic idea when applied to people in love. That "connection" mattered more.

She knew one thing with absolute certainty: she was still powerfully connected to Logan.

Emma pushed her bottom into the warmth of Logan's hip,

listening to the rain, thinking back to one of the very first dates she'd had with him.

Not even a date, really.

It was early in their freshman year at Princeton; they had met at an orientation mixer a few months earlier. Logan's father had come into town to visit and had invited him to bring along a friend to dinner. Logan had asked Emma.

It was the first time that she would be meeting Logan's father, and she was understandably nervous—a South Florida surfer girl being wined and dined by a financial titan whose face was familiar to anyone who watched CNBC or Bloomberg. She wanted desperately to make a good impression.

They'd had dinner at a venerable old steakhouse just up the road from the university. Emma had never been to the place— she couldn't afford it—but she had heard that it was renowned for serving its main course still sizzling in a pool of butter, un-adorned and alone on its own super-heated plate.

"Is it really true?" she asked when the waiter came to take their order.

"Is what true, ma'am?"

"That the plates are five-hundred-degrees?"

The waiter smiled and said, "Give or take a degree or two. As a matter of fact, we finish each steak on the plate itself. A minute or so on one side, give it a quick flip and run it out to you. That's why we ask all of our guests to *never touch the plates.* They're that hot."

"Five hundred degrees is hotter than the hottest setting on most ovens," she said.

"As I said ma'am, they're very hot."

He arched his eyebrows in mock seriousness.

"You don't want to touch them."

234

"Okay," she said. "Thanks for the warning."

Through all of this, Emma noticed Logan's father watching her with a kind of detached bemusement.

The steaks were delivered to the table with the predicted admonishments against touching the plate.

Which was, of course, the first thing Emma did.

"Ouch."

She looked over at Logan. He had his forefinger stuck in his water glass.

"He wasn't kidding."

Logan's father laughed and they both looked at him. He turned his attention to Emma and leaned across the table, pouring a little more wine into her glass.

"I'll bet that this place has been around for at least fifty years, Emma, and it's a bit of a Treverrow family tradition. I remember coming here with my father when I went to Princeton, and over the years, we'd come back for alumni events, or to visit Logan's big sister when she was here for school. So, I'd guess that Logan here has probably been to this steakhouse fifty times."

Mr. Treverrow looked at Logan for confirmation. Logan nodded.

"Probably close," he said.

"And every time they bring him his steak," the elder Treverrow resumed, "they tell him to not touch the plate. And every time, he touches the plate. And every time, he acts surprised."

He smiled as he set the wine bottle down.

"He's the only person I've ever known who absolutely has to touch the plate."

He took a sip of wine.

"Until you."

He sat back in his chair and smiled at both of them.

"I don't know if that's a sign of compatibility or what, but it's something."

At that moment, she wasn't sure whom she had a bigger crush on—Logan, or his dad.

Emma heard the sounds of little feet pattering down the stairs. She knew the next thing she'd hear would be the sound of a horribly loud cartoon as the kids turned on the set in the kitchen and went about the task of making their toast and cereal. Emma had taught the two how to make their own breakfast a couple of months earlier, and it was now part of their Saturday morning ritual. She'd even had a logo made at the agency (Make Breakfast! Not a Mess!) to hang on the fridge.

She loved the fact that they would whisper to one another ("Because we don't want to wake you up, Mommy.") while the television blared away at a level that could be heard three houses down.

She rolled over and looked at Logan. His eyes were open.

She nestled deeper into him and said, "Good morning, Batman."

"Batman?" he asked, a little groggily.

"You know, avenging the innocent. Mild-mannered citizen by day, crime fighter by night." She kissed him gently on the check.

"Batman."

"I think I'd rather be Aquaman." Logan said. "Cooler costume, and I can talk to fish."

Emma yawned.

"Aquaman it is."

Ironically, the sound of Super Friends drifted up from the kitchen.

"I guess I'd better sneak on out of here," Logan said, as he rolled out of bed and began to dress.

Emma nodded, grateful for not having to ask.

"I'll talk to you later today?" she asked.

"Sure. I'll let you know what I find out. I've got some stuff I need to do in the studio, and after that I'll probably jump in the car and see what I can dig up on Burrell Malin. I'll keep you posted."

"Logan—"

Logan put his finger on her lips.

"I know. We'll tackle all that later, sweetheart."

She smiled and nodded, tears beginning to well in her eyes. To lighten the mood, she asked, "So, how are you going to get out of here without Supergirl and Superboy seeing you, Aquaman?"

"I'm headed out that window," Logan said, pointing. "Across the roof, grab the gutter, easy twelve-foot drop, and a refreshing two-mile jog home."

"Aquaman uses windows?"

"Only when it's raining."

He leaned over and kissed her.

"The plate's hot, Logan." Emma said as she snuggled deeper into the covers.

"Please be careful."

Logan smiled.

"Not a chance."

CHAPTER 42

Silvano eyed his reflection closely in the bathroom mirror as he shaved and considered his Saturday options. He had planned on working on his tan down by the pool, but the rain was going to make that a non-starter. The good news was that Richie—just like his mom and all of his useless siblings—never woke before noon, so he had a solid five or six hours to himself.

A long breakfast and a two-hour spa package would fit the bill perfectly.

Silvano felt good. He'd made an early evening of it, getting out of the Cougar Club and back to the Four Seasons before 10 pm. A quick cordial at the hotel bar, and he was back in his room in time to catch a little bit of *Nightline* before falling asleep with the television still running. He awoke refreshed and ready to make the most of his downtime.

A one-hour Swedish massage, followed by a steam and whirlpool in the hotel's spa would help work out the kinks that had developed over the past few days of doing nothing more physical than pulling papers out of a file folder.

While no one would ever mistake Silvano for a cross-fitter, he was still a large and imposing presence. And at 55, keeping a muscular body from going to fat required more than simply watching his diet. Back home, he was a regular at his gym, mixing cardio work with weights and the occasional turn on the heavy bag. Having served as muscle for much of his career, he understood how perishable those skills were, and so—allowing for age and reality—he worked hard to keep his fighting trim.

Silvano rinsed off what was left of the shaving lather, toweled his face, and called downstairs to reserve a table for one for breakfast, and an hour with Francesca, a maniacally strong Belgian massage therapist. His last session with her had been so painful that he had actually been reduced to tears on the table.

Hanging up the phone, he donned what he considered appropriate casual wear for a Saturday morning breakfast in the Palm Beach Four Seasons' dining lobby: a pair of loose-fitting, slate-gray silk pants from Tommy Bahama, an off-white, long-sleeved linen shirt that he had picked up from Guy La Ferrera in Boca Raton, and a pair of dark-blue, suede Gucci loafers, worn sockless. He completed the ensemble with a stainless-steel and gold Rolex Yacht-Master.

By the time he reached the lobby, his table was ready—complete with his customary orange juice, ice-water and pot of fresh-brewed coffee. On the corner of the table lay fresh copies of the Wall Street Journal and the Palm Beach Post.

As he sat down, Silvano thought back to his conversation with Vadik the Bouncer. He imagined himself sitting down for an identical breakfast in a hotel run by Vadik. He imagined a guest a couple of tables over sending his eggs back because they were a bit underdone. He then imagined Vadik beating the hapless diner within an inch of his life for "fucking up in wrong hotel and with wrong manager."

Before leaving the Cougar Club, Silvano had actually gone to the trouble to leave an email address with the waitress named Jeannie; he had scribbled it on a cocktail napkin, telling her, "Vadik asked me to leave this with you. If you can pass it on to him, I'd appreciate it."

He'd handed her the napkin and a 50% tip, scooped up his loose change and cigar holder and left. On the way out, he had waved at Vadik, who was engrossed in a conversation on his cell phone and didn't acknowledge him.

There was no denying that Vadik was off-the-charts-weird —and in all likelihood, a complete and utter sociopath. But there was something about him that resonated with Silvano. He supposed it was that Vadik was had found a way *out*. How he did it, Silvano had no way of knowing. That kind of thing simply didn't happen in his world. And from what he'd heard, it didn't happen with the Russians, either.

Maybe Vadik was delusional; buying wholeheartedly into a fantasy that he'd created in his head. Maybe it would all come crashing down in an instant when Vadik's boss—whoever he was—got wind of the whole hotel thing and set Vadik straight on the terms of his employment and continued well-being.

Maybe. But then again, maybe not.

Vadik seemed to be that rare breed who actually had the last word in how his life played out. Not because of positon or authority; but rather because he was bat-shit crazy and savagely and unapologetically violent. Who was going to tell Vadik what he could and couldn't do?

Some fucking Russian tittie bar owner? Hardly.

And so, on that level, Silvano had a grudging respect for Vadik—even if Vadik's aspirations of becoming a hotelier didn't work out as planned.

"And how are you this morning, Mr. Mazzio?" asked Elaine, his regular breakfast server. "Would you like to order something from the menu today, or are you considering the buffet?

"I've got a massage in an hour, so I think I'm gonna keep it light, Elaine. Just the Continental this morning."

"Very good, sir." She leaned in conspiratorially. "Have you seen Francesca since your last visit?"

"No, why?" Silvano whispered, playing along.

"She's bulked up," Elaine said, winking. "You might want to stretch beforehand."

Silvano laughed and picked up his paper.

"Just let me know if you need anything, Mr. Mazzio," Elaine said as she walked off.

Silvano scanned the front page of the Post, which was running an in-depth article on a local Ponzi schemer who'd managed to scam dozens of investors—including several New York hedge funds—out of almost a billion dollars. The scam had something to do with selling bogus legal settlements. To keep the ruse going, the guy even forged some local judge's signature on phony settlement papers.

The balls. The guy made Ted Hodges look like a bush leaguer.

What fascinated Silvano was that this guy had been a completely normal, under-the-radar law-abiding citizen for forty-something years. A fucking lawyer, in fact. Then, one day—BOOM!—he up and decides to do something that would land him a federal pen for the rest of his life.

Silvano pondered what would make an everyday Joe, an average American adult with a legal means of earning a living, decide to go the other way. And he couldn't see it. Not because he couldn't get his arms around the moral implications—he was a career criminal, after all. Over the years, he'd mellowed a bit, as people tend to do as they get older. But he had no misapprehensions about who he was, or how his moral compass was calibrated.

He was a gangster, pure and simple.

He'd been part of a crew since he was seventeen. He'd planned and executed his first truck heist before he graduated

241

high school. He'd been made at twenty-two, and did his first jail stint at twenty-four.

Unapologetically.

Silvano understood who he was; more importantly, he understood how he became who he was. Hodges, on the other hand?

Silvano couldn't see Hodges finding his way into this way of life without some outside help. He was too spineless; too afraid of his own shadow to do something as stupid and rash as skimming a bunch of money from escrow accounts. No, there had to be someone else involved in the whole thing, and if there was, Silvano was pretty sure that Ritchie's account was just the beginning. He wondered how extensive the whole thing was, but he knew beyond the shadow of a doubt that Ted Hodges was up to his ears in shit.

The question was, did Hodges still have the cash? If he did, then Silvano had something he could work with. If he didn't (and most of the time in these kinds of situations, the first thing that disappeared was the cash) Silvano had a whole new set of problems.

Regardless, there wasn't much he could do about it on a Saturday. And with that, Silvano pushed Ted Hodges out his mind for the time being.

He had a massage to get to.

CHAPTER 43

I have a fairly well-developed sense of irony. But even I had a little trouble getting my head wrapped around the idea of doing the walk of shame out of the old familial homestead. The rain was really coming down when I hit the roof, so I did the sensible thing and tossed my shoes down onto the front yard before making it over to the downspout on the gutter. A quick swing and finger hold, and I was on the grass.

I stopped for a few seconds to get reshod, and started a slow trot out of the neighborhood and over the Intracoastal bridge.

By the time I got to my studio, I was soaked. Actually, by the time I got to the sidewalk in front of Emma's home, I was soaked. The good news was that I stored most of my working clothes at my studio, so within ten minutes of springing the padlock, I was toweled off, toasty, and sporting a complete but paint-spattered set of Sherwin-Williams' finest trade wear.

For the previous two weeks, I'd been working on a large side plate for the middle piece of the installation. I had already cut it to shape—a sort of slightly irregular circle— on my over-sized work bench; the next task was to weld it in place. I had a drilled a hole through the top edge of the piece large enough to accept a hook from my overhead gantry, but small enough to be covered in the weld pattern. Today's job was to feed the hook into the plate, get it up on the gantry, and position it close enough to the main piece that I could shoot a half-dozen tack welds to hold it together.

At that point, I'd step back, stare at it for a while, and figure out what to do next. If the thing looked right, I'd finish welding the rest of the seams—which was going to be a full day's work in itself. If I'd missed the mark on my mount, I'd have to break the welds, reposition the piece, and tack it again. You can't just wad up a piece of Iraqi tank and throw it in the garbage can.

Sculpture, I had discovered, had a certain raw power to it, but it lacked the quick and intuitive fluidity of drawing and painting. And once you're into a sculpture project, there's not much you can do but work your way through the entire thing until it's done—one way or another. I've had plenty of failed painting projects over the years and I've learned that once failures start to emerge, you need to step away. Run a knife through the canvas. Throw it in a dumpster. Or stack it in a corner somewhere out of sight and out of mind, until you feel like coming back to it sometime later.

It's a canvas. It's a couple of inches thick. You can stash them anywhere.

Sculpture? Different story.

I was pushing to finish this current project for a variety of reasons, but the big one was that it had completely taken over my studio. Pieces of it were everywhere; assembled, unassembled, on shelves, floors, tables and stools. Worse, the entire place was covered in rust. I'd had to move most of my paintings to a storage unit over on the mainland to keep them from getting ruined by all the rust and oil floating around in the air. (The Iraqi T-72 tank I had parted the metal from had been one of the early casualties of the first Gulf War, grinding to its final halt surrounded by burning oil derricks. Twenty-some years later, the pieces still stank like an oil field fire.) I wanted to get the piece done, get it sold, and get it out of here.

Moving the paintings meant that I was going to have to curate Friday's show in the storage unit, looking at the work under weak overhead fluorescent light—which is not the best way to make critical decisions about what gets shown, what doesn't, and how it should be priced. I made a mental note to bring a flashlight with me.

But first things first—I needed get a big piece of oily, stinky, rusted metal welded to an even bigger piece of oily, stinky, rusted metal. I pulled my gantry over toward the table, let out some chain, and began bolting a smaller hanging hook to the end.

The relatively mindless work gave me a chance to think about what just had happened with Emma. I was certain that she was already wringing her hands and whispering quiet recriminations. But I'd be lying if I said I had any regrets. Because I didn't.

If she had so much as nodded, I'd have moved home that morning. It would have taken me all of ten minutes to pack up and get over the bridge.

I had made a conscious decision when I moved out of the house (at Emma's request) not to get too rooted; I wanted to be able to chuck it all in a heartbeat if things changed and I was asked back. For the past couple of years, I had rented a little cottage on the island side of the bridge, near the studio and the restaurant. That kept me within walking distance of the three places that mattered to me.

I wanted the cottage to be a place that Zack and Isabella felt comfortable, so I stuffed it with chain store furniture that had taken me about 10 minutes to pick out. I owned a television that only Zack knew how to work, a refrigerator that held only beer and juice boxes, and a closet full of board shorts, t-shirts and work clothes.

My only extravagances were an incredibly expensive but insanely comfortable PranaSleep mattress and an oversized rain-fall showerhead powered by a 100-gallon water heater. When I had returned after ten years of overseas duty, the two things I'd decided I'd earned were a good bed and a shower with limit-less hot water.

Every night for the rest of my life.

The kids actually liked the cottage; in their minds, staying overnight was the equivalent of camping. They slept on a fold-out mattress in the living room with about three-hundred of their most important toys and stuffed animals. They had a "Dad's House" set of beach junk that I kept in the studio, along with bikes and scooters and various and assorted other stuff.

When I had Zack and Isabella, every meal we ate came from Casa Playa's. I'd take them over for dinner, and have breakfasts and lunches delivered. I enjoyed this because it was both fis-cally responsible (why throw money at the competition?) and hugely entertaining: It forced Devan, my increasingly diva-like head chef, to make stuff—macaroni and cheese, chicken fingers, peanut butter and jelly sandwiches—that he viewed as beneath his considerable talents. I tried to have him deliver Cap'n Crunch and milk for breakfast one morning, and he sent Aaron over instead with a handwritten note threatening to quit.

I loved having Zack and Izzie in my house, but it wasn't the same as having all of my family together. I realize this sounds a little disingenuous coming from someone who spent close to a decade away from his wife and family, along with another year petitioning for a chance to do it again.

But time and circumstance have a way of changing things, and I guess I'm one of those things.

I made sure that the hook was properly set in the plate; I didn't know what the thing weighed, but I guessed in the 400-pound range. If the hook slipped or the hoist failed, the plate would come crashing down and take off my foot like a guillotine.

Who says that sculpting isn't a high-risk profession?

I slowly fed chain through the hoist, lifting the plate off the table. Once it was swinging freely, I steered the gantry over toward the center assembly, positioning the plate about a foot away from where I wanted it. I wanted to make sure I had it hanging at the right height before pushing it in to where it was actually touching the sculpture.

I stepped back. The plate—which was probably five feet wide and four feet tall— looked like a badly crafted gong as it swung in the gantry. *What the hell*, I thought and grabbed a rubber mallet off the bench. I took a full-on, two-handed swing at the thing.

It sounded like a gong made out of a piece of Iraqi tank.

Cool.

I whacked it a couple of more times for good measure before powering up the Millermatic. I changed the wire spool on the welder to a thinner gauge and dialed the voltage up two ticks. A tack weld is different than regular welding; it's meant to be temporary—the metallurgical equivalent of glue dots. And in metallurgical terms, that meant going a little hotter, with a slightly smaller wire.

Since these dots were holding up a four-hundred-pound piece of metal, they needed to be *strong* dots. I did the math in my head again. Four-hundred pounds divided by six tack welds meant each dot had to hold sixty-six pounds.

I decided to shoot a dozen instead. I liked my foot.

I pushed the plate in toward the assembly. As I got closer, I made ever more minute adjustments to the hitch. Once the plate touched, I stopped and did another walk around, eyeing the thing like I was lining up a pool shot.

Everything looked right.

I walked over to the bookcase that held a vintage Sansui receiver, a restored Pioneer belt-drive turntable, and about five-thousand vinyl records. I dug through the stack and found my trusty copy of *Superunknown*—in my opinion, the single greatest welding soundtrack ever created.

I fired up both Soundgarden and the Millermatic, and got to work.

CHAPTER 44

Burrell Malin squinted at formula again on the print out; cross-checking his notes and making sure that he had it exactly right. From what he'd read and seen on YouTube, there was absolutely no room for error. Flash powder, while theoretically an excellent initiator, was also unstable as fuck. He needed to be spot on with his proportions, and he needed to move slowly and deliberately as he mixed the components.

Otherwise...

Actually, he didn't really know what would happen otherwise.

This sucked.

Burrell wished he was anywhere but in his own kitchen cooking up homemade gunpowder. But he had come to the conclusion earlier in the week that only way to get out of this thing with Becker was to do the job right the first time. Which, now that he thought about it, was good advice for pretty much anything—legal or not.

"Doing it right" in this instance meant utter and complete destruction of both the house and the evidence. It meant leaving a blackened hole at what once was the street address for a perfectly livable home.

His primary concern was making sure that there was nothing left behind that could ever be traced *back to him*. Back to any of the dozen-odd purchases he'd made over the previous couple of days. Back to his fingerprints. Back to his house. He'd seen enough Miami CSI to be terrified of fibers and DNA and trace blood amounts and fingernail clippings and whatever the fuck else they liked to trace. He wanted a guarantee that all they would find would be ashes.

From what he'd read, that meant more than a massive amount of accelerant (which was what the acetone was for.) To really do it right, he needed multiple simultaneous explosions next to stockpiles of flammable material and accelerants in multiple locations throughout the house. That was the only way to guarantee that the entire house would be completely engulfed in flames before first responders could get there. Once they arrived, there'd be nothing to do but wait it out until the entire thing collapsed.

Goodbye house. Goodbye evidence.

Nothing was foolproof, and fire chiefs and arson experts were masters at finding the chemical and smoke signatures that indicated arson. But, as Becker had pointed out at the ballpark, that wasn't necessarily a bad thing. Arson investigations took time, and the more time he and Becker could get on their side, the more time they had to disappear.

The wrinkle in all of this was that rigging an entire house to explode into an instant ball of flames wasn't as easy as it sounded. It required three things—a detonator, an explosive, and some kind of accelerant. None of which he knew anything about.

But he was a quick learner.

Malin had initially figured that the easiest solution would be about five hundred dollars' worth of high-end fireworks, and an electronic remote fuse kit—the kind that professionals used for 4th of July shows. Earlier in the week, he'd hopped in his Oldsmobile and driven down to the central Palm Beach County, where a half dozen fireworks stands hugged Route 441.

It took him about a half hour to determine that actual fireworks were a no-go. Every shop was absolutely covered in security cameras, which meant that even a cash purchase could be traced. And since the 4th had come and gone, a huge purchase would stand out like a sore thumb.

The electronic remote detonation systems, on the other hand, were too good to pass up. For less than two hundred dollars, Burrell had picked up six detonation kits (one for each house) from six different fireworks shops. The devices were wireless, had a range of 200 meters, ran on AAA batteries and could remotely detonate up to four separate stations simultaneously.

Throwing the detonators in the trunk of his Cutlass, Burrell had driven home, fired up his laptop, and after a couple of hours of research, determined that there was only one option for his explosive.

Flash powder.

He'd never heard of flash powder, but the instructions for making the stuff were pretty straightforward. There were dozens of YouTube tutorials on the subject; all pretty much the same: a grainy video of a laboratory table with a bunch of bottles of different colored liquids and powders. A disembodied slightly Eastern European-accented voice calling the play by play, like Wernher Von Braun back from the dead. Graphics popping up here and there indicating ingredients and proportions. And a pair of latex-gloved hands doing all of the measuring, mixing, shaking, straining, and sifting—very slowly and very deliberately.

He had decided to use primary ingredients that offered the best mix of stability and burn rate: dark aluminum powder and potassium perchlorate. To his surprise, getting his hands on these materials was about as hard as ordering a book off Amazon. A couple of keystrokes, and he had two pounds of each overnighted to him from a chemical supply house in Powell, Ohio.

Total cost, including shipping: $68.35.

He'd picked up a box of purple latex gloves—because that's what the YouTube guys were wearing—from Walgreens, and a plastic digital kitchen scale from Bed, Bath & Beyond. The rest of the stuff he needed he'd found around the house.

Using a plastic take-out spoon, he very carefully measured out seven grams of potassium perchlorate onto a square of paper he'd set on the scale. He returned the one-pound bottle of the chemical to a counter on the other side of the kitchen.

Just playing it safe, he figured.

The powder looked completely harmless, like baking soda. Nonetheless, Malin treated it like it was enriched uranium. Once satisfied that he had the right amount, he slowly lifted the square of paper off the scale and brushed the powder onto a larger sheet of paper next to the scale.

Just like Wernher Von YouTube did in the video.

He checked his notes again and reached over to his laptop and resumed the YouTube video, confirming that he needed to measure out three grams of aluminum powder. He hit PAUSE, and very carefully spooned the powder onto the square of paper on the scale. The stuff was so fine that it was a little hard to handle, but after few attempts, he had 2.97 grams, according to Bed, Bath & Beyond.

Close enough.

He placed the bottle of aluminum powder on the counter with the potassium perchlorate and walked back to the table. He clicked PLAY on the video and watched the guy transfer the aluminum powder to the big sheet of paper, making a small pile next to, but not touching, the potassium perchlorate. He hit PAUSE again, and very carefully followed suit.

So far, so good.

He looked at the two little harmless piles of powder—one grey, one white—sitting peacefully side by side.

He took a deep breath, grabbed the two ends of the paper and began combining the powder by alternately lifting one end of the sheet, then the other. As he did so, the powders ran to the middle, mixing slowly into a very fine, light-grey mass. The YouTube narrator called this "the Diaper Method," and emphasized that the flash powder needed to be mixed in this manner for at least fifteen minutes to ensure a complete mesh of the two chemicals.

As he mixed, Burrell nervously, but absentmindedly, rubbed his stockinged feet across the rug that lay underneath the kitchen table.

When he was satisfied that the mix was complete, Burrell cued up his YouTube video for the next step. Wernher demonstrated how to remove any clumps from the mixture by pressing a non-metallic spoon into the stuff and smashing anything that looked suspicious. He emphasized, for what seemed like the fortieth time, how crucial it was for the powder to be absolutely consistent and lump-free.

Burrell pick up his plastic spoon, and began running it over the powder, looking for lumps, as he continued to rub his feet back and forth on the kitchen rug. The plastic spoon was cheap and fairly flimsy, so when he came across a particularly troublesome clump, he would use his right thumb to push the spoon into the powder with a little more force. As he did so, he inadvertently picked up traces of powder on the thumb and outside edge of his pushing hand—something he didn't notice until he used that hand to click PLAY on his laptop.

Oops.

As he touched the metal surface of his aluminum MacBook, he felt the faintest hint of a static electricity charge, which arced in an instant to the flash powder residue on his gloved hand.

The resulting explosion was, to say the least, impressive. In a nanosecond, his arm, shoulder, and the right side of his face were engulfed in a bright green flash, which blew him out of his chair and sent him skidding across the floor. The flash was so bright he was blinded.

The only saving grace, he later figured out, was that the initial explosion knocked him out of the line of fire from the secondary explosion that came a second or so afterwards. That explosion, fueled by ten grams of newly-mixed flash powder sitting on a piece of paper on his kitchen table, wiped out his laptop, his Bed, Bath & Beyond kitchen scale, his kitchen table, and his hearing.

CHAPTER 45

A decidedly waterlogged Elliot Becker sat on the toilet in his master bathroom, his battered body swathed in three layers of six-hundred-pile Turkish cotton towels. He dialed Burrell Malin's number for the fourth time. Each previous attempt had gone to voice mail.

"It's Burrell. Leave a message."

He hadn't left a message. Not yet. Better to redial until the idiot answered.

"...Hello?"

The voice sounded strained, as if the person on the other end was in great pain.

"Burrell? Is that you?" Becker asked.

Apart from heavy breathing, there was silence on the other end.

"Burrell?"

More silence.

"BURRELL!!!"

A pause, then, "Huh?"

"BURRELL! WHAT'S GOING ON THERE? IS EVERTHING OKAY?" Becker yelled, slowly and distinctly, as if Burrell were a trapped miner at the bottom of a shaft, and English was his second or third language.

Another few seconds passed and then, "Oh, hey, Mister Becker. Did you ask me if everything was okay?"

Burrell sounded either drunk or delirious—Becker wasn't sure which.

"I'm calling you to see if everything's on track, Burrell. We discussed this. I told you I wanted to get everything rolling this weekend—"

"—Huh? I can't hear you, Mister Becker. I've...ah, fuck...I had an accident with some of this, uh...arson shit."

Becker blinked, mortified.

"What? Burrell, what the fuck are you talking about—"

"—I told you, Mister Becker, I can't hear a fucking thing you're saying."

Becker heard the sound of the phone dropping to the floor.

"I'm all fucked up." Becker heard Burrell say—apparently to himself—since he was no longer speaking into the phone.

"Burrell?..BURRELLL!" Becker shouted.

Becker pulled the phone away from his face and looked at the screen, as if that might help. It didn't.

"Fuck," he muttered and ended the call.

Well, this isn't good, he thought.

"Sasha!" he yelled.

She appeared in the bathroom a few seconds later.

"You okay?" she asked. "What do you need?"

"I need you to find me the address for Burrell Malin. I think something's wrong with him. I was just on the phone with him —"

"—I know," Sasha interrupted. "I heard you telling at him. Your language is atrocious, Elliot. Anyone ever tell you that?"

Becker ignored her. "—and it sounded like he's had some kind of accident or something. I'm not sure. Whatever it is, it didn't sound good, so I'm thinking I need to get up there and see what's going on. I think he lives up in Jupiter, but I'm not sure. I know we've got his address somewhere. I just need you to get it for me."

Sasha blinked. "If something's wrong with him, why don't you just call 9-1-1?" she asked.

"Wouldn't that be better?"

Becker just looked at her.

"Okay. Let me find the address." Sasha headed down the hall.

Becker stood, testing his equilibrium. Most of the ibuprofen had apparently worn off, since the more debilitating side effects were starting to subside. He could walk at least, which was a big step up from crawling. He headed for the bedroom to get dressed for the drive north.

He pitied his poor liver.

He was rooting through his sock drawer when Sasha came bouncing in, waving a post-it note.

"I found Burrell's address. What do want me to do with it?"

"Give it to me," Becker said as he snatched the piece of paper out of her hand. He scanned it. The address was listed as Jupiter, but up in the north end of Palm Beach County, municipalities tended to run together. He wouldn't know for sure where it was until he plugged it into the GPS on his Land Rover.

As he turned toward the closet, he was overcome with dizziness; he had to reach out and put his hand on the wall to steady himself.

"Elliot, you're not well. There's no way you're gonna be able to drive all the way to Jupiter. You'll run off the road." Sasha said.

"Alright, fine. You drive me." Elliot said. There was no point in arguing, and truth be told, Sasha was right. He looked forward to reclining the leather passenger-side seat as far back as it would go, and turning up the climate control to Maximum AC. He might even get a half hour's worth of sleep.

"In the meantime, grab me some clothes and get yourself dressed. I want to be on the road in the next ten minutes. There's no telling what went wrong up there."

Thirty minutes later, they pulled onto I95, heading north. Not bad timing, considering that Sasha had to dress herself *and* Elliot, who couldn't manage to stand on one leg long enough to pull his trousers on, and had to be helped.

He looked blearily out the window, watching the endless pavement and palm trees of South Florida whiz by at a dizzying speed. Among her other talents, Sasha drove like a moonshiner's daughter.

Forty-five minutes later, the BBC-inflected navigation temptress advised Sasha to take the next exit and go west. Sasha hit the exit at a solid 85 miles per hour, slowing only slightly to take the left that would lead them west. Within three minutes, they were out of metropolitan Palm Beach County and headed toward the sticks.

"Rustic," Becker said, apropos of nothing. He was having a little trouble holding a thought.

He saw a sign for something called the Bonette Hunt Club Banquet Lodge, which advertised a "Wild Boar Barbeque Every Sunday—Year-Round." He thought about that for a second.

"You ever eat wild boar, Sasha?" he asked.

"Wild boar? What, are you kidding me Elliot? I'm from

258

Massachusetts. I don't even think we got wild boar up there."

Becker said, "No, they got wild boar everywhere, including Massachusetts. Wild boars have fur and fat. It's not like they can't take the cold."

"Well then, I'm from the city. And we don't have wild boar in the city. So—no. I haven't eaten wild boar. And I don't like barbeque anyway."

BBC interrupted this conversation with late breaking news that Sasha needed to make the next left, which she did at full speed, the Rover's tires leaving a patch of rubber behind. They had apparently entered the last known outpost before the complete disappearance of civilization in Palm Beach County.

The neighborhood was a single paved road that ran maybe two miles, dotted with homes of all shapes and sizes—from aging ranch houses that looked to be from the early 1960's to brand-new, two-story colonials. The front yards were littered with boats, RVs, junk cars and children's toys. A pit bull came sailing around the side yard from a house to the right and began chasing the car, barking madly and nipping at the rear wheel. Becker watched it in his rear-view mirror.

"Probably ought to speed it up a little," he advised.

Sasha punched the gas and pulled away from the dog, which gamely tried to keep pace for another fifty yards or so before giving up and trotting home.

Charming.

Another hundred yards or so, and BBC announced that the destination was on the left. Sure enough, Burrell's piece-of-shit-Cutlass was parked in the driveway. Sasha swung the Rover into a U-turn and parked the beast in the swale.

What a fucking dump.

Becker would have expected a home appraiser's home to be a little more up to snuff. Instead, the place was a mess. Talk about zero curb appeal. The window awnings were rusted and drooping. There wasn't a stitch of grass in the entire yard. Mail spilled out of the mailbox and was strewn across the front stoop. The place had probably been last painted in the middle seventies. And there was a sagging couch in the carport.

"Well, this is tacky." Sasha pronounced.

"Which should make you feel right at home." Elliot retorted, tiredly.

They got out of the car and went to the front door. Elliot rang the bell.

They waited a few seconds. Nothing.

"I didn't hear anything." Sasha said.

"Whadaya mean?" Elliot asked.

"I didn't hear a doorbell sound. Maybe it doesn't work."

Becker just looked at her.

"Maybe we should knock."

Becker sighed and said, "Yeah, you're probably right," and began banging on the door, yelling "BURRELL!" every few seconds.

Still nothing.

Becker tried the door. The doorknob was actually unlocked, but the door itself was secured with a deadbolt. He sniffed. "Do you smell something?" he asked.

Sasha pursed her nose and screwed her eyes shut in concentration.

Jesus.

"Smells kinda like a fireworks show. Like, after."

She kept her eyes closed another second or so.

"And a barbeque. I told you, I don't like barbeque and I hate that smell."

A bad feeling started to grow in the pit of Becker's stomach. He was pretty sure it wasn't related to the ibuprofen. With his good hand, pointed toward the back of the house.

"Go around. Check if there are some windows you can see through. Or a door that's open. I'm gonna keep knocking here. Give me a shout if you find something."

Sasha nodded and headed toward the right side of the house, her four-inch heels sinking into the sandy soil as she navigated the denuded front yard. Becker kept knocking on the door, occasionally yelling for Burrell to open up.

Lacking anything else useful to do, Becker kept grabbing the doorknob and yanking at the door as he yelled for Burrell. He shouted to Sasha as well, but heard nothing from the back of the house.

The déjà vu was instantaneous as the door shot open precisely as he yanked it, sending him reeling off the front stoop and into the yard. This time—mercifully—his head hit nothing but dirt. He looked up. Sasha was standing over him, her eyes wide open, her mouth gaping like a goldfish.

"I told you to shout out if you found something, you idiot," he said as he slowly rolled over and pushed himself up with his good hand.

Sasha finally found her voice.

"Elliot, you gotta get in there right now. I don't know what happened, but it looks like a bomb went off in the place. And there's a guy in there—I guess it's Burrell— that's...that's—"

"Dead?" Becker asked, as he regained his feet.

"No, not dead." she said.

She looked back toward the front door, trying to process.

"He's just sitting on a chair. Just staring. I don't think he can hear. His clothes are kinda burned off, and his skin is all red and blistered."

She tugged his arm.

"You gotta get in there, Elliot."

Becker followed Sasha into the house. Malin was parked on a La-Z-Boy in the living room, staring into space. Sasha was right: he was a wreck. His clothes were literally burned off his body. What little hair he'd had on his head was singed to an almost translucent halo of tiny curls. His right eyebrow was missing completely. And his skin looked like a 7-11 hotdog that had been sitting under the heat lamp since yesterday.

Becker looked to the right toward the kitchen, where indeed, a bomb had gone off. There was no mistaking it. There was debris everywhere, and the smell of cordite or gunpowder —Becker didn't one from the other, but he knew it was the smell of an explosive—was hanging in the air, along with a whitish-gray haze.

Fuck.

Becker went over to Burrell and leaned down so that his gaze met Burrell's.

"What happened?" he asked.

Burrell just looked at him with bloodshot eyes. He pointed to his ear and shook his head. "Can't hear," he croaked. "Got my hearing blown out."

Becker shouted, "WE GOTTA GET YOU TO A HOSPITAL, BURRELL. OR AT LEAST TO ONE OF THOSE DOC-IN-A-BOX PLACES."

Burrell nodded.

"There's one of them mini-emergency places over in the Winn Dixie plaza about five miles east of here."

With that, Burrell resumed staring into space.

Becker stood and motioned for Burrell to follow suit. He pointed to Burrell's legs.

"IT LOOKS LIKE ALL THE DAMAGE IS UP TOP. YOUR LEGS SEEM OKAY. CAN YOU WALK?"

Burrell stood slowly.

As he did so, Becker noticed the stain that Malin's blistered skin had left on the La-Z-Boy and winced.

"Sasha! Go find some towels or a sheet or something."

His week had been bad enough. The last thing he needed was getting Burrell Malin all over the Land Rover's upholstery.

CHAPTER 46

Ted Hodges, Esq. ground his Toyota Camry to a halt in the one and only handicapped parking spot adjacent to the Hogs & Honeys Sports Bar and Grill in Islamorada, a little less than halfway down the Florida Keys island chain. In his defense, he'd been driving for five and a half straight hours in the rain—which had only just let up—and his mind and eyesight were both on the fritz.

He hadn't eaten before making his break from the marital domicile at dawn, so his stomach was acting up—and he wanted a cocktail.

Not just any cocktail.

A daiquiri.

Hodges had decided, as part of his new persona, that he needed a signature cocktail. And for the last two hours of his drive, he had been debating what would be his new signature cocktail would be. Something refreshing, certainly, but it had to be a drink that also reinforced his island credentials and masculine appeal. While on a stop for gas, he pulled out his new iPhone and googled "Ernest Hemmingway's favorite cocktail."

Which—depending on the source— turned out to be a daiquiri.

A few clicks later, Hodges learned that Hemmingway's daiquiri differed from the frozen version he was used to. Allegedly invented by a legendary Cuban barman named Constantino Ribalaigua Vert, Hemmingway's daiquiri consisted of four simple—but sublime—ingredients mixed in a cocktail shaker, and served ice-cold in a martini glass. Straight up.

As he drove, Hodges rehearsed the preparation instructions he'd deliver rapid-fire to some hapless barkeep; his persona a mix of James Bond and George Clooney, as he smiled roguishly at the attractive and unattached patron one stool over.

"Two shots of Flor de Cana Extra Dry Four-Year Rum, a jigger of fresh lime juice, a measure each of grapefruit juice and maraschino liqueur. Shaken. Not stirred."

He couldn't wait to try it out for real.

Stepping out the car, he was hit by the heat. The sun had broken through the clouds, and steam was rising off the Hogs & Honeys parking lot. His recently-liberated scalp hadn't felt UV light since he was in law school; he made a mental note to pick up a tube of high SPF sunblock at the next Walgreens he passed. He covered his pasty pate with his hand and hustled into the bar, noticing a long line up of Harley-Davidson motorcycles to the left of the entrance.

As he entered, it took a few minutes for his eyes to adjust. The décor was classic Florida dive bar. A couple of pool tables fronted the place. A U-shaped bar dominated the middle of the room. Looking past the bar, Hodges saw that Hogs & Honeys opened out into a little marina, with a couple of slips for small boats, a deck with outside seating, and a Tiki-style bar. Despite it being early lunch hour, the place was crowded. Still worried about burning his scalp, Hodges sidled up to the indoor bar and took the only available stool. To his left sat a large middle-aged man in a t-shirt emblazoned with a charter fishing boat called the Penelope III. To his right sat a twenty-something blonde in a bikini-top and shorts.

Just as he imagined.

The bartender, a late-thirties, tatted-up brunette wearing a Harley-Davidson tank top and a pair of Levis 501's, walked up, slid a menu across the bar and asked, "What can I get you?"

This was his moment.

"I'll have a daiquiri."

She looked at him, the boredom apparent on her face.

Dammit, he thought. *I should have just said "daiquiri."*

Without a word, the bartender turned away, walked to a frozen concoction machine and pulled a plastic cup from a dispenser. She filled the cup with a white slush, grabbed a bottle of Captain Morgan Rum from the well, and poured a quick shot over the top. She plucked a lime from the garnish bin, walked over to Hodges, and handed him his frozen daiquiri.

"I'm Marie." she said as she fastened the lime wedge to the side of Hodges' cup.

"You wanna order some food?"

Hodges wasn't sure what to do. His rollout had suddenly gone sideways.

"Um, well, actually, when I said 'daiquiri' what I meant was —"

"What? Strawberry?" Marie asked, unsmiling. "We only have Pina Coladas and regular daiquiris for frozen drinks."

He could feel the blonde in the bikini top glancing over his way; he was tongue-tied.

"I um...well, what I meant was a daiquiri that you *mix*."

The bartender grabbed a cocktail straw from behind the bar and—never taking her eyes off Hodges—stirred his frozen drink.

"How's that? Mixed enough for you?"

Hodges heard the blonde next to him laugh. His felt his face flush.

"Thank you," he managed to croak out.

"My pleasure. Lemme know when you decide what you wanna eat."

She walked off, her ass swinging languidly in her 501's.

Hodges took a morose first sip of his first cocktail on the first day of his new life in the Keys.

It was awful.

He picked up the menu and began scanning it desultorily for non-seafood items. Hodges hated seafood. (Which, on top of the daiquiri humiliation, had him wondering if the whole hide-out-in-the-Keys thing wasn't such a great idea after all.)

He was looking for a hamburger on the Hogs & Honeys menu when someone tapped his shoulder.

"You the dickhead driving the Camry?"

Hodges looked over. Standing between him and the charter boat guy was one of the largest human beings he'd ever seen. He had to be at least 6 feet 5 inches tall, and well over 300 pounds. He was wearing a leather vest over a Harley t-shirt that stretched across his massive chest, which Hodges assumed made him some sort of biker. A chain snaked from a belt loop on his jeans to his back pocket. His beard was full and flecked with gray. He wore a hoop in his left ear, and his head was so freshly-shaved that Becker thought he could see his reflection in it. Although he had to be at least 50 years old, he had the look of a man who only grew more dangerous with age. His lower lip bulged with dip of tobacco.

It took Hodges a second or two to collect his thoughts. His legal training kicked in instinctively, and instead of answering the question, he asked one of his own.

"And you are?"

The biker reached across the bar, grabbed Hodges' daiquiri, and spit a long stream of tobacco juice into it. He put it back in front of Hodges and said, "I'm a guy that just spit in your drink, douchebag. So—one more time—are you the dickhead driving the Camry?"

Hodges started to feel a swell of panic; he fought it back and stayed with his training: Be assertive. Stay on the offensive.

He said, "I'm sorry, but how is the brand of car I drive relevant? I wasn't aware that it was a crime to drive a Camry."

The biker tilted his head slightly and smiled. It wasn't a nice smile.

"You're right. It's not a crime to drive a Camry. It's unimaginative to drive a Camry, but it's not a crime."

Hodges started to say something, but the biker cut him off.

"It is, however, illegal to park the aforementioned Camry in a handicapped parking spot without a disabled driver permit."

"Excuse me?" Hodges asked.

"You parked in a handicapped spot, dipshit," the biker said, as he leaned in, bringing his face within inches of Hodges. Hodges was petrified and mesmerized as he watched the huge man adjust the wad of tobacco with his tongue.

"I can tell you're a fucking lawyer what with the answering-a-question-with-another-question-bullshit. They teach you that shit the first day of law school? I was a cop for twenty-five years, fuck face. Marine Patrol. I've seen a million of you assholes."

By now, everyone within earshot had turned their attention to his little corner of the world. He wanted to crawl under the bar and never come out.

"Anyway, given your extensive legal training, I'm sure

you're familiar with the Americans with Disabilities Act, which stipulates that establishments such as this provide ample parking for their handicapped patrons."

He paused long enough to deposit another stream of tobacco juice into Hodges' daiquiri.

"And that patron, as far as this place goes, is Jim Webb. *Also* ex-Marine Patrol, and one of my best friends. Gave up a leg in the line of duty. Wrecked a cruiser chasing a piece-of-shit drug mule up on Card Sound Road."

He looked at Hodges.

"That spot you parked in? That's *his* spot."

"C'mon, Karl, maybe it was an honest mistake," the guy in the charter boat t-shirt said.

"Are you kidding me, Tommy?" Karl the biker asked. "Since when does a lawyer make an honest mistake?"

Sensing that didn't have an alternative, Hodges spoke up.

"He's right, Karl—if I may call you that," he said, holding his hands up in a feeble attempt to forestall Karl from beating him senseless.

"It *was* an honest mistake. If I parked in the wrong space, it was purely an oversight. I've been on the road since about seven this morning, and I may not have been thinking clearly. What say I go out there and move the car, and—I don't know— the next round is on me?"

Karl looked at him incredulously.

"You wanna buy me a fucking daiquiri?"

Hodges' hands came up again.

"No! I mean yes! If that's what you want...I meant I'll buy you whatever you want to drink. Or eat, I guess. I was just trying to—"

Karl cut him off with a raised hand. He pointed toward the door.

"Pay your tab, Counselor. Then take your ass out of here, and your Camry out of Jimmy Webb's spot."

In thirty years of legal practice, Hodges had never been addressed as "Counselor." And now, in the span of two days, two different psychopaths 200 miles apart had used the phrase. *What are the odds?* he thought.

Hodges fished a crumpled twenty out of his front pocket and dropped it on the bar. Under Karl's menacing stare, he decided that it wouldn't be prudent to wait for change. He slid off the stool and hightailed it out of the bar.

"Drive safely, dickhead," Karl called as Hodges hit the door.

Outside, he made a beeline for his car. As he approached, he noticed that someone had used a fat black Sharpie to scrawl "DICKHEAD" in huge block letters across the driver's side door, along with a crude arrow pointing to the window.

Welcome to the Keys, Mr. Buffet.

CHAPTER 47

Silvano Mazzio lay face down on the table, gritting his teeth in anticipation of the next assault on his hamstring.

"Keep the breathing nice and steady, Monsieur Silvano," Francesca said soothingly, in her charming Flemish accent. "Tensing the body will undo all of the work we have already done."

With that, she dug her thumbs viciously into the juncture between his knee and the back of his thigh. His sharp intake of breath was automatic. He forced himself to slow down and breathe deeply and normally. He felt a tear leak from the corner of his eye as he fought the impulse to throw an elbow and knock Francesca across the room.

"Very good. Very good. Do you feel that knot? Right *there*?"

As she spoke, she jammed a finger directly into a tender spot midway up his hamstring. He about came off the table.

"That is sign of both tension and inactivity. Are you not getting in your stretching?"

Silvano tried to answer without whimpering.

"It's been a little hectic this trip, but I'm going to try to fit a couple of workouts in this weekend."

"Yes. I highly recommend that. Also, water. Are you hydrating sufficiently? I feel signs that you are not getting enough water each day. Very important. Especially today. We've released many toxins, and without proper hydration, you might feel a little sick later."

As she spoke, Francesca pushed and pulled on Silvano's leg as if she were smoothing a table cloth.

"A liter of fresh cold water before your steam bath, Monsieur. Oui?"

"Oui."

Francesca slowly unfolded the towel that was draped across Silvano's hips, covering his body from his shoulders to his ankles. Then, she began to apply a gentle pressure with her forearms across his buttocks, legs and lower back.

It was a signal that the massage was coming to an end, as well as the only relaxing moment of the session. Which was fine; he understood that relaxation came *after* the massage; not during it. He breathed in steadily through his mouth, holding the inhalation for a five count, and then slowly exhaling. He knew from past experience that he'd be lightheaded when he sat up, and that this breathing exercise would help him recover a bit more quickly.

In fact, it was Francesca that had given him the advice.

Francesca leaned down toward his ear and said softly, "All done, Monsieur. Take your time, there is no rush. Rise slowly, and I will meet you outside. Your robe is on the door. The light is fine? Not too dark for you to see?"

"No, the light's fine. Thank you, Francesca," he slurred through slack jaws.

He heard the door open and close quietly, and he was alone.

He kept his eyes closed, drifting to the edge of sleep. Silvano had no particular compunction to move just yet. He wanted a few more minutes to bask in the utter relaxation Francesca had coaxed into his body before making his way out of the treatment room, where a liter of infused water awaited him.

If everything went to plan, Silvano figured he could count on one more Saturday session with Francesca before making his way back up to New York. He's bought a one-way ticket down, not knowing how long it would take to get things sorted out with Richie. Based on what he had seen at Hodges' office, he was going to be here at least through Thursday, and if rolled into Friday, he might as well stay the weekend. Which was fine by him.

It wasn't his money.

Silvano slowly lifted himself into a sitting position, his feet dangling off the table. He looked down at his pale, hairless legs; at feet that were as white as cavefish. Almost translucent. *That's what thirty years of brogues and dress socks will do*, he thought. Silvano resolved to get a little sun while he was down here, even if it came from a tanning booth.

He slid off the table and fetched his robe, letting the towel fall to the floor. Cinching the belt, he opened the door and peered out. The coast was clear; all of the doors to the other treatment rooms were closed.

As was always the case after a massage, the world had a slightly surreal quality to it. The spill of light at end of the hall formed gauzy little halos everywhere, and the silence was almost overwhelming. He didn't trust his balance or depth perception, so he walked very slowly and deliberately.

Francesca was waiting for him in the Relaxation Area, which served as a sort of hyper-luxurious way station for spa guests between treatment sessions. Comfortable chairs were arrayed artfully around low tables covered with reading material and treatment brochures. Ambient music poured softly from speakers mounted in the ceiling. A small Zen fountain splashed tranquilly in the middle of the room, and an assortment of infused waters, juices, and light snacks were arranged on a side table.

"Here you are, Monsieur Silvano," she said as she handed him a glass of ice-cold water with a lemon slice floating in it. "Have a seat, relax, and take your time. I want you to drink all of this before even thinking about taking a steam. If you need anything, just ask Anna, and she'll take care of you. Is there anything else I can do for you?"

Silvano said, "You might want to put me in for the same time next Saturday, Francesca. It looks like I'm going to be here through the week."

"Perfect. I'll do that." She shook his hand firmly, smiled and walked back down the hall.

Silvano perused one of the coffee tables for something to read, deciding on a copy of *Florida Design*. He took his water and his magazine and settled into an oversized chair near the fountain. He took a first sip of water, which was cold and delicious.

"Lucky you."

Silvano looked up.

An attractive, middle-aged woman wearing a Four Seasons Spa robe was seated on a small couch to his right. She was smiling at him.

"I'm sorry?" he asked.

"I said lucky you," she said, still smiling. "Getting to spend a week in The Four Seasons."

Nice-looking broad.

"Well, I guess it's all in how you look at." Silvano said, politely returning her smile.

"How so?" she asked, as she drew her knees up and tucked

her legs underneath her. She was in her late forties or early fifties, with pale blue eyes, blonde-turning-to-gray hair, and a vaguely patrician air about her that hinted at a lifetime of WASP patronage.

Silvano said, "It's an extra week on the road, which isn't great. On the other hand, if you've got to spend an extra week on the road, you might as well spend it in the Four Seasons."

The woman laughed lightly in either agreement or appreciation of his wit.

"Well put," she said. "I'm Kathleen, by the way."

"Silvano."

And that's how it started. Over the next half hour, Silvano learned that Kathleen was divorced and living in Palm Beach, that her ex-husband had been "absolutely wonderful" in their divorce and was still a close friend. That she owned a two-bedroom condo in "one of the nicer buildings mid-century buildings on the Island," and that her kids were both off at college—the daughter at Vassar and the son at Florida State.

"And how about you, Silvano? What has you staying in the Four Seasons for a week?"

Silvano had a standard cover story for instances like this.

"I manage money and business affairs for a few wealthy families in the New York area."

Which was, strictly speaking, the God's honest truth.

"I get down here periodically because my clients have real estate and other business interests in the area."

"That sounds fascinating. Would I know the families?" Kathleen asked.

You would if you read the New York Post or watched MTV, Silvano thought, but answered, "Probably, but it's my policy to keep the relationships confidential. They like it that way."

Also, the God's honest truth.

Kathleen nodded and smiled. "Of course."

"Are you a member of the club here?" Silvano asked.

"Oh, heavens no," Kathleen said laughing. "My divorce settlement was nice, but not *that* nice."

They both laughed.

"A friend of mine gave me a gift certificate, actually. She's just launched a little local lifestyle magazine and I wrote a couple of articles for her as a favor. Before the kids, I worked in public relations, so it's been kind of fun to get back in the swing of things."

"What were the articles about?" Silvano asked.

"Oh, you know, a profile of a local Junior Leaguer, a restaurant review. That sort of thing."

"How was the restaurant?" Silvano asked with a smile.

"Four out of five stars," she said laughing. "The location was a little off the beaten path, but the food was fabulous—a mix of Caribbean and South American with a little bit of Old Florida thrown in for good measure." She took a sip of whatever she was drinking. It was green and looked sort of like a smoothie made from lawn clippings.

"So, it wasn't here in Palm Beach?"

She shook her head and said, "No—it's a little south of here down A1A. Very casual. From what I understand, it used to be this awful Mexican cantina kind of thing and changed hands a couple of years ago. I thought it was charming." she said, her eyes twinkling. "With the right company, I'd definitely go back and see if they can pull another star out of me."

Silvano signaled politely to the attendant that he'd like a refill. This woman intrigued him. She wasn't really what he'd consider as his type, but then again, he ran in a different circle up in New York. She had a kind of cool elegance to her that he found unique and very attractive.

"So, apart from the free meal, you got a gift certificate to the spa?" Silvano asked.

"I did."

"And you feel like you got a fair shake in the whole deal?" he asked with a smile.

She looked directly at him with those pale blue, twinkling eyes and smiled again.

"I'm starting to think I got a very good deal."

CHAPTER 48

I had just finished adding two quarts of oil to the Bronco when my phone rang. It was Emma.

"Hey there. How was your morning?"

"About what you'd expect when it's pouring rain and you've got two little hellions locked up in the house."

"So, you're now at movies, I'm guessing." I said as I closed the Bronco's hood.

"Exactly."

"I love going to movies with Zack and Izzie," I said. "I always fall asleep before the opening credits are over. It's great."

Emma laughed. "I'm actually looking forward to a little nap myself, now that you mention it."

"So, what time does it let out?"

"That's why I called. The weather's supposed to clear up late this afternoon, and I thought I'd take the kids to the beach after the movie. I wanted to see if you'd like to join us."

I thought about it for a moment. "That might work out fine," I said. "I'm headed up to that appraiser's place in a few minutes. He lives out west up by Jupiter or Palm Beach Gardens. If all goes according to plan, I'll be back down here by five or so."

"According to plan? You've actually got a plan?" Emma asked.

"Okay, 'plan' might be a bit of a stretch," I allowed. "Unless going up there and snooping around can be called a plan. On the other hand, it's a good forty miles from here, so I might actually come up with something more complicated on the drive up."

As I was speaking to Emma, I was loading an old pre-packed bolt bag into the back of the Bronco. Also known as a bug-out kit, it was stocked with the standard list of stuff that I had been trained to consider as essential—a 30-foot length of rope, three different knives, a magnetic compass, burner phone, matches, water, cash, an emergency medical kit, a Zero Trace flashlight, a lock pick, a change of clothes, duct tape, a couple of energy bars and my Sig Sauer. Not that I would need all that stuff— but I've learned that it's better to have it and not need it, than to need it and not have it. Besides, it would have taken longer to unpack it and cut it down than to just throw the whole thing in the truck.

"Do I need to tell you to be careful, Logan? Or is that going to go in one ear and out the other?"

"No worries, but thanks."

Emma sighed. "Okay. So, call me when you're headed back down this way, okay?"

"Hooyah, Master Chief," I replied. "I'll see you guys on the beach."

Emma said, "I love you," and hung up the phone.

I swung into the Bronco and pointed it north. Since the 30-year-old car pre-dated navigation systems, I'd popped Malin's address into my iPhone. He lived out toward the old Beeline Highway, which, in the northern part of Palm Beach County was effectively the middle of nowhere. No problem. I had a full tank of gas and a topped-off crankcase. I was good to go.

It was an exceptionally fine day for a drive; the rain had finally stopped, leaving behind a pink and azure sky laced with high-floating cirrus clouds and a light, warm breeze that hinted of the coming high-pressure system. As I made my way north, the urban jungle of Palm Beach proper gradually gave way to vast swatches of open land dotted with pine forests and scrub palm.

I loved this part of Florida; where the deep south meets the tropics. Gone were the Bentleys and Range Rovers, replaced with Ford F-150's and Chevy Silverados; transients (like myself) were outnumbered by native Floridians; and the landscape was like no other place in America. Look to the left, and you could swear that you were on the Florida/Georgia line; to the right, a line of Royal Palms stretched over the horizon. Overhead, red-shouldered hawks danced lazily on thermals, while yellow-eyed ospreys looked on down from tree-top perches. I kept my eyes open for black bear, panthers, and white-tailed deer—common sights along these roads.

I had friends from the service who had moved up here after coming home; their idea of a good time was knife-hunting for wild boar. At night.

I turned onto Indiantown Road, and headed west of the city of Jupiter. After about twenty minutes, I turned left onto Malin's road, which, according to Google Maps, ran parallel to a huge state wildlife management area and about two thousand retention ponds. Definitely a neighborhood for folks who wanted to get away from it all.

Malin's house—which was a complete dump—sat on the left-hand side of the road, about a mile down. An old Cutlass was parked in the driveway. As I swung the Bronco into a U-turn, I noticed two deep, parallel trenches in the swale in front of the house. Someone had left in a hurry. I parked the truck a couple of hundred feet down the road—as was my habit— got out, and went to the front door.

My "plan" was pretty straightforward: knock on the door and start asking questions. This wasn't what I had told Emma, of course. If I'd told her I planned on interrogating Malin, she would have blown a gasket. Too confrontational. Too much potential for escalation, she'd tell me. But I knew from practical experience in Iraq that door-to-door interrogations produced way more actionable intelligence that simply patrolling the streets looking for bad guys.

The key to an effective interrogation was to get a guy off balance right out of the box and keep him there. Obviously, this is pretty easy when you've breached a door by force with five guys stacked behind you.

In one-on-one situations, I liked to surprise the target with information he didn't know I had. Confused and wondering what else I had on him, he was no longer thinking about how best to bullshit me.

With that in mind, I wanted to be sure to use some variant of the word "arson" right out of the box with Malin, as in: "So, Burrell—I hear you're an arsonist." Or: "Funny—you don't look like an arsonist."

Either way, it would put Burrell Malin on his heels from the get-go. And once I had him there, I'd keep the questions coming, fast and furious. This was important, because the more time you gave people to think, the more complicated interrogations became.

I pushed the doorbell; I didn't hear a chime, so I knocked. The door itself had three small vertical slashes of frosted glass at eye-level. I tried to peer in, but couldn't see a thing. As I got closer, however, I could definitely *smell* something. I put my nose closer to the junction between the door and frame and sniffed again.

Flash powder.

I was immediately transported back to every close quarters combat situation I'd ever been in, from drills to the real thing. Flash grenades—sometimes called "flash-bangs," were standard protocol when breaching a room. Theoretically non-lethal (although I've seen evidence to the contrary), flash-bangs are designed to momentarily stun and blind the enemy in advance of a room breach. Flash-bangs are nothing more than a metal canister with a fuse and about 19 grams of flash powder.

And when they detonated, they smelled just like Burrell Malin's door.

My situational awareness—long dormant—suddenly kicked in. I paused for a second to take in my surroundings and knocked again.

Nothing.

I turned the doorknob. It was locked. I stepped off the stoop and walked back to the Bronco. I looked up and down the long road. There wasn't a car to be seen, and the nearest house on either side was at least an acre away. I opened the back of the truck, unzipped my bug-out kit, and dug out my beloved HPC ElectroPic, an aptly-named and very useful little tool for situations like this. I toggled the trigger to make sure the batteries were still good.

I was rewarded with a pleasant little hum.

I headed around back, reasoning that if I was going to break-and-enter a complete stranger's house, I should probably do it out of the prying eyes of some random Jupiter Farms resident.

The back windows were filthy—no surprise there—but I could see enough to confirm that something had definitely exploded inside. I moved to the door, which was secured with an off-the-shelf Kwikset deadbolt. I inserted the tension tool in the left-hand side of the lock, fed the ElectroPic's blade all the way into the drum, backed it out just a hair, and pulled the trigger.

If electric pick guns have a downside, it's that they can be a little noisy. I believe they more than make up for that by being fast. Which was the case with Burrell Malin's back door: after about three seconds, I felt the pins in the drum fall. I torqued the tension tool, and the bolt slid back.

Now that the breaking was done, I proceeded to enter.

This wasn't the first time I'd been in a bomb maker's workshop after an "accident." Being in a bomb maker's workshop in America, however, was a first. I looked around, working my way out from the kitchen, which had clearly been ground zero, to the other rooms in the house.

I was looking for a body.

It took me all of about thirty seconds to confirm that Burrell Malin—alive or dead-- was not in the house. Either he survived and walked out under his own power, or he was dead, and someone had moved him. I went back to the kitchen and looked around. A container of sodium perchlorate and another with aluminum powder sat on a counter, apparently unscathed by the explosion.

Classic flash powder ingredients.

I glanced at the overturned and badly-burned kitchen table. I could make out the remnants of an Apple laptop and what was probably a scale of some kind, along with some charred pages of handwritten notes. It was pretty simple matter to reconstruct what had happened: Malin was cooking up a batch of homemade flash powder and managed to blow himself up in the process. This wasn't surprising; the stuff was notoriously unstable. It could have been set off by almost anything. I remembered a CQC safety officer demonstrating that quality by tossing a small open tin of flash powder onto a concrete floor.

I couldn't hear anything for an hour.

Dead or alive, flash powder was pretty good circumstantial evidence for Burrell Malin being an arsonist. Or wanting to be one, anyway. It was too bad that his laptop had gone out with explosion. If I had been a cop, I could have sent it to some sort of crime lab, where they'd reconstruct the hard drive or something. But I wasn't a cop, so I started rooting around the house looking for the next best thing: paper documents. I was hoping to find something that would tell me which homes Becker and Hodges were targeting.

Addresses. Owners. Anything.

I was guessing there was a list on the laptop; if I was lucky, maybe Malin had printed it out. I found a printer in the back bedroom, but there was nothing in it. I went through each room methodically, opening drawers, rooting through closets, looking for filing cabinets.

Nothing.

As I searched, I was careful to replace everything exactly as I found it. I wanted no sign that I'd been here. I was standing in the living room pondering what to do next, when I remembered the pile of mail that I had stepped over on the front stoop. Maybe there was something in there that I could use. I turned to go out the front door, when I kicked something. I looked down.

It was a cell phone.

CHAPTER 49

Aleyev Vadik Antonovich closed his copy of *Der Spiegel*, took a last sip of iced tea, set the glass carefully on the table, and walked into the house from his back porch. As was tradition in the cottage on weekends, the French doors and windows were thrown open to catch the cross breeze that came off the ocean two blocks east. Shaded by the towering canopies of a pair of hundred-year-old Royal Poinciana and Banyan trees, the cottage stayed cool, even in the dead of August.

Debussy's *Clair de Lune* from *Suite Bergamasque* drifted in from the front room. It was a piece that Rheese loved fiercely and played beautifully. Vadik stopped and listened for a moment. An amazing composition; emotionally raw and structurally intricate; tranquil and utterly heartbreaking; its shimmering arpeggios leaping and descending into a sonorous, expressive calm. That Rheese could play the movement with such assurance and exquisitely articulated emotion almost moved Vadik to tears.

He walked quietly toward the front of the cottage, not wanting to disturb Rheese from playing; he wanted simply to watch. He paused in the arched entryway; Rheese's back was to him. As Vadik listened, he swayed ever so slightly, his gnarled hands pantomiming the complex rests and modulations that gave the piece such emotional breadth.

Rheese finished the movement, and without turning said, "So, were you fantasizing that you were Brad Pitt and you and all your buddies just cleaned out the Bellagio?"

Vadik smiled. "A little. Mostly though, I was watching you, Rheese. It is indescribable pleasure to watch you play. Like private concert."

Rheese stood up from the piano and said, "Flattery will get you everywhere, good sir. In fact, I think you've earned yourself a cocktail. I know I have."

"What are you in mood for? I'll make them." Vadik said.

"I dunno…surprise me. Let's sit out on the porch and enjoy the breeze. We can talk about the elephant in the room and make evil plans for the weekend."

Rheese walked off toward the back of the house, while Vadik pondered the elephant in the room.

Dmitrievich.

Vassili Dmitrievich was the last obstacle standing in the way of Vadik realizing his American dream—a life he couldn't have imagined when he was killing Chechen separatists for Spetsnaz. *That was what? Twelve years ago? Fifteen?*

It was a dream that began with his immigration to the United States—and the realization of what was possible with hard work, a little luck, and the freedom to be who you really were. It had distilled when he met Rheese at— of all places— the Cougar Club. And it had taken form when he and Rheese had bought the tiny but tasteful Palm Beach cottage they now called home.

Despite its reputation for sprawling oceanfront mansions, Palm Beach originally boasted a thriving colony of cottages when it was being developed in the 1920's. Over the years, the majority of these structures had been razed to the ground; adjoining lots were combined, and larger homes were built.

Others were moved.

But a few survived.

When one particularly noteworthy example had come on the market, Rheese had pounced, telling Vadik that this was a once-in-a-lifetime opportunity to own an original piece of Palm Beach. Rheese was beginning to make a mark in the merciless world of Palm Beach interior design; Vadik had saved eighty cents of every dollar he'd earned since coming to the United States and going to work for Vassili Dmitrievich. Financially, it was within reach; they just needed to pull the trigger.

It was the easiest decision Vadik had ever made.

Once they bought the cottage, they were confronted with a quandary common to almost everyone who acquires a landmark property in the Town of Palm Beach: modernize or restore? This was a not-so-easy decision, but there was only one that—at least in retrospect— was absolutely right: rather than erase history in an orgy of marble countertops, pasta faucets and recessed halogen lighting, Vadik and Rheese had chosen to restore.

Within reason.

The project had taken almost a year, along with most of their savings. But it had been worth it. The restoration was absolutely magnificent, down to the original hardwood floors and window casings. The cottage had twice been featured in architectural and design magazines, and Vadik and Rheese had acquired a reputation as a couple with impeccable taste and style among town's ardent community of preservationists. This, not surprisingly, had been very good for Rheese's business.

The only downsides were that the rooms and proportions of the cottage were authentic to the structure as it had been built some ninety years earlier, meaning small bedrooms, only two bathrooms, a formal living room (which held Rheese's baby grand piano), narrow hallways—and an exceedingly small kitchen.

It was into this tiny kitchen that Vadik walked, thinking it might be a good afternoon for something light. Maybe a Sangria. Saturdays were heavy workout days for him: a five-mile run with a weighted vest, and an hour of intense Krav Maga sparring. He was relaxed, but a little sore and tired. Better to not overdo it before dinner.

He rooted through the refrigerator, finding a bottle of inexpensive chilled Grenache wine, a lime, some berries, and a container of grapefruit juice. He sliced the fruit and mixed the ingredients, along with a tray of ice and a dash of sugar, in a large crystal pitcher. He put the pitcher and two crystal tumblers on a tray and carried it out to the porch.

Rheese was thumbing through *Der Spiegel*.

"The news always looks bad in this magazine. And I don't even read German."

Vadik said, as he poured the drinks, "The German word for beauty is *schønheit*, which should give you an idea of how harsh the language is. Everything in German sounds worse than it is."

Rheese took the offered drink and sipped.

"Perfect idea, Vadik."

Vadik smiled.

Rheese put the drink down.

"Alright, before we talk about the elephant, I wanted to throw out an idea for dinner tomorrow night. There's a little place down A1A that's been getting these breathless reviews for its Caribbean cuisine. It's supposedly kind of funky, but from what I hear, the food is to *die* for. I thought we'd pop in there and see what the buzz is about; maybe meet the chef with an eye towards recruiting him down the road—you know, for the hotel. I'm betting that it's packed tonight, but we can probably have our pick of tables on a Sunday night."

Rheese took another sip of Sangria.

"What do you think?"

Vadik smiled and said, "Caribbean food? I don't even know what that is. But okay, let's do it. What's it called?"

"Casa Playa's, I think. Or Constance's. Something like that."

"Count me in," said Vadik, as he tasted his Sangria.

Very nice.

Rheese said, "Okay, that's settled. Now, moving on—what are we going to do about dear Mister Dmitrievich? Because if we're going to make a go of this hotel, one of us is going to need to be there full time. And because I think we're still going to need the income from my design business—at least over the next year—that person is *you*, Vadik."

"I agree," said Vadik.

"So how are you going to deal with Vassili?"

"I'm just going to tell him that I'm moving on," Vadik replied. "That's all. Vassili Dmitrievich does not tell me what I can do, or what I cannot do. And, trust me on this Rheese, Vassili Dmitrievich does not want to get on wrong side of me. He knows better than that."

"Why? Because he knows you'd kill him?"

"Well, there's that," Vadik said chuckling.

There were no secrets between Vadik and Rheese.

He continued, "And the fact that I know where all the bodies in Vassili's world are buried. I know everything. Things he would not want other, more powerful people to know. Were he to cross me, getting killed by me would be best thing he could hope for. The alternatives would be far worse. He knows that."

Rheese said, "Still, I think it would be best if you could somehow resolve it so that we're not having to constantly look over our shoulder. Part as friends, and not as enemies."

"I agree with this also," Vadik said.

"So, how do you do that, Vadik?"

Vadik thought about it for a moment and picked up the phone.

"By calling him."

CHAPTER 50

Burrell Malin navigated the front stoop of his house, fishing in his pocket for his keys. Becker's administrative assistant, Sasha, gently held his elbow, as if the keep him from falling down. There was no danger of that, but he appreciated the gesture and enjoyed her touch, so he said nothing. Becker was still in the car, trying for the third or fourth time to get Ted Hodges on the phone.

Malin swung the door open and made a beeline for the La-Z-Boy. Sasha headed toward the kitchen, asking loudly, "Is there anything I can getcha, Burrell? A cold water? A beer? Something to eat?"

"A beer'd be nice, ma'am. Thanks."

Malin sat down heavily. A beer would definitely be nice. He rubbed his eyes and looked around at the mess. The kitchen table was overturned; parts of his laptop lay scattered across the floor; his kitchen rug was charred black, and the place still smelled like a fireworks factory. Still, considering the alternative, the news from the doc on duty at the emergency walk-in clinic had been as good as he could have hoped for.

"From what I can see, Mr. Malin, most of the burns are first degree, with some second-degree damage to your right arm and hand. You have a tympanic membrane perforation in your right ear—what's known as a ruptured eardrum—but your left ear seems to be a fine. A little traumatized, but fine," the doctor had said.

Loudly.

"So, what does all that mean?" Becker asked. "Does he need to go to a hospital?"

"No, I think he'll be fine at home. His skin and eardrum should heal on their own over the next couple of weeks, as long as he takes it easy and makes sure to use the topical antibiotics and pain relievers that I'm going to send home with him."

The doctor looked at Becker.

"What happened to your hand, if you don't mind my asking?"

"Nothing. Gardening accident."

With that, Becker had hustled him and Sasha out of there like the clinic charged by the minute. To his credit, Becker *had* covered the bill—if only temporarily.

"Seven hundred and fifty-seven dollars, Burrell. Fucking highway robbery. I'm putting it on your tab," Becker said, as they headed toward the Range Rover.

The entire drive back to Malin's house had been one long tirade about "fucked up timetables" and "carefully laid plans going off the fucking rails." Malin hadn't bothered to respond. What was he going to say? *Sorry I blew myself up?*

What an asshole.

At some point in all of this, Becker started babbling about "going to Plan B." From what he could make out, "Plan B" involved bringing Ted Hodges onboard, with Burrell relegated to coaching Becker and Hodges on the best way to burn down a house.

Like he knew.

"We'll push it back a couple of days, give you a chance to get your feet under you. Get Hodges in here, get him up to speed, and the three of us can do the first one, say Thursday. Maybe Wednesday, if you're feeling up to it. So, as of now, you're a fucking consultant, Burrell. You up for that?"

Malin grunted as he looked out the window. He couldn't really hear everything Becker said, but he got the gist of it: even after damn near blowing himself to shreds, he was still stuck with this asshole.

Sasha walked into the living room, carrying Burrell's beer.

"Here ya are, Burrell. Ice cold."

Malin took a healthy pull. *Jesus, that was good.*

"Where's Elliot?" Sasha asked. "Is he still out in the car trying to get hold of Ted? I told him the reception's awful out here. My phone's had no bars since we got off the turnpike. You get good reception out here, Burrell?"

Malin reflexively tapped the front pocket of his jeans.

His cell phone was missing.

Given everything that had transpired since Burrell had blown up his kitchen and Becker and Sasha had shown up, he hadn't needed to use—and hence, hadn't thought about—his cell phone. Now, it was like he was missing a limb.

"My phone. I lost my phone." he said, the panic beginning to rise in his voice. Like most people, Burrell's cellphone was more or less permanently grafted to his person. He began to feel what drug addicts would describe as the early symptoms of withdrawal.

"It's got all my contacts, all my emails, everything."

He stood and started rooting around the living room.

"I remember dropping it when I was talking to Mister Becker. It's gotta be in here somewhere."

293

Sasha joined in the search.

"I'm sure it's around here, Burrell. We'll find it. You sure you didn't have it when we took you to the doctor? Maybe it fell out in the car. Want me to go outside and check?"

"Check what?" Elliot Becker said, as he came through the front door.

"Burrell's lost his phone," Sasha answered. "He thinks he dropped it when he was talking to you this morning, and that's the last time he remembers seeing it."

"Well, he definitely dropped it when we were talking. That I can tell you for sure," Becker said, as he joined, rather desultorily, in the search for Malin's phone. He poked half-heartedly at a cushion on the La-Z-Boy.

"We NEED to find it," Burrell said, his voice on edge. "The wrong person gets hold of it, and it ain't gonna be good for any of us."

Becker stopped in his tracks.

"What do you mean, Burrell? What do you got on that phone?"

"All my contacts, for starters. Including you. All my emails, for another thing. Including yours. And all my texts, including the ones we've been sending back and forth all week about torching the houses. All of them."

"Yeah, but don't you have a password on the phone? A security lock? That kind of thing?" Becker asked. "Someone punches in the wrong code three or four times and the phone erases all the data. Isn't that how those things work?"

"Nope—I mean, *yeah*, that's how those security codes work, but..." Malin trailed off, feeling oddly *guilty*.

"I dunno...punching in the code every time drove me crazy, so I disabled it. I mean, it's not like I ever lost my phone before.

This is the first time *ever*."

Becker looked at him in disbelief for a moment before erupting.

"WELL, THAT'S JUST FUCKING GREAT, BURRELL! GREAT FUCKING TIME TO LOSE YOUR FUCKING PHONE FOR THE FIRST FUCKING TIME, DUMBASS!" he yelled, not necessarily so that Malin could hear him.

Now, Becker looked panicked.

"Sasha, go check the Rover. Maybe brainless here dropped it in the back seat. Check under the sheets. And get the sheets out of the car while you're at it."

Becker started pushing furniture around like a mover on crystal meth—bad hand and all.

"If we can't find it, I guess I'm gonna have to go back to the clinic and see if you dropped it there. Maybe we'll get lucky and someone ran over it in the parking lot. Speaking of that—"

Becker walked to the front door and yelled out to Sasha, "CHECK THE SWALE, TOO!"

Malin had given up looking for the phone. What was the point? He knew *exactly* where he'd dropped it, and it wasn't there.

Sasha came back through the front door. "Nothing. Not in the car. Not in the street. Not in the swale. Not in the yard."

"Great," Becker said. "Sasha, gimme your phone for a minute. I want to see something."

He grabbed the phone from her hand and punched at it, the frustration evident on his face.

"Sasha, what's your fucking—"

He sighed, handed the phone back to Sasha, and looked at Malin. "*She's* got a security code on her phone, genius. At least one of you has half a brain."

He turned to Sasha. "You still got all those texts between Burrell and you?"

She nodded.

"Pull 'em up, will you? I wanna see what kind of exposure we're talking about."

Sasha manipulated the device for a couple of seconds and handed it to Becker. Holding the phone in his good hand and flicking his thumb, he began to scroll through the screen.

"Man. oh, man, oh, man," he mumbled as he scrolled. "Fuuuuuck. Aw, man. This...is...not... good."

Becker looked up and met Malin's eye.

"You may not know this, Burrell, but I'm also a lawyer. And I know evidence when I see it. So, I don't know if you're the praying type, but this might be a good time to start."

CHAPTER 51

For the second time in less than twenty-four hours, I sat in my Bronco, parked behind Casa Playa's, scrolling through a cell phone. Only this wasn't my cell phone.

It was much, much better.

CHAPTER 52

"To Sunday nights."

Vadik clinked glasses with Rheese and took a sip of his ice-cold Tito's martini.

"To Sunday nights," he echoed, as he looked over the Casa Playa's menu.

It was oversized and handwritten. Almost every inch of space was covered with densely packed descriptions of appetizers, soups, salads and main dishes. Vadik didn't know where to start.

Rheese said, "If the food lives up to the menu, I'd say this place is the find of the year."

Vadik nodded. "What is Triple Tail?" he asked, as he continued to scan the menu.

"Kind of like grouper, but a little sweeter. You'd love it."

A tall, fit man with longish blonde hair who'd been talking to a couple at a nearby table turned toward them.

"Not that I'm eavesdropping, but if you want the Triple Tail, you should probably tell me now and I'll go back and save you a piece. We don't get it in that often, and it sells out fast."

He was wearing faded Levi's and a white Greg Noll long-sleeved t-shirt. He looked like a lost surfer.

"Sorry to interrupt. I'm Logan, the owner."

Rheese looked at Vadik, shrugged and said, "Well, nice to meet you, Logan. I'm Rheese, and this is Vadik. This our first time here."

The man named Logan smiled and said, "You're gonna love it, that I can promise you."

"Well, that's the buzz, around the Island." Rheese replied with a smile. "Everyone's talking about Casa Playa's."

"Really?" Logan asked, a little incredulously. "You two came down from Palm Beach to eat *here*?"

"Yep. You must have a really good publicist." Rheese said.

Logan laughed. "If I have a publicist at all, this is the first I'm hearing about it."

Vadik asked, "So—what is owner's recommendation, Logan?"

"Everything on the menu is great. But if it were me, I'd definitely do the Triple Tail. Maybe on the salad."

"Okay," Vadik answered. "Then I will take you up on offer to save piece for me. Thank you."

"No problem," Logan said and looked at Rheese, raising an eye.

Rheese said, "Are you kidding? I'll eat some of his and try something else."

"Smart move," Logan said, smiling. "Let me go tell the cook. Enjoy your meal, and if you need anything, let me know." He walked off.

They sat in silence for a minute, each absorbed in Casa Playa's menu. Which was fine with Vadik. He needed some time to think. The call to Vassili hadn't gone as expected. Vassili had been far too agreeable; too immediately accommodating: *"Of course, Vadik. I completely understand. You have to do what you have to do. There comes a time when we all have to move on and do our own thing."*

This was complete bullshit.

Vadik had known Vassili for years; he had once seen him nearly beat a bouncer to death when the guy got a job at a competing tittie bar. Because Vassili accommodated no one. Conceded nothing. Vassili Dmitrievich only took. And this kindly uncle thing?

Vadik knew what that meant.

"Are you going to keep your nose buried in that menu, or are you going to tell me what's going on?"

Vadik looked up at Rheese.

"You've been in your own world all day, Vadik. Actually, you've been in your own world since you hung up the phone with Vassili yesterday evening. So, why don't you tell me what's on your mind, and we'll figure out how to fix it?"

Vadik thought for a second, blew a thin sigh and said, "I am about ninety-percent sure Vassili is planning to kill me."

Rheese cocked an eyebrow. "Seriously? Because, from what I could tell from your phone call, Vassili seemed fine with it. He told you he understood, and he even wished you good luck. I heard him."

Vadik leaned forward.

"That is thing, Rheese. Vassili wishes no one 'good luck'. And Vassili only 'understands' what Vassili wants to understand. This is a feint. This is to get me off my guard. Until he has someone kill me."

"And you know this how?"

"Because I have seen this Mister Nice Guy act before with Vassili. Many times. It is purely to put someone at ease. Not defensive. Not looking over shoulder."

Vadik thought back to how relaxed and cocksure Elliot Becker was in the five minutes proceeding his finger amputation.

"So that when time comes, they never see it coming. It is all a ruse, trust me."

Rheese was silent for a minute.

"Why would he want to kill you, Vadik?"

Vadik shrugged. "Because I know too much about his operations, I suppose. That makes me a threat. I could go into business for myself, use what I know against him. I could go to a competitor. Any number of problems I would create—all of which are solved by killing me.

Vadik paused and took a sip of his drink. He looked up at Rheese over the rim of the martini glass.

"In retrospect, I was wrong to assume he would leave me alone. The more I think about it it, if I were him, *I* would have me killed. No question. It is the right thing to do, business-wise."

Rheese chuckled. "My mother warned me about you."

Vadik smiled, and said, "Here comes waiter."

The two ordered quickly.

Vadik said, "I can promise you that ten minutes after that call, Vassili was on phone recruiting freelancers for job."

"Freelancers? What are freelancers?" Rheese asked.

"A person from outside the organization. He would never give this job to someone that works for him, because it would be clear signal that he has no loyalty to his own people. That would be poison for him, because he needs that trust. Also, no one would want to take on job of killing me because of the high level of risk involved. I am not an easy man to kill. They know that."

"So, where would Vassili find freelancers?"

"There are people around with the right kind of skills that he could reach out to. Problem for him is that I know most of them; I am not the only ex-Spetsnaz or GRU in South Florida. We all know of each other, and to turn one against the other would be very hard. There is a loyalty there. Would cost a lot of money."

"What makes you so sure that Vassili would keep this an all-Russian affair?" Rheese asked.

"Because Vassili has no friends outside of Russians. Business arrangements? Yes. Friends? No. Only Russians. He would not trust this to anyone other than a Russian. On this, I am certain."

"So, what are you going to do?"

Vadik answered, "I've already reached out to a couple of old comrades. If Vassili starts looking, one of them will hear about it. And they'll let me know. In the meantime, I maintain situational awareness, keep my guard up, and act as if I suspect nothing."

"And that's enough for now?" Rheese asked.

"When I understand what Vassili has planned, I can begin to lay in countermeasures. But until then, this is going to have to be enough."

Rheese sighed. "I hope you know what you're doing, Vadik."

Vadik reached across and patted Rheese's hand. "Not to worry. Vassili's not first guy who decided he wants to kill me."

"I probably don't want to ask what happened to the other guys."

Vadik smiled. "You could, but unfortunately, they're not

around to answer."

CHAPTER 53

At precisely 9 am Monday morning, Silvano Mazzio and Richard Pizzuti walked to the front door of AA Top Title, rang the buzzer and waited for the solenoid to click.

Silvano was still steaming.

"I don't know what you're so pissed about, Sal. We made it here right on time."

No thanks to you, asshole. Silvano thought.

When he'd hit the lobby of Tower One at eight, Myron the security guy was nowhere to be found. Silvano found him two minutes later, as he exited the elevator in front of Ritchie's penthouse. He was pounding one the door, yelling, "MISTER PIZZUTI! MISTER PIZZUTI? IT'S MYRON, FROM DOWNSTAIRS! ARE YOU AWAKE?"

Mazzio had politely gestured for Myron to move aside, as he fished in his pant pocket for the key to the unit.

"Mr. Mazzio, I'm sorry. He wouldn't answer the phone, so I came up to get him. I musta reminded him ten times this week-end that he needed to be ready at eight am sharp. He kept telling me 'no problem,' and that he'd be there."

"That's okay, Myron. Not your job to get his lazy ass out of the crib. He's a grown man. Ought to be able to wake himself up."

Mazzio pushed the door open and walked into the apartment. Ritchie was snoring away on the living room couch. Mazzio headed into the kitchen, grabbed a bottle of water from the refrigerator, walked over to the couch and poured it on Ritchie's head.

The budding DJ sat up sputtering.

"What the *fuck*, Sal?!"

"You just had your shower, Ritchie. Now, you need to get dressed. You got ten minutes. And dress respectably. Not some rapper getup. This is business."

Silvano parked himself on the edge of a leather easy chair, his hands on his knees. He looked expectantly at Ritchie.

"Well?"

Ritchie groaned and stood up.

"Now you got nine minutes."

To his credit, Ritchie emerged from the back of the condo five minutes later, wearing a pair of jeans and a blue, button-down shirt. His wet hair was neatly combed.

"Jeez, Uncle Sal, I don't know why you're getting so worked up over all of this. It ain't like they're going anywhere."

"Really, Ritchie? You know that for a fact, do you? Lemme tell you something—this was *my* million bucks, I'd be a lot more worked up than you seem to be."

He stood and headed for the door. Ritchie followed.

"You think this kinda shit just *solves itself*? Is that what you think?"

Mazzio shook his head.

As they came through the lobby, Myron tried again to apologize. Mazzio waved him off.

Climbing into the back of the black Chevy Tahoe, Mazzio said to the driver, "You get there one minute late, and this is the last fare Star Studded Limousines ever gets from me. Understood?"

Properly motivated, the driver hit the gas like someone had waived a starter's flag. At five minutes to nine, the car pulled up in front of AA Top Title's office. Ritchie started to get out, but Mazzio held him back.

"Precisely at nine. Not before. Not after. *Precisely*. That's how you start building a reputation, by doing exactly what you say you're gonna do."

A few seconds after 9 am, the solenoid clicked and Ritchie and Silvano entered the lobby. Silvano went directly to the phone and dialed.

"Good morning. How can I help you?" It was the attractive assistant that Silvano had met on Friday.

"It's Silvano Mazzio and Richard Pizzuti. We're here for Ted Hodges," he said. "He's expecting us."

Silence.

Silvano waited a second. "Hello?"

Nothing.

Silvano assumed the connection was lost. He started to re-dial when the door at the back of the lobby opened. It was the assistant. And she looked nervous.

"Mister Mazzio?" she asked.

Silvano walked toward her, gesturing that Ritchie should follow.

"That's me. We met Friday, if you recall. Ted and I set an appointment to follow up this morning. This is Richard Pizzuti. He's got an account here. Maybe you know that."

The woman nodded. Tears were beginning to well up in her eyes, and she was starting to shake like a leaf.

"Hey. *Hey, there.*"

Mazzio reached out and gently held her at arm's length. He tilted his head slightly and leaned down to make eye contact.

"Is everything okay? Where's Ted?" he asked in a low, soothing voice.

The tears were streaming freely now, mascara running. He could feel the terror in the woman's body.

"It's alright. What's your name, hon?"

"Mar...Marcy," she said.

"Okay, Marcy. Everything's gonna be fine. Just tell me where Ted is."

Marcy buried her face in her hands and said, "I don't know. I haven't seen him since Saturday." She was verging on hysteria.

"Since *Saturday*?" Silvano asked, confused.

"Saturday morning," she said. "Ted's my husband. I woke up Saturday morning, and he was gone; his car was gone, his clothes were gone, *everything* was gone. No note, no nothing. He hasn't called me. He sent me *one* text, saying he was safe and for me not to worry. Two sentences. That's it. He didn't even take his hairpiece, which is not like him at all."

She paused for a second and looked at Silvano through her tears. "And I *knew* something was wrong on Friday after you left, and after that asshole Elliot was here, and—"

"—Wait...*who? Who is Elliot?*" Silvano interrupted. "Who is Elliot?"

She looked confused.

"He's a mortgage broker. I thought you *knew* him. I thought you were in on whatever they were doing."

Silvano held up his hands and said, "I don't know anyone named Elliot, hon. I'm here on business that's completely un-related to whatever Ted has going on with Elliot, but I gotta tell you Marcy, it's really important that you help me find Ted. Really important."

He looked at her with all of the kindness he could muster.

"I don't know what he told you, but—"

"—He didn't tell me anything." She interrupted. "He came home completely drunk Friday night, said he didn't want to talk about it, said it would be better for me if we didn't talk about it. He went straight to bed, and when I woke up Saturday, he was gone."

Mazzio fought to remain calm.

"Tell you what, Marcy. Let's you and me go back into the office, and see if we can't figure out where Ted is. I don't think I need to tell you this, because you appear to be a very smart person, but it is imperative that I find your husband. A not-insubstantial amount of money is involved here, and it would be very bad for all concerned if we don't resolve our little issue. You understand?"

She nodded through her tears.

"What are you going to do when you find him?" she asked, trembling.

"*Nothing*, Marcy. Ted will be fine, I promise you. I just want to get this resolved. It's the best thing for Ted and the best thing for you. You gotta trust me on this."

Silvano said this with all the sincerity that he could muster. He looked over at Ritchie, who had taken a seat and was busy playing a game on his cell phone, completely oblivious to what was going on around him.

"We're going back there," he said, nodding toward the back office. "I'll be a while. You stay here."

"Okay," Ritchie said, never looking up.

Idiot.

Two solenoids later and they were in Hodges' office. It looked exactly like Mazzio had expected it to look.

"I don't know what to tell you, Mr. Mazzio. I've already looked through everything in here. There's nothing."

"Can you show me the text he sent, Marcy? Maybe's there's something there."

Marcy left briefly and returned with a brand-new iPhone.

"He has the same model. We got them together, for our anniversary. He's still figuring out how to use it, but he loves texting me. Normally, he texts me all day long, even when we're in the office."

She gave the phone to Silvano. The last text read, *"I'm safe. Don't worry."* That was it. Silvano scrolled up, looking through earlier texts between Hodges and Marcy. Lots of *"I love U"* and *"I love U more"* and crap like that. One particular conversation, however, caught his eye.

"While you're at Publix, we need Diet Coke." Marcy had texted.

"How did U know I was at Publix?" Hodges had texted back.

"Find My iPhone. I set it up on both of them."

"I need to delete that on mine. LOL."

"Marcy," Mazzio said, as he handed her the phone, pointing to the exchange. "Do you know if Ted ever disabled that?"

She squinted at the screen and drew in a quick breath.

"I forgot about this. No. There's no way. I had to set his phone up in the first place. All Ted knows is how to text, how to Google, and how to make calls. He wouldn't even know where to start."

Mazzio leaned back in Ted Hodges' office chair.

"Alright. So, what do you gotta do to find out where Ted's iPhone is right now?"

"I just need to open the app and log on. Give me a second," Marcy said as scrolled through several screens on her device. After a few seconds, she stopped scrolling. She furrowed her brow, looked up at Mazzio and handed him the phone. The screen showed a small phone icon interposed on a street map.

"Where is this?" Mazzio asked, pointing to the screen.

Marcy reached over and pinched the map image, which zoomed out to reveal water on both sides.

Five minutes later, Silvano walked out of the office and across the parking lot toward the Tahoe.

"Hey, Uncle Sal! Where you going? Are we leaving?" Richie called from the front door.

Mazzio ignored him and rapped on the driver's side window.

"You ready to leave, Mister Mazzio?" the driver asked as the window rolled down.

Salvano opened the door and motioned for the driver to get out of the car.

"Change of plans."

CHAPTER 54

Special Agent Harley Slavnick was having a busy Monday. He'd spent the first half of the morning on the phone with the Bureau's Financial Intelligence Center in Washington—commonly referred to as the FIC—getting a crash course in mortgage fraud. What he thought was a big problem was, in fact, a *huge* problem. So huge, in fact, that the FBI wasn't the only governmental agency involved in investigating and prosecuting the crime. There were intra-agency task forces, working groups run by the Department of Justice, special investigatory groups, and more.

"You guys in Florida are ground zero for this stuff. We prosecuted more than a hundred people down there last year alone," an FIC staffer told him. "If it weren't for Florida, California, Nevada and Arizona, we'd be out of business."

Florida. Always Florida. Harley thought.

"Probably the best place to start is with a mortgage fraud dataset targeting package and a SARs run on the title company. What's the name again?"

"Double A Top Title." Harley answered, reading him the tax ID number.

A few hours later, Special Agent Harley Slavnick was giddily awash in data. Because real estate transactions are generally public record, the challenge wasn't necessarily *getting* the information; it was making sense of it. In that regard, the FBI's ability to exploit data was mind-blowing—and rivaled only by the NSA.

He started with the Suspicious Activity Reports—or SARs, as they were known— generated by banks doing business with AA Top Title. SARs are usually triggered by large cash withdrawals or deposits, or wire transfers to sketchy offshore entities.

Harley recalled the scene in *Scarface* in which Tony Montana and his buddies carried duffle bags of cash into a local Miami bank. SARs laws were passed specifically to root out that kind of activity, making it harder for terrorists and money launderers to go undetected. In almost every case of financial malfeasance that Slavnick had ever investigated, a string of SARs was one of the earliest indicators that something wasn't quite right.

It turned that four different banks had filed five separate SARs against AA Top Title in the last year alone. Not good, but in and of itself, not enough to prove anything. Large cash transactions were still legal in the United States. Suspicious maybe, but legal nonetheless. What made a SAR meaningful was a deeper context; other stuff that pointed to fraud.

Slavnick kept digging.

He pulled a list of every mortgage that AA Top Title had administered in the past two years. This was breathtakingly easy through the FIC databases. There were close to six hundred in the system, with a total loan value of almost $300,000,000. Assuming the average borrower put 3% into escrow (a conservative estimate, Slavnick figured), that meant that Double A had acted as custodian to at least nine million dollars over the last twenty-four months.

A big number.

Slavnick had learned in his conversation with the FIC that a high correlation of mortgages to home equity loans—commonly known as HELOCs— was a good indicator of fraud. With that in mind, he began cross-referencing the mortgages he had pulled to every HELOC processed by AA Top Title. He was looking for common borrowers in both groups. After about an hour of data crunching, Slavnick determined that for every three mortgages Double A had managed, two showed matching HELOCs with the same borrower. Almost four hundred people.

That seemed high. Really high.

Slavnick (marveling again at how easy it was) extracted the Social Security numbers attached to the HELOCs and ran a quick credit report on each. Seventy-four came back with 90-day late notices on their loans.

Including Emma Treverrow of 255 Blue Water Lane.

"You've been a naughty boy, Ted Hodges," he said under his breath. This was getting fun, and he was just getting started.

He picked up the phone and dialed a number.

A woman answered.

"Double A Top Title."

"Hello. This is Special Agent Harley Slavnick with the North Miami office of the Federal Bureau of Investigation. I'd like to speak with Ted Hodges, please."

A brief pause as (Harley imagined) the woman's stomach dropped, and then, nervously: "Mister Hodges is not available at the moment. Can I give him a message?"

In an exasperated tone, Harley asked, "Is Mister Hodges not available because he is otherwise engaged, or because he is not in the office? If it's the former, I'd suggest you interrupt him and let him know the FBI is on the phone."

He wasn't exasperated. Actually, he was exhilarated. He always enjoyed this part of being a Federal agent—the ability to instill utter fear in someone simply by stating his name and his employer. Let his Harvard classmates have their little year-end bonuses. He had something far more satisfying: power.

"He...he's not in the office at the moment. Can I give him a message?"

"When is he expected in?"

"I don't know, sir. I haven't heard from him. I'm not even sure he's coming in today," the woman answered.

"Please have him call me as soon as he gets in." Slavnick rattled off his office number, said "thank you," and hung up. He turned to his workstation, googled Hodges's name and business address, and in short order—courtesy of the Federal Bureau of Investigation—had his cell phone number.

Hodges didn't answer.

Slavnick left a message—the exasperation in his voice real this time. It was never a good sign when people ignored the FBI. He considered sending a request up the chain of command to run a trace on Hodges' phone, but he knew that would require a lengthy conversation with Agency legal counsel, and he didn't want to get mired in paperwork and conference calls at this point. He thought about calling Logan Treverrow and letting him know what he'd found— but thought the better of it.

Let it play out a bit more.

He decided that his best course of action was to continue to mine the data and give Hodges a couple of hours to either come to his office or come to his senses. If he didn't hear from him by close of business, he'd pay AA Top Title a little visit.

Hodges smiled.

Federal law enforcement was like a love affair: it was always so much better in person.

CHAPTER 55

I was standing in my storage unit, a small tactical flashlight in my teeth, trying to decide whether to put the painting I was holding on the pile to the left, or the pile to the right.

Right meant gallery. Left meant it continued to live in the storage unit.

I looked over and did a quick count of the pieces in the pile on the right. When it comes to gallery walls, I'm partial to white space, so I was being careful not to take too much stuff. The exhibition was scheduled to run for at least a month; if it went well and some pieces sold, I could always pull something else out of the unit.

I was looking forward to the opening on Friday. Invitations had gone out the week before, and from what the gallery owner was telling me, attendance was going to be strong. I had done my part, passing out invitations to the artsy types frequenting Casa Playa's—who were becoming increasingly commonplace, I'd noticed. The evening before, I'd even met a couple from Palm Beach—Vadik and Rheese—who told me that everyone on the Island was "buzzing about Casa Playa's".

Right.

Palm Beachers only leave Palm Beach if the town is on fire—and they'd stop at Buccan on the way out to grab a quick bite. The idea that they'd eat somewhere off the Island is anathema.

Anyway, I gave Rheese and Vadik an invitation, too. Rheese had mentioned that they were in the process of opening a hotel, and I figured it couldn't hurt.

Hotel lobbies have a lot of wall space.

I added two more pieces to the gallery pile and randomly decided I had the perfect number for paintings for an art opening. I walked out to my Bronco and grabbed an oversized roll of postal wrapping paper. I cut two five-foot pieces, laid them crossways on the floor of the unit, plopped half the stack of paintings in the middle, and wrapped it up. I repeated the process with the remaining stack, loaded the two packages into the truck, and headed toward Palm Beach.

I still needed to name, tag and price each painting, and the gallery had a large workspace in the back—which was kept at a constant and artwork-friendly 72º—that I could use. Anything was preferable to another minute in my mini-storage unit.

Two hours later, I was done, leaving me with plenty of time to do some recon work—courtesy of Burrell Malin's lost phone.

I'll never understand the faith that people put into the almighty cellphone. By training and inclination, I have a deep mistrust of technology. Not only can technology be hacked or lost, it can be turned against you without your knowledge. The willingness to let a wireless company track your every movement simply to make it easier to find an Applebee's is beyond me.

Burrell, apparently, hadn't gotten the memo about never leaving anything on a cellphone that you wouldn't want everyone to see—friend and enemy alike. From what I could tell, Burrell either didn't know how or didn't care to delete *anything*. His browser history, his texts, his inbox—even his Google Maps searches—had at least two years' worth of history.

Among the useful stuff I found on Burrell's cellphone:

A shopping list of arson supplies (helpfully titled "Arson Stuff")…An endless text exchange with someone named Sasha regarding arson timetables, along with an ongoing narrative of everything he'd bought on his "Arson Stuff" shopping list… A series of arcane Google searches on subjects ranging from "arson accelerants" to local fireworks stands.

And this was just the useful stuff—the not-so-useful stuff ranged from deviant to deranged.

Identifying the target homes was simply a matter of filtering Malin's inbox to include only Modern Properties-related correspondence—and doing the same thing with his texts. I found five different homes mentioned in either an email or text exchange, each with the owner's name and an address. I took a quick look at his Google Maps searches, and—sure enough—he'd run all of them. The homes were within a ten- or fifteen-mile radius in Palm Beach county, split between swanky neighborhoods in towns like Boca Raton, Delray Beach and Ocean Ridge.

The only thing I couldn't find was an actual *schedule*. There was nothing on his device that told me when—or where—all of this was going to start, other than the timetable being "moved up." Which probably meant this week.

At this point you may be wondering whether I felt guilty looking through the seedy details of Burrell Malin's digital life.

Nope. Not in the least.

As far as I was concerned, Burrell Malin had given up all rights when he threatened my family. He was part of a criminal enterprise that had stolen Emma's identity and committed fraud in her name. He was a budding arsonist who, if everything went according to plan, would be adding to the homeless population in the next couple of weeks. On top of that, he was an idiot.

And idiots deserve what they get.

I took me a little less than an hour to case every house on the list. A couple of the homes were in gated communities, but Burrell had thoughtfully included the appropriate key codes in his Notes app. I did a slow drive-by at each address, looking for anything out of the ordinary. In those neighborhoods, anything other than a BMW or Lexus parked in the driveway qualified as out of the ordinary.

I saw nothing to give me pause. No pickup trucks, or panel vans. No broken-down Oldsmobiles. Every home looked calm, peaceful, manicured, and ordinary.

Maybe the explosion pushed the timetable back a couple of days, I thought.

Afterwards, I swung by the offices of Modern Properties, Inc., which were located in the kind of low-rent office building one associates with businesses that are just barely in business. The company was on the second floor, at the end of a dingy hallway. No name; just a suite number.

I tried the door, but it was locked. I rang the buzzer and waited.

Still nothing.

I looked at my watch.

It was 4:30 pm. Still in the heart of the business day. I assumed that Becker had come in early, gotten his wire transfer, and cleaned out the place. I doubted he'd ever be back.

As I walked to my car, I thought back to my time in Iraq. When we'd get hold of an insurgent's cell phone, one of the first things we'd do would be to call every number in the memory. We wouldn't say anything; we'd just dial and see what happened. Usually, we'd get nothing. But occasionally, we'd make something happen. I wondered what Becker would do if I called *him* on Burrell's phone. Would he answer it?

Would he panic?

I decided to find out.

CHAPTER 56

"**P**ut everything in the Rover," Elliot Becker ordered. "We'll park it in the garage when we get there and unload the stuff with the door closed. That oughta keep the neighbors from snooping."

They were standing in Burrell Malin's living room, looking over a pile of bags, cans, boxes and loose items.

"Where we going?" Burrell asked.

"Boca. We're gonna start out with Joanne's house."

"Why Boca?" Malin asked.

"I figure we might as well go big right out of the box."

Malin said nothing.

Becker said, "So, you need to come up with a reason to get her and her old man out of the house tomorrow, Sasha. Give them a gift certificate to Olive Garden. They got Olive Gardens in Boca?"

Sasha said, "Probably not."

"Alright. Then Houston's or something."

Sasha nodded.

"Alright," he said, looking at her. "Sasha, you'll follow us in Burrell's car. Once we've got everything unloaded, you can take off."

"I bought enough stuff for five houses," Malin said. "Want to leave some of it here?"

"Nah, pack it all up," Becker answered. "I don't wanna find myself in a position where we need more of something and we don't have it. What we don't use tomorrow, we'll pack up in a box and store it over at Hodges' place. He's got room."

Elliot made a mental note to call Hodges—again. Ted had clearly been dodging him, but Becker knew that eventually, he would crack and answer the phone. He was too weak-willed not to. In the meantime, Sasha would have to pitch in with the loading and unloading, since he and Burrell only had two good hands between them.

Using his foot, pointed to a large square can. "What's that?" he asked.

Burrell hadn't heard him, so Becker nudged him and asked again.

"Acetone," Malin said. "You pour it over the stuff you want to light up first. Burns real fast and real hot, so that other stuff —walls, furniture—catches fire faster. They call it an accelerant."

Becker smirked.

"See Burrell? You know more about this shit than you thought you did."

Malin nodded morosely.

"Anything more we gotta add to this stuff?" Becker asked.

Malin thought about it for a moment and said, "All my flash powder's gone, so we probably ought to stop by a couple of those fireworks shops and pick up some Roman Candles or stuff like that. We'll need them for initiators."

"Accelerants. Initiators. I'm telling you, Burrell, you got a real future in the arson business. No problem. I'll pick it up tomorrow morning."

Becker paused for a second and added, "One thing I see missing in all of this is a *gun.* You got a gun, Burrell?

Burrell looked at him, a little surprised.

"A gun? Like a pistol?"

"Yeah, like a pistol," Becker answered. "Given everything, I'd feel a lot more comfortable if I had a gun. So—you got one?"

Burrell sighed. "Yeah. I've got one. Walther PPK. Holds six rounds plus one in the chamber."

"Is it easy to use?"

"It don't get any easier."

"Good. Go grab it. I'm gonna need a quick run-thorough, though. I'm no gunslinger to start with, and I only got the one good hand."

Burrell headed toward the back bedroom.

"Sasha, get moving," Becker ordered as he fished his phone out of his pocket. "I gotta make a quick call." He walked toward the kitchen. His head and his hand were throbbing. The ER doctor had told him that he'd need to take it easy for at least two weeks; give his body time to heal and adjust. Which wasn't this.

Becker scrolled through his contacts and found Vassili Dmitrievich's cell number. The previous evening, he'd had an epiphany; a way to transform this debacle into a coup de grace. Every problem solved in a single, fiery instant.

All he had to do was to get Vassili Dmitrievich to go along.

His thumb was poised to dial Vassili when the phone rang. Becker watched as the screen shifted to display the incoming call information.

It was Burrell Malin.

CHAPTER 57

*H*OT NURSES #7 - *Tight teen nurses are eager to do any-thing help make their patients feel better! (95 minutes / $8.99).*

DESPERATELY HORNY HOUSWIVES - Whether it's her neigh-bor, the cable guy, or some random guy off the street, this smoking hot MILF has only one thing in mind! (120 minutes / $9.99).

Ted Hodges couldn't decide. The nurse video was less ex-pensive, but the MILF selection seemed to offer better value. He used the remote control to scroll through other "Adult Se-lections" available on his in-room On Demand entertainment system, looking for anything to take his mind off his present circumstance.

For the last two days, he'd been hiding away in the Key West Inn, which, oddly enough, was not located in Key West. It was in Key Largo, just off US 1, at Mile Marker 100. The Key West Inn was neither Key West-ish, nor inn-like. It was a four-story, cinderblock affair with nondescript rooms that opened to an outside walkway overlooking a parking lot large enough to accommodate tractor-trailer trucks. Hodges' room was three doors down from the ice and soda vending machines on the second floor.

If he opened the curtains, he could look out the window and see his Camry, parked at the back of the lot, "DICKHEAD" still visible on the driver's side door. From Hogs & Honeys, he'd driven straight to a CVS drugstore, where he'd purchased a large bottle of fingernail polish remover and a roll of paper towels. He'd pulled the car behind the store and went to work on the lettering, promptly taking off most of the door's paint. "DICKHEAD" however, had stayed stubbornly in place.

Wracked with indecision, he'd driven north for an hour until, overcome with exhaustion, he pulled into the parking lot of the first hotel he saw. He needed eight hours of sleep and sanctuary, and for $79 a night, the Key West Inn promised both.

Now, sitting in his room, he debated sending Marcy another text. He'd sent one early on Sunday afternoon, assuring her that he was safe and that she shouldn't worry; he wasn't really sure what he'd say in follow up:

Don't worry. I'm humiliated?

Or:

Don't worry. They painted DICKHEAD on my car?

The room was littered with wrappers and bags from fast-food places up and down US1. After Hogs & Honeys, he had no interest in actually entering a bar or restaurant of any kind. He took advantage of the Key West Inn's free breakfast buffet each morning, and only left the property to run to a drive-through for lunch and dinner. He drove straight back to the hotel, consuming double cheeseburgers and chalupas to an unending stream of hotel-quality in-room porn. He figured that by now, his OnDemand bill was about equal to his room charge.

He didn't know what his next move was, but at eighty dollars a day, he had plenty of time to figure it out. He could hunker down here for weeks; for months, if it came to that. He clicked ORDER on *Hot Nurses #7*, rooted through a stray Taco Bell bag, and pulled out a cold Dorito's Cool Ranch Taco Supreme. Just as he was settling back on the bed, he heard a sharp clacking on the front window of his room.

He came to his feet in a panic, his taco spilling onto the floor. He waited a second. The clacking started again. He couldn't see who was out there, because he'd drawn the curtains when he'd come back from his noontime Taco Bell run. It sounded like someone was rapping something metal–a set of car keys, maybe—against the glass. The was a pause and the noise started again.

Whoever is was tapped out *Shave and a Haircut*. Becker turned off the beside light (a useless gesture, since it was three in the afternoon) and idled cautiously toward the window. He edged himself against the doorframe, and slowly pulled the curtain aside.

Standing there was Silvano Mazzio.

Mazzio leaned slightly to the right toward the window, peered inside and made eye contact with Hodges. He tapped on the window again—with the biggest handgun Hodges had ever seen. He shrugged fatalistically and pointed the gun directly at Hodges.

He mouthed, "Open up."

CHAPTER 58

V adik took a sip of strip club coffee as he finished his notations on the previous evening's cash reconciliation form. All in, the Cougar Club's register drawers were less than $100 short on total receipts of a $6,825.

Not bad for a Monday night, considering the club's reliance on independent contractors, i.e. strippers. When Vadik had taken over as General Manager of the Cougar Club, the drawers had been short hundreds—even thousands—of dollars. Every single night.

Not anymore.

He'd fired two bartenders and a DJ his first day on the job, and beat the shit out of a bouncer who was dealing ketomine in the bathroom. He needed to set new standards, and the best way to do that was to make public examples out of people who didn't meet those standards. One of the surviving cocktail waitresses took to calling him "Dalton"—an homage Patrick Swayze's character in *Roadhouse*. Vadik didn't take offense.

He loved *Roadhouse*.

He did a quick final count of the previous night's cash, zipped it up in a deposit bag, and headed down the hall to Vassili's office. It was 9:00 am, and the club was blessedly quiet.

Vassili was sitting at his desk drinking an Ultimat screwdriver, while he scanned an online edition of Pravda on his desktop computer. He glanced up at Vadik and asked, "How was it?" as he lit a cigarette.

"Little over sixty-eight hundred," Vadik answered, as he tossed the deposit bag and register tapes on Vassili's desk. He was being careful to behave exactly as he did every Tuesday morning at the Cougar Club. Vassili offered him a cigarette, and as usual, he politely declined.

"Always with the healthy choices, Vadikim. You will live to be a hundred."

Vadik smiled the same smile he smiled every Tuesday at this joke, as he pulled up a seat. Vassili never came to the club on Mondays, so Tuesday mornings had become their time to catch up and discuss business.

"I heard there were problems with a motorcycle club Saturday night. Anything I should know about this?" Vassili asked.

"I am sure for those bikers, Saturday night was problem. For club? Not a problem." Vadik said, dismissively. "They will not be back to Cougar Club anytime soon."

"You're not anticipating problem with police?"

"No, Vassili. I am not anticipating problems with police. These are not types to go to police to fight their fights for them."

"Okay, Vadik." Vassili said, his hands up in placating manner. "Just making sure."

Vadik pulled a list of items he needed to go over, as Vassili did the same. For the next hour, the two stuck to the business of the Cougar Club: food and beverage orders, how the new valet parking company was working out, repairs to the sound system, and the same list of grievances the dancers bitched about every week—which Vadik and Vassili ignored every week.

Vassili said, "If this place is such a sweatshop, fucking dancers can go to Cheetah for all I care. There is always another dancer who needs a shift."

Vadik looked at his watch. "Speaking of which, it's ten am. Let's go meet some."

With that, both men stood and headed out of Vassili's office and into the club's main room. Tuesday mornings were reserved for dancer auditions. Unlike other clubs, which allowed aspiring entertainers to audition during regular hours, Vassili had long maintained that the real test of a stripper was how well she performed stone cold sober in an empty room.

Vadik looked at his list.

"We have three entertainers trying out this morning. One from Scores in New York City—or so she says—one from Rachel's down in Hollywood, and one rookie."

The two men took a seat at a table next to the main stage. Vadik was uncomfortable with the entrance to the club being at his back, but there was nothing he could do about it—other than keeping an eye on the mirrored wall across the stage.

It was Vassili's policy to hold auditions with the house lights on and no choice in music—just a single downtempo tune by Portishead—possibly the most depressing group in the history of contemporary music.

"Levels out the playing field," he was fond of saying.

As the first dancer climber onto the stage, Vassili leaned over and said to Vadik, "Remind me to talk to you about Elliot Becker. I got a call from him yesterday, and there's something I need you to do later."

Vadik didn't know what that meant, but he felt reasonably sure that Vassili wouldn't try to have him killed before he did whatever Vassili needed him to do. Which meant he didn't need to kill Vassili. Not yet, anyway. For the moment, he could relax.

If only slightly.

CHAPTER 59

Silvano Mazzio signaled that he'd like a warm up for his coffee.

"That's two cups over your two-cup limit, Mister Mazzio," his server admonished gently.

"I know, Elaine. Thanks for looking out for me." Silvano said. "I had a pretty hectic day yesterday and didn't get much in the way of sleep last night. Just trying to get a move on this morning."

"You know, Mister Mazzio, there's no law that says you can't head right back to your room, draw the blackout shades, and crawl in bed for a couple of hours," she said. "This is a resort, after all. A little vacation is to be expected."

Mazzio snorted. "Don't tempt me."

He was exhausted.

In the last twenty-four hours, he'd driven to Key Largo and back, kidnapped and imprisoned Ted Hodges, and still managed to meet his spa crush Kathleen for a nightcap at Bice. He'd slept fitfully and awakened early. He took a two-mile walk on the beach to clear his head and spent the rest of the morning hunched over a laptop in his room, navigating between an Excel spreadsheet and five different offshore banking sites he kept on hand for occasions just like this.

Finally, at 10:15, he'd headed down to the dining room for a late breakfast. He didn't tell Elaine that he'd also had two cups of coffee sent up to his room. He'd need the boost, because today was going to be busy.

And very likely unpleasant.

Try as he might, Silvano couldn't come up with a word or phrase that adequately described the goat rodeo that Hodges and his little pal Elliot Becker had gotten themselves into. And with whom. The day before, speaking to Hodges' wife Marcy, Silvano had assured her that his business was completely unrelated to whatever it was Hodges had going on with Becker. Turns out that wasn't the case. Not by a longshot.

Mazzio had taken Marcy's iPhone along with him when he'd commandeered the Tahoe, and the thing had zeroed in on Hodges' device like it was a fucking homing pigeon. Amazing. He made a mental note to call his broker Monday and short Blackberry.

He found Hodges holed up in a cheap roadside hotel in Key Largo. Before he'd left AA Topic Title's offices, Mazzio had asked Marcy what kind of car Ted drove—and sure enough—a beat up red Toyota Camry was parked in the back of the hotel lot. Someone had written DICKHEAD on the driver's side door with a Sharpie.

Mazzio pulled the Tahoe up to the entrance, went in and told the desk clerk that some asshole in a red Camry with DICKHEAD written on it had hit his car in the parking lot of the 7/11 down the road. The clerk wanted no part of a possible confrontation.

"The guy's in room 204. Just please take it outside."

As soon as he saw the gun, Hodges had folded and opened the door. Walking in, Mazzio took note of the food wrappers and crushed tacos.

"Looks like you've already eaten, Ted. That's good. We won't have to stop. You gotta make a pee-pee before we get on the road?"

Hodges shook his head as he silently shoved his belongings into a beat up roll-on suitcase.

"Okay. Go pay your bill. I'll meet you out front."

Five minutes later, Hodges exited the lobby tugging his bag behind him. Mazzio popped the lift gate and watched through the rearview mirror as Hodges loaded his luggage into the back.

"You got anything in your car you need to get, Ted?"

"No, I have everything," Hodges said in a low, defeated voice.

"You sit in the back seat. Passenger side. And don't forget to buckle up. These fucking drivers are crazy down here."

The ride back had been illuminating, to say the least. Once Hodges got talking, it was everything Mazzio could do to get him to shut up once in a while so he could process what he was hearing. Mazzio had seen this type of thing before; some guy who's been living a double life for so long that when the realization comes that it's over, that there's no more reason to lie, he can't put a cork in it. He spills *everything*—even shit you don't wanna hear.

That was Hodges on the drive back: Providing detailed breakdowns of every scam he and Becker had been running, down to the dollar...Hodges' suspicions that Becker was secretly screwing him over...How *he* was secretly screwing Becker over...The growing lack of intimacy in his marriage, and how a blowjob from a stripper named Sasha had marked the beginning of his long fall from grace.

Jesus.

"A couple of things, Ted. Go back to Ritchie's escrow account. How much did you say was in there last Friday when you did the wire transfer to your buddy Elliot?"

Hodges answered, "Four hundred and forty-three thousand dollars. Exactly."

"And that's what you wired to Becker?"

"Except for a hundred dollars. I left that in the account to keep it open." Hodges said, almost giddily.

"And how much you got in that money market account of yours? The money you skimmed behind Becker's back?" Mazzio asked.

"Three hundred thousand and change."

Mazzio did the math.

"That puts you about two-hundred and fifty thousand short, Ted. With interest, closer to four-hundred thousand. Any ideas on making up the difference?"

For a few blessed seconds, there was silence, as Hodges thought about it.

"Vassili Dmitrievich," he said.

"The Russian you told me about? The guy your idiot friend borrowed all the money from?" Mazzio asked.

He watched as Hodges nodded in the rearview mirror.

"I'm sure he's got it. We've already paid him more than a half-million dollars out of the Pizzuti account."

Mazzio thought about his options. None of them were good. But a quarter of a million dollars wasn't something you just wrote off. Especially to a Russian gangster and two half-assed con men. There was a principle at stake here; reputations to consider.

Fuck.

"Alright," he sighed. "Where can I find him?"

"He owns a nightclub up in West Palm. Elliot says he's always there."

"A nightclub. You know the name of the place?" Silvano asked.

"It's called The Cougar Club."

Mazzio sighed again.

The Cougar Club.

Of course.

He'd cross that bridge when he came to it. The first order of business was to get Ted Hodges stashed away safely for a couple of days.

After the little Keys adventure, Mazzio didn't trust Hodges as far as he could throw him. A little time on his own to reflect what he'd admitted to Mazzio, and it was entirely possible that Hodges would try to make another break for it. He pulled out his Blackberry and dialed a number.

"Tower One Condominium. This is Myron."

"Hey, Myron. Silvano Mazzio. I got a quick question for you."

"Sure thing, Mister Mazzio."

"Is the unit next to Ritchie's still vacant?" Silvano asked.

"Yep. The sales people use it during the day as a model unit."

Which meant it was both vacant *and* fully furnished. Perfect.

"Great. I'm gonna need you to leave me a key at the front desk for that unit, and a note to the sales folks that there are some repairs going on tomorrow, and that it's off limits. Got it?"

Ted didn't even pause. "Sure thing, Mr. Mazzio. The key will be here."

An hour and a half later, Silvano had Hodges handcuffed to the outflow pipe of the bidet in the master bathroom of Tower One Sales Model Unit A.

"If you lean over a little bit, Counselor, you can see the TV there in the bedroom. I'll even give you the remote. And you got all your favorite foods right here..." On the way into West Palm, Mazzio had stopped at a Turnpike rest stop and stocked up on Burger King.

"...and Ritchie will come and check on you every couple of hours and cut you loose to take a leak and whatnot."

He paused and looked Hodges in the eye. "But the best thing you can do, Ted, is sit tight, don't make any trouble, and keep your trap shut."

Mazzio made Hodges call his wife at home and tell her that he was back in town and not to worry; that Silvano was taking care of him, and that he'd be home in the next day or so. When he finished the call, Mazzio put both of the Hodges family phones on the kitchen counter. He didn't need anyone tracking *him*.

"There you go, Ted. Your iPhones have found one another. Together at last."

In the now-empty Four Seasons dining room, Mazzio took a last sip of coffee and mentally ran down a checklist of everything he had put in place, and everything he had to do today. He figured the Cougar Club wouldn't open until sometime around noon.

He decided to take Elaine's advice and get a couple of hours of sleep. He didn't know if it was physically possible to fall asleep on six cups of Four Seasons coffee, but he was going to try.

He probably wasn't going to get another shot at sleep for a while.

If ever.

CHAPTER 60

When an August swell happens, everything else takes a back seat. A rare high pressure system settles on the east side of the Bahamas Bank, and the southeast trade winds push a groundswell over sandbars that have had a chance to rest and replenish through the mid-summer doldrums. For a day or two, it looks like Malibu. But it's rare—which was why I spent most of Tuesday morning in the water. Outside of a hurricane, this was likely the last decent swell we'd see until a September Nor'easter. The lineup was predictably heavy; I could sit on my board and count the number of sick days that had been called in that morning.

It started to blow out a little around 11 am, so I packed up my gear, jumped in the Bronco and headed up to the gallery. I wanted to get the bulk of my paintings hung early in the week so I could focus on my increasingly interesting day job as secret agent man.

The calls to Becker's phone had gone pretty much the way I thought they would:

"Who is this?"

"Where did you get this number?"

"Where did you get this phone?"

"I don't know who you think you are, but you're making a

big mistake, my friend."

"WHO THE FUCK IS THIS?!"

I said nothing; just let him babble. My thinking was that I'd either drive him into action, or force him to abandon the whole idea out of sheer paranoia. Either outcome was fine with me: If he sped up his timetable, I'd be there. If he took off, I'd call Slavnick and tell him that I had visited AA Top Title the previous week and overheard a heated discusion between Hodges and some guy with a bum hand that sounded "suspicious."

Which was technically the truth—and probably just enough to get Harley Slavnick and his Federal Bureau of Investigation boys all tangled up in things. It occurred to me that this was probably the thing I should do anyway, but that didn't seem nearly as interesting as chasing down this stuff myself.

On that score, Emma was probably half right: I wouldn't say I was bored, but I wasn't going to pass up a little August action if it came my way.

Life's short. You've got to jump in when you can.

By three in the afternoon, I had most of the gallery walls done. The owner—a hipster 40-something named Campbell whose grandparents were founding members of the Everglades Club—was arguing mildly with me over where to put the biggest canvas in the collection. Campbell was smart and rebellious, had impeccable taste and was fun to argue with.

She wanted the painting to sit on the floor, leaning against the wall, like it was in some SoHo lot.

I said, "Why don't we just lay it flat on the floor and let everyone walk on it? We can claim that I'm part of the Jackson Pollack school of abstract expressionist drip painting."

She ignored me.

"And how about I work on it during the exhibition, like it's performance art? I can get drunk and go outside and wreck my

Bronco."

She kept ignoring me.

"My friend Kathleen called," she said as she propped the big canvas against a wall. "She's coming Friday and wants to interview you for a piece she's doing for that new Island magazine," she said.

"What new Island magazine? Who's Kathleen? I asked, conceding the argument over the canvas placement.

"I forget the name of the magazine, but she did a review of Casa Playa's last month. They ran it. She gave you four stars, incidentally. You remember her? Blonde, mid-fifties? Great style? Very WASPY?"

"Sort of," I said. "Is four stars the tops, or was she holding back?"

"I think five's tops. Anyway, hunt her down on Friday and be charming. She's bringing a date. Be nice to him, too."

"Fine," I said. "Kathleen something plus one. Noted."

I looked at my watch. It was getting toward three o'clock, and I wanted to do another run-by of the houses on Malin's hit list.

"I've gotta bounce," I told Campbell. "We're good here?"

She waved without looking at me, her attention fixated on the details of a painting on the north wall of the gallery. "See you tomorrow, Jackson."

I was walking out when my phone rang. It was Emma.

"What's going on, Aquaman?" she asked.

"Nothing much. Finishing up stuff at the gallery," I answered in my best superhero-artist voice.

"What's happening with our favorite loan sharks?"

"I'll know more in a little bit. I'm getting ready to check out the houses."

"I know I've asked this before," Emma said, "but what happens if you find them? Do you have plan?"

"I have a framework of a plan," I answered. "Which is all I need."

"Which means that your plan is that you're improvising," Emma said.

"Nope, not at all. It means that I'm smart enough to know that the dynamics of the environment will define the tactics."

"Sounds like the kind of double-speak they teach you in War College."

I find people who are much smarter than me to be incredibly frustrating.

"I'll give you a call if I see anything interesting."

"Okay. I love you."

"I love you, too."

I jumped in my Bronco and pointed it south.

CHAPTER 61

E mma was hanging up the phone as Constance walked into the section of theatre balcony that served as her office. What she wouldn't give sometimes for four walls and a door.

"So, how's Logan?" she asked.

"How do you know that was Logan?" Emma asked.

"Who else would you tell that you loved them? Besides me?"

Emma smiled.

"Logan's fine. Surfing. Getting ready for the opening Friday."

"Has he heard anything from the FBI guy yet?"

This was sticky. Between his illegal recording, breaking and entering, and stolen cell phone, Emma was pretty sure that Logan had broken more laws than Elliot Becker and Ted Hodges combined. She loved Constance, but telling her anything was akin to putting up a billboard. There was a reason that Constance was in advertising.

"He didn't mention it, so I'm assuming not. But with Logan, you never know."

"Logan gave you one of the guy's cards last week. I loaded it into your contacts yesterday. Special Agent Harley Slavnick.

Why don't you give him a call yourself? After all, it's your name on that loan. Not Logan's."

Emma said, "Yeah, I know, but this is actually the kind of thing Logan's really good at. The FBI only got involved in the first place because one of the agents is a friend of Logan's from the Navy. I think for now, I'm going to take a back seat."

Constance nodded and said, "Okay. Suit yourself. In the meantime, we have the new spots for Athletica spooled up in the media room. Thought you might want to take a look."

"Okay. I'll be down in a few."

Emma thought about what Constance had said.

What can it hurt? I won't tell him anything. I'll tell him I'm just following up.

She scrolled through her contacts and dialed.

"Federal Bureau of Investigation, Miami Division."

"Agent Slavnick, please."

"Agent Slavnick is out of the office. Can I give him a message, or would you like to be connected to his voicemail?"

"That would be fine," Emma answered. "I'll just leave him a message."

"Thank you. I'll connect you."

"This is Special Agent Harley M. Slavnick with the FBI's Miami Division. I'm not able to take your call at the moment, but if you leave me a detailed message along with the time that you called, I *will* return your call."

It sounded more like a threat than a promise. The line beeped.

"Hi, Agent Slavnick. This is, um… Emma Treverrow…Logan Treverrow's wife—or, ex-wife, I guess. I'm calling to, um…"

She was tongue tied. *What was it that she was going to say?*

Why was she so nervous?

"I was calling to check in on your, um…"

She stopped. *What was she doing?* She'd dropped this problem in Logan's lap because she knew he would know what to do —or figure it out along the way. That's what Logan did best.

The least she could do was let him deal with it the way he saw fit.

Emma put the phone back in its cradle and headed down the indoor hill to the media room.

CHAPTER 62

Special Agent Harley Slavnick tried the door to AA Top Title.

It was locked. He punched the button to the right, and a few seconds later a solenoid tripped. He entered the firm's lobby, taking in details as he proceeded to reception desk and dialed extension 115, per the laminated sign's instructions.

"How may I help you?" asked a female voice.

"This is Special Agent Slavnick from the Federal Bureau of Investigation. Are you the person with whom I spoke yesterday?"

Silence and then a meek, "Yes...sir."

"I am here to speak to Ted Hodges. Is he in the office, or are you going to tell me again that he is not available?"

"Sir, if you'll wait just one minute, I'll come out and meet you in the lobby."

"Fine," Harley said.

As he waited, Slavnick did a slow pirouette, noting the aging furniture and cheap artwork. For a firm with clients that routinely bought and sold homes worth a half-million dollars, Hodges didn't seem too concerned with keeping up appearances. Slavnick heard the buzz of a magnetic lock opening somewhere in the back office, followed a few seconds later by another buzz at the door that opened into the lobby. A frightened-looking middle-aged brunette said, "Agent Slavnick?"

"Yes," Slavnick said, as he opened his credential wallet and held it up for her inspection. He loved doing that.

She squinted at it briefly and cleared her throat.

"I'm sorry sir, but Mister Hodges is not here. We haven't seen him all week. Normally he's the first one here on Monday mornings—well, along with his wife—"

"—wait. His *wife* works here as well?" Slavnick interrupted.

"Yes, sir. Marcy."

"I'd like to speak with her, then. Now, please."

The woman shifted uncomfortably. "I'm afraid she isn't here, either. She came in yesterday, but left around noon and never came back. She seemed really upset."

Slavnick looked at her closely and asked, "Where do you think she went? And I didn't get your name, Miss…?"

"Webster. Susan Webster. I work in admin here. Anyway, I don't really know where she would have gone, other than home. She was crying and everything. I know when I feel like that, all I want to do is go home and crawl in bed."

Slavnick scrolled through his phone, stopping on an address in his contacts. He held it up to Susan Webster.

"Is that the Hodges' correct home address?"

The woman squinted at the device and nodded uncertainly. "I think so. It looks right to me."

"Alright," Slavnick said. "Thank you for your help."

He turned to leave, stopped and turned back to the woman. He handed her a business card. "If either of them show up at the office, please give me a call immediately. My cell number is on the card."

She just looked at him and said quietly, "Okay. Sir."

Slavnick walked out and headed out to his government-issued Chevy Malibu, relishing the thought of a house call.

CHAPTER 63

Silvano Mazzio let the Tahoe idle in the nearly-empty Cougar Club parking lot as he finished up his phone call with Kathleen.

"By the way, thanks for the nightcap, Silvano. You really didn't have to. You looked exhausted."

Mazzio replied, "Yesterday was a really long day, I'll admit. But it was nice way to end it. Don't worry, I'll be rested up for Friday."

"Good. I'm looking forward to it. You'll love Campbell, the gallery owner. She's a stitch."

A stitch.

Another WASP phrase, he assumed. Dating Kathleen was like entering entirely new world.

"Any friend of yours is a friend of mine," Silvano said, as he glanced at his watch.

Time to get to work.

"So, I'm at my appointment. Can I call you later?"

"Sure," Kathleen said. "Have a good day."

That wasn't going to happen, he was certain.

"Thanks. You, too."

It was a little after three in the afternoon and staffers were clearing the lunchtime buffet. Silvano moved across the club toward what had become his regular booth. He scanned the place for Vadik, figuring he had a better shot of getting to the owner through the crazed Russian bouncer than by asking a hostess or bartender.

A few minutes after he was seated, Vadik emerged from the double doors at the back of club, engrossed in conversation on his cell phone. He walked with purpose, his head down as he crossed behind the bar. Silvano waved his server over.

"Jeannie, right?" he asked.

"Good memory, hon," she said, smiling. "What can I getcha?"

"Vodka tonic. And if you can send Vadik over, I'd appreciate it."

Jeannie's eyebrows arched. "Is everything okay? You're not still mad about the steak sauce thing, are you? I'm sorr—"

"—everything's fine, Jeannie. Vadik is an old friend, that's all. Just tell him it's Sal." He smiled to reassure her.

"Oookay," she said uncertainly. "I'll get your drink and tell him you're here."

She walked off toward the bar.

Onstage, a bored-looking blonde kicked off the first of her three-song set with *Tainted Love*. Mazzio watched with mild interest as she swung herself into a tight spin on the pole. Beyond the stage, he could see Jeannie talking to Vadik, who still had the phone to his ear. She pointed in Silvano's direction.

Mazzio leaned back in the booth and considered how best to open the conversation with Vadik as he watched the blonde segue from *Tainted Love* to *Closer*, by Nine Inch Nails. *That is one unhappy stripper*, he thought.

Vadik walked up, his normally-placid features knotted in concern or anger. Silvano couldn't tell which.

"Dressed casually today, Sal. I like the Yacht-Master. Very nice."

"Hi, Vadik. Thanks for coming over."

Silvano extended his hand and Vadik shook it. The bouncer was clearly distracted by something; maybe it was call he'd just finished.

"What can I do for you?" Vadik asked as he sat down.

Jeannie approached the booth and set down Silvano's drink, along with a glass of ice water for Vadik. The two remained silent until she left.

"I got a bit of a favor that I wanted to ask you, Vadik. I'm a little uncomfortable about all this, and I don't want to put you in an awkward position, but I don't see no other way at the moment."

Vadik waved his hand dismissively. "What can I do for you, Sal?"

Silvano paused a second and said, "I need to speak with your boss. I believe his name is Vassili Dmitrievich. I have a certain business issue that's come up, and I was given his name by an associate who told me he might be in a positon to help with this particular problem."

Vadik frowned. "Vassili? You want to speak to Vassili?"

Silvano nodded. "Not want to. *Need to.*"

The two men looked at one another for a moment until Vadik said, "And that is all you're going to tell me?"

"For now, I think that's best. I got no problem with you being part of the conversation, but I imagine that will be Mister Dmitrievich's call."

Vadik shifted his gaze from Silvano to his glass of ice water. He tapped his fingers lightly on the table as he considered the request. The tapping stopped, he looked up and said, "Please wait here, Sal. I'll see if Vassili is available."

CHAPTER 64

What the fuck is this about? Vadik thought, as he walked across the main room of the Cougar Club and toward the back offices. This was the last thing he needed—especially given the phone call he'd just finished.

Vassili had apparently found someone stupid enough to try and kill him.

He'd been in the kitchen trying to get the buffet put away when he'd gotten an encoded text on his BlackPhone.

A contract on you has been accepted. $250,000. Half in advance. Terms specific to time and location. Details to follow if possible, but no guarantees. Watch your six.

He had to admire Vassili.

$250,000 was about five times the going rate for high-end wet work in South Florida, which probably meant that Vassili had to keep upping the ante until someone bit. Exiting the kitchen, he had dialed a number over his secure voice platform.

"What else do you know?" he'd asked.

"Everything I know was in the text. I am trying to get more information, but nothing is forthcoming right now. I will not tell you to be patient, because for all I know, the operation may already be staged."

"Any thoughts on the taker?"

There was a brief silence.

"Kramnik, maybe? Yevgeny Kramnik? You remember him? Staff Seargent? We had him with us in 2003 or 2004…what the fuck was the name of that shithole town in the Caucuses?"

"Shali." Vadik answered. "It was Shali. 2003. Yes, I remember him. Very capable killer."

"And he's here now. Works for that cheap fuck Antonin Bodelenko, which means he needs the money. So—maybe him. But that is pure speculation, Vadik."

"Alright. I appreciate your help. Keep me apprised of what you learn."

His contact had been right about one thing: the time for patience and watchful waiting was over. Vassili had made his move; it was time for Vadik to begin making his. Which was why Sal's request to meet Vassili Dmitrievich couldn't have come at a worse time.

Vadik assumed he'd know what all this was about soon enough; he was certain that Vassili would insist on his presence at the meeting. Vassili hadn't gotten this far by being careless—which meant that Vadik needed to be very careful about raising any eyebrows at this particular time.

Vadik knocked on Vassili's door, opened it and leaned in.

"Man in booth forty-eight says he needs to talk to you about something. Did not tell me what it was."

Vassili looked at him.

"Did he asked for the owner or did he ask for me by name?"

"By name."

"You know this guy?"

"I know *of* this guy. Has been here three times, including

today. Well behaved. Good tipper. Drinks vodka tonics, gets occasional table dance, smokes nice cigars. Doesn't want any trouble."

Vassili looked at him, musing the pros and cons. Or so Vadik imagined.

"Okay. Bring him here. And you stay."

Vadik closed the door and walked back to the booth. The fucking music—some industrial shit about bowing down and getting what you deserve—was giving him the mother of all headaches.

"Vassili has agreed to see you. Would you like another cocktail to take with you?"

"No, this one's fine. But thanks for asking."

"Of course. Please follow me, Sal."

CHAPTER 65

Special Agent Harley Slavnick knocked with his usual authority and waited.

He glanced around at the tidy ranch home that was purported to be the LKA of Ted and Marcy Hodges. No cars in the driveway, but that didn't mean anything. The neighborhood was well-kept middle class, median home value probably in the mid-300's. Not the kind of over-the-top, living-large South Florida mansion normally associated with successful white collar criminals.

He could hear a small-variety dog losing its mind inside somewhere. He rang the doorbell to agitate it further. Maybe someone needed to be awakened.

A few minutes later, the door opened a crack, the security chain still in place.

Slavnick peered through the opening. Female. Mid-forties. Clearly attractive and well-tended, although her eyes looked red-rimmed from crying. Or sleeping. She was dressed in a pair of sweatpants and a man's oxford cloth shirt.

"Are you Marcy Hodges, ma'am?"

Nothing.

"Ma'am, are you—"

"Who's asking?" came the reply from behind the door.

"Special Agent Harley Slavnick with the FBI, ma'am."

Slavnick held his creds up to the crack in the door.

"I'm looking for Ted Hodges. I went to the offices of Double A Top Title and was told that he has not been into work for the past couple of days, and that you left work yesterday and have not been seen since."

"Why are you looking for him? What do you want with him?"

"Ma'am, if you could just open the door and let me enter the house for a few minutes, I would appreciate it."

The door closed briefly as the security chain was slipped.

Framed in the midafternoon light, Marcy Hodges smoothed her rumpled shirt, pushed the hair out of her face, and dabbed at the corners of her eyes with a wadded-up Kleenex. She sniffed briefly, met Slavnick's gaze and said, "Please come in."

The home was tasteful without being ostentatious. Comfortable furniture, dark hardwood floors, framed Clyde Butcher prints on the walls, fresh flowers everywhere. Slavnick had the distinct feeling that the home reflected Marcy Hodges' tastes and sensibilities, while the offices of AA Top Title reflected her husband's.

"Please have a seat," Mrs. Hodges said, as she indicated a stool next to a marble countertop that separated the kitchen from the family room.

"I was just making some tea. We can chat here in the kitchen."

Slavnick pulled the stool out from underneath the counter and sat.

"Can I offer you something? Tea? Ice water, perhaps?"

"I'll join you and have some tea, thank you," Slavnick said, as Marcy Hodges pulled a kettle off the stove and plucked two china tea cups from cupboard. He sat silently, admiring her composure, as she steeped the two cups. Underneath the counter, he could feel the little dog sniffing frantically at his shoes. He shook his head when she offered sugar or cream.

As she set the cups on the counter, Slavnick cleared his throat to begin his questioning. Marcy Hodges held up her hand, cutting him off before he could speak.

"Agent Slavnick," she began calmly. "Before you ask, I have no idea what is going on at my husband's office, but I am fairly certain something *is* going on. I am even more certain that it has to do with a man named Elliot Becker."

Slavnick didn't know what to say. He wasn't used to being cut off. He cleared his throat again. "Mrs. Hodges, if I could just ask you to—"

Marcy Hodges pushed her hand toward Slavnick in a STOP! gesture. The last person he'd seen do that was a power-hungry crossing guard in sixth grade. Apparently, Mrs. Hodges was going to speak her piece, and he was going to sit and listen until she was finished.

Slavnick pulled out his notepad and pen.

CHAPTER 66

"So, Vadik tells me that you and I have some sort of business problem. Or business opportunity. He did not elaborate on which one it is."

"A little of both, perhaps," Salvano replied. He thought carefully before continuing.

Vassili Dmitrievich sat behind a large desk. On a credenza behind him, a bank of flat screen monitors displayed high-definition camera feeds from every angle and every room in the Cougar Club. The office was apparently soundproofed as well, since Nine Inch Nails was no longer being hammered into Mazzio's head.

Vadik had escorted Salvano into the office and made the appropriate introductions in his formal but stilted English, before switching to a rapid-fire discussion with Dmitrievich in Russian. Since Salvano had no idea what the two men were saying, he sat placidly until they were finished.

Dmietrivich raised his eyebrows in a "I'm waiting... " gesture.

"The best way to put it," Salvano continued, "is that I'm looking for a straightforward conversation aimed at resolving a matter *before* it becomes a problem."

Vassili scratched his temple lazily and said, "So Sal, what is this matter that is not-yet-but-could-end-up-being problem?"

Mazzio said, "I have a business associate. His name is Ted Hodges. Runs a title office here in town. You may have heard of him."

Vassili frowned slightly and shook his head.

"No? Doesn't matter," Mazzio resumed. "Anyway, it turns out that this associate of mine also has a business relationship with a certain Elliot Becker, whom I have been led to believe is a business associate of *yours*. And from what I understand, someone who owes you a considerable sum of money."

Silvano looked to Vassili for confirmation, but the Russian simply stared at Mazzio, his face giving away nothing. Russians, for whatever reason, had the best poker faces in the world. Silvano glanced at Vadik, who was leaning against the wall with his arms crossed, his eyes fixed on the bank of monitors. Silvano couldn't tell if he was listening or not.

Mazzio leaned forward and said, "Let me say upfront, Vassili, whatever arrangement Mister Becker has with you is no concern of mine. I want to be clear about that. He owes you money? Fine. He needs to pay you what he owes you. I don't know any of the details, and I don't need to know any of the details. That's between you and Elliot Becker."

Vassili pointed a large finger at Mazzio and said, "I sense this is where the 'problem' part comes in, Sal. Am I right?"

Mazzio smiled diplomatically; almost apologetically.

"Long story short, Vassili, I believe that over the past six months or so, your friend Elliot Becker may have funneled money out of my associate's business operations to meet certain financial obligations he had with you. Unfortunately, that money was not Mister Hodges' money to give to Mister Becker. And it was not Mister Becker's money to give to you. That was *my* money."

Mazzio paused and met Dmitrievich's half-interested gaze.

"And I'm gonna need it back."

The two men sat silently for a minute until Vassili said something in Russian to Vadik. Snapping out of his reverie, Vadik answered angrily in the same language, shrugging and shaking his head. Vassili turned back to Silvano.

"And the fact that you have been in my club not once but two times in the last week? What am I to make of that?"

Silvano figured that would come up. "Purely coincidental. What can I say? You do nice taxi ads."

Vassili looked at him for a second and shrugged, accepting the compliment.

"I'm still not sure if it's the girls or the Porterhouse, but they seem to work. Anyway, for the sake of conversation, Sal, how much money are we talking about? This guy—Hodges— he owes you what?"

"About two hundred and fifty thousand, before interest. Closer to four with the vig."

Dmitrievich smiled.

"*Vigorish*? Why do I get the sense, Sal, that you have been down this road before?"

"Because you're a smart guy, Vassili. That's why."

Mazzio held Vassili's gaze for a long moment. He wanted— no, *needed*— Vassili to understand who he was dealing with without having to spell it out. In the long run, that would be better for all concerned.

He said quietly, "You don't build up the kind of business you got, Vassili, without being a smart guy."

Without taking his eyes off Silvano, Vassili said something else to Vadik in Russian. Vadik barked back at him, and both men became increasingly heated as the conversation increased in volume. Mazzio sat serenely, sipping the vodka and tonic he'd brought along. There wasn't really anything he could do at the moment. He'd left his gun in the Tahoe, so if they wanted to kill him, they would. After a few minutes, Vassili returned his attention to Silvano.

"Alright, Sal. I need to make a few phone calls to see if and how we can resolve our matter before it becomes an issue, as you say. If it would not be inconvenient, I'd like to ask you to wait for a few minutes and enjoy the floor show in the main room. We have some real talent out there on Tuesday day shift, I can tell you that."

Silvano nodded.

"No problem."

CHAPTER 67

"Alright, let's get moving," Elliot Becker said as he pulled the Range Rover into Joanne Sander's garage. The two-story, four-bedroom Mediterranean-style home was empty, thanks to the two $100 gift certificates —one for Boca Town Center Mall, and one for the Grille on Congress—that Sasha had dropped off earlier in the afternoon as a 'thank you' gift for being "such loyal clients."

"But they're only good for *today*," she emphasized, per Becker's instructions. Once Joanne's live-in boyfriend and useless sister were assured that the restaurant certificate also applied to beverages, the three of them were up and out of the house by 2:30 in the afternoon.

Perfect timing.

"Sasha, close the garage, and go park the Cutlass in the driveway. Neighbors around here are likely to complain if they see a car parked in the street. Then, start unloading this stuff. Pile it near the laundry room door."

Becker killed the ignition to the Rover, reached across his body with his good hand, and opened the door. Burrell exited from the front passenger-side seat.

"Burrell, let's take a quick walk through the house and plan out where you want to put this shit. What's the technical term? 'Stage?'"

"Yeah," Burrell answered. "Stage. We're gonna want to stage it in at least three separate places in the house—hopefully, kind of spread it out so that it all burns inward. That's what the fireworks and the remote detonators are for. We can make it all go up at once."

"Dude, you don't gotta yell. I'm right here." Becker said in exasperation.

Burrell had healed nicely in the day since the flash powder explosion, but his hearing was still iffy, and he spoke too loudly as a result.

"By the way, where's the gun?"

Burrell reached behind his back and pulled a small automatic pistol from the waistband of his jeans. He handed it to Becker and said, "Safety's on. The magazine's loaded, and there's a round already in the pipe."

"I don't know what the fuck that means, Burrell," Becker said, as he slid the small weapon into his front right pocket. "But I hope it means that it's not gonna go off in my pants."

"No, you're good for now," Malin said.

"Alright, you can show me how to work it later. In the meantime, let's see what we got inside. And keep an eye out for the kind of setup that we talked about."

They passed Sasha in the kitchen.

"Get moving, Sasha. I want all this set and ready to go an hour before sundown. And I want my Range Rover to be at least twenty miles away when this all goes up."

Sasha saluted and headed toward the garage as Becker and Malin looked around. Becker pulled his phone out and dialed Hodges' number, which went straight to voicemail, as usual. Which was fine.

It was time to leave his one-and-only voicemail.

"I told you a long time ago, Ted: you're *in* this, whether you wanna be or not. So—tonight, we're in Boca. Remember Joanne whatshername in Boca? I'm sure you do. Anyway, we moved everything up, and I'm gonna need you to get your ass here—one way or another—by eight pm tonight. Or it isn't gonna be good for you—or your wife. Sasha's gonna text you the address in case you forgot it. I'm not fucking around, Ted. Call me or don't, but have your ass here by eight."

Becker disconnected the call.

"Burrell, where are you?" he called. "What are you thinking? Did you find what we needed?"

Burrell came around the corner and said, "There's a master bedroom on the main floor with a big walk-in closet that we can put the safe in. There's also a small office kind of room in the front of the house that we can use."

"Does the office have doors that we can close off?" Becker asked.

"Yep."

"And if you stage one of your fire setups in there, what's gonna happen?"

"Don't know for sure, but I'd guess a lot of it would go out the window. The walk in-closet would be better, because there's all kinds of clothes and boxes and stuff that would go up like tinder."

Becker thought about it for a moment. He could make that work.

"Fine. We'll put the safe in the walk-in closet."

He pulled out his phone, set it on a side table and texted Hodges with his one working hand.

Check your voicemail.

Next, he texted Vassili Dmitrievich the address of the home

in which he was standing, along with a time: *9:00 pm.*

Becker pocketed the phone and thought about the next five hours. If this worked, he was home free. If it didn't, he was beyond fucked.

He found Malin in the kitchen, on his hands and knees, looking under the sink.

"A lot of wood cabinets in here. Which is good. If we rig one here under the sink, we might get lucky and have a bunch of these cleaning products go up. That'd get it going really fast. That would take care of the back of the house."

"Do we need to set one upstairs? One of the bedrooms, maybe?" Becker asked.

"Heat rises, so my guess is that once it gets moving up the stairwell, it's all over," Malin said. "On the other hand, there're probably firebreaks built into the ceiling. Maybe do one up there, just to be safe."

"I just noticed something," Becker said. "Your rash. I can't smell it anymore."

"I know," said Malin, shaking his head. "It's the damndest thing. I think the fire burned it off or something. It's gone."

"Well, how about that?" Becker said. "A medical miracle. God bless us all."

Sasha had started carrying the supplies into the house. Becker handed her a handwritten list.

"I need you to make three separate piles in the living room, each pile containing the stuff you see here," he said, pointing to the list. "The rest goes back in the Rover. You got any questions, ask Burrell."

Sweating in her four-inch heels and skintight jeans, Sasha nodded and trudged off toward the garage.

Becker walked to the front of the house and looked out

the window at the perfectly manicured lawns and gracefully maintained homes. At little kids riding by on bikes and skateboards. At neighbors chatting with one another with their properly-leashed Standard Poodles and Golden Retrievers sitting at their sides, pooper-scoopers at the ready.

This time tomorrow, these people wouldn't know what hit them.

And with a little luck, neither would Ted Hodges and Vassili Dmitrievich.

CHAPTER 68

I t took me four tries, but I hit pay dirt in Boca Raton.

After leaving the gallery, I worked my way south through Delray Beach and Ocean Ridge. By 3:30, I'd driven by three homes, seeing nothing unusual at any of them. Emma had called me twice; there wasn't much to update her with. Just normal homes in normal neighborhoods, with normal neighborhood stuff happening.

"But you'll let me know if you see something unusual?"

"Yes," I answered. "I'll let you know if I see something unusual. I'm headed down to Boca now. There are two houses—one over by the mall, and the other one a little further south."

"Okay. Keep me updated."

"Yes, dear." I said.

I wondered why she was so worked up. I don't do well with micromanaging, and she knew that better than anyone.

It was coming up on four o'clock as I entered an upscale neighborhood in the heart of Boca Raton. The homes were pretty much all the same: two story, Mediterranean-style affairs perched on undersized lots. I'd done a quick county tax roll search on all of the target homes listed on Burrell's phone; this one was owned by someone named Joanne Sanders. And while I wasn't a realtor, according to the records, she appeared to have wildly overpaid for it. Especially if all she could afford to drive was the beat-to-shit Cutlass Sierra parked in the driveway.

I'd seen that car before, parked at Burrell Malin's house.

As I passed the house, the Cutlass' driver-side door opened. I kept the Bronco moving and watched through my rearview mirror as a tall redhead in stripper heels and tight jeans got out and walked inside. Not exactly how I'd imagined that Burrell Malin would look.

I drove a couple of blocks further, took a right into a street that ended in a cul-de-sac, parked, and considered my tactical situation.

I assumed that Burrell Malin, Becker and Hodges were inside the house, probably staging a burn rig. If they were smart (which was debatable), they were staging multiple burn rigs.

I doubted they'd do anything until nightfall. There were too many neighbors out and about for them to leave without someone noticing them. My best guess was that they'd stage the rigs, lay low for a couple of hours until the sun went down, slip out under cover of darkness, and remotely detonate the units from a distance.

That's what I would do, at any rate.

The neighborhood was less than a mile from the freeway; with a decent head start, they could be a hundred miles away before anyone even thought to start looking for them.

I figured I had at least three hours, maybe longer.

Hodges and Becker had seen my Bronco before at the offices of AA Top Title; there was no point in raising any flags with another drive-by.

I'd seen enough, anyway.

The bugout bag in the back of the truck had everything I'd

need, with the exception of dark clothing and a good pair of Merrell boots.

I started the Bronco, took the long way out of the neighborhood, and headed toward the Town Center Mall.

I needed to go shopping.

CHAPTER 69

I n combat, you are either killed by forces beyond your control, or by situations you fail to control. As a professional, Vadik was trained to never worry about the former, and to make certain the latter never happened.

The key, of course, was being able to distinguish between the two.

After depositing Sal in the club's main room, Vadik had returned to Vassili's office. Since it was the middle of the afternoon, the club owner had switched from screwdrivers to iced shots of Ultimat. He offered Vadik one as he sat, which Vadik accepted.

"This guy is a problem, Vadik. Big problem." Vassili said as he poured. "I don't know where he's from, but I can tell you right now he is not going to go away."

"So, you are not going to give him the money?" Vadik asked.

"Fuck no, I'm not going to give him the money!" Vassili barked. "This guy can't manage his own affairs and this is suddenly my problem? We are reverting to socialism now? Is my job to help the downtrodden and fuckups? This is why I left Soviet Union in first place."

"Okay. So, what is it you want to do, Vassili?" Vadik asked.

"Only thing there is to do, Vadik."

Vadik blanched. "You want to kill this fellow?"

"No, Vadik." Vassili answered. "I want *you* to kill this fellow."

"Vassili—"

"—Vassili, what?" Dmitrievich interrupted. "You tell me you're moving on, but until then, while I still pay you, you are now wanting to decide which orders from me you follow and which ones you don't? That how they did it in Spetsnaz, Vadik?"

Vadik fought the urge to take the letter opener from the desk and ram it through Vassili's eye.

Instead, he said, calmly, "I am only asking if you have thought this through. This man, Sal…it is apparent he is not an amateur. Clearly he has connections that—"

"—need to be severed *now* before I have half the New York *La Cosa Nostra* breathing down my neck!" Vassili snapped.

He took a breath to calm down.

"The longer we let this drag out, Vadik, the more friends and associates of Silvano Mazzio we're going to have to deal with."

Vassili leaned back in his chair.

"My guess is he hasn't said anything to any of his bosses. Yet. Why would he? He would try to deal with it on his own first. See if he can get it resolved without publicizing the fact that he let some bullshit title attorney and his con man buddy take him for a quarter million dollars."

Vadik leaned against the credenza and slowly sipped his vodka. His mind was racing to stay ahead of Vassili.

"When?" he asked.

"*Now*." Vassili replied. "We do this now, we limit the damage."

Vadik thought about it for a moment.

"I'll do it in here. With a wire."

"How?" Vassili asked.

"I'll bring him back in. You need to have him positioned so that his back is against the door."

"Why not have him sit there?" Vadik motioned to a chair in front of his desk. "I'll sit here. Keep him distracted."

"No. That will not work." Vadik said, thinking. "He is professional. He will sense me coming from the look in your eyes. Too much risk. Better for both of you to be standing in front of monitors, watching the feeds. Backs to door."

"Alright," Vassili conceded. "Maybe I'll run feed of you breaking those bikers in half. More fun than a UFC pay-per-view."

Vadik grunted.

Vassili continued, "Okay, that's settled. Tonight—that thing I mentioned this morning. I need you to meet Becker at some house in Boca. I'll text you the address later. He has a safe there—or so he says—with a couple of hundred thousand in cash. He wants to buy a couple of months from us. Says he needs the time to get his business in order. Wanted me to come personally, but I think I prefer to stay hands-off on this one."

Hands off?

The warning bells started clanging in Vadik's head as Vassili paused to light a cigarette.

"You go. Get the money. Tell him he has six weeks until next profit disbursement is due. Break something small to remind him of our seriousness in this matter. An elbow, maybe. Something like that. I'll meet you back here at, say, midnight."

He looked at Vadik. "*Dah*?"

Vadik nodded, turned and went to retrieve Silvano Mazzio.

CHAPTER 70

Special Agent Harley Slavnick pulled into the parking garage of the Tower One condominium complex in downtown West Palm Beach. He found a spot marked GUEST, parked and headed toward the elevator that would carry him to the lobby. He wasn't exactly sure where he was going, but he had a couple of possibilities in mind.

The smartest thing Slavnick had done was to shup up and let Marcy Hodges talk. She had been a wealth of information; the fact that he didn't prod her too many with questions had probably yielded more useful information than if he'd tried to pull it out of her.

She'd had her suspicions about what was going on at Double A over the past year, coinciding with the arrival of an individual named Elliot Becker. She couldn't give him particulars beyond "odd loan requests" and "a couple of techie kids who were always doing stuff in Photoshop" but she knew something wasn't adding up. Slavnick didn't go into detail about what he thought was happening, because he didn't want to steer her in any particular direction. He wanted her impressions; her take on what was going on.

The fact that he wasn't the first person to show up at the office looking for her husband was interesting; Slavnick assumed that whoever this Mazzio fellow was, he didn't have Ted

Hodges's best interests at heart. That, combined with the fact that they had found Hodges' phone in the Keys, indicated that Hodges was on the run. From what or whom, Slavnick didn't know for sure, but the odds were good that it was Silvano Mazzio.

He said to Marcy, "You mentioned that two men showed up yesterday morning. Who was the other one?"

"Richard Pizzuti. He's a client of the firm, buying some mansion by-owner. We're doing the title and escrow work. I was kind of surprised when I saw him, because I'd always assumed he'd be older. But he was a kid in his early twenties."

Pizzuti. Why did that name sound familiar?

"Do you recall how much was in Mister Pizzuti's escrow account?

"Not the exact number, but it was a lot. Close to a million dollars, I think."

Bingo.

"When your husband called you, did he sound stressed or frightened?" Slavnick had asked.

"Not really," she'd replied. "If anything, he sounded relieved. I don't know, it's hard to explain. He told me he was with Silvano, and everything was fine. That the whole mess would be cleared up soon, and not to worry."

"But you don't know from where he was calling?"

"No. Mr. Mazzio actually took my phone with him, so I couldn't access the app that finds his phone."

Slavnick had thought about that for a second and pulled out his own iPhone.

"All I need is your husband's ID and password, and I can find his phone on mine. Yours as well. I'm assuming you have that, yes?"

Like the rest of the FBI, Slavnick considered Find My iPhone a godsend. It was like a LoJack for people. In the few years since its introduction, the Agency had apprehended literally thousands of fugitives with it. He couldn't believe that people would actually install technology on a device they carried on their person that made it easier for other people to keep tabs on them, but they did.

Will wonders never cease?

Within a few minutes, Slavnick's screen showed a green dot pulsing at an intersection in downtown West Palm Beach. He zoomed out. There were at least 4 different condominium and apartment buildings in the area.

The accuracy of the Find My iPhone app depended on a lot of variables: the strength of the Wi-Fi network, whether it was inside a building or not, and whether the phone was turned on or off. The only thing that Slavnick could confirm for sure was that Hodges' phone had been in this general vicinity the previous evening.

He put in a call to his office to determine an LKA for both Silvano Mazzio and Richard Pizzuti. Mazzio came up with an address on Long Island. Richard Pizzuti came up blank.

He'd have to case every building in the area.

It was approaching five o'clock when he approached the faux-cherry front desk of Tower One Condominiums—the fourth building on his search. He cleared his throat, waking a geriatric security guard from his afternoon siesta. His name tag read "Myron."

Slavnick held his credentials out.

"I would like to speak with Silvano Mazzio, please. Can you call him or give me the number of his residence?"

The security guard squinted closely at the credentials for a second and replied, "There's no one living here by that name. I been here five years. Know all the residents. Who are you?"

Slavnick blinked. "I am Special Agent Harley Slavnick with the FBI. As my credentials attest. You're telling me that no one named Silvano Mazzio lives in this complex? I'm going to ask you again, because an untruthful answer on your part could have serious consequences."

The security guard looked supremely unconcerned.

"Nope. We got no one living here by that name. Is that it?"

"No, that's not it," Slavnick replied. "Additionally, I would like to speak to Richard Pizzuti. I know he lives here, because there are literally hundreds of pictures of this building on Mister Pizzuti's Facebook page, along with references to his quote 'penthouse crib' unquote."

Truth be told, there weren't actual pictures of the *building* on Richie Pizzuti's Facebook page. Just pictures of the unit itself, which was apparently Party Central for a random collection of sketchy music industry types, to judge by the gold chains and sideways hats. Slavnick had tried the fib out on the receptionists at the previous four buildings—all to no avail.

This security guard, however, looked a little less cocksure.

"How do I know you're for real? How do I know that badge ain't a fake?"

Slavnick said, "If it will make you feel better, Myron, I'll be happy to have you taken in and locked up for interfering with an ongoing federal investigation. How's that?"

Myron knew when he had met his match.

CHAPTER 71

Vadik closed his office door and walked to a locked filing cabinet. He'd deposited Silvano in Vassili's office next door, excusing himself to "retrieve some banking records," as Vassili put it.

He unlocked the top drawer to the cabinet and reached into the back, behind the old invoices and purchase orders, and pulled out a custom-made garrote fashioned from two wooden dowels and 30 inches of piano wire fed through the center of a similar length of 550 Paracord. Vadik had learned during a two-year stint as a contract assassin for the GRU that wire garrotes—popularized in so many movies—had an unfortunate tendency to decapitate the victim. The Paracord-and-wire combination was a perfect compromise: it was strong, bit deeply into the neck and, used properly, killed just as effectively.

Without the fuss and mess.

He was closing the file drawer when his BlackPhone vibrated with an incoming text.

He pulled the phone out of his pocket and scrolled to his new messages screen.

Yevgeny Kramnik is confirmed as hitter. He is recruiting a driver. Infil is a private home in Boca Raton. Does this mean anything to you?

Vadik sighed and put the phone in his pocket.

He sat behind his desk for a moment to calm his breathing and heart rate, and to give Vassili time to get himself and Silvano positioned with their backs to the door, watching the security monitors. He reviewed various methods he might use, settling on the classic "back to back" approach. Given the target's weight and height, this technique offered the best chance for success with the least risk. Executed properly, it was indefensible.

He hadn't garroted a person in years; he worried he might be a little rusty. So, he closed his eyes and visualized the movements of the technique. He ran the scenario over and over until the movie in his mind was smooth, graceful and mercifully fast.

If he'd had more time, he would have spent ten minutes in middle-density meditation. Instead, he took a sip of ice water, did five box breaths, and held his hands out in front of him.

They were steady.

He looked at his watch. Enough time had passed to safely assume that Vassili had the two of them positioned where Vadik needed them. He got up and grabbed the garrote, wrapping the cord around his right hand.

As he opened the door, he glanced both ways to ensure that they'd be receiving no surprise visitors in the next few minutes. He moved quickly down the hall, his eyes roving, his situational awareness dialed up. When he'd left Vassili's office, he'd purposefully left the door slightly ajar, allowing him to enter silently with just a slight push.

As he entered, he moved to his right to avoid having his reflection caught in the monitors on the credenza. Sal and Vassili were positioned perfectly, both unaware that Vadik was in the office.

He moved toward the two men in smooth measured strides as he unwrapped the garrote and finalized his grip on the handles. The weapon had a springy responsiveness to it that he'd forgotten. He reminded himself to allow for some elasticity in the ParaCord.

Three feet from the target and still closing, Vadik lifted his chin slightly and brought the garrote up, whipping it up and over the target's head, snapping it back as it crossed over the jugular.

It bit immediately.

CHAPTER 72

Vassili had made Silvano wait almost an hour while he did whatever he needed to do to get the situation resolved. On the other hand, he had to give Vassili credit for his hospitality. Fresh drinks were delivered every five minutes or so; Jeannie had even offered to go back to the kitchen to fix him a plate from the buffet. An endless stream of entertainers stopped by his table, insisting on giving him table dances and refusing payment. Even tips.

It was the first time Silvano had seen a stripper actually turn down money—let alone an entire day shift of them.

"It's on Vassili," a big blonde from Mississippi told him. "If you want, we can go back to the Cougar Den and have some private fun. That's on Vassili, too."

Silvano had declined. He needed to keep his mind in the game.

By the time Vadik came to collect him, he was scrolling through old emails on his Blackberry, more or less ignoring the redhead dry-humping his right knee.

Vassili stood as they entered the office, his hand outstretched.

Silvano went immediately on guard.

"Please, Sal, come in. I think I have just about gotten this mess of ours fixed. I've been on the phone with my people for the last hour trying to get to the bottom of this. If you have your banking information handy, we can get on the phone and execute a wire transfer for the two hundred and fifty thousand. I thought about it, and while I am happy to make good on the disputed amount I received from Becker, it seems to me that the interest should remain a private issue between you and Mr. Hodges. Yes?"

Silvano thought about it for a second and nodded.

"Seems fair enough. Sure."

Vassili smiled.

"Okay. Vadik, if you can go and find the account numbers and wire transfer passwords that I need, we'll get this issue over and done with."

Vadik nodded and left.

"In the meantime, Sal, let's have a quick drink together," he said as he poured two rocks glasses half-full with iced vodka.

Handing one to Silvano, he said, "Vadik says good things about you. He doesn't miss much, Vadik. So, if he says you're okay, that's good enough for me."

"Vadik is a good guy," Silvano replied. "From what I can tell, you're lucky to have him. He's definitely got your club under control."

Vassili smiled. "Ah, yes. Vadik told me you were here Saturday night. You saw what he did to bikers?"

Silvano said, "I didn't see it actually happen, but I saw the results. I was by the valet stand when they came stumbling out."

Vassili's eyes brightened.

"Then you've got to see this, Al. It's the footage of Vadik taking those guys apart on the security cameras. It is hilarious.

I was watching it all morning."

Vadik clicked the mouse on his desk and waved Silvano over.

"Over here. On this one," he said, pointing. "I've never seen anything like it, and I've seen a lot."

Silvano got up and walked over to join Vassili in front of the video bank. He watched on one of the monitors as Vadik jabbed a pen into the biker's throat.

So that's how that got there, he thought.

He was stunned how quickly Vadik moved. The whole thing was over in the blink of an eye. After delivering what appeared to be a lecture of some kind to the broken and bleeding men, Vadik leapt up on the table and began kicking the bikers. Vassili laughed uproariously at this, pointing to the monitor.

"Is hilarious, no?"

His attention still fixed on the footage, Silvano heard a faint whistle in the air, as if a bullwhip were about to snap nearby. His body tensed as he turned to his right and looked toward Vassili. He watched as a thin cord slipped over the club owner's head and was yanked taut at his neck.

Vadik was on the other end.

Pulling back on the two wooden handles attached to the cord, Vadik ducked and pirouetted so that his back was to Vassili's. This movement crossed the cord over itself, forming a closed loop that instantly cinched Vassili's neck. With the handles now over his own two shoulders, Vadik snapped forward violently at the waist, pulling Vassili up onto his back, feet dangling inches above the floor. Vassili's hands pawed desperately at thin air, trying to find something—anything—to grab onto.

Silvano stepped back slightly, just out of Vassili's flailing reach.

As Mazzio stood transfixed, Vadik pulled harder on the handles, drawing Vassili further up his back. Vassili's eyes began to bulge as his faced turned a mottled red, then purple. Not a sound escaped from him.

Vadik spread his feet and walked forward a few steps, bouncing Vassili along as he pulled even harder on the handles, clearly waiting for the struggling to stop.

He didn't have to wait long.

Vadik let Vassili's now-limp body slide off his back, and fall to the floor.

Silvano looked at Vassili, and then at Vadik.

The silence in the room was profound.

CHAPTER 73

Harley Slavnick knocked on the door to Richie Pizzuti's penthouse crib. Based on what he'd seen in depressing fifteen minutes he'd spent scrolling through Mr. Pizzuti's Facebook page, he had an idea of what to expect.

He could hear a television playing loudly in the unit, so he knocked again—this time with more force. He stepped back and readied his credentials.

"It's open!" he heard someone yelled from inside the unit.

Stepping into the foyer, Slavnick was almost overcome by the thick stench of marijuana and what he imagined to be cigar smoke. He'd learned in the Academy that this was how the drug was smoked these days—the cigar was opened up, the marijuana was sprinkled in, and the cigar was re-wrapped for use.

He believed the term was 'blunt', but he wasn't sure. He didn't run into habitual marijuana abusers all that often in the Financial Crime Section.

Slavnick walked slowly straight ahead, one hand holding out his credentials, the other hovering over his holstered .38. The sounds of some kind of televised carnage grew louder as he went deeper into the unit.

"This is Special Agent Harley Slavnick from the FBI. I am approaching the living area. Please have your hands where I can see them," he called out in a stern voice.

He turned the corner to find two men lounging on a huge leather couch playing a video game. A large bowl of marijuana sat on the table next to a tall orange bong, and a package of Swisher Sweets cigars. There were beer cans and fast food wrappers everywhere.

The two men—Pizzuti and Hodges (minus the toupee)—didn't even look up.

They just kept playing.

Slavnick cleared his throat and took a position in front of the television.

"Dude! What the fuck?" Pizzuti protested.

Slavnick didn't move.

"Yeah. What the fuck, dude?" Hodges said, giggling.

Slavnick held out his credentials and said, "I've been looking for you, Mister Hodges. I have some questions for you—and not incidentally, your wife is very worried about you."

As Slavnick was speaking, Pizzuti pointed a remote at the television and clicked it off.

Hodges took a sip of beer from a can on the table and said, "I'm fine. I'm just sitting here playing video games with my friend Ritchie. There's no law against that. I should know. I'm a lawyer."

"True, but there are laws against the possession of marijuana, Mister Hodges," Slavnick said, nodding toward the bowl. "Particularly in bulk quantities—an indicator of trafficking—which is a federal crime. I should know, because I'm a lawyer *and* an FBI agent."

Pizzuti groaned. "Fucking weed, dude? Give me a break. You don't even have a warrant."

"I don't need a warrant, Mr. Pizzuti. You invited me in."

An appliance of some kind started pinging in the kitchen. Pizzuti looked at Hodges and said, "Your Whopper Junior's ready, dude."

Hodges and Pizzuti looked at each other. Pizzuti started giggling, and a few seconds later, Hodges joined in.

Both men were clearly very high.

Hodges looked at Slavnick and said, "So what do you want to ask me about? My fucked-up title company? Fucking Elliot Becker?"

"Among other things. I'm going to need you to gather your things and come with me."

"All my stuff is in the other place," Hodges replied. "I gotta go get it. And I gotta eat my Whopper Junior."

He struggled to extricate himself for the deep confines of the couch. Slavnick walked over and reached out a hand to pull him to his feet.

"Dinner is going to have to wait. Where exactly is the other place?" he asked.

"Right next door, dude," Pizzuti answered. "It's the model unit. Very sweet."

Hodges found his footing and barreled toward the foyer. "I'll show you the way, Agent Slutnick."

Forty-five minutes later, Slavnick had Hodges packed up and ready to go. He'd relented and let Hodges have his Whopper Junior. There was no telling when they'd have a chance to eat, and the man wouldn't stop whining. As Hodges wolfed down his burger, Slavnick took a final look around. He noticed two iPhones and a pair of handcuffs on the counter.

"Are these your phones?"

Hodges nodded, his mouth full of food. "One of them is. The other's Marcy's."

"And the handcuffs?" Slavnick asked.

Hodges shrugged. "I don't know. They were here when I got here. Maybe the salespeople use them on each other."

"Mind if I take a look at the phones?"

Hodges nodded. "Knock yourself out."

There were two text alerts on the home screen of Hodges' phone. The first advised Hodges to "*Check your voicemail.*" The second was an address in Boca Raton, followed by: "*Be there by 8 or you're fucked.*"

Both were from Elliot Becker.

CHAPTER 74

Aleyev Vadik Antonovich—former Senior Warrant Officer, Spetsnaz GRU, recipient of the Medal of Valor for the Russian Federation, newly-unemployed Russian mob enforcer and future part-owner of a high-end boutique hotel in the heart of Palm Beach— looked at the body of Vassili Dmitrievich.

"So. That's that."

He turned to Silvano Mazzio.

"I am sorry you had to witness that, Sal. For to make you feel better, please know that Vassili here was expecting *you* to be on the end of the garrote. Not him."

"I'll bet that came as a surprise." Mazzio replied, a little shakily.

"And I'll bet it stung a little too," Vadik said, rubbing his shaved head with one hand and letting the garrote drop to the floor.

"Not that it's your problem, Sal, but he was planning to have *me* killed this evening as well. How is that for multitasking? Have me kill you and then, three hours later, have an old comrade from my military days kill *me*?"

Vadik smiled, almost wistfully. "He was a complicated guy, Vassili was."

The two men stood silently.

After a moment, Silvano asked, "So, where do we go from here, Vadik?"

Good question, Vadik thought. For the last hour and a half, he'd been running on adrenaline. Analyzing the situation as it unfolded, making decisions instantly, never looking any further out than the next few minutes. Precisely as the tactical environment had demanded. Now, it was time to take a longer view on things.

He walked over and leaned against the credenza, rubbing his eyes and bringing his heart rate down. Thinking.

"Two things come to mind," he said. "First, we will need to find a place to store Vassili until dark. There can be no hint of what just went on here. It needs to look like business as usual."

Silvano interrupted. "*We?*"

Vadik nodded. "Yes. We are going to have to work together on this. It is in both of our interests. Not that I have to remind you Sal, but that could be you lying there."

Silvano looked at him warily. "I realize that, Vadik. I'm just not sure how much of a help I can be in this."

Vadik snorted. "Don't play coy with me, Sal. We both know this is not first body you've had to dump. We both know who you are. In fact, I am counting on your professionalism."

He paused. "And your Chevy Tahoe."

"My Tahoe?" Silvano asked.

"Yes. The Chevy Tahoe you drove to Cougar Club. The one that is parked next to the valet stand. I saw you park and exit the vehicle earlier today on security cameras."

Silvano asked, "What about your car? It's your corpse, after all."

"I drive a Fiat Five Hundred, Sal. Classic, throwback-European style. But tiny. Barely big enough for me, let alone Vassili."

"Okay," Silvano said. "So, we store Vassili in the Tahoe. How long?"

"Until nightfall. Then, we drive out to the Everglades and get rid of him. After that, we head to Boca Raton, to a certain house where your friend Elliot Becker is waiting. That is the setup I mentioned. The one where Vassili was planning to have me killed."

Silvano shook his head as he tried to process all of this.

"You're saying that you want to walk right into a setup that Vassili arranged to have you killed? You just wanna waltz in there? And bring me along with you? Are you out of your fucking mind, Vadik?"

Vadik smiled slightly. "Since I know about the setup, Silvano, the element of surprise is gone. Without element of surprise, risk drops dramatically. I am certain that I can convince my old comrade Yevgeny Kramnik that there is no point in carrying out the hit, since the guy who was going to pay him is no longer around. He will be more than happy to put this behind him and go back to breaking knees for Antonin Bodelenko. Trust me on this."

Silvano just looked at him.

"Which brings me to Elliot Becker," Vadik continued. "I know for fact that Becker has a private banking account with more than four-hundred thousand dollars in it. Not investments. Cash."

Silvano said, "Yeah, Hodges told me about it. It's the money he cleaned out of my nephew's escrow account. What about it?"

Vadik said, "It just so happens I have all of the account information needed to transfer that money into any account you'd like, Silvano. Tonight. We can set it up in advance. All I need is the PIN number to authorize the transfer. Which I am confident Elliot Becker will supply."

Silvano looked at him in amazement. "How did you get your hands on that kind of information, Vadik?"

Vadik smiled. "Elliot Becker's girlfriend and office administrator is my sister. And Sasha tells me everything. And because Sasha tells me everything, I know Elliot Becker better than Elliot Becker knows himself."

CHAPTER 75

I'm not a shopper.

Whole decades can go by without me stepping foot in a mall. Especially a mall like the Town Center Mall in Boca Raton. As I navigated the parking lot, the sheer number of stores and choices and arrows pointing this way and that made it even more confusing. I decided the most efficient strategy would be to find a single department store that carried the three things I needed: a dark shirt, dark pants, and dark boots.

I passed a name I recognized: Nordstrom.

It had an outside entrance that opened directly into the store.

Perfect.

I parked and walked into what looked to be both the shoe *and* men's department.

Even more perfect.

I shopped quickly, hustling through the shoe department and pointing to a pair of dark brown Merrell hiking boots.

"Eleven and a half, please. I'll be back in five minutes."

I barely broke stride as I grabbed a black, long-sleeved cotton pullover off a stack and a matching pair of dark cotton chinos, and brought both back to the checkout counter in the shoe department.

"Can you just ring all of this up, and point me to a dressing room?" I asked. "I'm kind of in a hurry. Late for a thing."

"Absolutely!" the overly-enthusiastic clerk exclaimed. She scanned the items and punched a couple of keys on the register.

I couldn't believe the total: $1,259.

"Are you sure that's right?" I asked.

The girl nodded. "Prada pullover. Hugo Boss pants. Merrell boots. It's a gorgeous ensemble. If you'd like, there's a Gucci belt that would really finish the whole look. Let me just—"

"—No. That's fine," I said, fishing out my wallet.

Fifteen minutes later, I was back in my car, gorgeously ensembled, and ready to recon an American neighborhood.

How far I had fallen.

The neighborhood had a common-use pool and clubhouse with a small parking lot about a block from the Sanders home. That seemed to be the best place to leave the Bronco. I parked as far away from the streetlamps as a I could, opened the tailgate and rummaged through my bugout bag. I pulled out my Sig Sauer and placed it in the waistband of my new Hugo Boss pants. The Gucci belt that I'd relented on (because the salesperson simply wouldn't shut up) held it snugly. The Prada pullover hid it nicely.

I slid an extra mag in my pocket and pulled out a small nylon bag that held a night vision scope I'd gotten from Cabela's a couple of years earlier. The bag was nondescript, so I could carry it through the neighborhood without raising any eyebrows. I popped a small flashlight in the bag, checked to make sure I had my phone, closed the tailgate and locked the truck.

Night was beginning to fall as I made my way toward the house. As approached, I stopped a couple of houses north and crossed the street. I found a spot in between two homes behind a pair of air conditioning compressors and a pool filter. The vantage point—which was sort of caddy-corner to the Sanders home— gave me a clear shot of the entrance, and the racket of the pool and AC units covered any noise I might make.

The Cutlass was still parked in the driveway. There were a few lights on in the house, but I saw no one walking past any of the windows. I fished out the scope and adjusted the optics to the fading light.

And waited.

CHAPTER 76

"**W**e need you hold there, Harley."

"But—"

"—But nothing, Agent Slavnick. You have no idea what you're walking into. Your suspect is under the influence. You have no backup. You will wait until backup arrives, and together, we will determine the appropriate course of action."

"But—"

"End of story, Harley."

Special Agent Harley Slavnick blew a sigh, regretting that he'd even made the call.

"Agents Briggs and Stoneside will be there in less than twenty minutes. Get their take on the situation. You're a great agent, Harley, but you don't have a lot of field experience. They do. You don't want to be going hell bent for leather into a situation that you haven't prepared for, with a bunch of unknowns. If the situation warrants, we'll reach out to Boca PD and have them send a cruiser to the scene. But until we get a handle on this, you stay put."

Slavnick knew there was no point in arguing. Strictly speaking, his supervisor was right. But he had a feeling that there a clock ticking; something was going to happen. And if he didn't get moving, it was going to happen without him.

"Yes, sir," he said and hung up the phone.

He re-read the text on Hodges' phone.

What was going to happen in Boca?

He looked over at Hodges, who was rooting through another Burger King bag.

"Want some chicken fries, Agent Saltlick?"

Slavnick shrugged.

"Why not?

CHAPTER 77

"You're sure this stuff is gonna work?" Elliot Becker asked as he and Burrell Malin walked into the kitchen.

"As sure as I can be," Malin answered.

He was exhausted. In a little under four hours, he had staged three different burn rigs—with almost no help from Becker. With his recent pyrotechnic misadventure still fresh in his mind, each installation had been nerve-wracking. He referred continually to the handwritten schematics that he'd prepared in advance. He was fairly confident that the things would work—putting a flame to flammable stuff *always* worked—but until he saw it with his own two eyes, there would still be that small element of doubt about how *well* it would work.

"Don't start second-guessing yourself now, Burrell. We got four more to go after this."

Burrell nodded absently.

"Okay," Becker said. "Last thing we gotta do is roll the safe into the closet. Sasha!"

"What do you need?" she asked, as she walked into the kitchen.

Burrell looked at her with puppy eyes. Over the last couple

of days, he'd developed an unmitigated crush on the redhead. In addition to being beautiful and sexy, she was always positive and willing to help. Always a nice word for him. It was a shame that she had picked such an asshole for a boyfriend.

"Grab the hand truck and help us get the safe in the closet. Then you and the Rover can get out of here."

She nodded and headed toward the garage.

"Okay, while we got a minute, Burrell, show me how to work this gun." Becker reached with his good hand into his right pocket and extracted the Walther.

Burrell winced at how casually Becker was handling the gun.

"You got to rack it to make it work. Just pull back on the top and let it fall into place."

Watching Becker trying to seat a round was a nerve-wracking experience, given his heavily banged hand and the resulting need to prop the gun clumsily against his stomach as he pulled back the slide. Burrell was surprised neither of them were shot in the process.

Once Becker had a round in the pipe, Burrell took a relived breath and said, "Now, move that little lever on the left. That's the safety. That de-cocks the hammer."

Becker did as Burrell instructed and asked, "So, if I want to shoot it, what do I do? Just pull the trigger?"

"Well, you gotta take the safety off first. That little lever you just pushed. Move it back the other way."

After doing so, Becker asked, "Now it's ready?"

"Yep. Just pull the trigger."

Becker pointed the gun at a photograph of Joanne Sanders and her sister. He made gunshot noises as he pantomimed shooting them. After about ten fake rounds, he looked at Burrell.

"Alright. Good. This might just come in handy."

Malin winced again as Becker shoved the small gun sloppily back in his pocket.

"Let's get this fucking safe set and get Sasha out of here. What time is it?"

Burrell looked at his watch. "Almost eight," he answered.

Becker smiled slightly.

"Right on time."

CHAPTER 78

Mazzio pulled the Tahoe into a flood-lit gas station off US Route 441 and parked it next to the vacuum and air dispenser.

"They got a water hose here. Let's take a few and get the muck off our shoes, then I'll fill up. You might wanna pop in the mini-mart there and grab us some water and stuff. I'm thirsty as hell."

"*Dah*," Vadik said as they exited the vehicle.

"How far is it to this house in Boca?" Silvano asked.

Vadik looked at the navigation screen on his phone. "Half hour or so. Maybe forty-five minutes. That will put us there right about nine o'clock, which should be fine. Becker's not going anywhere."

"How do you know that?" Silvano asked.

"Just got text from Sasha. She says she's leaving in a few minutes and that Becker and some other guy are there waiting for Vassili and your friend Hodges."

The two men took turns with the hose, trying to remove the rich black mud. It was everywhere—on their shoes, their clothes, and on their hands. Vadik pulled the table cloth they'd covered Vassili with from the back of the SUV. They used it as a makeshift towel. Once it was covered in mud, Vadik took it around behind the mini-mart and stuffed it in the dumpster.

"You were smart to go with the black interior, Sal. Really hides dirt well." Vadik said appreciatively, as he walked back to the car.

"Thanks, Vadik."

Is this guy for real? Silvano thought, for the hundredth time.

With Vassili safely six feet under, the two had managed to relax a bit. Vadik had used the drive time wisely, setting up the wire transfer protocol on his BlackPhone. All that remained was to input Becker's PIN number, and $442,900 would be instantly wired to the numbered Caymen Islands bank account that Silvano had specified.

Once safely in that account, the money would instantly be rerouted through four different offshore accounts—each with different corporate ownership—until finally coming to rest in a Swiss UBS merchant account owned by the same real estate development firm that was turning Tower One condo. Exactly as Silvano had designed it earlier that morning—thinking at the time that it would be Vassili's money taking the whirlwind tour. Silvano, of course, mentioned none of this to Vadik. What happened after the initial transfer was *his* business.

Vadik headed toward the mini-mart, while Silvano moved the Tahoe to a gas pump. While the tank filled, Silvano pulled out his Blackberry and scrolled to Kathleen's contact information.

Looking forward to Friday.

Inside of ten seconds, he got a text back.

Me too. Hope your appointment went well today!

If you only knew.

He looked at what he'd typed, sighed and punched the back button repeatedly.

Thanks.

He hit SEND and put the phone back in his pocket as Vadik emerged from the store, his arms laden with bottled water and power bars.

Power bars? What's the matter with a simple Three Musketeers?

The pump cut off. Silvano replaced the handle, climbed in the car and dialed up a classic rock station as Vadik settled into the passenger seat. Silvano gunned the Tahoe out of the lot and pulled into traffic as the cars rolled south out on 441.

Like waves crashing on the beach, Salvano thought.

CHAPTER 79

The garage door to Joanne Sanders' Boca Raton home opened, revealing a late model Range Rover with its brake lights illuminated. The garage itself was dark. The big SUV lurched into gear and backed quickly out of the garage and into the street. Inside the garage, a hand reached through the door and hit the control to close the door.

I already had the scope pointed to where I thought the car would come to a halt and shift into a forward gear. I wasn't exactly on the mark, but I was close enough to confirm that it was a woman driving the car. I assumed it was the redhead, but the poor image quality of the night vision gear prevented me from being absolutely certain.

Not that it really mattered; I was after Ted Hodges and Elliot Becker. As long as they were still in the house, I wasn't going anywhere.

It was coming up on 9 pm. Except for light spilling out of windows, the neighborhood was completely dark. I decided to give it a few more minutes and then move closer to the house to get a sense of what was going on inside.

I'd been crouching for a while, and my knees aren't what they used to be. I stood briefly to stretch out, being careful to keep my body close to the wall and hidden from view. I was unkinking my calf muscles when a black Chevy Tahoe turned onto the street and drove slowly toward the Sanders home. It stopped three houses short and parked by the curb. I slipped back into my crouch and felt around for the night vision monocular as both doors opened and two men got out.

Even from a hundred yards, there was something familiar about both of them. As they walked down the street toward the home, I slowly pulled the scope up, my index finger on the zoom button. I pointed the device about ten yards ahead and waited for them to walk into frame.

As they came into view, I noted that each man carried a sidearm. One was dressed in all black; the other as if he were about to go yachting. I pressed the zoom function and moved my frame of reference up to catch the faces.

The first guy wasn't a huge surprise. It was Mazzio—or at least the person I *assumed* to be Silvano Mazzio: the large, violent-looking man I had seen leaving AA Top Title the day I'd shown up at the office. In the conversation that I had recorded, Hodges had confirmed that Mazzio was the guy with him when Becker and I had stumbled into the lobby.

I was surprised to see that I also knew the second man. It was Vadik—the Russian half of the Palm Beach couple I had met at Casa Playa's the previous weekend. The hotel owner. Why he would be walking into an arson-rigged home in Boca Raton with an Italian mobster and an automatic weapon was beyond me.

I sat stock still, secure in my hide, and watched the two men approach and take flanking positions by the front door. Vadik reached over and turned the knob.

The door swung open.

With Vadik taking first position, both men entered the house, guns up. The door closed behind them. Very professional.

I was up and moving immediately. The probability of the shit hitting the fan in the next twenty seconds was very high; anyone in the house who had been watching the street before Vadik and Silvano hit the door was now otherwise engaged. Of that I was certain.

I ran across the street toward the house, pulling the Sig from my belt. As I approached, I slowed down slightly and angled toward the right side of the house. I moved down the side yard, stopping at an iron gate. I opened it quietly.

The backyard was dominated by a kidney-shaped pool and a large stone patio. A wide span of sliding glass doors started about fifteen feet from the corner of the house. I looked back toward the pool, which had a large waterfall feature at one end. There were no lights on in the backyard; I moved fifteen feet away from the house and crouched behind the jutting rocks and landscaping of the waterfall. Well outside of the pool of light spilling out of the sliders, I was effectively invisible. And because the glass doors spanned almost the entire back wall, I could see everything that was happening in the house. From the kitchen on the left to the main room in the middle, to what looked to be the master bedroom on the far right.

For the time being, I was content to simply watch. I wasn't there to save anyone—least of all Elliot Becker or Ted Hodges.

CHAPTER 80

Elliot Becker was in the master bedroom's walk-in closet with Burrell Malin, pushing the cheap safe into position.

"Alright, that oughta do it. It doesn't have to look perfect. Just like it's got money in it." He pulled the safe door open slightly. "There we go."

The idea was simple: lead Vassili into the closet where the money was supposedly stashed. Put the pistol to his head and have Malin secure him with a pair of zip-ties that Becker had in his right front pocket. One Vassili was secured, turn the gun on Hodges (assuming Hodges paid attention to the texts and got his ass to the house) and do the same thing. In one elegant move, he'd have the two biggest problems in his life tied up next to about a hundred pounds of fireworks, and closet full of flammables. After that, it was just a matter of pushing a button.

Problem solved.

He looked at Malin. "You ready?"

Malin held up a device the size of a television remote control with a small LED light and four buttons fared into the plastic housing.

"Laundry room. Upstairs bedroom. Kitchen. Closet," he

said, pointing to each button in sequence. "Boom. Boom. Boom. Boom." He paused and added, "Bonfire."

Becker nodded. "Cool."

The two men heard what sounded like the front door closing as they exited the closet.

Becker put a hand on Malin.

"Stay here."

Becker walked toward the bedroom door slowly as Malin retreated back into the closet.

"Ted? Is that you?" Becker called.

Nothing.

"Vassili?"

Still nothing.

He took a tentative step into the hall and felt something cold and hard press against his temple.

"Hello, Elliot."

Fuck.

"Vassili couldn't make it. How's the pinky finger?"

Fuck. Fuck. Fuck. Fuck.

Elliot felt the barrel of the gun shift against his head. He was being steered.

"Let's go to the kitchen, Elliot. My friend is famished."

Prodded by the gun, Elliot complied.

In the kitchen, Becker was surprised to find Silvano Mazzio making himself a sandwich. The big Italian smiled at Becker and pointed to Vadik.

"Guy's a total fitness freak. All he eats are power bars. Me? I need something more substantial, if you know what I mean."

Tell me this isn't fucking happening, Elliot thought.

The gun pressed harder into his temple.

It was definitely happening.

"So, Elliot. Here's the deal," Mazzio said, as he slathered mustard on his sandwich. "You got four-hundred and forty-three thousand dollars in an account that you're gonna wire to me. All you need to do is tell us PIN number. We got everything else all set up. Easy-peasy."

Mazzio took a bite of his sandwich and looked at Vadik. "You want a sandwich, Vadik? I got everything all laid out here. Take me two minutes."

Vadik shook his head. "Thank you all the same."

Mazzio shrugged and looked back at Becker.

"See what I mean?"

Becker fought to remain in control. To think ahead. To buy some time.

"Where's Vassili? I thought Vassili was coming. I had a deal with Vassili—"

"That deal is now off table, Elliot," Vadik said, conversationally. "This is new deal. In this deal, you give us your PIN number, and we don't blow your fucking head off. Probably not so good a deal as you'd like, but that is deal nonetheless."

"I...I need a second to catch up," Becker said, holding up his hand. "I swear to you—I don't have a fucking clue what you're talking about. I don't have that kind of money. If I had four hundred thousand dollars, I wouldn't be here. I'd be—"

Keeping the pistol trained on Becker's forehead, Vadik pulled out a cellphone and scrolled through a couple of screens. He held it up where Becker could read it.

It was a text containing all of the pertinent information

for his Modern Properties account. Routing number. Account number. Balance. And user ID. The only thing missing was the Personal Identification Number.

Becker looked at Vadik. "Where did you get this?" he asked, as he looked at the top of the screen for the sender.

"Who is *Snezhana*?" he asked.

"My sister." Vadik replied, apparently waiting for Vadik to catch on. He sighed in exasperation.

"*Your* girlfriend, Elliot."

Sasha? That bitch.

Just like that, Elliot Becker realized the extent to which he was fucked. There would be no Plan B.

"Speaking of my sister, she mentioned you were here with someone else. The arsonist. This person is in back bedroom, I'm assuming?"

Becker closed his eyes and nodded.

"Silvano, could I bother you to go and collect friend of Elliot's? What's his name, by the way?" Vadik asked, turning to Becker.

"Burrell. Burrell Malin."

"Burrell. Of course," Vadik said. "Sasha always tells me you treat this Burrell fellow like a dog."

Becker shrugged, as Mazzio wiped his hands on a paper towel, drew a Berretta from the waistband of his pants and headed toward the bedroom.

"Be right back."

"So, Elliot. Really—how is finger?" Vadik asked.

Becker was struggling to frame a reply when Mazzio came walking backwards into the kitchen, both hands on the Berretta.

"Vadik?" he said. "We got a problem."

Mazzio's gun was pointed at something—or someone—just around the corner. As Mazzio continued his retreat into the kitchen, a tall man with a shaved head followed him in. He had a large pistol pointed at Mazzio.

"You know this guy?" Mazzio asked.

Vadik glanced over and nodded.

"Yes, I know this guy." He smiled tightly.

"Silvano, meet Yevgeny Kramnik. We served together in Chechnya. How are you, Sergeant?"

With that, Vadik swung his gun from Becker toward the large man, as Kramnik moved his pistol from Mazzio and trained it on Vadik.

"I am fine, sir. You're looking fit, if I might say so."

"Thank you, Yevgeny. It's gets a little harder every year."

Becker fought the urge to vacate his bowels.

"So, you are here to take me out, Yevgeny? That's what I've been led to believe."

Both men looked intently at one another.

Kramnik said, "Unfortunately, yes. Specifically, to terminate you and to recover two-hundred thousand dollars in cash from a safe here in the house."

"And for this, you were promised two-hundred and fifty thousand dollars, I believe?" Vadik asked, his gaze and his gun never wavering.

"Yes."

"Vadik? Talk to me." Mazzio said, his pistol still trained on Kramnik.

"Keep your gun on Yevgeny, Silvano." Vadik replied calmly.

411

"But no need to fire just yet. I think once my old friend gets a better sense of big picture, this problem will resolve itself."

Vadik turned to Kramnik and said, "So, Sergeant, there is no good way to tell you this, but—"

With that, Vadik switched to Russian. A few seconds into the exchange, Kramnik's eyes arched in surprise. Vadik shrugged and continued on in Russian as both men kept their pistols trained on one another.

No one was paying attention to Becker. He slowly moved his good hand toward his right pocket.

CHAPTER 81

From my hide by the waterfall, I watched in fascination as a bizarre Mexican standoff played out. I had no idea who the new player was in all of this, but I doubted it was Burrell Malin.

This guy looked ex-military. Probably ex-special forces.

The sliding glass door to the kitchen was slightly ajar, but my distance from the house made it impossible for me to hear everything that was going on. Nonetheless, I was impressed by the civility of it all. There were no raised voices, no sudden movements. Just three professionals trying to resolve a sticky situation without a bunch of unnecessary bloodshed.

Sitting in the dark watching a brightly-lit tableau of three men with guns trained on one another, I felt like I was screening a mid-seventies B-movie with the sound turned way down.

The only person out of place in all of this was Becker.

From my vantage point, I had a clear view of his face. He looked like he was going to fall apart any second. His mouth was quavering, and he kept pulling his knees together as if in great gastric distress.

The conversation suddenly switched languages. I continued to watch, fascinated as the two Russians began gesticulating with their free hands. Mazzio looked on impassively, his pistol still trained on the stranger.

I doubted he understood Russian.

Suddenly, Becker started to contort; reaching in with his one good hand, he was struggling to extract something from his pocket. Whatever it was, it was stuck. Using his over-wrapped hand to hold his pants taut, he yanked at the pocket frantically.

His pocket went off.

The three men turned to Becker, who had gone down in a heap, his right foot a mangled, bloody mess.

I sprinted across the patio, slipped through the door and walked into the kitchen just as the new guy proved to be the first to get his wits about him. He was raising his pistol toward Vadik, who was focused on a bleeding and screaming Elliot Becker.

"I wouldn't, friend." I said, my Sig trained on his center mass.

CHAPTER 82

From the safety of the walk-in closet, Burrell Malin listened intently to the conversation going on in the kitchen—which was difficult, considering his newly-burst eardrum. When it switched to Russian, he decided he had heard enough.

He stood and carefully pull the remote detonator out of his pocket. Tentatively, he poked his head out of the closet. It was clear.

He mentally mapped out the next few moves. Leave the closet, head to the back of the master bedroom. Quietly slide open the door, slip out of the house and head around the north side. From there, it was ten steps to his Cutlass—and less than a mile to I95-and freedom.

He'd have to make one stop along the way, of course. About three houses down, he figured. Just long enough to punch four quick buttons in succession.

Boom.

Boom.

Boom.

Boom...Bonfire.

Problem solved.

CHAPTER 83

In a brief moment of clarity, Elliot Becker decided that blowing a foot off with a pistol actually hurt more than having a pinky snipped off by a Russian mob enforcer.

He was not happy to be in the position to possess such information.

He looked up through his tears to see *yet another* armed stranger standing in the kitchen. It looked like the surfer guy from Hodges' office. He was pointing a pistol at the man Vadik had called Yevgeny Kramnik. Becker tried to recall the surfer guy's name.

Logan Treverrow.

"First of all, fellas, I want to congratulate each of you on exceptional trigger discipline," Treverrow said. "I've been watching from the back yard, and it's hard to believe that the only gun that's gone off so far is Elliot's."

Vadik brought his gun up and trained it on Kramnik.

"That's two on one, Yevgeny," he said, calmly. "Even if you take me first, you won't get off another shot. This guy is SEAL, I think."

Seal? Becker thought, deliriously. *The singer? I thought Seal was black.*

"How did you know that?" Treverrow asked.

"Sig Sauer P226 MK25 with Tritium night sights and a threaded barrel. Anchor insignia. Nicked rails. Not a collector's gun. A shooter's gun. A SEAL's gun."

"Good eye," Treverrow said.

"By the way, I didn't get a chance to tell you other night, but the Triple Tail was excellent. Rheese can't stop talking about the place."

"Thanks. Assuming we all live through this, I'll tell the chef."

"Vadik?" Mazzio interrupted. "You wanna get this moving along?"

"Oh, yes. Sorry, Sal." Vadik turned his attention toward Kramnik.

"Okay, Yevgeny. Like I told you, there is no longer a Vassili Dmitrievich to pay you for this hit. Also, I'm guessing that Vassili told you to take your advance from the money here in the house."

Kramnik nodded sheepishly and said, "Correct comrade."

"Sadly, Yevgeny, there is no money in this house. Am I right, Elliot?"

Vadik looked at Becker and waited.

Becker, whimpering and with a string of snot running from his nose, shook his head.

Vadik continued: "So, if you take me out, Yevgeny, you'll be doing it for free. And you'll most likely die in the process. On the other hand, if you want to walk away, I'm willing to give you one-time pass. I'll forget the whole thing, as comrade in arms. This offer that is good for the next ten seconds."

The room was silent as Kramnik considered his options.

417

"Okay," Kramnik said, as he dropped his gun to his side. He looked downcast. "Sorry for inconvenience, sir. We'd have none of this trouble if Antonin Bordelenko paid his people what they are worth."

Vadik and Treverrow lowered their guns as Silvano Mazzio picked up his sandwich and resumed eating.

"Understood, Sergeant. Give me a call in a couple of months. I might have something a little more in line with your skill sets by then."

Kramnik nodded appreciatively.

"Now, do me a favor, Yevgeny. There is another person here in the house. His name is Burrell Malin. Can you find him for me and bring him back here?"

"Yes, sir," Kramnik said, and went off.

Turning his attention toward Becker, Vadik said, "Elliot? Can you stop crying like little girl long enough to give me the PIN number please?"

Becker racked his addled mind for a counter strategy. Maybe a fake PIN.

"If you're thinking about a fake number, Elliot, you should know that we're inputting it right now in the kitchen where we are standing. We'll know if it's right or wrong immediately. If it's wrong, I'm going to blow your other foot off first, and ask again. I'll keep blowing body parts off until there are no more body parts to blow off."

Becker gave in. "One-seven-seven-six-four-two-five. Capital *I*, lower-case *w*."

"You got that, Vadik?" Silvano asked.

Vadik was tapping his phone. "Give me second."

He looked up. "Transfer complete."

Along with the cash, Becker felt his last vestige of hope drain out.

Vadik said to Treverrow, "That is a very nice pullover, by the way. Prada?"

"Yep."

Kramnik came back into the kitchen.

"There is no else one here in the house."

Vadik looked at Becker questioningly.

Kramnik continued: "But there are at least two burn rigs that I found staged—one in the master bedroom closet, and one upstairs."

"Where is Malin?" Vadik asked Becker.

Treverrow said, "He's probably hauled ass, Vadik. And I'll bet he's got a remote detonator with—"

The front of the house burst into flames.

CHAPTER 84

Special Agent Harley Slavnick took the lead on the drive from West Palm Beach to Boca Raton. Briggs and Stoneside followed in a Bureau-issued Yukon. As a material witness in an ongoing investigation into a possible case of arson, Hodges sat in the back seat of Slavnick's car. As a suspect in an ongoing case of mortgage fraud and/or knowingly running a Ponzi scheme, he was also Mirandized and handcuffed.

It wasn't the lawyer in Slavnick that compelled him to keep reminding Hodges that he had the right to remain silent. He needed a moment to think—and Ted Hodges simply wouldn't shut up.

It had taken a good twenty minutes for the other agents to show up, and another twenty minutes to get them up to speed. In that time, the Whopper Junior had done its job, as Hodges appeared to have sobered up a bit. After listening to the voicemail and Hodges' recounting of Becker's plans to torch a series of homes in the area, everyone had finally gotten the go-ahead around 9 pm.

Slavnick hoped it wasn't too late.

He had called his supervisor to get some guidance on informing local law enforcement that there might be an impending arson case in a Boca neighborhood.

"We're discussing that right now. If we're wrong—if this

asshole Becker is just blowing smoke—we'll look like idiots. So, it's a little sticky. What I need you guys to do is get moving now. We'll let you know what we decide in a few."

"Yes sir. Any direction on what you want us to do with the Pizzuti kid?"

"Was he breaking any laws, besides the weed?"

"Not that I'm aware of, sir."

"Kidnapping? False imprisonment? Battery?"

"Uh, no, sir. He and Hodges were actually just sitting there, playing video games."

"Then leave him there."

A sign along I95 read *Boca Raton—Next 4 Exits*. Slavnick maneuvered the Malibu toward the right-hand lane. He looked back at Hodges and asked, "Do you know if Becker has a weapon? A pistol? Anything like that?"

Hodges snorted, "Are you kidding? He wouldn't recognize a gun if it went off in his pocket."

Slavnick thought about it for a second. He hated the idea of going in blind on something like this. He grabbed Hodges' cell phone off the passenger-side seat, scrolled to a number and handed it to him.

Hodges looked at him questioningly in the rearview mirror as he cradled the phone in his cuffed hands.

"What do you want me to do with this?"

"I want you to call Elliot Becker. I want you to tell him that you're on the way. That you're running late. I want you to find out what's going on. I want to know what we're facing there, and you're the only one that can get him to tell you."

Hodges looked at him dubiously, but punched the CALL button nonetheless.

With both hands, he put the phone to his ear and waited a few seconds.

"Elliot? It's Ted. I'm on the way there with Agent Slutnick from the FBI. Anyway, he wants to know what's going on down there, because he doesn't want any surp—."

Slavnick swerved across three lanes of highway as he reached back and jerked the phone out of Hodges' hands.

"What? I thought you wanted me to—"

"I DIDN'T WANT YOU TO TELL HIM YOU WERE WITH A FEDERAL AGENT, YOU IDIOT!"

Slavnick tossed the phone into the passenger side floorboard and pounded his steering wheel in frustration. If his supervisor ever got wind of this, it'd be his career.

"Hey, look Agent Shiplap. There's a Wendy's at the next exit. Can we stop?"

Slavnick sighed and picked up his phone to call Briggs and Stoneside.

CHAPTER 85

"**B**ack door. NOW!" I yelled.

I grabbed Becker by the ankle and started dragging him toward the sliding glass door that I'd used to enter the kitchen. Vadik grabbed the other ankle. We were moving so quickly that Becker almost went airborne, his head bouncing along the tile.

"Don't forget this idiot has an unsecured pistol in his pocket," I said as we pulled Becker through the door and deposited him onto the patio. Mazzio and Kramnik hit the door right behind us, just as the cabinets in the kitchen went up, followed by a burst from the bedroom to the right. Within a few seconds, the entire back of the house was engulfed.

Once again, Vadik and I grabbed Becker and hauled him away from the house and onto the pool deck. He was flopping around and screaming in pain until Vadik leaned down and jammed his AF-1 pistol into his mouth.

"Now is not time to be crybaby, Elliot," he said.

Becker managed to get it down to a whimper as I reached in and extracted the pistol that had blown his toes off, along with his cell phone and—surprisingly—a pair of zip ties.

"Walther PPK." Vadik said. "Elliot's a real James Bond, huh?"

I motioned for Vadik, Kramnik and Mazzio to join me by the

pool's waterfall, out of Becker's earshot.

"I figure we have about three minutes to exfil," I said.

All three nodded in agreement.

"So, let's spend those three minutes getting on the same page. I think we can all agree that none of us were here, right?" I asked, looking into each man's face. "I know I wasn't."

They nodded again.

"Good. The question is—what are we going to do with him?" I asked, pointing at Becker.

"Kill him." Vadik said. "He could ID all of us if we leave him here."

"ID us for what?" Silvano asked. "Stealing his stolen money? We kill him, and that's gonna be the one thing they *can* pin on us. Other than that, they got nothing. Let Becker sing all he wants."

"How about Vassili?" Vadik asked.

"All he knows is that Vassili was supposed to be here tonight, and he wasn't. Beyond that, he's clueless." Silvano said.

I had no idea who Vassili was, or what had happened to him, but I was smart enough to not ask.

"Silvano is right," I said. "Becker's problems are his own problems. And he shot *himself*," I pointed out, as I wiped the Walther clear of my prints.

"Okay, so what do we do with him?" Mazzio asked.

Before any of us could say anything, Becker's phone rang. I looked down.

It was Ted Hodges.

I motioned for silence, put the phone to my ear and said, "Yeah?" in my best Elliot Becker imitation.

I listened for a few seconds and smiled.

"I know what to do with Becker." I said, as I tossed Becker's phone into the pool. "Anybody got a pen?"

Mazzio pointed to Vadik.

"Absolutely."

CHAPTER 86

Special Agent Harley Slavnick ignored the *Kids at Play - Please Drive Slowly* signs as he barreled through the neighborhood toward Joanne Sanders' house. In the back seat, Hodges whooped every time the Malibu jumped a speed bump. Briggs and Stoneside were right behind in the Yukon.

Although he'd punched the address into his navigation system, Slavnick didn't need it anymore. All he had to do was look up and drive toward the brightly burning house in the middle of the subdivision. Or, alternatively, follow the firetrucks.

Dammit.

The front of the Sanders home was blocked by what looked to be every piece of equipment the Boca Raton Fire Department owned. Slavnick was forced to park a couple of houses down.

"You're staying here in the car," he told Hodges, who nodded agreeably. He slammed the door shut, locked the car, and walked toward the Sanders home. Briggs and Stoneside caught up with him in front of the house.

Brandishing his credentials wallet, Slavnick walked up to trio of firefighters working to feed a hose to a team positioned in front of the house.

"Where's the chief?" he yelled. One of them pointed to a tall, middle-aged man in PPE gear barking orders into a handheld radio. The three agents walked up, credentials in front of them.

"We're here as part of an ongoing arson investigation," Slavnick said as they approached the man.

"Looks like you're a little late," the chief said as he turned back to his radio. He reeled off a fast set of instructions, using acronyms and terms that Slavnick wasn't familiar with.

"Look, Chief," Slavnick said. "I don't want to get in your way. I know you guys are busy. I just need a few seconds of your time to catch me up. We'll stay clear, I promise. But can you tell me what you know?"

The fire chief looked at him for a second and said, "Well, you're right about one thing. It was definitely arson. Place went up like a roman candle. Probably at least three separate burn rigs staged. I'm guessing we'll get tags for acetone, gun powder, kerosene—who knows? But it was definitely deliberate."

"Have you been able to determine if anyone was in the house?"

"Nope. Still early for that. But the residents weren't home. We know that, because they're over there talking to the cops." He pointed to a woman who was sobbing uncontrollably. "Told us she lives here with her sister and boyfriend. They were out to dinner when this happened."

"How long before you think you guys will be able to get in there?" Slavnick asked, pointing to the house.

"Another hour, at least. We've got it pretty well contained, but at this point, it's gonna have to burn itself out."

Slavnick was about to ask another question when someone yelled "Chief!" from the front yard. They turned to see a team of firefighters carrying a body.

"We found one!"

A group of EMTs emerged from an ambulance with a body board and portable gurney and converged toward the team. Slavnick and the other agents, along with the fire chief, rushed toward the victim; a middle-aged man in filthy khakis. He had a large bandage on his left hand and his right shoe was covered in blood. He was struggling to free himself from his rescuers.

"I've had it! I've fucking had it! Let me go, you assholes!" he yelled as the firefighters deposited him on the body board.

"You're not gonna to believe this, Chief, but this guy was zip tied to a palm tree in the back yard. With this pinned to his shirt."

The firefighter held up a ragged piece of paper.

It read: *Attention: Special Agent Harley Slavnick.*

CHAPTER 87

"**I** like having your paintings in one place, Daddy. It feels all cozy."

I looked away from my phone and into the most beautiful face I have ever seen. "Thank you, sweetheart. Does that mean you're having fun?"

My eight-year old daughter Isabella rewarded me with a nod and a perfect, snaggle-toothed smile. Then she turned and walked away, her little white dress and blonde ringlets disappearing into the crowd of art lovers, scene-makers and society hangers-on.

Looking to torture her little brother, or smother her mom in kisses. One of the two.

I put the phone back to my ear.

"Thanks for the call, Ben. Let me think about it."

"You don't have to think about it. You just have to do it."

I laughed, remembering the hundreds of times he'd told us the same thing in Coronado. Over a bullhorn.

"I'll talk to you later, Master Chief."

I looked across the room and winked at Campbell, the gallery owner. I pointed to the large painting sitting on the floor, leaning against the wall. It had a red dot next to it, indicating "sold."

You were right, I mouthed.

I'm always right, she mouthed back. She surreptitiously pointed to an attractive middle-aged blonde plucking two glasses of champagne off a tray.

She pantomimed writing.

I assumed that meant that the blonde was from the magazine. Kathleen something or other. Plus one.

I dutifully made my way toward her.

"Hello, I'm Logan Treverrow," I said.

She smiled at me and held up her champagne flutes.

"If you'll relieve me of one of these, Logan, I'll shake your hand."

I took one of the glasses and she nodded at the champagne and smiled.

"Please. I grabbed an extra one for my friend, but he can fend for himself," she said, her blue eyes twinkling.

We each took a sip and I asked, "Are you enjoying the opening?"

Campbell had done two of my previous gallery openings, and she was constantly warning me against asking people if they *liked* the work. I thought that was the objective of a gallery opening, but—as I mentioned earlier—there's no point in arguing with Campbell. So instead, I always asked people if they were *enjoying* the opening.

Whatever.

"Of course!" she said brightly. "And I *love* your work!"

Take that, Campbell, I thought.

Everyone seemed to be enjoying the evening, and judging

from the number of red dots on the wall, the work was being very well received. With three successful openings under my belt, my career as a fine artist was on a nice trajectory. (The jury was still out on my future as a sculptor. If I didn't get that monstrosity out of my studio and sold to someone—soon—I was going to lose my mind.)

Of course, this should have made me very happy; and on one level, it did. On the other hand, the most fun I'd had in the last three years wasn't painting. It certainly wasn't sculpting. It wasn't even kite surfing.

The most fun I'd had in the last three years was running head long into a Mexican standoff between two Spetsnaz and a Mafioso, with a fully-loaded and cocked Sig Sauer.

How twisted is that?

My conversation with my old BUDs instructor Ben Gray hadn't helped matters.

"I just got off the phone with Harley Slavnick. You should be a meteorologist, Logan. Your ability to predict things is uncanny," he'd told me earlier that morning.

"What do you mean?" I asked.

"Harley just got transferred to the Manhattan office," Gray replied.

I asked, "I'm guessing that's a good thing for him?"

"Mostly, I'd say. Lots bigger fish for him to chase there, but probably boring for a guy who considers himself the reincarnation of Elliot Ness."

I thought about that.

"Yeah. Boring sucks. I definitely get that."

Gray laughed. "I know you do. That's why I know it was you who trussed up that little shit Elliot Becker in the back of that burning house."

My stomach dropped a bit.

"I don't know what—"

Gray laughed even harder. "Don't even try to deny it, Logan. I would have done the same thing. Like we always said, call the cops—"

"—and see who gets there first," I finished.

"Exactly." Gray said.

"So. Does Slavnick know?" I asked.

"He suspects, but he's not going to pursue it. What's the point? From what it looks like, all you did was drag Becker out of a burning house and tie him to a tree. It's pretty clear he shot himself."

I started to breathe a slight sigh of relief.

"On the other hand, *how* you knew where to find Becker is a whole other question. If we were to follow up on that, I'm guessing we'd find some shit on you. Stolen phone, maybe. Breaking and entering. We found an ElectroPic at Malin's house, did you know that? I remember how you used to love that thing."

Damn. I *knew* I had forgotten something that day.

After a few seconds, I asked, "So where does that leave us, Master Chief?"

"Glad you asked. Until this thing came up, I didn't know you came from money. You're worth more than a couple of small, hot countries, according to Slavnick."

"So?" I asked.

"So—it turns out that a guy with your training and re-sources could be very useful to me in certain situations."

"What kind of situations?" I asked.

"I don't know," Gray replied. "Getting someone who's not

supposed to be somewhere out of there. Buying up weapons before they get in the wrong hands. Intel gathering. Recon. Security work. Thinning the herd once in a while. Stuff like that."

"So, stuff where it would be a little sticky explaining why the FBI has personnel on the ground doing stuff they shouldn't be doing, somewhere they shouldn't be," I finished.

"You were always a smart guy, Logan. That's why you went to Princeton and I went the Michigan State."

"Go Spartans," I said.

"You'd need to pull some people together. Start with a fire team. Four guys. Grow it to a squad down the road; maybe a platoon. For operating capital, you'd probably have to keep somewhere between two and three million liquid. You front the expenses, and bill me back as a consulting fee. Trust me, Logan—you'll make a ton of money. You wouldn't believe the budgets we have for these kinds of operations."

Gray paused.

"Best of all, any potential investigations into Logan Treverrow never get off the ground."

Gray let a few seconds pass.

"So, what do you think?"

I hesitated.

"C'mon. I know you're bored," Gray said. "You wouldn't have stuck your nose in as far as you did if you weren't. Not to mention, you're getting rusty. You wouldn't have left the ElectroPic if you'd been on your game."

That stung.

"Alright. Give me a day or so to work through some of the details in my head. I can't think about this right now. I've got an art opening tonight that I have to attend."

"You're quite the Renaissance man, Logan." Gray said. "But in your heart, you're still an operator. Rusty. But still an operator."

"Fuck you, dude." I said.

Gray laughed. "I'll call you later."

Which he had—right in the middle of my gallery opening —to tell me that Burrell Malin had been picked up in a Winn Dixie breakroom in Yeehaw Junction. Even there, his Cutlass had stood out like a sore thumb.

"—and I told my friend that we absolutely must find our way into your charming restaurant."

I looked up.

"I'm sorry, what?" I asked.

"Casa Playa's," Kathleen the magazine writer said. "Your restaurant."

"Oh, yes. I'm sorry. The hearing in my right ear is a little sketchy," I said, hoping to cover my gaff. *If I blow this, Campbell will have my ass,* I thought.

I was trying to think of something witty or charming to say when Silvano Mazzio walked up and put his arm around Kathleen.

"I leave you for ten seconds and you're already carrying on with the guest of honor?" he said.

We all laughed—Kathleen sincerely.

"Logan Treverrow, I'd like you to meet Silvano Mazzio, my friend from New York, and a man with impeccable taste."

We shook hands. "I feel like we've met before, Mister Treverrow," Mazzio said, the corners of his eyes crinkling into a smile.

"Call me Logan, please." I said. "Probably at a house party."

He laughed.

"Will you two excuse me for a moment?" Kathleen said, touching Mazzio's arm. "I want to say hi to someone. Logan, please tell Sal about your restaurant."

She walked off.

"You're the 'plus one'?" I asked.

"It would appear so," Mazzio answered. "Although, I gotta say, I really like your work. I bought one, in fact."

"Really?" I asked. "Which one?"

He pointed to the large painting sitting on the floor.

"That one."

"That painting's priced at seventeen thousand dollars." I said. "It's the most expensive painting in the gallery."

"Yeah, I know. But I figured you got screwed by Hodges, while I got some of mine back. Anyways, thought I'd help out if I could."

I was oddly touched.

"Thanks, Silvano."

"No worries. It ain't my money anyway."

We stood there in silence, until I asked ,"You hear from the Feds?"

He smiled. "Quick phone call. They had me on a Double A's security camera and visitor's log, plus whatever bullshit Hodges babbled to them. I said I was there looking to see what happened to my nephew's escrow deposit. I had a legit beef with the fucking guy, you know?"

He paused a second.

"They knew from the get-go they had nothing on me. And that it'd be a royal pain in the ass to try to pin something on me. At twelve hundred an hour, the only people that'd win in that scenario would be my lawyers. I know that. They know

435

that. So, they were just checking off the boxes."

He looked at me. "How about you?"

"Pretty much the same story," I replied.

"Yeah, well, in this instance Logan, I wouldn't get myself too worked up. If there's one place I have connections, it's in the federal corrections system. Doesn't matter where these three idiots wind up, word'll get to them soon enough that silence is a virtue."

Emma walked up and kissed me on the cheek.

"Hi sweetheart."

"Emma, I'd like you to meet Silvano Mazzio. He just bought the big canvas."

To her credit, she recovered quickly.

"It's okay, sweetie," I said. "Silvano and I are old friends."

"Old friends or Super Friends?" she said, smiling.

I laughed. "Super Friends."

I hadn't given Emma any of the particulars on what had happened, telling her she'd be better off pleading ignorance if anyone ever came asking—but as I said, she's a lot smarter than me.

"Good to meet you, Emma," Silvano said, shaking her hand.

She looked at two of us and smiled crookedly.

"So if Logan's Aquaman, who are you, Silvano?"

Silvano thought about that for a second and smiled broadly.

"Iron Man. He's Italian on his mother's side. Antonio Stark."

Emma laughed. "You're quick, Silvano. I'll give you that."

She pointed over toward the bar.

"There's the couple from the other night. Vadik and Rheese.

I'm so glad they made it."

Silvano looked at me. Before he could ask, I answered.

"Yep."

EPILOGUE

T he device in my hand vibrated briefly. I glanced down, punched in a 13-digit security code, and accessed my incoming texts.

Done.

The one word I was looking for. I moved to a quiet corner of the hotel lobby, as far from the crowd as I could, and dialed a number. Roughly 4,000 miles south, a satellite phone rang.

"That was quick," a slightly echoing voice with a distinctly Russian accent observed.

"Where's my money?" I asked.

"Exactly where it started, sir."

"Well done, Sergeant." I replied.

I made a slight adjustment to the custom-fitted inductive Bluetooth device in my right ear. Unlike conventional earpieces, this model was virtually invisible—something I appreciated in moments like this.

"It's a little crowded here," I said in a low voice. "So, you're going to have to do most of the talking."

I made a final tweak to the earpiece and continued. "Let's

start with the inventory."

"You got something to be writing with?"

"I've got a good memory," I said, as I smiled charmingly in the direction of a septuagenarian heiress Botoxed within an inch of her life.

"Okay," came the reply. "Here we go."

There was a pause as notes were scrutinized.

"Forty-eight M4A1's with SOPMOD Block 3 upgrades and a half a million rounds of 5.56 ammo..." Another pause. "A bunch of shitty Chinese Kalashnikovs... I don't know why they bothered with those, to tell you the truth."

I let that pass without comment.

"Let's see...thirty-six FIM-92 Stinger missiles with reprogrammable microprocessors."

"Holy shit," I whispered. "*Three dozen* stinger missiles?"

"Yep. At sixty thousand each, those alone set us back almost two million."

"What else?" I asked.

"The rifles and SAMs are the big ones. There's lots of little things...some M67 fragmentation grenades, a hundred thousand rounds of Wolf 7.62 ammo for AK's...some limpet mines —"

"—Alright," I interrupted. "So—total for the whole mess?"

"Four million American greenbacks. I rounded up a bit. Nice even number. They didn't even bother quibbling. Took the money and ran."

"And Gray?"

"He already rerouted the buy money back into our account and moved the inventory out of the region. Like we never even existed."

"You hope." I replied.

"If I may ask, how is opening ceremony for hotel going?"

"It's called a grand opening. Not an opening ceremony. And it's going fine," I said as I looked around the room. Vadik and Rheese had commissioned thirty pieces from me for the hotel lobby and restaurant alone. I had used the money to pay down the HELOC, since the bank had been unwilling to negotiate—fraud or no fraud.

A waiter dressed in an all-black ensemble—including a Prada pullover—approached me. He held a small tray upon which stood a single vodka martini in a frosted glass and a handwritten card.

The card read: *Attention: Special Agent Harley Slavnick.*

"Excuse me, sir, but the group at the bar sent this with their compliments."

I looked over.

Silvano Mazzio—the charming bastard—was holding court with Kathleen, Emma, Sasha and Rheese. He'd come down for the opening and to do a little financial consulting for our small, but growing enterprise. Silvano definitely knew his way around banking.

The four of them waved.

I shot Silvano the finger, smiled and turned away to finish my call.

"Anything else, Yevgeny?" I asked. "When are you out of there?"

"Mopping up now. Exfil at twenty-three hundred, local," he replied.

Two hours. That would put them back in South Florida around 6 am, assuming fair winds and a bit of luck.

"Okay. I won't hold you up. We'll see you at, let's say, o-seven thirty, usual place. Good job."

"*Da.*" The line clicked off.

I looked across the room, caught Vadik's eye and winked.

He nodded.

I set a smile on my face, and commenced to mingle.

THE END

About the Author

C.D. Boswell roamed all over the US and Europe before settling in South Florida more than thirty years ago. A former college linebacker, he's made a living as a lifeguard, bartender, musician, copywriter and creative director over the years. For a year or so in his early twenties, he even cleaned the swimming pools of the rich and famous in Beverly Hills—far and away the weirdest job he ever had. These days, he lives with his wife, daughter and an assortment of large and small animals off a little stretch of waterway in Palm Beach County and is happiest when he's on his boat, just out of sight of land.

Visit CDBoswell.com for information about upcoming events and book releases.

Made in United States
Orlando, FL
02 February 2022

14326606R00241